MASKED

M Greenhill

2 Little Monkeys Limited
Auckland, New Zealand

For More Information:
www.mgreenhill.com
Cover By: L1graphics
First Edition October 2017

To Leo, Sebastian and Dominic with all my love.

Without your support, this book would not have been possible.

Who's Afraid of the Big Bad Wolf?

San Francisco

No dead bodies, no stabbings, and no domestic disputes had marred his uneventful evening. Sure, there were a few bar fights he was called in to deal with—and the robbery at the 7/11 put a little variety into things—but so far, his shift had been ordinary.

Now, not so much.

After overhearing yet another conversation between the dispatchers, Officer Nigel Hardy threw his half-eaten donut in the gutter and groaned. "You have got to be kidding me, not tonight of all nights."

Officer Hardy cursed under his breath as he climbed into his cruiser. Throughout the evening, a series of peculiar attacks had been reported in the Marina District, which had since moved on to the Financial District. The emergency operators were convinced somebody was running an elaborate prank, but the reports had his left eye twitching uncontrollably and his mouth forming a rigid grimace. A sure sign something was off.

The police dispatcher who took the latest complaint debated aloud whether to call animal control, the circus, or the local mental institution to check for a missing patient.

Some panicked callers told 911 operators that a large, rabid dog was terrorizing the public. Others were adamant a dirty and ill-looking naked man was running around biting people. Further callers reported the dog and the man were together.

Officer Hardy monitored the conversation across the police scanner with a growing sense of unease. He had no choice but to intervene. He reached for the two-way radio. "Dispatch, this is Unit 233. I'm near the vicinity of the last sighting. Will investigate. Over."

The speakers crackled, followed by a series of blips. "Confirmed, Unit 233."

Mindful of what he could be walking into, he sped through the deserted streets with lights and sirens muted.

Officer Nigel Hardy was a police officer bound to serve and protect the citizens of San Francisco, but his fellow officers and the public were unaware of his true allegiances. Officer Hardy was a Werewolf, and his primary objective was to protect his own kind. He, and other Werewolves like him, occupied strategic positions on the front lines of law enforcement departments across the country. They monitored Werewolf activity across pack boundaries to ensure their existence remained a myth to Humans. He had come from a long line of protectors, and he wasn't about to fail his race— not on his watch.

Within five minutes, Hardy arrived at the scene, only to confirm his earlier suspicions had been correct.

A petrified couple was huddled in a darkened doorway of a store. Less than two feet from the pair lurked a snarling wolf. Its eyes were wild and mean. Bared fangs drooled copious amounts of saliva, and what could only be blood, dripped from its powerful jaws. The wolf's shoulders were hunched, its head low to the ground as it prepared to attack. A growl ripped from deep within its chest, and the guttural and raspy undertones raised the hairs on the back of Hardy's neck.

He got out of the car and surveyed the area. "Crap." Unlike the other witnesses that evening, Hardy understood the ramifications of the crisis playing out before him.

He took a closer look at the creature. In their distraught state, the couple did not notice what his superior vision detected. The wolf looked...*unnatural.*

Tufts of dark brown fur had fallen off the animal's body and left its skin exposed. Instead of a smooth surface, the skin appeared scabrous and coarse, as if irritated and clawed at for hours.

How the hell did he get like that?

Hardy glanced back at the couple. Despite his fear, the man had positioned himself as a shield between the canine and the woman. Just as the man held up an arm to protect his body from imminent attack, the beast snapped its jaws at the couple. The man flinched and shrank farther into the shadows.

Instead of lunging, the creature howled, followed by a cry of pain and a series of whimpers. A distinctive creak, like timber as it strains and resists before it breaks, punctured the night air.

The hairs on the back of Hardy's neck bristled. "Double crap."

The Werewolf was beginning the transition into its Human form. He needed to do something before this became a disaster of gigantic proportion. His eyes darted around the area and considered his limited options. Not seeing an alternative, he unholstered his SIG Sauer P226. The handgun was the only weapon he had with any chance of dealing with the other Werewolf. "I'm going to fire my weapon to distract him. When I do, I want you both to run and don't look back. Understood?"

In spite of their terrified state, both nodded profusely, their eyes fixated on the creature.

He discharged a bullet into the air, and an ear-stinging crack echoed through the deserted street. The sound shifted the animal's focus away from the couple. Now the wolf's massive, mangy head faced him.

The couple edged around the doorway and broke into a full sprint.

When Hardy was sure they were out of earshot, he addressed the unstable Werewolf in a quiet, even tone. "Friend, you need to calm down. You're in a heap of trouble. I can't overlook this. Not only have you exposed yourself to Humans, but you've also bitten them. You're just lucky no one has died...yet."

He continued to assess the Werewolf. An odd, putrid odor wafted from the creature. He had failed to notice it before, perhaps due to the intense fear that had radiated from the terrified couple. A cold, foreboding chill ran up and down Hardy's spine. His eyes remained glued to the slow and agonizing transformation of the unknown male wolf. The change from one form to another should not take this long, or be as haphazard.

Hardy pulled out his phone and hit the first number on his favorites list, while still watching the conversion. He did not need to wait long before the call was answered. "Alpha Locke, we have somewhat of a situation here that I'm going to need help with."

A deep, authoritative voice responded. "Situation?"

Hardy briefed his alpha on what had just occurred. This wasn't the first time he had been required to deal with a rogue wolf that had almost exposed them.

And it won't be the last.

His only consolation was that Alpha Daniel Locke would know what to do and would take the problem off his hands.

Hardy stopped mid-sentence and stood transfixed. The Werewolf had completed his painful change into a man. Now more pronounced, the rancid stench of rotting meat made his skin crawl. In all his ninety-two years, this was something he had never experienced.

The man was covered from head to toe in black oozing pustules. There were patches on his scalp where hair used to be. A chunk of his right bicep was missing, as if bitten by ragged jaws. The hole in his upper arm was a mixture of gray and charcoal tissue.

Hardy scratched the back of his neck. What he was seeing was not possible.

"Hardy, are you there? Report."

Silence.

The two Werewolves stood immobile on the darkened pavement. Neither moved, not once breaking eye contact. A bulb from a nearby street lamp flickered and died, bathing the area in near darkness. The movement triggered a reaction in the injured Werewolf. The last remnants of sanity left the Werewolf's eyes, and a menacing growl from somewhere deep in its chest reverberated. Hardy's stomach plummeted.

In an instant, Hardy dropped his phone and discharged his gun. He fired several shots in quick succession at the Werewolf's heart. The body fell to the ground, dead before the last bullet hit its mark. In the ensuing silence, Hardy heard Alpha Daniel Locke's deep voice booming from the phone on the pavement.

"Hardy, what the hell is going on?"

"Crap." Hardy removed his hat and scratched his head. "The paperwork on this one is gonna take me into next week."

Officer Hardy approached the Werewolf, still not sure what had just happened. His chest tightened in horror as he gazed at the odd-shaped boils that covered the body. The sharp smell made him nauseous and, if possible, it was stronger than before.

How the hell am I going to explain this?

ONE
Wildfire

Nederland, Colorado

Daniel Locke ended the call and threw his phone on the desk, where it slid into the back of his laptop with a distinctive thud. Throughout his conversation with Hardy, he had remained the stoic and commanding alpha everyone expected him to be. Inwardly, his rage bubbled just below the surface as Hardy described the condition of the downed Werewolf. His people were dying in the worst possible way, and he had no idea how or why. Up until a month ago, Werewolves did not get ill. Now bodies were piling up across the country, and he had no way of predicting when the next victim would appear and potentially expose them all.

He hit the nearest wall with his fist and put a large hole through the surface. Wood splintered as the support beam cracked under the pure, brute force.

Simon poked his head through the door and eyed the damage. "Do we feel better now?"

He glanced at his hand, which bore no marks to show it had made contact with anything, let alone destroyed a portion of an office wall, and shrugged. "Much."

Simon leaned against the door frame and crossed his arms over his chest. "And I'm sure that the poor, defenseless wall had it coming."

He chose to ignore his friend—who also happened to be one of his betas—and headed back to his mahogany desk.

Simon, unable to hold his tongue in the best of situations, inspected the damage and chuckled. "How the hell am I going to expense the fix? I'm pretty sure I don't have a GL code for—in a fit of rage." He shook his head and turned toward Daniel. "I overheard some of the call. You know, it's okay if you don't have all the answers. This isn't your fault, you can't save everyone."

Daniel's green eyes flashed a warning at his beta. "I'm not having this conversation."

Simon's brows rose and he folded his arms. "Man, do you need to get laid."

"That's right, because if there's a problem, getting laid is always the answer."

Simon pretended to think about it for all of two seconds before he winked. "Yep."

Daniel rolled his eyes and snorted. "We all know that lately there's only one thing on your mind."

Simon put on his best offended face. "Nah. Sex solves everything was my default position before I met Lyssa." He jerked a thumb toward the damaged wall. "She finds very creative ways to calm me down before I get to that point."

Daniel frowned and crossed his arms over his chest. He stood to his full height, towering over his beta. "Well, we don't all have the luxury of having a mate, so I'll have to take your word for it. In the meantime, we have somewhat of a problem on our hands."

Simon's mood deflated, and he shuffled his feet under the scrutiny of his alpha.

As soon as the words were out of his mouth, Daniel regretted snapping at his friend. Simon only had his best interests at heart, and only wanted him to find the same contentment he now experienced. But his friend's pity at not having a mate irked him. Moments like this, he regretted the ability to communicate telepathically with his most trusted advisors and was thankful it did not extend to the rest of his pack.

"I just think you gave up too soon," Simon said.

He threw his friend a look that made it clear this particular topic was off-limits. He had long since grown weary of the politics that centered around this subject, and it did not help that his wolf echoed his friend's sentiment.

Simon got the message and plopped down on the oversized, brown leather Chesterfield tucked in the corner of the office. "So, Wildfire has made its way to the West Coast."

He nodded. "From what Hardy described, it certainly seems that way, but we will only know for sure once we get the autopsy results. The body will be sent to the San Diego pack. Once there, Alice can tell their doctor what to look for and what tests to run."

"Why bother when you already know the results?"

The same thought had crossed Daniel's mind. If the others were anything to go by, the autopsy would find multiple organ failures, tumors rampant in the brain, and unidentified bacteria saturating the tissue and blood. To make matters worse, when they investigated the victim, Hardy would discover the dead man had bottles of a little-known herbal medication called Wildfire stashed in his belongings. The toxicology screens would indicate trace amounts of the drug in the bloodstream, but nothing that would fell a full-grown Werewolf in such a horrifying manner.

Daniel leaned against his desk. "For the same reason as the last twelve bodies—we need to know if this is just a coincidence, or if they have something in common apart from being unaligned."

While many of the packs disapproved of Werewolves not aligning themselves to a pack, Daniel understood that a portion of their community, either through choice or circumstance, chose to go it alone. As long as they kept a low profile and stayed out of trouble, he had no issues with their choice. It was when they turned rogue he took exception. Their race's biggest risk of exposure was from this small sector. And the growing animosity between the pure and mixed blooded Werewolves did not help. As far as he was concerned, all Werewolves were equal, no matter their heritage. Any Werewolf who thought differently was not welcome in his pack.

"Has Alice confirmed the link between Wildfire and the deaths?"

"All we know for sure is that the drug has no effect on Humans," Daniel said.

The frustration with their lack of progress weighed heavily on Daniel's shoulders, adding to his ill-temper. Werewolves, as a race, had no need for internal medicine. They did not get sick or suffer diseases in the same way as their Human counterparts. Each pack had their own doctor, but they were trained to deal with physical injuries only. Understanding diseases and the workings of bacteria and pathogens was an alien concept. He was lucky that Dr. Alice Hayes, his pack's doctor, was a Human doctor before she met her Werewolf mate and made the choice to turn. She at least had some knowledge, even if it was decades out-of-date.

Daniel headed to the wet bar and poured two glasses of single malt. He handed one to Simon. "Has your team worked out how they're getting it?"

Simon took a sip and cleared his throat before he answered. "We think they are ordering it online."

"Pardon?"

"You know, on the internet. That inter-webby thingy."

"I bloody well know what online is," Daniel said. "What have you found out?"

"Turns out, Wildfire is freely available for sale on herbal health sites. Thousands of them. Well, actually, more like hundreds. Anyway, none of the retailers manufacture the product, nor do they ship or stock the goods." Simon swung his legs off the couch. "The entire delivery chain works through a third party that only transacts on the internet. To make matters worse, the dietary supplement pills are FDA regulated, and as they have no adverse effect on Humans, we can't get Wildfire removed from the online stores without attracting attention."

Simon let out a frustrated groan. "The problem is, we don't have the knowledge, or the ability, to deal with this. We've tried to buy the stock out, but you can only order a single bottle at a time. Who knows how long it would take us? We don't have the expertise to hack into those sites and bring them down." He raised a brow and snorted. "Not to mention half of them are on porn sites. I had a hard time convincing Lyssa I was on there for work. She even threatened to tell my mother."

The ramifications of allowing this to continue did not even bear thought. Not only could the drug be bought easily, but they needed to be prepared for the possibility Wildfire could be given to an unsuspecting victim. He posed the question that had plagued him since hearing about the distribution method. "Are we sure this drug is targeting Werewolves and isn't a side effect of the Human weight loss product it's marketed as?"

"You've seen the bottles. What do you think?"

Daniel had to admit, if the logo of a wolf paw print wasn't a giveaway, the Lupine brand on the bottle sealed it. Caught up in his own thoughts, he considered the possible consequences. If they could not stop the progression of the disease once contracted, they needed to stop it at its source.

He ran a hand through his dark hair and let out a deep breath. He would need to convene an emergency meeting of the Alliance Council. If someone was targeting them, it would not be long before they were exposed. The last time that happened, it had brought them to virtual extinction—an event that had taken over three centuries to recover from.

He dismissed Simon and picked up the phone with a heavy heart.

Simon passed through the doorway, but halted mid-step. "We're out of our depth here. We have no idea about the digital world, and we are literally chasing shadows." He paused and tilted his head. "You know who we need to call in, don't you?"

He could not believe this subject was being raised again. "It's not going to happen." His voice came out as cold as ice. Over his dead body would he allow that to happen.

Simon scurried out of the room, muttering under his breath, "I wouldn't bet on it once the council gets involved."

Alliance Council Meeting, Idaho

The venom in Daniel's tone was unmistakable as he brought his fist down on the table. "No. Absolutely not!"

The council had decided this particular meeting warranted a physical gathering rather than their usual video conference. Within twelve hours they had convened on Brandenburg pack land in Idaho, and within the first thirty minutes of the session, the conversation had turned into his worst nightmare.

Morgan, one of the elder statesmen in the room and their host, pinched the bridge of his nose. "Daniel, be reasonable. This is the only choice we have. We can't involve anyone else, and even if we could, Parker is still the best."

Daniel crossed his arms over his chest and leaned back in his chair. "Find someone else."

"There is no one else."

"You seem to forget Parker is not one of us."

Members of the council whispered among themselves. Some around the large table viewed him as cold, distant, and unapproachable. His outburst probably shocked them. They were keeping their own counsel, waiting for one of the senior members to step in to dilute the situation.

Morgan rubbed the crown of his salt and pepper hair and took a deep breath. "I beg to differ. Parker has been accepted by me, my family, my pack, and the majority around this table. Someone who, may I remind you, is protected by my pack. The old ways are gone, and this council is responsible for guiding and leading our people. All of them."

From the other end of the table, a deep growl broke into the heated discussion. Heads swiveled to Abraham. He leaned on his cane as he stood and made eye contact with each of the twelve alphas present. "Enough! I have heard enough. Are you listening to yourselves?"

Abraham drew his bushy white eyebrows together, planted his gnarled hands on the table, and leaned forward. No one dared speak over the oldest member of the council.

Tamas, his grandson, and the Texas pack's alpha, helped steady Abraham. He shooed the younger man away. "I'm old, not disabled."

Abraham's wrinkles etched further into his skin as he pierced Daniel with a penetrating stare "We are losing our people to this mess, and we have no idea how to stop this plague. The longer this goes on, the more at risk we are to exposure and annihilation. If Parker can help get us through this, I don't care what *chutzpah* or prejudice you have Daniel, you will get over it. We need to act now or everything we ever knew—everything we have worked to achieve—will disappear in the blink of an eye."

An unfamiliar feeling of shame descended on Daniel while Abraham addressed the room. He needed to bury his personal issues and put his people first. Otherwise, Abraham was right; there would be no future for them. Despite his misgivings, his opinion of Parker would need to take a back seat.

He leaned forward and drummed his fingers on the table. There was no choice. He had to concede to the council's resolution. "I'll go along with your decision to seek Parker

Johnson's help, but mark my words, I know from experience that we shouldn't trust this Human."

Out of the corner of his eye, he saw Simon's self-satisfied smirk. Daniel growled and opened a telepathic link to his beta.

For that, you are on patrol duty for the rest of the month.

TWO

The Summons

Portland, Oregon

Parker leaned back in her chair, pushed her glasses up, and pinched the bridge of her nose. While she enjoyed being busy, this was a little over the top, even for her. After a crick of her neck from side to side, she sighed and refocused on the monitors on her desk.

The latest round of ransomware sent chills down her clients' collective backs. It wasn't surprising, then, when demands for forensic security audits flooded in. No matter how much she tried to convince them they were protected, they insisted on the extra precaution. She even had a few offers to double her hourly rate to put them at the top of the pile. However, charging anyone eight hundred dollars an hour, even if they could afford it, did not sit well with her.

To top it off, she had spent the better part of the morning fielding calls from a raft of new clients who were in desperate need of bolstering their network security. As with the rest of corporate America, they had just received a huge wake-up call. Most were referred to her by one of her existing clients, or they heard her lecture at one of the many conferences where she was a guest speaker.

She had been so focused on the computer monitors flashing lines of code, and the files scattered across her desk, that she did not notice her personal assistant was standing in front of her until Beth cleared her throat. Parker leaped back in her chair and put a hand to her chest. "Jesus Christ, Beth. The way you just appear isn't natural. You need to wear a bell around your neck."

Beth tossed a stack of unopened mail on Parker's desk. "Well, if you'd answer your phone, I wouldn't need to interrupt you."

She shifted a mound of paper and files to reveal her office phone. Nothing on the display revealed any missed calls. "What do you mean?"

"No, not your landline. Your cell. That sexy cousin of yours called. He's been trying to reach you."

Parker fished her phone out of her over-sized handbag and groaned. She had missed eight calls from Bobby. "I forgot I put it on silent this morning."

Beth sifted through the remaining mail and headed to the door. "Well, you better call him back, he said it was urgent. And Marc wants to see you. He's found a problem with Blue Horizon's firewall."

Beth popped her head back around the corner with a wicked grin on her face. Her distinctive purple hair was hard to miss—no matter how much people tried. "If he is coming to visit, let him know I am more than happy to show him all that Portland has to offer." With a sly wink, she was gone.

Parker rolled her eyes and dialed Bobby's number. She did not know who to be more concerned for—her cousin or her PA.

"Hey, how's my favorite cuz?" Bobby said.

A broad smile spread across Parker's face, and she sat back in her chair. "I thought you'd be in New York. Hasn't that weirdo convention started already?"

"Nah, it starts this weekend—and that would be Awesomeness Con, to you. Parks, have some respect, you are speaking to the grand prize winner of an audience with Mr. Freaking Stan—the legend—Lee. Booyah!"

Her head dropped to rest on the palm of her hand, and she shook her head from side to side. Bobby's obsession with comics was a little extreme, but he could have worse hobbies.

"I head off tomorrow," Bobby said. "Hey, Parks, umm..."

He went quiet, as if struggling to find the right words. "We were wondering...that is, Alpha Morgan was wondering...if you would come to Brandenburg to meet with him."

"Sure, no problem, I was planning on driving up this weekend to catch up with Clara anyway. Didn't she tell you?"

The line was silent. Parker frowned and checked her phone, thinking they had been disconnected. "Are you still there?"

Bobby stuttered as he spoke. "Um, Parks, do you think you could come out sooner...like tonight, perhaps?"

She bolted upright, took her reading glasses off, and placed them on the desk. "What's going on? Is everything okay?"

"I'm fine cuz, don't panic, but they need you here ASAP."

She glanced at the time on her computer monitor. "Okay, I'll try to beat the city traffic out of town. I should be there before ten." She paused. Being summoned wasn't a usual occurrence. Something was up. She swung her chair around to face the Portland skyline outside her office window. "Bobby..." Her voice caught in her throat. "What are you not telling me?"

There was another short silence before he answered in a mumble. "Alpha Locke is here."

Parker drew in a sharp breath, and a heavy rock plummeted to the bottom of her stomach. Her hands trembled, and she nearly dropped the phone. "Oh."

"You still there?"

The initial shock slowly wore off, and she rubbed her temple as her mind went into overdrive. "Y-yes. I was just checking my calendar."

"I gotta go and let Alpha Morgan know you're on your way. See you when you get here."

Parker took a long moment to digest the conversation. She frowned. Morgan wouldn't request help unless the situation was serious. Her hands continued to tremble at the thought of Daniel Locke. She looked down at them and groaned. *You have got to get a grip.* If she did not, she wouldn't be able to make the five-hour drive from Portland to Payette.

No longer able to put off the inevitable, she bolstered her courage, called for Beth, and gathered up the folders on her desk.

Beth poked her head around the door. "Yes, boss?"

"I'm leaving early, and I might be away for the next day or so. I need you to reschedule my meetings, and let McMillan know I'll email him my final report in the morning. Tell Marc I'll swing by his desk on my way out."

Beth took notes on her phone. "What about the Van Wyk event tomorrow night?"

Parker cringed. She had forgotten about the gala. She and her team had tracked down Van Wyk's former CEO, who had fled the country with millions of embezzled dollars. The CEO had been caught, extradited back to the States, and was now in jail awaiting trial. Thanks to her team, the money had been retrieved—mostly.

"Just make something up."

She locked the folders in a secure filing cabinet and dashed out of her office.

At home, she packed an overnight bag, grabbed two laptops and a VPN security key, and tossed them into her late model Chevrolet Blazer. She made a thermos of her special tea for the trip, alarmed the house, and headed out. When she had cleared the city limits, driving east on I-84 toward Idaho, she finally allowed herself to contemplate what this summons meant.

This visit was not optional. It was a command to make an appearance on pack grounds.

One of the few Humans aware of the existence of Werewolves, she was an extended member of the Brandenburg pack, and had been since Bobby was turned against his will a decade ago. Morgan and Clara Bergman, the pack's alphas, had taken her cousin in when it seemed his life was falling apart. She owed them everything. There was no question of whether she would help or not.

Her mind, however, struggled to understand why Daniel Locke was there, especially in light of how he felt about her. Their last contact had not ended on amicable terms. She shuddered at the memory. Three years later and it still terrified her. She pressed a button on the dash.

"Call Bobby."

He picked up before she heard the first ring. "Do you know how to get ketchup out of a shirt?" Bobby's voice was panicked. "I just dropped some on my Iron Man vs. Iron Maiden t-shirt. I can't meet Stan Lee with a dirty shirt."

"Good grief, Bobby, wear something else, then."

"I can't, it's the only thing I have left without holes."

That did not surprise her in the least. Her cousin was an absolute slob.

"Bobby, you're a grown man, I'm sure you can handle your wardrobe malfunction on your own."

Bobby mumbled under his breath, and the line went quiet. Parker frowned. "You still there?"

"Are you on your way yet?"

Parker rolled her eyes. From the way in which Bobby posed the question, she suspected she was about to be dumped with a smelly t-shirt and a bottle of detergent.

"Yes. I managed to sneak away without anyone noticing."

"It's hardly sneaking when you're the boss."

"About that. Um… Bobby…."

Bobby, clearly aware of what she was about to ask, stopped her. "I can't tell you why you've been summoned. Only that there was some secret squirrel meeting, and I was sent word to get you here ASAP. Other than that, I don't actually know."

Well, that at least answers the question of why Daniel Locke's involved.

Before she could say anything further, Bobby cleared his throat. "I'm assuming you'll arrive with a supply of your special tea?"

She narrowed her eyes and snapped at him. "It's Calendula, and I think you already know the answer to that."

"You know, Parks, they already believe you're strange with no unique scent. I don't want to be around when they discover that you've been deliberately masking it. They'll think you're trying to hide something."

Parker took a deep breath before replying. This conversation had been replayed countless times over the years, to the point that she was sick to death of the subject. This was the only topic that caused friction between them.

"You know damn well why! How the hell am I supposed to function around Werewolves when you know what I'm feeling before I do? You use this to your advantage when you deal with us Humans, and I won't put up with it. Besides, my feelings and thoughts are nobody's business."

"Chill, Parks. I won't say anything."

Bobby wisely changed the subject, and they discussed his trip to New York. She now knew more about the Marvel exhibition and Stan Lee than she ever wanted to. Period. By the time he finished and they had ended the call, she was seventy-five miles closer to her destination. She focused on the road ahead and sifted through recent conversations with Clara and Morgan, the Brandenburg alphas. There was nothing that stood out to warrant her summons, nor the Alpha Commander's presence.

Parker turned up the music. She needed something to distract her. The insides of her stomach were tied in knots. Being stuck with the sharp end of Daniel Locke's wrath over the phone was one thing, but how on earth was she going to deal with the insufferable man in person?

Parker pulled into the familiar driveway of the Brandenburg compound just outside of Payette, Idaho a little after nine o'clock in the evening. The lights from the three-story stone villa lit the last of the way to the front entrance. It was a welcoming sight. Her limbs were stiff from the long drive, and she was thankful to get out and stretch her legs. She had just opened her trunk when she was picked up and enveloped in her cousin's strong arms.

"Let me down, you big oaf." She attempted to disengage herself from his grip. "I can't breathe."

A broad grin spread across Bobby's wide face as he let her slide to the ground with a thud. "Not my fault you're a bit on the weak side."

Parker grabbed her bags and handed them to Bobby. As usual, his hair looked like it hadn't been combed in a week. "Since you are so big and strong, you can carry my luggage."

"Sure. Hold this."

Parker looked down at the stained t-shirt in her hand and groaned.

She jogged to catch up with him. "Do you know any more about what's going on?"

She was disappointed, but not surprised when he had no answer.

Bobby left after he deposited her in one of the guest rooms in Morgan and Clara's house. She was grateful for the chance to collect herself. There was no way she was going downstairs until she was fully equipped, and scentless. She pulled a change of clothes from her bag and was about to head to the bathroom when a knock on the door interrupted her. Without waiting to be invited, Clara breezed in.

The matronly female alpha pulled Parker into a warm, but firm embrace. "Hey, *Liebe*, how was the drive?"

She felt a familiar warmth spread through her. Not only was Clara the pack's second Alpha, but over the years, she had become a surrogate parent.

Clara loosened her grip and clicked her tongue with a disapproving tsk. "Are you eating properly? You don't have enough meat on your bones."

Clara had been taken from her native Germany over two centuries ago, but her very German nature had never wavered.

Clara held Parker at arm's length and assessed her. Her sharp brown eyes missed nothing. "You must be exhausted. Get freshened up and come downstairs to the kitchen. I won't have you starving yourself. You will have something to eat before you see Morgan and Alpha Locke. They can wait."

She stiffened at the mention of the Alpha Commander. The blood drained from her face in an instant. Her panic must have been evident because Clara leveled a stern look at her. "I realize you have bad blood between you, but that needs to be put aside." Clara paused, and her forehead crinkled with worry. "There is more at stake here than misplaced pride and stubbornness—both yours and Alpha Locke's."

Her stomach tightened "What's going on?" It must be something serious for Clara to be so direct.

She was frustrated when Clara shook her head and sighed. "Sorry, *Liebe*, but you'll need to wait until you meet with Morgan and Daniel."

"But—"

Clara cut her off and headed for the door. "Parker, I know what you're thinking, but you both need to…how do they say…build a bridge." She glanced back and continued in her no-nonsense tone. "And that's the last I am going to say on the matter. Be downstairs in five minutes."

Parker remained quiet. She dared not contradict Clara when she was in this sort of mood. Not game to keep Clara waiting, she rushed into the bathroom, showered, and changed in record time. She soaked Bobby's shirt to tackle later, and raced downstairs before Clara sent up a search party.

A sense of panic overtook her at the top of the stairs, and she stopped to wipe her hands on her jeans. She took a deep breath. *Get a grip.*

Parker slipped into the large country kitchen, relieved to see Clara was the only other occupant. She made her way to the breakfast bar and climbed on one of the stools, just as the older woman placed a dish of Pasta Carbonara in front of her. Her stomach took the opportunity to grumble and she cringed. She hadn't eaten since early that morning.

Clara poured two glasses of Chardonnay and took a seat next to her.

She raised a questioning eyebrow at the choice of drink.

"I think you need something stronger than your usual tea before we go to the library."

Parker's heart skipped a beat. Whatever was going on must be serious. To calm her anxiety, she changed the subject. "I like your new do, by the way, very Helen Mirren."

Clara smiled and touched the back of her hair. "You like?"

Parker nodded and they discussed Clara's sudden jump from grey to honey blond.

As soon as Parker finished her meal, Clara whipped away the dishes and slid them in the dishwasher. "We'd better go. I suspect Alpha Locke will be getting a little impatient about now."

At the mention of his name, Parker's stomach lurched. The nervous energy escalated, and she jiggled her foot before slipping off the stool.

She followed Clara to the library. Just outside the door, Clara halted and placed a gentle hand on Parker's arm. "It's not my place to tell you why you've been asked here. But before we go in, I want to assure you, whatever your decision, both Morgan and I will stand behind you."

Parker let out a nervous laugh, and she broke out in a cold sweat. "You make it sound like I'm walking to the gallows." She had the sudden desire to flee the building, get into her car, and make a run for it.

Clara pushed her into the library before she changed her mind. The room, with its floor to ceiling bookcases lined with ancient, musty books, always unsettled her. Having to meet Alpha Locke within its imposing walls reinforced her apprehension.

Morgan stood by the window, deep in conversation with a man she did not recognize. The man wore the brightest pair of board shorts she'd ever seen. From his slim frame and open, mischievous expression, she figured he couldn't be an alpha.

Morgan looked up, and an affectionate smile spread across his face. In three giant strides, she was enfolded in a fatherly bear hug. As with most alphas, Morgan towered well above her, and she felt like a twig wrapped in his powerful arms.

Despite his age, Morgan was a striking figure. He had graying salt and pepper hair and a body that men in their prime would envy. Both he and Clara looked to be in their mid-sixties, but she knew they were at least ten times that in reality.

Morgan turned to his companion. "Parker, I'd like to introduce you to Simon Dumas. He's a Mountain Pack beta who also doubles as the chief financial officer for Locke Industries."

Simon grinned. "Nice to finally meet you, even if it isn't under the best of circumstances."

She shook the offered hand and recalled that they had spoken in the past. His boyish charm and blond hair were irresistible, and she found herself returning the smile despite her nerves. Unlike Morgan, Simon was only a few inches taller

THREE

The Meeting

Parker's hand trembled as she held the photo. Her other hand flew to her mouth, and she felt sick to her stomach.

Jesus, she's just a baby.

She cleared her throat to dislodge a lump that refused to budge. Even if she wanted to, she was not sure she could speak. For the better part of the last hour, Daniel had brought her up-to-date on the mounting deaths across the country. With each horrific case, her dismay escalated.

She wasn't alone. The other Werewolves let out low growls as Daniel relayed the facts of each death, though he kept a stoic face. The story of Wildfire and its effects bombarded her brain, and a volley of questions popped into her mind. One question rose above the rest.

How was this possible?

Her analytical mind swept through the possibilities. Werewolves' metabolisms were so resilient that it took a large quantity of any narcotic for their bodies to experience the slightest of highs. It was impossible for a Werewolf to become addicted to any drug. Binging on alcohol was easier and cheaper than spending over five hundred dollars to get a three minute buzz.

Werewolves don't get ill.

Their natural healing abilities fought illnesses and diseases that Humans fall prey to every day. Bobby was a testimony to this. Her cousin, diagnosed with type 1 diabetes as a child, had been sentenced to a life of insulin shots. Once he survived the long and painful change, his new-found healing abilities repaired his pancreas and ensured his body produced the appropriate amount of insulin.

She glanced down at the table. Photos of dead Werewolves were scattered across the polished wood. Each one was more tragic than the previous. The pictures were evidence that someone, or something, was tampering with nature in a gruesome and terrifying way.

Why?

Her gaze fixed on the image of a young girl not more than seventeen years old, and her heart broke. The girl's body, disfigured by large, dark sores, lay crumpled by a dumpster, as if she were garbage.

Parker closed her eyes and cleared her mind. Even though she knew the answer, she had to ask. "Do you have any idea who might be behind this?"

Daniel replied for the others in the room. "No."

"Do you have a cure or are you close to one?"

"No."

"Do you know who else might be infected right now?"

Daniel rubbed his forehead and sighed. He stared straight at her and let out a low growl. "Are you able to help us or not?"

It was fleeting, but she saw it. For the briefest of moments, a flash of anguish and concern washed across Daniel's face. She quashed her compassion for his pain. Even with the stone-cold expression that took nothing away from the incredible specimen of male beauty, he was still the same person who had threatened to ruin her and tear her to pieces if she ever stepped foot on his territory.

She had turned down several lucrative jobs because they might have required her to travel through Colorado. While her rational mind realized he would never carry out his threat, the part of her that understood Werewolves' capabilities did not want to push her luck.

Parker glanced around the room. The others looked at her for an answer.

As if I had a choice?

Daniel Locke would not get the upper hand. She lifted her chin. "Of course, I can. You wouldn't have gotten me involved if you didn't think so."

Daniel's brows bumped together in a scowl. "Ms. Johnson, I think you are under the illusion I am requesting your services. It is Alpha Morgan and the Alliance who want your help. I am charged with ensuring your safety." He paused, and she flinched under his unrelenting stare. "And to minimize the damage that your involvement will undoubtedly result in."

She narrowed her eyes. *And there you have it.*

That insufferable man she had the misfortune of dealing with three years ago was back. The haughty, arrogant, and unreasonable individual that made her life a nightmare during the abduction incident was present and accounted for.

Her frayed nerves changed into hot, livid heat. She would not take this sort of crap from Locke—no matter how gorgeous or powerful he was.

She tossed the photo on the table and clenched her fists. "Mr. Locke, you seem to forget that at no point was I supplied with the full details about the situation three years ago. You decided what information you deemed fit to give me. Which, by the way, was nothing." Her chest rose and fell with rapid breaths. "Had I been aware of the full circumstances, I would've been better prepared, and you would've gotten the information you needed that much sooner."

Her fists twitched. Never before had she had such an overwhelming desire to physically assault another person.

Daniel crossed his arms over his chest. "Had you done your job, we wouldn't have lost a good man." His voice was low with barely restrained hostility. "Not to mention, someone I love wouldn't carry the scars of your incompetency with her for the rest of her life."

Her chest tightened at the memory. Doing her best to ignore it, she was about to throw a retort back at Daniel when Morgan's voice boomed. "I have heard enough!"

She stopped short and snapped her head around to face Morgan and the others, who looked on with shock.

Morgan glared from one to the other. "You two are acting like immature cubs. You both need to forget what happened in the past and focus on the situation at hand."

Parker's shoulders slumped. She was humiliated. Daniel had destroyed her composure and civility in an instant.

She sat down and drummed her fingers on the armrest. "He started it," she said under her breath.

Morgan frowned at her as if she was a petulant child. "You know I heard that."

An uneasy silence descended over the room. Clara hovered beside Morgan, the older woman's expression commanding her to see sense.

Parker groaned inwardly—she had made a right spectacle of herself. Her anger evaporated as quickly as it began, and she let out a deep breath. "Of course, I'll help Mr. Locke and his team. I'm just surprised that you didn't reach out sooner."

Now that her rational mind was back in control, she stood and took charge of the meeting. "Okay, we need to come up with a strategy to deal with this situation. I have some suggestions on how we should proceed."

Morgan and Clara visibly relaxed.

Parker pointed to the empty bottle of Wildfire that lay in the middle of the table. "From what you're telling me, we're dealing with someone who exists only in the digital world."

***

Daniel lay in the dark and stared up at the ceiling. Sleep had eluded him, and he found his mind playing over the events of the evening. He had occasionally encountered someone who challenged his authority over the years. As Alpha Commander, he was adept in dispensing with them in a quick and efficient manner. Most sane people would shy away from any suggestion of a confrontation with him, knowing it could be a death sentence.

He was baffled at how this little Human not only defied him, but pushed back and challenged him, and did so with fire and courage in her expressive blue eyes. He did not know whether to be concerned for her sanity or impressed by her bravery. From the moment she walked into the room, she had unnerved him, and he had been blindsided by her lack of scent. Not once had he ever met someone like her.

He was used to being able to gauge a Human's emotions. They had so little control over their bodies' reactions to what they were thinking or feeling. The greater the emotion, the easier for him to read them. Except for Parker.

From her horrified expression, Parker was affected by the photos, but once the initial shock had worn off, she schooled her features and erected a wall. It confused him. She should not have the ability to control her body's emotions so tightly that it failed to produce a physical reaction and scent.

I'll speak to Morgan about it in the morning.

His wolf stirred, letting him know in no uncertain terms to be quiet and go to sleep.

His mind was conflicted. He struggled to understand how he had let a Human ruffle him. He did not trust her. No matter that he could get lost in those eyes that exploded with sparks when they locked with his and refused to back down; or how soft and small her hand felt in his. He couldn't trust her. How could he, after she was responsible not only for the death of one of his men, but the irreparable damage inflicted on an innocent child?

She was right you know… His wolf yawned, trying to find a better position.

"About what?"

We didn't tell her everything.

He declined to comment, knowing his wolf spoke the truth.

We like her.

"No, we don't. She's Human, argumentative, and disrespectful."

Don't care. Sleep now.

He grunted at his wolf and promised he would find out everything about her from Morgan.

After all, this is war. Know thy enemy.

He sighed as he drifted off to sleep. His mind emptied of all but a set of almond-shaped bright blue eyes, fanned by thick dark lashes.

FOUR

An Uneasy Truce

Daniel thumped his pillow and grumbled under his breath. He'd managed to fall asleep, only to wake up less than an hour later, his mind in chaos, working overtime with images of bodies littered across his valley. Each one was covered with the tell-tale black sores of Wildfire. He would not allow that to happen to his people. His pack looked to him for protection. No matter what it took, he would make sure he found out who was behind this drug and make them pay for murdering innocents.

He rose and took a shower, then wandered downstairs. His mind ran through the list of what he needed to organize, all the while grinding his teeth together and grumbling under his breath. The idiotic decree by the council that the Johnson woman be under his direct protection was going to cause more problems than it was worth. He should be in San Francisco, leading the charge on whoever was behind the deaths of the Werewolves. Instead, he had to babysit her until Trevor, one of his enforcers, arrived in Portland to take over and escort her to Nederland.

He rubbed his chin and sighed. Hopefully, the delay in going to San Francisco would not leave the trail cold for any potential leads on whoever was behind Wildfire. There would be hell to pay if it did. But first, he was on a mission in search of coffee.

He strode into the kitchen and stopped short. *You have got to be kidding me.* Of course, she would be here. Parker was sitting at the large breakfast bar, staring at her laptop.

Startled, Parker looked up. Her smile froze midway and turned into a frown. She turned back to the monitor and resumed typing. Her fingers moved with such speed they flew across the small keyboard. The only sound in the kitchen was the quick tapping of the keys as they made contact with the surface.

He shrugged his shoulders. They could both play that game. He headed to the elaborate coffee machine installed on one of the kitchen counters and stood in front of it, perplexed.

What the hell am I supposed to do with this?

The massive machine staring back at him resembled the high-tech contraptions he had seen in top-end restaurants and cafés. An array of knobs, dials, taps, buttons, and graphic displays adorned the apparatus. Not one of them appeared to have the words *"push this button to instantly receive your coffee"* on it.

He grabbed one of the green coffee cups on top of the unit and placed it where he thought it might go. Not to be outdone by a machine, he poked and fiddled with the knobs to see what they would do, but nothing that resembled coffee came forth. He let out a low growl. Then, manna from heaven, one of the metal cylinders on the side dripped water.

Yes.

He quickly moved his cup underneath to catch the coffee that would undoubtedly soon follow, and eyed the machine with a look of absolute triumph.

Without warning, the metal spout that had been dripping water sizzled, and a high-pitched squeal echoed throughout the room. *What the?* Hot water, which quickly turned into steam, bounced off his cup and spurted all over the place, soaking anything and everything in its path. The display at the top of the unit flashed, and a constant and irritating beep permeated the kitchen.

Daniel took a quick step back and glared at the machine.

What the hell is wrong with this thing?

Parker pushed him away. "Oh, for Christ's sake, move, will you." She reached over, pulled out the offending cup, and pushed a few buttons. The appalling sound stopped, and the room was once again silent.

He let out a breath, thankful for the silence.

Parker reached for another cup and placed it on one of the drip trays. She removed a handle from the apparatus and filled it with ground coffee beans, which were dispensed from one of the containers. After pressing it with a tamper, she locked the handle back in place and pushed a few more buttons.

Daniel breathed in the luxurious aroma of fruit and spice as coffee slowly poured out of two small nozzles. When the cup was half full, she unceremoniously deposited it in front of him. Still not speaking, she returned to her seat and resumed tapping away at the keyboard.

He picked up the cup and stared at the liquid. While he knew he shouldn't push her buttons any further, something in him wanted to tease her a little. A grin tugged at his lips, and he raised an eyebrow. "What? No foam?"

Parker threw him a glare that would fell a lesser man, and, for the most part, attempted to ignore his presence. No matter where he went, people fell over themselves to get on his good side. But not Parker. Curious, he deposited himself in the seat next to hers and enjoyed his coffee. As the silence drew out, he cocked his head, and his gaze wandered over her. She was alternating between sipping what looked and smelled like herbal tea, and working away on her laptop.

Parker tucked a stray curl behind her ear. He sniffed the air. Her luxurious chestnut hair smelled of flowers and honey. In fact, that was the only scent he picked up from her. He had to ask Morgan to explain her lack of scent.

The silence grew awkward. He tapped the side of his cup and shifted in his chair. "Thank you."

Those same eyes he could not get out of his head the night before looked up, a confused frown marring her otherwise lovely features. Even though he disliked the woman, he had to admit she fascinated him.

"For what?"

He glanced down at his now half empty cup. "The coffee. It's very good."

Parker turned back to her laptop and resumed her tapping. "Don't mention it."

He held back a grin and peered over her shoulder, curious as to what had her rapt attention. A window was open on the screen, and she was typing line after line of text he did not recognize. Many of the words were in English, but more than a few seemed to be in an unintelligible language. None related to the five languages he knew.

Curiosity got the better of him. "May I ask what you are doing?"

There was a short silence. Daniel smiled inwardly, he might not be able to determine what she was feeling through smell, but her expressive face and eyes gave him all the information he needed. Even her red-rimmed glasses could not hide everything. An internal battle waged on whether to ignore him or relent and answer his question.

Parker's shoulders relaxed, and she let out a sigh. "I'm writing a web crawler that will search all sites selling Wildfire or any product that contains the ingredients. I'm also coding the crawler to search the deep web for any mention of the drug."

He raised a brow. "Deep web?"

"The portion of the internet that is indexed by standard search engines like Google is called the Surface Web. The bits outside this are the Deep Web. It's this part that's harder to reach, and about six hundred times larger than the Surface Web. Part of the Deep Web is a criminal playground. I'm hoping to find some clues from there. It will take a bit longer, but usually gives us good results."

He considered this new information. "Okay, so once you've found the sites that are selling it, what then?"

Parker tucked another loose strand of hair behind her ear. "Basically, we hack into the online trader's database, get the order information, and then start the real work." She took a sip of her tea. "The way I see it, we have two separate goals. The first is to contain the existing exposure. The second is to find out who's doing this."

"So, you can get the person's details from the order, and my men can track them down from there?"

Parker nodded. "Exactly. I can give you their names and addresses. However, you will need to work out if they are Werewolf or Human."

His previous animosity with her temporarily forgotten, he discussed options on how to proceed once they had located affected Werewolves. Once those on the drug were tracked down, they would need to be quarantined. The only question was—where would they hold these individuals? Wherever it was, they would require medical care.

For the first time since the onset of Wildfire, Daniel felt in control of the situation, and a small portion of the weight on his shoulders lifted. The packs were already on high alert, and he would ensure his first responder teams spread the word to the unaligned communities. The problem was, what kind of devastation would this cause before they brought the virus under control?

He rubbed his jaw and tried to settle his unease. While Parker continued coding, he contacted the appropriate people to start arrangements for a temporary hospital on his pack's grounds. Not caring whom he had to wake up to get things organized, he reached for his phone. If this was to work, they needed to be ready.

Just as Daniel ended his third phone call, Morgan and Clara wandered in and surveyed the paper strewn across the table and floor.

Daniel swallowed a grin when Morgan involuntarily twitched at the mess.

"Good morning," Parker said.

Morgan raised an eyebrow.

"What?"

Morgan shrugged and pulled his gaze up from the floor. "Oh nothing, just amazed the only thing littering my floor is paper, not blood."

Parker grimaced and glanced at the mess. "Sorry. We've already made a start."

Clara scolded Morgan and grinned at Parker. "Don't worry about him and his OCD tendencies. You do what you need to do." She placed a pan on the iron gas cooktop and ignited the flame. "You look hungry. I'll cook you up some pancakes and bacon."

Daniel's eyes lit up. Now that his thirst was sated, his stomach had been calling out for food.

Morgan stood near Clara, who busied herself in the kitchen. Every so often, he grabbed some bacon and popped it in his mouth before she hit him with a spatula.

Daniel shook his head and smiled. The man was taking his own life in his hands messing with Clara's kitchen.

Morgan wolfed down another rasher and focused his sharp eyes on Parker. "How are we going to track down whoever's behind this?"

Daniel pocketed his phone. Parker had already covered this with him so he was only half listening. The aroma coming from the skillet was making him ravenous.

"That's the hard bit." Parker grabbed a pen and drew a diagram on a pad to help illustrate her point. "My team will need to follow each transaction individually and track it through the banking system. This is going to take time. We don't have a warrant, and since we'll need to do it without getting caught, we can't use the standard channels. I already have my team working on finding their way through the back door of the central banks, so that should give us a head start. Once we do that, then we can—"

"What do you mean you already have your team working on this?" Daniel glared at Parker and closed the distance to the table in a heartbeat. The woman was a menace. He couldn't believe she would do this after assuring them she only had their best interests at heart. "I knew you couldn't be trusted."

Parker threw her hands in the air. "What the hell are you talking about? Are there no batteries included in that brain of yours?"

The room stilled. The only sound was the sizzle and pop of the bacon cooking on the skillet.

Daniel's jaw clenched, and the muscles in his face twitched. This creature blatantly and publicly defied him every step of the way—and had the audacity to question the state of *his* mind. What possessed Morgan to allow her to walk around free after she had discovered their existence he would never know. She should have been killed or imprisoned, anything but be allowed to roam around in public and risk the lives they had so carefully rebuilt.

How could he have been so blind as to think she would understand their need for secrecy? She had involved Humans without their permission. His mind churned through options to contain this new problem. *I'll have to act fast before any damage is done.*

Simon entered the room and mumbled, "Awkward." He busied himself by pretending to read one of the newspapers left on the table.

Unable to contain his frustration any longer, Daniel let loose. "Did we," he said through gritted teeth, "or did we not, agree that this needed to be handled carefully, and that no Humans were to be involved?"

Parker stood her ground. She lifted her chin in defiance and crossed her arms over her chest. "You mean, *you* agreed."

"Just answer the question."

He had expected Parker to show some form of remorse for the danger she had put them in. Despite the obvious threat, she was staring at him as though he had taken leave of his senses.

Before he uttered another word, a sharp laugh erupted from Morgan. "You two are so entertaining. We should sell tickets."

Daniel received another of Parker's withering glares as she reached for her laptop and snapped it shut. "That's it, I'm out of here." With that, she stormed out of the kitchen, as if the devil himself were on her heels.

Simon ducked his head behind the newspaper. "And then *that* happened."

Morgan chuckled. "Daniel, Parker didn't get any outsiders involved. You have my word."

Daniel ran a hand through his hair. "How can you say that? We can't risk exposure! You heard her. She already has, and she did it behind our backs." He cast a disgusted glare at the door through which she had disappeared. A low growl reverberated in his chest, and he recalled his original misgivings. "I should have pushed back when the council came up with this ridiculous plan."

Morgan let out a loud exhale and shook his head from side to side. "My friend, I know for a fact that Parker hasn't put us at risk. The team she was referring to belong to my pack."

This halted Daniel in his tracks, and his brows shot up. "What?"

Morgan eyed up the food Clara was preparing. "Parker employs two of my brightest omegas."

Clara smacked the back of Morgan's hand when he attempted to steal one of the pancakes from the stack. He threw her a cheeky grin and continued. "It's getting harder and harder for us to hide in plain sight. Our people have an expiration date—ten years. That's as long as we can stay in a single job before Humans notice we don't age. We have been lucky so far. As you know, each one of our packs have built up successful businesses that more than support our people and provide employment in the areas we are adept at."

Daniel tensed his shoulders. "And this relates to your omegas how?"

Morgan looked directly at Daniel, his expression no longer jovial. "We have ignored the technology age for far too long, and it's going to be our downfall."

Clara served up brunch and nodded for them to take a seat at the nearby table. "You know yourself, Daniel, it was easier in the early days." The worry lines on her forehead were more pronounced than normal. "We could swap outdated paper records with forged ones."

Simon put his newspaper down, eyed the huge plate of food, and rubbed his hands together. "I even remember one pack burning down their local city hall so the paperwork would be destroyed," he said, referring to the infamous incident from eight decades ago. "I think they pinned the blame on the local KKK Chapter."

Morgan picked up his cup of hot coffee and consumed half the contents. "That avenue is no longer an option for us." He put the cup down. "Everything is now stored on computers. Records of births and deaths, driver's licenses, school transcripts, the list is endless. Every part of what allowed us to hide in the Human world is now stored in zeros and ones, completely outside of our control."

Daniel folded his arms. "I am already aware of this." He was still unsure where the conversation was headed, or how it related to Morgan's omegas—or even their current situation for that matter.

It was true that each generation of Humans came with a new raft of problems. The computer age had caused more than its fair share of trouble for the Werewolf race. So far, they had minimized their exposure, but even he knew that would not last.

Morgan pushed his hands into his pockets and stared at his feet, and sighed. "Technology is here to stay. We have neither the skill nor the knowledge to be able to navigate it. As a race, we are at a disadvantage, and we can't wait until the Werewolves born into this age are mature and capable of the commitment required."

Morgan nodded in the direction Parker had escaped. "Parker has taken two members of my pack that displayed a keen interest in computers under her wing. Over the past two years, she has been training them. They're still young, and their wolves can only stay still for a few hours at a time. Because of this, Parker has them working in a separate office from the rest of her team. They come and go as they need to satisfy their wolves."

Daniel scowled. How come he was only hearing about this now?

Morgan paused and looked directly at him. "My friend, this is a different world from the one you and I were born into, but this is the world we live in. We need to make sure that the next generation is prepared. Parker is helping us set the groundwork. If it works, we can expand the program beyond my pack."

A part of Daniel wished that Morgan's belief would come true. They had always known they needed real world experience to help their race through the digital age. He knew as well as Morgan and every other alpha in the Alliance and beyond, that the only way this could be achieved was through training. However, the intensity of the training came at a price and had destroyed more than one Werewolf. When they were young, their wolves demanded control. A lot of control, which meant at least half their time would be spent in wolf form. If denied, they could lose their sanity.

Daniel felt his chest tighten, and he rubbed an eyebrow. "Why have you never mentioned this before?" He was an alpha, damn it. How had this been kept from him?

Morgan looked surprised. "But we have. Simon knows about it. We have been looking for new recruits from your pack."

Simon raised his hands. "In my defense, I did try to tell you on more than one occasion, but because Parker was involved you didn't want to know about it."

This announcement put Daniel in unfamiliar territory, and he was consumed with a foreign emotion—guilt. It appeared, in this instance, he had misjudged Parker. How had he let his emotions get the better of him? It was as if Parker was his Achilles heel, and he couldn't see beyond her actions of three years ago. Could he risk his people's safety and trust her to guide them to whoever was behind this? He struggled to reconcile his loathing for the woman against his need to protect his race.

Say sorry now. His wolf was less hesitant.

Daniel was still dubious. *No, she has been nothing but disrespectful.*

We like her. She makes nice coffee. Say sorry.

No.

But even he had to admit, they needed her. Daniel clenched his jaw. The tenuous working relationship they had reached earlier needed to be salvaged. If it meant he had to apologize; so be it. There was a first time for everything.

Daniel grunted, stood up, and marched out of the delicious-smelling kitchen.

***

Parker groaned as she exited the house and headed toward her Blazer. *Why is Locke leaning against my car like he owns it?* She cursed Bobby. If she hadn't rushed over to give him his clean t-shirt, she might have left before Daniel had a chance to come after her.

Daniel watched in silence as she approached. Nothing in his expression gave away his current state of mind. Not wishing for another argument with him, she scooted around to the back of the Blazer and dropped her bags in the trunk. To her dismay, she discovered a small black suitcase and a suit bag that had not been there before.

She narrowed her eyes and her brows bumped together in a scowl as she slammed the trunk closed and made her way to the driver's side. She tapped her foot and waited. Would he get the hint and leave?

Daniel was the first to break the silence. "I believe I might owe you an apology."

She raised an eyebrow. "Might?"

He ran long, masculine fingers through his hair and took a deep breath. "Okay, I'm sorry. I may have over-reacted."

She raised her other eyebrow. "May?"

Her buzzing phone interrupted their escalating animosity, and when she looked up again, he was eyeing her. Her initial reaction was to ignore him, but common sense overrode her gut instinct. This was Werewolf business and lives were at stake.

"Zeke hacked into one of the sites the crawler found. He now has a set of names and addresses for us."

Her phone buzzed again.

"Thirty-two names and addresses to be exact. He's having difficulty with a couple of firewalls, so I have to get back."

"You're not going alone."

Parker jumped at the sound of Morgan's voice.

Morgan handed Parker two plastic containers. "There's one for each of you, and I suggest you polish everything off. Clara will be most displeased if anything is left."

Parker looked in the containers thrust into her hands. "I can't eat all that."

Morgan grinned. "Didn't you hear what I just said? There's one each. The second is for Daniel. I'm sure you'll get hungry on the drive back to Portland."

"What?"

Morgan chuckled. "Tickets, I tell you. I would make a fortune." His face turned serious. "Parker, the moment you accepted this assignment, your life was in danger. We have no idea who is behind the killings, nor what information they have access to. The council have made your safety Daniel's responsibility. As far as they are concerned, you are joined at the hip until this mess is over."

Parker's pulse raced, and she nearly dropped the warm containers. She knew Daniel had been made accountable for her safety, but she did not think they were going to go to such extreme measures. She glanced across at Daniel. He looked as pleased as she felt—perhaps even less so, if that was possible.

"Besides," Morgan said, "Daniel will get a chance to meet Zeke and Jay before you all head to Colorado."

A sharp pain pulsed behind her left eye. She rubbed her eyelid to alleviate the discomfort. This wasn't going to plan. She had assumed she could talk Morgan out of the stupid idea of her going to Nederland. "You do know I don't need a babysitter."

Morgan shrugged and cocked his head. "If you want to argue the point, how about I send Clara out here?"

"No, no need." She already knew what Clara would say if she thought her safety was in jeopardy.

Morgan looked between Parker and Daniel. "Thought you'd see it my way." He winked and held his hand out to Daniel. "Let me know if you need anything."

Daniel shook the offered hand and nodded.

Morgan made his way back to the brick and stone mansion, but just before he reached the steps, he turned and called out to Daniel. "Before I forget, watch out for Beth." With that, he took the steps two at a time, and disappeared through the double doors.

Still not thrilled at the sudden change in her plans, Parker shook herself out of her personal pity party and sighed.

Nothing she said would change their minds. "Okay, then. We'd better be off."

She attempted to navigate around the towering man.

Daniel blocked her path and held out his hand, palm face up. "Give me the keys, I'm driving."

She blinked rapidly, and her eyes opened wide. "I beg your pardon?"

Before she could say no, he extracted the keys from her fingers, got behind the wheel, and turned the engine over.

A low growl came from inside her Blazer. "Get in, now."

She shook off the stupor. "I-I will do no such thing."

Daniel leaned over and opened the passenger door. He swung his gaze back to her and pierced her with a playful grin. "You seem to forget—you answer to me. And, as I have been placed in charge of this investigation, anyone you bring onto the team needs to be approved by me. If you want your omegas to stay involved, you'd better get in."

Parker hesitated. Five hours trapped in a moving vehicle with Daniel Locke was going to be torture. It did not matter how ruggedly handsome he was, or how nice his lips were, this was above and beyond.

Nice lips? A flutter rose up from the pit of her stomach. She mentally rebuked herself as she stomped around to the passenger door. *The last person's lips you should be contemplating are Daniel Locke's.*

FIVE

Something Wicked This Way Comes

Middlemarch Estate

Elijah's key scraped in the metal lock. He smiled sardonically as the rats scattered. Their sharp nails scratched against the damp stone floor in their flight to safety. The vermin were about to get more food to chew on. He threw the door open and stepped aside to allow the newest prisoner to be welcomed to her new home.

François, his colleague, propelled the latest test subject past him, and she fell to the floor in a crumpled heap before struggling to rise.

Her tiny whimpers ignited Elijah's ever-present hunger. If only he'd been allowed to play with her first. His fingers ached to trace his trusty blade across her soft skin, and to inhale the sweet metallic scent of her blood as it seeped from each jagged scar.

Elijah sighed. It wasn't to be. She was special. They needed her for the doctor's experiments. No matter. He was supplied with enough playthings to distract him from taking things he should not.

A shuffle from the far corner caught his eye. Their other prisoner peered through the darkness at his new cellmate.

Before Elijah could say anything, footsteps broke through the woman's low moans, and he stood at attention. He smirked when the shackled prisoner shrank back into the darkness as his leader stood in the doorway. *At least you didn't wet yourself this time.*

"Chain her."

The voice was cold, unfeeling, and powerful, as though dealing with an errant speck of dust.

François rushed to carry out the order. The new prisoner's ankles were forced into rusty iron shackles, a size too small so her circulation was limited. Her restraints were secured to chains attached to a metal ring bolted to the floor. Francois yanked the cloth sack off her head with such a violent pull that her head cracked back when her vertebrae objected to the harsh treatment.

Elijah held back the bolt of desire rippling through his body. Her pain was his pleasure.

Once François was satisfied the woman was secure, he followed their leader out of the cell and down the narrow corridor.

Elijah allowed his gaze to wander across the new prisoner's broken form. He licked his lips, almost tasting her fear. When an icy "Let's go," echoed down the corridor, he pulled the door closed and locked it. The dungeon returned to darkness, but unable to push down his inner need, Elijah peered through the small peephole.

Another whimper escaped from the new prisoner, and she struggled to rise from the floor. She was blind in the dark, but he made out the outline of the two prisoners and the rotting body. The prisoner felt around in the dark, then stiffened when the scrape of chains from somewhere near rang out. The movement from the existing prisoner was followed by a series of sniffs.

A croaked, almost inaudible male voice broke the silence. "You're Human."

Elijah couldn't help grinning as the prisoner moved away from her unknown cellmate. With barely any light, she felt along the stone floor, and her hands bumped against something. She crawled closer to the object and ran her palms over the oddly shaped form. Parts of it were soft and wet. Her fingers were sticky when she pulled them away. She continued to feel around the object she had found in the dark chamber.

Elijah chuckled as he closed the peephole and followed the others up the stairs. The stench from the rotting corpse was overpowering, and he looked forward to the fresh air above ground. As they emerged from the underground dungeon into daylight, the woman's screams reached her captors.

"She's found Jim, then," François said.

For such a large person, the maniacal giggle that followed was eerie.

Elijah rolled his eyes and ignored François. He continued his conversation with their leader. "We've increased the number of online channels for the product, and we are ready to move into the next phase on your say so."

The three continued toward a heavily guarded building not far from the dungeon. The guards, dressed from head to foot in black, were armed to the teeth with automatic rifles and concealed weapons. They stood to attention when they saw who was approaching.

Their leader barely acknowledged the guards as they passed. "Continue with the expansion plan, and make sure there's no way they can trace it to us."

As they entered the building, Elijah glanced around the pristine room. Dr. Fridericks and his assistant, in their ever-present white lab coats, waited beside a medical table. Beside them, strapped to the table, was another test subject. He was naked and gagged.

When their leader came into view, the man's eyes grew wild with panic, and he struggled against the restraints.

Elijah glanced across at François and murmured, "I don't know why they try and break free. It's pointless, if you ask me."

Their leader stood over the terror-stricken man, and motioned for the doctor to proceed.

"Make no mistake, we cannot fail in our goal to rid the earth of those abominations once and for all. Not even that stupid Alliance, or their joke of an Alpha Commander, can stop us this time. Start the procedure."

Fridericks reached for a biopsy needle. "Yes, Alpha Lauzon."

SIX

Mind the Personal Space

For the first half hour, the drive back to Portland was spent in relative calm. The fact that neither of them spoke probably had more to do with that than anything, and Parker chose not to destroy the peace, but as the miles flew by, the situation became more awkward. Unable to withstand the pressure any longer, she cracked. "I'm assuming Morgan told you about the training program."

She glanced across at Daniel's profile in time to detect a hint of a smile threatening to emerge from his stern exterior. A wave of heat rushed through her body.

God, I need to stop staring at his lips. This is disturbing, to say the least.

When her phone beeped, she breathed a sigh of relief for the distraction, and scanned the message.

"Tell me about your two prodigies," Daniel said.

She thought about the question for a moment, then shrugged. "Not much to say really. Both of them are good—very good—truth be told. It's just going to take a while to get them to a level where they can train others."

Parker replied to the message from Jay, and continued. "It's been interesting. Zeke's just turned twenty-two, so his wolf isn't mature. It wants out, but Zeke has an innate need to finish what he starts."

She twisted in her seat to face Daniel, a grin on her lips. "I sometimes walk into the lab and find him having a conversation with his wolf. They are forever negotiating. It's like listening to divorced parents arranging custody of the kids. Except in this case, it's for who's going to have custody of his body."

Daniel let out an amused chuckle. "I know what you mean. We have a bizarre relationship with our wolves. It takes years before we find the balance that suits both sides." He turned the air con dial up before continuing. "What does your firm do exactly?"

Parker settled into her seat and considered the best way to explain. "The work is different based on the client's needs, but, in a nutshell, we offer computer intelligence forensic services. Which is a fancy way of saying we track and analyze information hidden in computers, and help organizations stop the gaps in their security."

She glanced down at her phone. "My company works on anything from following money trails to finding discrepancies in accounts, and in some cases we track down people. We spend hours and hours finding the information, and then even more time pouring over data and interpreting it. Our clients come to us when they need us to find information they have lost or are after, or if they have information they want to keep behind locked doors."

Daniel checked the rearview mirror and readjusted his grip on the steering wheel. "How do the omegas fit into all of this?"

"Well, both Zeke and Jay have different skills. Zeke is, without question, our hacker. Jay, on the other hand, is brilliant at analysis. He can take seemingly unrelated information and form a connection to give it meaning."

"So, if they were both petty thieves, Zeke could break into anything, and Jay could then tell you what was worth stealing?"

Parker grinned. "Not bad. We just may get you into the twenty-first century yet."

"How have you dealt with the omega's needs? I get that it requires dedication and a lot of commitment, what I don't understand is how Zeke and Jay can get the job done effectively."

Parker bit the inside of her lip as she considered the question. "I don't assign them any jobs that require us to track down people. That type of work is mission critical, and I don't have the luxury of time. They get assigned the stuff that can be worked on piecemeal."

She furrowed her brow and attempted to find an alternate way of explaining how the arrangement worked. "It's simple, really, they work on the task until their wolves get antsy, and then they let them free. When they're ready, they return to work and continue on the project."

"With that kind of inconsistency, doesn't that mean they will never become skilled enough?"

She shook her head and smiled. She, Morgan, and Clara had spoken at length since taking on the two omegas, on this exact topic. "Hackers and developers are a complete subspecies. They exist on pizza, caffeine, and energy drinks. They're happiest when left in their own little world. Both Zeke and Jay are no different in that way. It's just that they can't be in that world for as long as the others. They will get there. It will just take them longer."

Parker pushed her glasses up onto her head. The slow progress to master this skill was something Morgan and the others had first struggled to come to terms with. "I think your problem is that you don't know how to fail. The professions you do take up, you excel in. You can do most things faster and more efficiently than your Human counterparts, but, when it comes to any of the sciences, you have shied away. It's these areas that require a commitment of time as well as mind—time that a young Werewolf can't possibly achieve in the same timeframe as a Human."

Daniel flicked the indicator on and sped up to overtake a slow vehicle. "Are you sure their wolves are coping with the restrictions you are placing on them?"

Parker sighed and settled back into her seat. She knew he was referring to an earlier disaster—one that put to rest any plans the Werewolves had of mastering technology that was now a part of everyday life.

"It took a little time for them to work out the right balance, but after a while, they developed compromises so that everyone was happy. Jay is older than Zeke, and I can already see the difference in the relationship with his other half. Jay's wolf is allowing him more time. Zeke's is still as demanding as a child. Either way it's working, and it's a win-win."

Parker's phone rang. Beth's name appeared on the dashboard monitor, but before she reached into her bag and picked up her iPhone, Daniel, who was attempting to turn down the radio, accidentally answered it.

She threw Daniel a look of exasperation and said, "Hi Beth, is everything okay?"

"Hey Boss, how's that sexy cousin of yours? Is Bobby's ass still as fine as I remember it?"

Parker cringed. She felt her cheeks burn red. "Beth, you're on speaker."

"And?"

She shook her head and rolled her eyes. She loved her PA to bits, but the girl had no common sense. "Nothing. What is it, Beth?"

"We have a problem."

Her shoulders tensed. *I've been away less than a day.* How could there be problems already?

Beth let out a deep breath. "Mr. Van Wyk wasn't too thrilled that you wouldn't be attending the gala tonight. I sorta…kinda…mighta said that you would try to make it."

Parker groaned and rubbed her forehead. "And why on earth did you say that?"

She cringed when Beth's high pitched "Uhhhhh..." hurt her ears.

This can't be good.

"Well..." Beth paused a moment before blurting out, "he mentioned that Peters and Mallory will be there. I may have said you were out of town meeting a new client, and that you would try to get back for it." Beth took another deep breath. "So how mad are you?"

Parker hit the back of her head on the headrest. "Shit, shit." Then for good measure added, "Shit."

"So, Boss, what do you want me to do?"

Parker looked at her watch and bit her bottom lip. "Okay, I'll be there, but I'll be late." She reached over to the dash and stabbed the end call button. "Shit."

"Why is the gala a problem?" Daniel said.

She rested her head and considered the ramifications if she did not attend. "Peters and Mallory are joint chairmen of a major client I have been after. They are impossible to track down. If I miss this opportunity, it may not come again."

Daniel nodded. "Okay."

Parker was thrown by his choice of words. "Okay, what?"

"Okay, we're going to this party."

"We are what now?" Her voice rose an octave. "You are going nowhere with me. When we get to the city, I'll drop you off at a hotel, and I'll arrange for you to meet the boys tomorrow."

"I don't need a hotel. I'm staying with you." Daniel, noticing Parker's gaping mouth, said, "You seem to forget, the council has decreed that you are to be monitored 24/7 until this is all over. Until I can put a team on you, that means me."

She closed and then opened her mouth to protest, but was cut off.

"Parker, don't argue with me. I always win. Am I clear?"

She snapped her mouth shut and folded her arms over her chest. She still had hours of being trapped in a moving vehicle with an arrogant alpha who, it appeared, always got his way.

Parker narrowed her eyes and lifted her chin. *Well buddy, you're dreaming if you think I'll put up with your crap. I've got four hours to work out how to get the council to change their minds.*

***

Daniel and Parker walked into the Kridel Grand Ballroom at the Portland Art Museum a little before nine p.m.

Daniel surveyed the richly appointed ballroom. *I've got to hand it to Mallory and Peters. They know how to schmooze with the best of them.*

He glanced at Parker and held back a smile. If her current mood was anything to go by, she wasn't going to take the news he knew the men she was here to see, well. As if on cue, Parker raised her chin and walked past him without saying a word. Daniel smirked as she failed to disguise her irritation at their close proximity. Even after an entire day in her presence, he still couldn't scent her state of mind, but was quickly learning how to push her buttons. He schooled his expression to be as neutral as possible as his gaze wandered over her for the hundredth time.

After arriving at her home and going for a quick run, he had showered, and changed only to be kept waiting while she did whatever women did when they got ready to go out. It was worth the wait. He replayed the moment she descended the stairs in a pair of black strappy high heels. His vision had fallen on a perfectly shaped calf emerging as she stepped through the sinfully long split in the floor-length black evening gown.

Unable to help himself, his gaze had continued upward, taking in the generous hips and small waist the figure-hugging dress enhanced. The man in him appreciated how the silky material clung to her breasts, hiding the perfectly shaped orbs from view.

He had almost dropped the glass of Scotch when she walked past him, and the back of her dress came into view. While the front was demure, the back was the complete opposite. Apart from two thin strips of material across her shoulder blades, the remainder of her back was bare, the material resting dangerously low across her waist and hips. His body responded as if set alight. The need to reach out and touch her, possess her, was all-consuming.

Her cool demeanor, and attempt to ignore him, brought him back to reality, and put him firmly in his place.

Daniel forced himself back to the present. He pushed his errant state of mind to one side as he reminded himself that in no way, in any universe, should he be having these thoughts—especially when it came to this woman. She was a means to an end. As soon as they had tracked the Wildfire culprit down, she would be out of his life for good.

He circled the ballroom, keeping an eye out for any threats, as Parker glided farther into the room in search of her team. Provided the noise levels did not become much louder, he should be able to listen in on her conversations. And, from his vantage point, he could see everything.

Parker had not wandered too far before an excited voice from within the crowd called her name.

Parker's irritated frown dropped as she turned toward the woman and broke into a warm smile. "Beth, sorry I'm late."

Beth squealed breathlessly as she stopped in front of her, grabbed her arm, and dragged her over to the rest of Parker's employees. "I thought you mightn't get here. I'm sure they thought I'd stolen my invite when I walked in the door. You'd have thought they'd never seen a colored woman in Dior before."

Daniel grabbed two glasses of champagne from a passing waiter and raised an eyebrow at Beth's comment. From the subtle twitch of Parker's lips, she mirrored his thoughts. Neither her color nor her attire had anything to do with the looks she undoubtedly received.

This was confirmed a moment later when Parker said, "You might try toning down the purple hair. And a classic Dior cocktail dress doesn't normally get matched with bright pink gothic boots with more studs than the Golden Gate Bridge."

Beth shrugged. "I can't help it if they don't recognize class when they see it."

Parker shook her head, and her eyes crinkled. If her expression was anything to go by, she adored Beth, but it looked like the girl sometimes wore her patience thin.

He made his way towards Parker and her entourage.

Parker turned her focus on her small team, who were milling to one side of the ballroom.

A man with a ponytail and wearing an ill-fitting suit let out a wolf-whistle. "Hey Boss, looking rather nice tonight."

Daniel materialized at her side and placed a champagne flute in her hand. "Yes, she is, isn't she?"

Before he registered what had happened, Beth latched onto his right arm and beamed up at him. He couldn't help but balk at the radioactive hair. If it was possible, the color was even more vivid this close up.

Daniel fought off the urge to disentangle himself and take refuge behind Parker. The tiny woman was clearly used to getting her way. She looked like she wanted to eat him alive, and the way in which she touched him as she spoke left him in no doubt about what she was offering. Not only that, he smelled her intentions a mile off.

"And you are?" Beth said.

"Where are my manners? Daniel, this is Beth Winston, my PA," Parker said.

Daniel reassessed the small woman, and he remembered Morgan's parting words.

I can see why he warned me about you.

"Beth, this is Daniel Locke. He is…" Parker frowned as she trailed off.

Daniel, realizing Parker's dilemma, came to her rescue. "Your new client. Parker has agreed to take on a project for me, one that will require her to travel."

Parker wordlessly thanked him for the save as he shook hands with Beth.

To his relief, Parker then introduced him to the remainder of her team, allowing him to put some distance between himself and the aggressive PA.

From the moment he approached, he identified Morgan's omegas. Unfortunately, they had also recognized him and were now standing in a submissive position, staring at their shiny shoes, not sure how to proceed. Before their strange behavior was noticed by their colleagues, he stepped up to them and said in a low voice, "Relax, it won't serve your alpha or Parker if your behavior comes into question."

He then cleared his throat. "I understand that you both will be working on my project with Ms. Johnson?"

Zeke and Jay bobbed their heads in unison.

"I and the rest of the alp–board members are grateful for your help. I know it won't be easy." Daniel shook each of their hands in turn.

Zeke and Jay stood up straight, their earlier meek demeanor gone, and pride replaced their previous apprehension. Jay's face relaxed, and a small smile broke through. "We understand fully what is at stake, sir. We won't let Parker or you down."

He continued to make conversation with the omega's while still keeping an ear out as Parker mingled with her people.

Unaware he could hear her, Beth pulled Parker aside. "Parker, I know I demand you bring back souvenirs when you go away, but you have outdone yourself this time. He is yummy." She openly gaped at him. "Can I have him? Can I have him, please?"

Parker rolled her eyes. She glanced around the room as if looking for someone, but not wanting to make it obvious. When she ran her hands down her dress, he guessed she had found whomever she was after.

Before she left, she threw a cheeky grin at Beth. "Go for it. I'm not sure you'd know what to do with him, though. I hear he's an animal when he wants to be."

Daniel had to stop himself from laughing out loud at Parker's play on words.

He followed Parker's progress as she gracefully navigated the throng of guests and joined a small group on the far side of the floor. When she laughed at something the man next to her said, he looked closer and realized he knew the man she was talking to. Andrew Mallory, chairman of Trask Enterprises. Not liking how close they were standing, he made his excuses and strode across the room. As he drew nearer, the man looked up and smiled. "As I live and breathe, Daniel Locke. I thought it was you arriving with Parker. What brings you to these parts?"

He took Andrew's outstretched hand and shook it. "Andrew, it's been a while."

A small, smug part of him was pleased that Andrew believed Parker was with him. Why it made any difference was something he did not wish to explore. Too long without a woman was clearly affecting him—that was something he would need to rectify before things got out of control. Not only was Parker not his type, but she was a means to an end, and out of bounds.

"You're just in time," Andrew said. He indicated Daniel should join them. "We have been discussing an industrial espionage problem."

After the introductions were made, the discussion again turned back to business. Parker seemed astonished with the level of insight he had into the men's business. Daniel leaned toward her and placed his hand on the small of her back. "In case you're wondering, I sit on a number of boards with Mallory and Peters."

Parker's expressive blue eyes widened.

"What?" he said. "Did you think all I do all day is chase deer and argue with impossible women?"

SEVEN

Hidden Alliances

Parker's feet pounded the pavement. Unlike her chaotic thoughts, her stride was sure and stable as her feet marked time with her elevated pulse. The day before yesterday life was uncomplicated. The only thing she needed to worry about was computer viruses, demanding clients, and keeping her business running. Today, it felt as though the weight of world rested on her shoulders. She had hoped an early morning run would clear her head, but her thoughts once again strayed. At the end of the evening, Daniel received word that another victim of Wildfire was found dead in New York. Her stomach churned at the memory of the disturbing image on Daniel's phone. As with the others, the young woman was unaligned, having chosen to leave her pack years before.

Her pace increased. In all likelihood, there would be more victims before they tracked the culprit down. When Bobby's face swam into view, it was as if someone had clamped a vice around her heart. While he did not fit the profile of the victims, he'd done some stupid things in the past. Parker's pace faltered. He was headed to New York.

Give him some credit. Morgan has briefed the pack on the deaths, and the link to Wildfire. He's not a kid anymore.

She needed to stop thinking about worst-case scenarios. Sweat trickled between her breasts' cleavage, and she pushed herself toward exhaustion before finally turning into her driveway. The moment she reached the top step, Daniel stormed out of the front door, and hauled her into the house before she caught her breath.

"Where the hell have you been?" Daniel slammed the door shut. His nostrils flared as he glared at her.

Parker pulled the earbuds out, and her forehead crinkled. "I went for a run. What's it to you?"

"Are you that deaf you didn't hear what we told you? You are to have someone with you. Always."

Her hands locked into fists. "You must be delusional if you think I'm in danger. Morgan and the others are just being overprotective. I'm Human. Remember?"

Daniel grabbed her by the arm and jerked her shoulder upwards. "You are the delusional one. If you think of pulling this rubbish in Nederland, I'll have you under lock and key."

She pulled out of his grip. "Oh please, you don't want me on your pack grounds any more than I want to go. The council will just have to get used to the fact that I'm not going."

Daniel let out a low growl, and his face grew stormy. "What part of Werewolves are dying from something that shouldn't be possible, did you not understand? I have been charged with protecting you, and that's exactly what I'm going to do. Do you really think I want you anywhere near my family after what you have done to them?"

Parker's body began to shake, and her vision clouded over. Her hand took on a mind of its own, and she slapped his face with as much force as she could muster. "How dare you!"

The moment she heard the crack of her hand against his skin she knew she had gone too far. In an instant, he had her wrists in a vice-like grip and had trapped them behind her back. Daniel lowered his head down to hers and uttered in a low, icy tone that sent shivers up her spine. "Make no mistake, you will be going."

The warmth from his breath distracted her as it brushed against her ear.

"Whether I have to drag you kicking and screaming the entire way, or you go of your own free will, is entirely up to you." Daniel paused for a moment before snarling. "At least with the first option I can put duct tape on that argumentative mouth of yours."

Tingles ricocheted across her body, and her tongue skimmed her trembling lips.

Daniel's eyes dropped to her mouth, and he let out a low moan. He fisted his hand in her hair and pulled her toward him in one fluid motion, crushing her mouth to his in a searing kiss.

Her body, instead of being repelled by the treatment, wanted nothing more than to feel his lips against hers.

He sought entry to her mouth, and a bolt of desire ripped through her when he slid his tongue deeper. Without thinking, she returned the kiss and relished the taste of his anger. She relaxed into his arms, and he pulled her flush against his body.

I need to stop this.

Self-preservation kicked in, and she pulled away from him. He was too male, too larger-than-life, and too demanding for her to allow this to happen. She needed to retain some dignity.

Out of breath, they faced off against each other. Anger emanated off him in waves, and after their earth-shattering kiss she was finding it difficult to concentrate. She took another step back and wrapped her arms around her waist. What had possessed her to lose control like that?

Daniel's breath was labored as he ran a hand through his hair. "Two days. You have two days, or we are going with my preferred option."

She stormed upstairs to get changed for work. She was white-hot livid and wished nothing more than to rid herself of the insufferable man.

Parker smirked. She couldn't help it. Daniel was the filling in a bus sandwich, and he hated every second of it. He fidgeted until the elderly woman on his right threw him a disgusted glare when he bumped into her and she dropped her book—yet again.

If he wanted to take his mission seriously, then she wasn't about to make it easy for him. After their fiery kiss, no way she was going to spend any more time than necessary in his company, not without witnesses. His discomfort at being wedged between commuters almost made her stay on the bus a few extra stops to extend the torture.

She needed to remove all possibility of a repeat kiss. Next time, she mightn't have the strength to pull away.

Trevor, her personal bodyguard, was waiting at her office. How she was going to explain Trevor to her employees was anyone's guess. To her further disgust, a second bodyguard was stationed with Jay and Zeke. The council deemed that they too, could be in danger.

She led Daniel and Trevor to her office, and Daniel closed the door behind them so her staff couldn't overhear their conversation. He wandered across to the large window that looked out over the city. "Before I go, there are some ground rules that you will adhere to."

Her eyes flicked across to Trevor. Instead of throwing Daniel a snide comment, she held her tongue. This wasn't the time or place to air their animosity.

She did not resume breathing until Daniel left for San Francisco.

The second her phone vibrated, Parker awoke. She shifted her position to get more comfortable, lifted her head from the window where it had fallen in her sleep, and yawned. The drive from the airport to Nederland was the longest stretch of sleep she'd had in the past two days. She reached for her phone. Bobby was in nirvana at the Awesomeness Con convention and somehow believed she shared his extreme love of Marvel, Dr. Who, and something called Legend of Five Rings. Her phone was full of his selfies from New York. She shuddered to think how cluttered her phone would be when he met Stan Lee.

The hum of the car engine over the soft strains of country music was a perfect backdrop to what lay outside her window. She marveled at the mixture of evergreens indiscriminately scattered amongst harsh rock and boulder-encrusted ridges reaching high above the highway on the right, while a sea of lush Colorado Blue Spruce blanketed the valley between two hills to the left.

Simon chuckled from the driver's seat. "You know you drool when you sleep?"

She lifted a brow and nodded to the road ahead. "Keep your eyes on the road, and I do no such thing."

Simon winked at her with a knowing smile and concentrated on the drive ahead.

Daniel's beta had picked her up, along with Zeke, Jay, and Trevor at Denver International Airport. Dressed in lime green shorts and bright red flip-flops, they could not miss Simon at the arrivals' area. Since then, he had kept them entertained with his straightforward, but cheeky, personality.

She resumed admiring the unfolding beauty of nature as they proceeded along the winding road and ignored the jibes from the driver beside her. For the millionth time today, she mentally ran through her checklist. She was sure she'd provided Simon with the complete list of what they would need. However, in her rush, she might have overlooked something.

They turned off the main road and passed through a set of gigantic wrought-iron gates that opened to a secluded gravel road lined on both sides with thick spruce and pine groves. When they finally arrived at a large compound set into the foothill, Parker was unprepared for the setting.

To her left was a car park, full to the brim with late model and classic vehicles of all shapes and sizes. A vast clearing dotted with giant elm trees sprawled out to her right. The expanse extended to the edge of the plateau and gently dipped into a verdant green valley. A path followed the slope. Larger than a walking track, but smaller than the width of a road, the path spread out over the valley like a river with endless tributaries. The valley itself boasted scattered dwellings hidden amongst the trees, each log house as lovely as the next one.

In addition to the houses, three long buildings stood halfway down the incline. She guessed these were the packs' dens and barracks. Near the middle of the clearing, with its back to the hill, was a massive log chalet. The building, which was the pack's communal house and operated like a town hall, was a hive of activity. Huge windows and doors adorned the building and overlooked both the clearing and the picturesque valley.

At the other end of the clearing, happy, laughing children swarmed ropes, swings, and ladders attached to ancient oaks. A stone path cut into the mountainside ran past the children's play zone.

Her breath caught as she spied a breathtaking piece of architecture nestled into the mountain. The mansion could only be the alpha's house. Daniel's pack ran a successful construction conglomerate, part of which would be operated from the house, but she had never realized just how successful.

As with the Pack house, the building was constructed of giant spruce logs and local river stone. Large decks wrapped around the outside of the building, and from what little she could see, the patio boasted at least three separate areas with an assortment of outdoor furniture. The mansion had large floor to ceiling windows that must provide uninhibited views of the compound and the valley.

Simon opened the trunk. "So, did you guys want to get started, or settle in first?"

Parker looked across at Jay and Zeke, who were both taking photos of the valley with their phones. "You two go have a run first and then come find me."

Simon glanced around the compound. "I'll get someone to show you the boundaries." He spotted someone and called out, "Hey, Hanson, get your butt over here."

The man changed direction and jogged over to them.

"Computer geeks, meet NSYNC. NSYNC, Computer geeks," Simon said.

The man rolled his eyes and held out a hand to Parker. "Ignore him, my name is Kyle."

Parker's brows drew together, and she glanced across at Simon. "I thought his name was Hanson?"

Simon lifted his shoulders and grinned. "What can I say, I keep on forgetting the pretty boy's name."

From the good-natured faces they pulled at each other, this was a long-standing inside joke. Simon gave Kyle instructions on showing Jay and Zeke where to take their runs. The boys picked up their bags and followed Kyle down the trail that led to the den to drop off their gear.

They hadn't gone far when Simon called out with a huge grin, "West Life, make sure you bring them back in one piece."

The only response he received from Kyle was a one-fingered salute.

Simon laughed, then turned back to Parker and indicated she should follow him. "We've set you guys up in Barracks One." He pointed to a building a half-mile down the valley. "The hospital is being set up in Barracks Two, which is on the other side. The pack's infirmary isn't large enough to house the expected numbers."

Parker shouldered her tote bag and reached for her briefcase. "Have any victims been located yet?"

He nodded. "They should be here by tomorrow."

When they arrived at Parker's new working quarters, Simon opened the door and stepped aside. "We got everything you requested. I'll have someone come and help you move things to where you want them."

She stepped inside and surveyed the interior.

"The barracks normally house trainees who come here to do specialized tracking training. It's not much, but it should do," Simon said.

Parker had expected to find it bland like a typical army barrack, but she was pleasantly surprised. Three large workstations had boxes piled on top, waiting to be unpacked. A multi-tray Xerox printer was pushed up against a far wall, and three large electronic whiteboards adorned the walls. A recreational area, including a lounge and a kitchen, occupied the far end of the room.

She turned to smile at the beta hovering behind her. "This is great, although you might have gone overboard with the whiteboards. I only asked for one."

Simon looked sheepish as he scratched the back of his neck. "Well actually…" He cleared his throat. "By spending that little bit more, we qualified for a free iPhone."

Parker laughed. "You mean you qualified, don't you?"

Simon's face broke into a mischievous grin. "Hey, don't knock it. The way I look at it, it's a win-win situation. There's gotta be some perks to being the CFO."

"What's a win-win situation?"

Parker hitched her breath and froze. She had not heard Daniel walk into the room, and jumped in before Simon could reply. "We were just discussing the setup. The sooner we begin, the sooner we supply you with those lists of possible victims."

Simon moved behind Daniel and mouthed a silent thank you. However, from Daniel's expression, he knew she was covering for his beta. Without saying anything further on the subject, Daniel indicated for the three others who had followed him to step forward. "Ms. Johnson, you obviously already know Simon. These are my other betas, Samuel, Adam, and Vic."

Parker stepped forward and shook hands with each of the betas. When she got to Vic, she asked out of curiosity, "Short for—?"

The stocky woman glared at Parker, and she instantly regretted asking the question. Somehow, she had gotten on the bad side of this beta without knowing how.

Vic barked a clipped "Victoria" before she stepped back into line.

All righty then.

Once the introductions were finished, Daniel said, "If you require anything while you are here, you can ask any of my betas. They are aware of the reason you are here, and they will make sure you and your team are comfortable. You have free reign within our village. If you need to leave the grounds, one of them is to accompany you."

Parker held back the sudden desire to stick out her tongue at Daniel. He was treating her like a child. Instead, she held her temper in check and waved her hand dismissively. "I don't need a babysitter. What do you think I'm going to do, take off with the family silver?"

Samuel, Adam, and Vic flinched. Simon, on the other hand, smirked like a Cheshire cat.

Daniel's jaw tightened, and a muscle twitched. "Leave us. NOW!"

Not having to be told twice, the betas scampered out of the room. Simon threw her a supportive glance on the way out.

Once they had left, Daniel towered over her. "While on my grounds you are to afford me the respect I deserve." He grabbed her wrist and backed her against the nearest desk, pinning her into place with his powerful body. "I am the alpha here. What I say is law. Do I make myself clear?"

Her anger caused spots to dance in front of her eyes. "First of all, Mister High-and-Mighty-Alpha, I am not one of your pack that you can command with the click of your fingers. And for your information, where I come from respect is earned, not given."

Before she could continue her tirade, a woman entered the barracks and squealed. "Well aren't you the cat's meow. Sorry I'm late, I was hoping to meet you when you arrived."

The woman flew across the room to Parker, threw her arms around her shoulders, and almost squeezed the life out of her.

Daniel's eyes widened as he stared at the woman whose jet-black hair, styled in a short, stylish bob, so closely matched his.

"Jessica, I can't breathe," she said in a broken voice. "Remember, you Werewolf, me Human."

Jessica loosened her grip, held Parker at arm's length, and looked her up and down. A look of pure disbelief crossed her face. "Chickadee, I can't believe you're here! I need to pinch myself." She embraced Parker again.

Parker couldn't help but smile, and she returned the hug. Warmth spread through her chest. The only upside of coming to Daniel's pack was that she would finally meet her friend— even if she had deliberately ignored Jessica's calls over the last two days.

Jessica stepped back and glanced between Parker and Daniel with a knowing look. "So," she said, with a wink, "what are we talking about?"

The room fell silent. From Daniel's stiff posture and rigid muscles, he was taking this as well as Parker expected—not well at all. She groaned inwardly. *I thought she'd tell him before I turned up.* Clearly not.

Daniel cleared his throat, and his Adam's apple bobbed with the effort. "I see you know my sister."

She nodded mutely. In hindsight, perhaps she should have warned him.

Daniel's jaw tightened and he turned to his sister. "It appears we need to have words."

Jessica waved him off. "Pfft. Horse-feathers. You must be off your trolley if you thought I wouldn't reach out to her. I got my baby back because of Parker. Just because you're focused on what almost happened, doesn't change the fact that the life of my child, your bloodline, was saved that day."

"But that's the problem," Daniel said. "Mandy almost died. We sat by her bedside not knowing if she would survive. Or have you forgotten that?"

"Her scars remind me every day." Jessica's eyes narrowed and her voice rose. "You seem to forget that the only reason she is with us today is standing in this room."

Daniel raked his fingers through his hair. While he was prepared to argue with her at the drop of a hat, it appeared his sister was another story. "We will discuss this later."

Jessica placed her hands on her hips, but before she could respond, Daniel stormed out of the building, barking orders at his betas.

Jessica's gaze followed his path, and her hands dropped to her side. "That went well, don't you think?"

Parker rubbed her forehead and shook her head. "I think we have different views on the definition of well."

Parker chatted with Jessica throughout the afternoon, catching up on events since their last Skype call two weeks ago. Their regular contact had begun three years beforehand, not long after the incident with Daniel. The incident which, it turned out, involved the kidnapping of his eight-year-old niece—Jessica's daughter.

She only became aware of the true nature of the potential disaster once it was all over. Even then, the details had come from Jessica, not Daniel. She still remembered the knot in her stomach when Jessica told her that a group of well-organized rogues had taken Mandy while they were on a shopping trip. The rogues had overpowered the minders and snatched Mandy from her mother's arms. In the space of a single phone call, Parker's take on the run-in with Daniel had gone from surprise to mortification. At no point during the unfolding drama, had she realized that the thing she was tracking down was a child. She'd just assumed the "something precious" she was after was some sort of family heirloom. Even now, after all the time that had passed, she was still sick to her stomach each time she thought about it.

No part of Mandy's body was left undamaged, and for a while, it had been touch and go. Daniel had also lost one of his men. In his grief, Daniel blamed her for the delay in providing him the information that would have gotten them to the rogues earlier.

Once the dust had settled, Jessica called Parker to thank her for all she had done. A long-distance friendship developed between the two women in the three years since, and they regularly spoke via phone or Skype. At first, Parker hadn't known how to take Jessica's energetic personality, which often bordered on mania. Jessica buzzed from one subject to another, and her vocabulary was stuck somewhere in the 1920's. She was the complete opposite of Daniel.

"I see you and my brother are still nursing that beef," Jessica said, not long after they began to unpack the boxes.

She raised an eyebrow and looked over the top of her glasses. "You think?"

Jessica pulled the lid off a box and inspected the contents. "You need to cut him some slack. It went against everything he believed to ask for your help three years ago." Jessica paused and looked up at Parker, her expression now serious. "Considering how he felt about the outcome, it's even harder for him this time."

Jessica handed her a box of whiteboard markers and sighed. "He may be hard-boiled, but he really is a good egg.

You need to remember he has seen a lot in his two and a half centuries, more than most. He distrusts Humans and has experienced first-hand the genocide inflicted on us as a race."

She remained quiet. Morgan and Clara had given her an abridged version of their histories. While she suspected they left a lot out, what information they did impart left her ashamed of her own people. She bit the inside of her lip. Worrying about a handful of employees was bad enough, but to have the weight of an entire race on her shoulders? As much as she did not want to, she empathized with Daniel's need to protect his own.

But when she recalled his confining her to pack grounds, she ripped one of the boxes open with more effort than required. *That doesn't mean he gets to order me around like he would the rest of his little army.*

Parker was so focused on her work she failed to notice the sun had slipped low on the horizon and turned a vivid orange as dusk approached. She switched the lights on. While Werewolves may have incredible vision, she was cursed with normal Human eyesight.

Just as she sat back at her desk, Jessica rushed in with a large box, set it down, and clapped her hands excitedly. "Gotta get my wiggle on, Chickadee. Ray's back with Mandy. See you at the barbecue?"

She cringed and made her excuses. "I'm a bit tired. I might finish up here and head over to the Den."

Jessica made a face, her lips pursed, and her brows bumped together in a scowl. She was apparently not taking no for an answer. "Don't be a piker. You have to come, it'll be swell."

Parker rubbed the back of her neck. How was she going to say no without offending Jessica?

"Mandy wants to meet you," Jessica said. "And besides, now that it's jake to mention your name, Ray would like to thank you as well." Jessica grabbed her arm, and pulled her out the door and toward the main compound. "Come on, be a blue serge. You are coming, and that's that."

Parker gave in, albeit with reluctance. "Okay, but I need to shower and change first."

"I know, I'm showing you to your room."

Parker stopped moving the same time her heart stopped with a thud. "What do you mean? The Den is that way."

Jessica threw a confused look at Parker and giggled. "You slay me. Why do you think you're in the Den? You're up at the main house."

Parker's eyes flew wide open, and she had the sudden instinct to flee.

There must be a mistake.

She followed Jessica up the path toward the alpha's house, and was struck by an overwhelming feeling she was walking into on-coming traffic. How could she possibly share the same living quarters with Daniel Locke?

EIGHT

Into the Public Arena

Daniel sped through the thick forest that flanked the valley, thankful he was alone. He struggled not to lash out. He was already overtaxed with the Wildfire disaster, and now Jessica had gone behind his back. Not only that, but she had lied to him for the past three years. He did not need his own flesh and blood stacking another layer of stress on him. He clenched his fists. His own sister. How could he ever trust her again? *Damn!* He knew Parker was trouble. The only question was, how much more damage would she inflict on them before this was all over?

Daniel recoiled. He had never had so little self-control over his emotions. While his temper often seethed below the surface, he always had enough control to channel it elsewhere. Now he had argued with Parker in front of his betas. His stomach dropped. What must they be thinking.

He stopped and looked up into the forest canopy as if the trees held the answers he was after. Not finding any, he leaned against a tree trunk and rubbed his forehead. Much to his irritation, Simon was more than happy to voice his opinions aloud, albeit when they were alone. If he heard his friend utter the term *sexual frustration* one more time, he would punch him into next week. The man's answer for everything was always the same, no matter the situation.

I am not attracted to Parker. She's too outspoken, too argumentative, and far too infuriating.

He let out a low growl and rubbed the back of his neck. He needed to find a way to get through this with his sanity in check, but if she kept countermanding his orders, there was very little chance of that.

He jerked and felt alarm projected through his telepathic link with Simon. *Alpha, you had better get back here now.*

He raced through the forest toward the house, a sour taste in his mouth. What now? The trees blurred as he navigated the miles with ease. In less than five minutes, he was in the house and heading toward the offices. He heard bickering coming from down the hallway.

"Hit the AV button and then select the channel," Adam said.

"No, it's the TV/Sat button, dipshit," Simon said.

As soon as he walked into the room, Daniel rolled his eyes at the sight of his four betas crowded around the flat screen TV, arguing over the remote. They stopped and he looked from one to the other and shook his head. He scowled and grabbed the remote from Simon's grip, pushed a button, and the TV came to life.

"What was so urgent that it couldn't wait?"

Simon pointed to the phone on his desk. "Nigel Hardy in San Fran just phoned in. He's on speaker." He pointed to the TV. "Change it to KGO."

The words *Breaking News - Brutal Massacre - San Francisco Peninsula - Locals Terrified* ran along the bottom of the screen. Behind the police cordons and tape, the cameras focused on four covered bodies, while both police and crime scene investigators swarmed the area. Dozens of reporters and photographers hounded the city's outgoing Chief Medical Examiner.

Daniel turned up the volume.

"Dr. Hart, Dr. Hart, can you tell us the cause of death?"

"Was this carried out by a single person, or do you suspect it was a gang-related incident?"

"Dr. Hart, is it true an animal ravaged the bodies?"

"Do the police have any suspects yet?"

"We understand that the victims were high school students. Can you give us the name of the school they attended?"

Dr. Hart turned to the flock of reporters. "I have no comment at this time." If her haunted expression was anything to go by, she was struggling to come to terms with what she had just seen.

Dread overwhelmed Daniel as he watched the news piece. "One of ours?"

The question hung in the air.

"Yes," the pained voice of Officer Nigel Hardy said. "We tracked him down before anyone got to him. He went to ground in an old abandoned warehouse. When we got there, he was as messed up as the one from the other night."

Daniel closed his eyes and inhaled. "Is he still alive?" While the Werewolf needed to pay for his crimes, they needed answers. Answers a dead man couldn't provide.

There was a slight pause. "We had no choice. He was out of control." Hardy's voice cracked. "In the end, it took all three of us to finish him."

Daniel focused on the speakerphone. He trusted Hardy and knew there would have been no other option. However, that also meant they had lost their best lead to tracking down who was behind the murders. "Damage control?"

"We have all the victims' cell phones, there was no CCTV and, so far, no witnesses. The local authorities don't know what to make of it, and the ME's office is backlogged and understaffed."

Daniel rubbed his jaw and worked through a list of containment actions. "Those bodies can't be autopsied until we know there's no evidence that can be traced to us."

Like a well-oiled machine, he quickly communicated the actions they had repeated far too often in recent weeks. "I'm sending an extraction team. The evidence on those bodies needs to disappear. This will be high-profile, so we need to tread carefully."

Daniel turned to his betas. "Adam, put a clean-up team together. We won't be able to get to the airport before the last flight, so we'll leave first thing." He leaned closer to the phone. "Hardy, you need to make sure we can get in and out without being seen."

"What about the photos?" Simon said.

Hardy broke in. "Already taken care of. When they get back to the lab, the techs will discover that all the SD cards are missing."

"Have you identified the Werewolf?" Daniel said.

"Working on that, sir. It doesn't look like he was a rogue. His family's affiliated with the local pack, and he went to school with the victims. From what I can tell, the kid's wolf emerged earlier this year. I'm waiting on Alpha Bryant now. We're going to speak to the family as soon as he arrives."

"I want a report as soon as you have further information."

"Yes, Alpha."

He ended the call. The room remained silent, each digesting the scene still playing out on the now-muted screen.

Daniel sighed. "I think we'd better prepare ourselves. This situation is only going to get worse."

For a long while after he had dismissed his betas, he sat in silence, sifting through the possible aftermath these deaths could cause. His mind flashed to Jessica, and what they went through when it looked doubtful Mandy would ever come home.

This has got to stop.

He was about to notify the council when he noticed Jessica and Parker heading up from the valley. His fists clenched as he watched their progression. How could his sister have forgiven and forgotten so quickly? He let out a low growl. He now had the misfortune of Parker camped in his home until this mess was over. Damn Morgan and the council for putting him in this position.

His only consolation was that the house was so large he might get through this ordeal without having to bump into her each day.

He turned back to the TV, which was still focused on the deaths of the teenagers in San Francisco. He stared at the body bags and let out a tortured sigh. He and Parker needed to find a middle ground if they had any chance of finding out who was behind this massacre.

NINE

Peace Offering

Parker begged off from attending the pack barbecue once she found out about the teenagers' deaths in San Francisco. After a quick shower, she headed back to the barracks to finish setting up. Every hour they did not have answers was another hour closer to the next needless death.

Night had well and truly fallen when she heard a child's giggle, followed by a man's deep baritone. The door opened, and Daniel strode in, followed by a young girl holding a plate of food.

She could hardly miss who the child was, considering Mandy was a full head taller than most her age, and the spitting image of her mother. Her heart skipped a beat as she laid eyes on the jagged scars across the girl's neck and face. More were hidden underneath her t-shirt and jeans.

Mandy's face exploded into a thousand-watt grin, and she thrust the plate into Daniel's hands. "Parker!" She broke into a run, closed the distance, and threw her arms around Parker.

Parker laughed as she embraced the young girl. "It's nice to finally meet you, Mandy. Your mom tells me you've been using those oil paints I sent. I would love to see some of your artwork while I'm here."

Mandy let out a squeal and tightened her grip. "I made one just for you."

Daniel placed the plate on a desk, and stood at attention with his hands behind his back. "Mandy wanted to come and say hello." He nodded toward the barbecued steak and coleslaw. "She was also a little concerned that you hadn't eaten."

From his stiff tone, she couldn't help but feel that both the food and the child were a peace offering.

Her throat tightened, and the back of her eyes prickled. She was well aware what it took for him to bring Mandy to her and appreciated the gesture. "Thank you, Daniel."

She turned to Mandy and smiled. "How about you sit next to me, and we can chat while I eat?"

By the time Daniel informed Mandy he needed to get her home, both she and Daniel had managed polite conversation without throwing barbs.

"Can I show you my paintings tomorrow?" Mandy said.

Parker, unsure of how to answer, looked toward Daniel for guidance.

He rustled Mandy's hair. "As long as it's okay with Parker and your mom, I'm sure we can arrange it."

Mandy let out another happy squeal and threw her hands around Daniel's leg.

The loving bond between the young girl and her uncle tugged at Parker's heart.

Daniel bent down and picked her up. "It's way past your bedtime, and your mother is already going to be angry with me for keeping you up so late. We'd better go." He turned to Parker. "Providing things go to plan, the first set from your list, will be here tomorrow. If you find Jessica in the morning, she'll introduce you to our pack doctor."

Parker stood and placed her hands in the back pockets of her jeans. "Hopefully, I'll have another set of names for you before they get here."

Mandy blew a raspberry on Daniel's cheek, and he half-heartedly growled at her. Mandy giggled, and he glanced back at Parker. "If you do, pass the list on to Simon. I'm heading to San Francisco with the team. We need to contain and limit the damage from the latest deaths." He carried his niece to the exit.

"Night Parker," Mandy said.

She stared at the closed door with her brows knitted together. The loving uncle she had just witnessed was a far cry from the volatile alpha she had come to expect. What had happened to warrant the drastic change?

She turned back to her computer, knowing she wasn't about to get an answer from thin air. She had hours of work ahead of her before she could rest.

The sun was well and truly up by the time Parker awoke the next morning. She yawned. Three hours of sleep was not enough, but she had made progress.

By the time she headed down the valley, her mind was in overdrive. Hopefully, Zeke and Jay had made sense of the instructions she left them, and had made a head start on the lesser known banks. Unless they found the money trail, they would have little hope of tracking down the potential victims or the perpetrators.

The pack, a lot larger than the one she was used to, was a hive of activity. More than once she had to stop as people came up to introduce themselves. She was surprised to discover they were aware of who she was and why she was there. They were worried that whatever was infecting the other Werewolves would make its way into the packs. As far as they were concerned, the sooner she found who was behind it, the sooner their alpha could stop it from spreading.

Her stomach churned. *No pressure then.*

Instead of the twenty minute walk she was expecting, it took her an hour to reach the barracks where Jessica was standing beside a woman in a white coat.

Jessica waved her over. "Hey, Chickadee."

She introduced Parker to Alice, the pack's doctor. The petite redhead was the last person Parker imagined to be a Werewolf, let alone a doctor. Alice looked around the same age as her. In reality, the woman could be anywhere from thirty to three hundred.

"We were just having a chinwag about the digs for our new arrivals. I think we have everything ready for them," Jessica said.

"How many did they track down in the end? Did they find more than the initial three?" Parker said.

She felt uncomfortable from the doctor's unwavering stare. Had she said something wrong? Perhaps the doctor was still under the assumption they weren't to have contact with her. She endured the glare, but felt on trial.

"Yes," Alice said.

Parker waited for the doctor to add more information. And waited.

She mustn't be much of a talker then.

"Do you know what sort of condition they're in?" Parker said.

"Yes...sort of."

Jesus. It's like getting blood from a stone.

Alice glanced down at the clipboard in her hand and then back up again. This time, Parker detected less reservation in her tone. "I understand that you identified the victims."

She nodded. "I had help. We are still working on compiling more names. Unfortunately, the list gets longer each time we look at it." She paused. "Dr. Hayes, do you think I could speak to them? It might be helpful if I asked them a few questions when they get in, in particular how they knew where to get Wildfire in the first place."

Alice fell quiet and glanced toward the makeshift hospital. "I can't promise anything." She pulled the clipboard tight against her chest and fidgeted with the pen she held. "I'm a little out of my depth, and I don't know what condition they'll be in when they get here."

The doctor's face was pinched, and she had dark circles under her eyes. Alice bit the inside of her lip, and her expression grew worried. "I'll assess them when they arrive and let you know."

Parker nodded. "That sounds fair."

Alice continued to clutch the clipboard, but gave her a hint of a smile.

Her gaze darted to Jessica and then back to Alice. Perhaps she had misjudged the doctor. Being responsible for the medical care of Werewolves who had contracted the fatal disease mustn't be easy. She frowned. The more she thought about it, the more she was convinced Alice was frightened of what was about to descend on them.

Once Alice left to make final preparations for the Wildfire victims, Jessica filled Parker in on the other comings and goings of the pack. "Daniel took a team with him and left early this morning. Reports are also trickling in about missing Werewolves."

"Do they think it's related to Wildfire?"

Jessica shrugged. "The beef is, the packs don't like to air their dirty laundry. That first list you gave us had thirty-two names. Twenty-five were Human. Of the remaining seven, we found four alive, and have confirmed two dead. We know the last one belongs to the local pack and, as it turns out, he has been missing for a while. They've been searching for him without any luck."

"That doesn't mean that the missing Werewolf is taking Wildfire," Parker said.

Jessica did not look convinced. "Daniel confirmed that the Werewolf who offed those high school students went missing two weeks ago. We can't treat his disappearance, followed by their deaths, as a coincidence. To make matters worse, he wasn't on your initial list."

A few hours later, after she had kicked off her latest web crawler, Parker took a break to clear her thoughts. She headed to the nearest building and found Alice talking with a small group.

Once the doctor was finished with them, she wandered over to Parker. Her face was pinched with worry. "They've not arrived."

She gave Alice a warm smile. The woman looked like she could do with a drink—or ten. "I know. I thought I'd see how you were and if you needed any help."

Alice shook her head. "Most of it is sorted. I'll send word to Tech House after we have them situated, if you like."

She raised an eyebrow. "Tech House?"

"Barracks One." Alice nodded toward the group she'd spoken with. "Some of the younger Werewolves have dubbed your new home Tech House—for obvious reasons."

Parker chuckled. Nothing was sacred in a pack. She looked around the large room, empty except for the metal-framed beds. A chill ran up and down her spine as her gaze rested on the metal chains scattered across the room. Iron rings were bolted to the floor beside each bed.

My God! This isn't a hospital, it's a prison.

Alice pushed her hands into her jacket pockets. "I know it looks barbaric, but based on reports from the New York, San Francisco, and San Diego first responders, we'll need to restrain the patients for their own safety, as well as ours."

Parker gulped. This was becoming too real. "There's a very comfortable couch and a fantastic coffee maker in Barracks One, I mean Tech House. How about you join me for a cup?"

Alice's eyes darted around the makeshift hospital. "I'm not sure I should. There's still a few things I need to finish."

She beckoned Alice to follow her. "Nonsense. This might be the last chance you get to take a break. I insist."

Parker handed Alice a cup of freshly brewed coffee. "So, how long have you been the pack's doctor?"

Alice took a sip of the scalding hot beverage, and scrunched her nose. "I worked with the previous pack doctor for about two decades until he passed, which means I've had the role for about forty years."

"Do you enjoy it?"

The doctor stared at the floor for a while before responding. "Well, it's not what I thought I would end up doing in medicine."

"Oh?"

"I was born Human." Alice held her cup in both hands and polished off half the contents of her coffee. She placed it back on the table and rested her hands on her lap. "Before I met John, my mate, I graduated from Albany Medical College and worked at Ellis Hospital in New York."

Parker quickly did the math. "It must have been difficult being a female doctor in the 1950s."

Alice shrugged. "I was lucky. Ellis employed a few lady doctors, and we helped each other through the difficult times."

"Do you miss it?"

The room fell silent as Alice considered the question. "I don't regret my decision to turn. It took a while for me to take that final step, it's not an easy thing to go through, but once I did, I didn't look back."

She put herself in Alice's shoes. It couldn't have been easy to walk away from a life she worked so hard for. She was thankful she would never have to make that decision. "Did you keep in touch with the other female doctors?"

Alice nodded. "For a short while, yes. But as time passed, it became too apparent that they were aging, and I still looked the same. I kept tabs on them over the years, but most of them are gone now."

Melancholy shadowed Alice. Parker tilted her head as she studied the pack's doctor. The more she got to know the woman, the more she realized her first impression of Alice was wrong. Whether Alice had always been careful in letting her real emotions show, or whether it was only since the change, she would never know, but she was warming to the doctor.

"I have to say, the whole aging thing freaks me out. Bobby, my cousin, was two years older than me when he was turned ten years ago. I've aged normally and look a decade older. He, on the other hand, looks as though he's still twenty-five."

Instead of weighing up her answer, Alice did not hesitate. "Staying younger, longer, is one of the perks of being a Werewolf. Once I turned, I helped Dr. Montgomery, the previous pack doctor, but our duties were unexciting. The only thing we did was re-break bones that healed too quickly. A few major injuries changed things up a bit, but apart from that, until now, there hasn't been much to do." Alice's shoulders drooped, and her expression returned to one of concern. "None of us pack doctors are prepared for this."

Parker sighed. *I don't think any of us are.* "So, what else do you do with your time?"

"I have been fortunate. Alpha Locke has indulged my passion for internal medicine and genetic sequencing. My studies focus on Werewolves, rather than Humans."

Both brows shot up. "Werewolves don't get sick, so how does that work?"

"My research has focused on the differences between Humans and Werewolves at a genetic level. I have also carried out studies over the years on why some Humans turn when bitten by a Werewolf, and others don't." Alice stopped as if she'd said too much.

"Go on," Parker said.

Alice leaned forward as if sharing a secret. "None of that has prepared me for this disease though. I'm a little out of my depth."

Her heart went out to Alice. The poor woman had been thrown into the deep end of something she hadn't been trained for. No wonder she appeared reluctant to share information. Alice did not know anything more than the rest of them did, which was next to nothing.

Out of the corner of her eye, Parker spotted someone waving. Jay and Zeke were frantically attempting to get her attention. She let out a deep breath. As much as she thought Alice needed someone to talk to, her trainees needed her more.

Parker patted Alice's knee. "You'll be fine. I'm sure you're worried for nothing, but I'd better go before one of those two burst a blood vessel."

A small smile graced Alice's lips as she put her cup on the small table. "I'd better go as well." She stood and pushed her hands into the pockets of her white doctor's coat. "Thanks for the coffee, and the…you know, umm…chat."

Parker had a sudden urge to reach out and give Alice a hug. Instead, she waved and headed over to Jay and Zeke.

"Spill."

Zeke huffed and pointed to his monitor. "Boss, we've come up against a gnarly firewall I've not seen before."

Parker pulled her reading glasses from her hair and leaned closer. When she saw the screen, a cold, hard stone dropped to the bottom of her stomach. "Shit!"

Jay jumped up from his seat and came closer. "What is it?"

Her eyes narrowed, and she cursed under her breath. "It's the new Cisco firewall."

This wasn't one she'd had a chance to train them on yet, which meant that she had her work cut out for the next few hours. Not only would she need to break through an extremely sophisticated firewall, but she would need to train Zeke and Jay on how to do it next time.

For the remainder of the morning and well into the afternoon she immersed herself in the task at hand. Even when Jessica breezed in to inform her that the first set of patients had arrived, she remained at her workstation. When Zeke's stomach grumbled, yet again, like a freight train, she sent the boys off to the Pack House for a late lunch.

She grabbed two cans of soda from the fridge, and made her way to the other building to see the infected patients. They might give her more clues on where to look for the people behind Wildfire.

The makeshift hospital was teeming with people, the majority of which were Daniel's enforcers standing guard over the three patients. Her brows knitted together. *Anyone would think they were prisoners.*

When she moved farther into the hospital, their dire condition became more apparent, and she found it difficult to hide her shocked reactions. Dark festering sores covered the patients' exposed limbs, and they resembled the more extreme disheveled, homeless people who wandered the streets of the big cities. One of them looked to be in a feral state. Enforcers were restraining him while Alice injected something into his arm. The second, while not as agitated as the first, wasn't far off.

The third patient was a young girl who could not have been more than eighteen. The teenager was huddled in her assigned bed, her back against the wall, and her chocolate brown eyes darting around looking for the best avenue of escape. Restraints kept her shackled to the bed.

Parker's heart ached for the young girl. She looked malnourished, her hair was matted and dirty, and her clothes torn and ragged.

Alice came to stand beside her.

"Do they have to be chained up like that?" Parker said.

"They've been restrained for their own safety and are in differing stages of agitation. Those two over there are barely lucid and became increasingly violent during the trip here. We will have to post guards on them."

Parker pointed to the teenager. "What about her?"

"That's Abigail. It looks like she is at the beginning. She's only nineteen." Alice sighed. "They picked her up hiding in an abandoned warehouse."

"Is she able to speak to us?"

Alice tipped her head to the side as she studied her patient. After a moment, she nodded. "Can't see why not. Who knows how long before her condition deteriorates. She knows you want to speak to her."

Careful not to frighten her, she and Alice approached as non-threateningly as possible. Parker held her breath as they drew closer, and her fingers tightened around the soda can she was holding. Even with chains, the girl was stronger than her and could do a considerable amount of damage before anyone else reacted. She held up the can of soda and raised an eyebrow at Alice.

Alice nodded and she passed the girl a can of Coke Zero. In hindsight, she should have grabbed the sugared version. "Hi Abigail, I'm Parker. I understand Dr. Hayes mentioned I'd like to have a little chat?"

Abigail nodded and cautiously took the offered drink. She glanced at Alice, then at the can, before tearing the tab off and finishing the contents in four long chugs.

Parker breathed easier and sat down on the bed. "Abigail, can you tell me how you knew about Wildfire?

Abigail wiped her mouth with the back of her hand. "Gail."

"Pardon?"

Abigail glanced down at the empty can and picked at the lip. "Gail," she said, "my friends call me Gail."

Parker smiled. "Okay, Gail. What do you know about Wildfire, the drug you took? How did you learn about it?"

She placed her phone on the bed between them and pressed the record button.

Gail fidgeted on the cot, clearly uncomfortable with this line of questioning. "I don't feel so well." She tossed the can onto the mattress. "Can you get me some? I haven't had any in a while. Please? I promise I'll be good."

Parker, not knowing what to say, looked to Alice.

At first, she thought the doctor was about to crumple under the pressure. However, Alice squared her shoulders and determination set in.

Good for you. Don't let this get to you.

Alice moved closer and rested a gentle hand on the teenager's shoulder. "Gail, the drug isn't safe and is causing your body to shut down." She indicated the affected areas. "Those sores you have developed on your arms and legs are the result of what it's doing to you."

Alice held up a syringe and showed it to the scared girl. "I'm giving you a dose of morphine. It should dull the pain."

Once the painkiller took effect, Parker repeated her question.

At first, Gail looked as though she wasn't going to answer, then tears welled and threatened to spill over her eyelashes. "I was partying with some of my friends, we were at a club. They were doing their usual thing and getting high. It doesn't affect me, so I didn't bother. They were giving me a hard time because I wouldn't join them." Gail took a deep breath before continuing. "You don't know how hard it is. I just wanted to be like them."

She lightly touched Gail's hand and gave her a tentative smile. "Okay, so what happened then?"

Gail shifted on the bed, brought her knees up to her chin, and wrapped her arms around her legs. "We were dancing, and this dude came up to me and told me he had something that would help me get high, just like my friends." She stopped and looked at both Parker and Alice.

When she nodded, Gail continued. "At first, I didn't believe him, but then I thought—hell, why not try it? What's the worst that can happen? Right?" She looked down at her blemished arms, took a deep breath, and let out a broken sob.

Alice placed a reassuring hand on the girl's shoulder.

"He gave me this red pill and told me to swallow it. You won't believe how wonderful it was." Gail smiled. "The rush I felt—as though I could do anything. I could finally fit in with my friends, and I didn't want it to stop."

Parker's heart beat faster. What type of person would actively go out of their way to make a young girl like Gail become a drug addict? "How long did it last?"

"About an hour."

Parker's eyes widened. *No wonder she went back for more.* "So, what happened next?"

"Well, the dude that gave it to me, who was a Were, by the way, told me if I wanted more, I could get it online. He said it was totally legal." Gail's shoulders sagged. "I ordered a bottle the next day, and pretty soon after I couldn't get enough of it."

Parker jotted down a few notes. "How long ago was this?"

"Umm…" Gail squinted. "Probably about six weeks ago."

Parker glanced up. "Do you know who the guy at the club was?" She held her breath.

When Gail shook her head from side to side, Parker let it out again. Of course, it wouldn't be that easy.

"Do you remember what he looked like?"

Gail lifted her shoulder in a half-shrug. "I hadn't seen him before. The only thing I remember was that he had a really cool accent, European or something…" She trailed off and toyed with a lock of hair. "He was a bit of a creep though, if you ask me. He was too touchy-feely."

Parker checked her phone to make sure it was still recording. "And you're sure he was a Werewolf?"

Gail nodded and bit her bottom lip. "Oh yeah, definitely. I could smell it."

"Did he tell you which website to order Wildfire from?"

"No, he said to Google it. He told me the first hit was free, but I would need to pay if I wanted more." Gail stiffened and drew in a sharp breath.

She reached out and held on to Gail's arm. "Are you okay?"

Gail closed her eyes and grimaced. "I don't feel so well." She opened them again and looked directly at Parker. "Am I going to be okay?"

The innocent brown eyes imploring her for answers shook Parker to her core, and she broke out in a cold sweat. How could she tell the girl she did not know? That none of them knew.

Parker swung her head around and exchanged glances with Alice. She too, had no answers.

Bolstering more courage than she felt, she turned back to Gail. "Sweetie, we are going to do everything we can to get you better. That much I can promise you." She squeezed Gail's shoulder. "I'm going leave you in Dr. Hayes' capable hands. Thank you for agreeing to talk with me."

Parker rose from the bed, but Gail's hand snapped out and tugged on her arm. The teenager's eyes were wide with unshed tears. "Will you come and visit with me later?"

Gail's desperate plea was nearly Parker's undoing. She took a deep breath before answering. "Of course, I will."

She returned to Tech House and replayed the recorded interview. After listening to it twice, she listed all the relevant information she could use to track down the bastard who had infected Gail. If he was responsible for her addiction, he was responsible for others as well. The teenager wouldn't have been his only target.

One thing was for certain, she needed to let Daniel know that Werewolves were behind Wildfire.

TEN

Death Comes to Nederland

Simon was just getting off the phone when she walked into his office.

"We have an updated list of people who purchased Wildfire from the second and third sites we found. It should be in your mailbox. I cross-referenced against local hospitals, GPs, and pharmacy records. I figure if they have been hospitalized at some point, or have a prescription for anything, they are most probably Human. This, at least, gives you a better starting point."

"Good thinking. It took us forever to get through that first list," Simon said.

"Alice and I spoke to one of the patients you brought in. It looks like Wildfire is being distributed by Werewolves."

Before she could continue, Simon's phone rang.

By his abrupt change in demeanor, she knew who was on the other end. Simon's shoulders pulled back, his muscles tense and ready for orders as he listened intently. "Parker's with me at the moment, and she pretty much said the same thing."

Simon activated the speakerphone, and Daniel grilled her about her conversation with Gail. She summarized their discussion, including who was behind the drug.

"She can't remember what he looked like, only that he had an accent."

"That supports the information we've received. Except instead of a club, we think it was a customer at the restaurant. The name of the Werewolf who killed those kids is Tyler. He worked at the restaurant," Daniel said.

Parker considered the available options. "It may be a long-shot, but if we can get hold of the security footage from the club that Gail was at, we might be able to identify him."

Daniel agreed to Parker's suggestion and instructed Simon to make the necessary arrangements.

"There's still one thing bugging me…"

Daniel's concern echoed through the phone. She had the same fear. "How are these Werewolves being targeted? I can't imagine anyone I know wanting to try Wildfire in the first place. Gail was susceptible because of the group of kids she hung with. She wanted to fit in. So naturally, it didn't take too much prompting to push her over the edge."

"I would say it wasn't too difficult at this end either. Tyler's pack shunned him. No other pack would take him in. As a result, he was feeling isolated."

Simon sat back in the chair, strain and anger evident on his face. "So, assuming that they are actively preying on vulnerable Were's, how the hell do they know who to target?"

The question hung in the air. The unknown force threatening the very existence of Werewolfkind was one step ahead of them.

"We need to regroup. There are names on the new list near where I am now. We'll see if we can track them down, and then head home. It should only take a couple of days." Daniel paused. "Parker, whatever you need, just let Simon know."

Once the call ended, she and Simon discussed the best ways in which to acquire the security footage. She suggested an option, but Simon zoned out mid-sentence.

Parker had been around Werewolves long enough to know he was having a telepathic conversation. Based on his expression, it wasn't a good one.

"Feck." He bolted out of his seat and rushed out the door.

Parker trailed after him. They made their way to the Pack House, and she spotted a white van speeding up the road. It entered the compound and skidded to a halt. No sooner had it stopped than three large men emerged from the vehicle.

Despite the van being stationary, it was rocking from side to side.

She froze when the doors opened. The patients brought in earlier had only minor visible blemishes that indicated something was amiss. The thing that emerged from the vehicle in restraints was neither man nor wolf. It was caught somewhere in between. Four enforcers were required to escort him out of the van and into the hospital.

Disfigured beyond recognition, the thing was covered in black abscess-like pustules. The smell that came from him was overpowering, and his tortured howls echoed across the valley. Dusk had settled across the valley, and responding howls from wild wolves were heard for miles.

The pack members witnessing the spectacle quickly rounded up the children and spirited them away. A cold chill ran up and down her spine, but she gathered her wits and ran ahead to warn Alice of the new arrival. The enforcers dragged the man, now almost manic, inside and chained him to a bed. Alice dosed him with morphine as soon as she could get near him.

"W-why does he look like that?" Simon said.

Alice, who was taking the man's pulse, cast a compassionate glance over her new patient. "He's frozen mid-change, and it's putting his body under a great deal of strain.

We need to get enough painkillers into him to let him change back."

Parker cringed when Alice injected another dose of morphine using a large needle. His hardened skin initially resisted, but gave way with additional pressure. Her stomach lurched, and she held back her body's natural reaction to the scene.

The man howled in agony, but slowly the morphine took effect, and the Werewolf transformed into a man, bones cracking and snapping throughout the process.

Alice examined him. Her look of concern increased exponentially with each new trauma she discovered. "Femurs and tibia on both legs have snapped. He has broken ribs, and his shoulders are dislocated. In his condition, I don't think his body is going to heal the damage."

Simon, who had remained in the background while Alice did her job, stepped forward and watched as the man continued to pull against the restraints and scream obscenities. His bright Hawaiian shirt and colorful flip flops were a direct contrast to the black mood which had taken over the room. "What can we do?"

Alice looked down at the man, her quick mind assessing her options. "I don't know. I will need to run some tests."

Her unspoken words were clear. She did not hold out much hope for his recovery.

Parker met Simon's concerned look. His body had become stiff and a light sheen of perspiration erupted across his brow. "I'll see what I can do about getting some screens for privacy," he said

For the next hour, the man continued to fight against the restraints, reacting like a man possessed. No one could get near him. Foam pooled around his mouth, reminding Parker of a rabid dog. Alice upped the dosage of morphine until he finally calmed down enough to stop pulling against his chains.

The Werewolf remained quiet for some time, then he opened his eyes, blinked, and looked around in confusion. "Where am I?" His words came out in a raspy croak.

Alice approached and took some readings. "You're safe. Can you tell me your name?"

The man struggled to remember. "Tony." He sucked in a breath. "My name is Tony."

"Tony, you're ill," Alice said. "You were brought here so we can take care of you. Can you remember what happened?"

They watched as he tried to make sense out of his scattered mind. "I remember walking down an alley. I was hungry, and I saw a homeless man digging through the dumpsters at the back of a restaurant, and then I remember..." He broke off, his eyes widening as a memory flooded his mind. "Oh Luna, please, no! I didn't mean to. Please, m-make the pain go away."

The Werewolf began to lose his tenuous hold on lucidness.

With a gut-wrenching scream, he cried out. "Please kill me, just kill me!" He was pulling so hard on the cuffs that he had cut through his skin, and the metal rubbed against exposed bone.

Simon, wide-eyed, glanced around the room and snapped his gaze back to Tony. A mixture of fear, sorrow, and horror crossed his face. "Can't you give him anything else?"

Alice placed the used hypodermic needle onto the tray. Her hands shook as she reached for another glass vial, and she dropped it twice before she managed to secure it tightly in the palm of her hand. "Nothing works... we have pumped enough morphine in him to kill an elephant five times over."

Parker's head was spinning. Things were too real. This man. This place. This situation was more than her brain could process. She was supposed to be behind a computer monitor, not watching someone die in such a horrific manner. It was like her legs were stuck in concrete. She was unable to move, and no matter how much she willed her body, it was frozen to the spot.

The man's eyes alternated between amber and hazel, both man and animal in frenzied madness. Foam poured from his mouth and nose. His skin darkened as the minutes passed. The room filled with moans and wails, and Parker felt sick to her stomach. And yet, her body refused to move.

Minutes dragged into hours as the witnesses held vigil, and awaited the inevitable outcome. The moans from the bed finally gave way to a low whimper, a tentative gasp for air, and then nothing. No sound, no moan, no wail. Nothing. Silence. Deathly silence.

Alice searched for any vital signs. Her shoulders slumped in defeat. She stood back, her eyes fluttered closed, and she exhaled. "It's over. He's gone." A single tear trickled down her cheek.

Parker remained rooted to the spot, staring at the still-warm body. The pain and anguish that twisted his face had faded. He was now shrouded in peace. Silence descended upon the room, and she was sure her heartbeat could be heard for miles. She took a labored breath, but the sharp, rancid smell of his festering sores was almost too much for her gag reflex, and she fought back the rising bile.

Time stood still. The lifeless body disfigured by the disease deliberately inflicted on it lay limp on the bed. Eyes still open, still chained, still dead.

Simon placed both hands on his head. "This is only the beginning."

Parker's legs began to shake and threatened to buckle. She took deep breaths and clenched her fists to fight off the lightheadedness. The pulsing of her blood as it rushed through her veins and her racing heart working overtime was deafening. A moment later, something snapped, and her body stilled. Then, like a backdraft, rage took hold. She allowed it to consume her. Its white-hot flames welcomed her like a long-lost friend. Now able to break free of the inertia that had overpowered her, she bolted for the door.

"Where are you going?" Alice said. Her voice was thick with pent-up emotion and sorrow.

Her brows furrowed, and her mouth set into a grim line. "To break a dozen state, federal, and international laws. Those sites are coming down. I don't care how."

Hell House

Five days later

"Parker."

The familiar voice drifted into her dreams, and a soft hand on her shoulder rocked her gently into the land of the living. At first, she was sure it was only an echo of some distant memory, but the persistent shake of her body brought her out of her much-needed rest.

"Parker, wake up."

Her eyes opened. She raised herself up from the desk and blinked as she stretched her weary body. Alice hovered over her with a look of concern. "God, what time is it?"

Alice's worry lines deepened. "It's three-thirty in the morning. You should go to bed."

Parker shook her head and yawned. "I can't, I need to see if the virus has replicated. I need to make sure it's done its job." She mentally crossed her fingers. If it worked, it meant they could bring down the sites selling Wildfire as soon as they were listed. It had taken her five long days and nights to write the code, but they were almost there.

She checked the monitors. Satisfied that there was nothing of concern, she turned back to Alice. "What about you? How's Hell House?"

Alice shrugged. "No change, still hell. Just came over for a five-minute break. You have the best coffee, and I didn't think you'd mind."

Parker let out a dry laugh. "Once Simon heard he could be eligible for a PlayStation from my usual supplier, he was more than happy to have the beans shipped in for me. Urgent delivery to boot."

Alice gave her a wan smile and headed to the recreational area.

Parker couldn't help but notice how worn out the doctor looked. "Alice, I'll make it. Put your feet up for five minutes."

She made them both a hot drink, handed a cup to Alice, and collapsed on the couch beside her. "How bad?" Did she want to hear the answer?

In the five days since witnessing their first death by Wildfire, their lives had become unrecognizable. Time was supposed to be relative. For Parker and the others, time had frozen.

With each passing day, the pressure on Parker and her team to find out who was behind the devastation increased. To date, they had found over three dozen Wildfire victims with still no clue as to who was behind the drug. She did not think she could stomach watching any more people die in such a horrific, heart-wrenching manner.

Over the past week, the doctor had found the courage to ease the poor souls' pain as she presided over the patients in the makeshift hospital, now only referred to as Hell House. Assisted dying. While Parker hated the term, it was apt. The majority of those near death chose this route, rather than enduring the final hours of agony.

Alice sighed. "We lost two more, and we have seven others moving into the last phase. They're being caged now. And the teams are finding more from your lists every day."

Parker yawned and rubbed her eyes, fatigued beyond belief. She jumped when her laptop emanated a flurry of high-pitched beeps. Her heart sank when she glanced at the screen. "Nuts."

"What is it?" Alice said.

"I triggered one of their security protocols."

She held her face in her hands and shook her head. "Which means I'll need to go in another way."

"Sounds like you're going to be busy." Alice placed her cup on the table. "Thanks for the coffee, but I've got blood work to analyze. I'll—"

Alice was interrupted by Daniel's abrupt and unexpected arrival. By the manner in which he stormed into the room, he was clearly agitated. "Leave us."

Alice left as though the devil were on her heels.

Oh God, what now? I'm too tired for this.

She let out a weary sigh. "We weren't expecting you back until tomorrow."

Much to Parker's surprise, Daniel included her in all discussions, and they had spoken via phone on a regular basis throughout the week. They had spent hours strategizing and going over the current developments and any issues she was having, as well as his frustration with the lengthy process of tracking down the people she had identified. At some point during the week, the animosity between them dissolved and was replaced with an easy working relationship, which only made Daniel's current mood the more unexpected.

"What the hell are you doing here?"

She froze at his angry tone.

"You were told to get some rest. Both Simon and Jessica have repeatedly advised you to do so. I know for a fact I ordered you earlier today to take tonight off. And what do I discover when I arrive back at four in the morning? You, not in your bed asleep. Instead, you're still down here working!"

Parker rolled her eyes. "You need to stop taking your job as my watchdog so seriously. I'm not doing anything that the others aren't doing. I want to get those bastards just as much as they do."

Daniel grabbed her by her arms and lifted her into a standing position. Her body pressed against his rock-hard chest, and she was close enough to see the fire blazing in his eyes.

"Unlike them, you are an irritating Human who doesn't know when she has reached her limit. We can cope with minimal sleep. You can't. You are of no use to us if you are unable to function properly. And as much as I hate to admit it, you are our only chance to find whoever's behind this."

Trapped, but unable to tear her gaze from his, she met his angry stare. His face was so close she felt the heat of his breath fan across her cheek.

"I want you in bed. Now." His voice was earthy and low.

His eyes subtly changed from green to amber and then back again. Heat radiated through her body, and an unfamiliar feeling of desire pushed up from her core.

Daniel let her go, and pushed her in the direction of the door. "Let's go."

She was unable to snap out an answer before he growled again. "I wouldn't challenge me on this, if I were you. You wouldn't like how that would turn out."

With as much dignity as she could muster, she gathered her wits and errant pulse, and stormed ahead of Daniel up the darkened pathway toward the house.

TWELVE

Subject Thirteen

Middlemarch Estate

Order was everything. Without it, how could one function? Dr. Hans Fridericks relished the fact he was a neat and methodical person. As such, he insisted on a perfectly sterile working environment. There was a place for everything, and everything was in its place.

Satisfied he was prepared for the next round, Hans ran a critical eye over the room. From the medical monitors to the heart and lung unit, to the mobile 160,000 lux halogen mobile surgical light, no expense had been spared. In fact, the room was better equipped than many of the top hospitals' operating rooms around the world.

He ordered his assistant to recheck the spotless instrument table placed the perfect distance from the medical table. The table itself was laden with surgical knives, scalpels, forceps, and the other myriad of equipment required to carry out his work. Each implement, carefully and lovingly cleaned and then set on the stainless-steel trays in perfect order, was set exactly one inch apart.

He rechecked the monitors and machines that would be used for the procedure, and confirmed everything was in working order and within acceptable parameters. He was taking no chances with this one. It would not do to have another one die on his table—it would take far too long to prepare another test subject.

Time he did not have.

His alpha was becoming less and less tolerant. Hans needed a breakthrough to complete the formula that would be used to carry out their objective. Without it, their work to date would have been in vain. He would never get back to their main experiment. Moreover, he did not wish to suffer the same ending as his predecessor. His alpha was unforgiving when it came to this particular matter.

Failure meant death, and he had come too far to die now.

Hans glanced at his watch, ensuring everything was in order to begin when the alpha arrived. "Tighten the straps," he said to his assistant. "We don't need a repeat of this morning."

"How much longer do you think this one will last?" his assistant said.

Hans raked his gaze across Subject Thirteen's body. "So far we've had positive results. Hopefully, he will make it through the entire procedure." He tilted his head and considered his options. "However, we should start prepping another control subject just in case."

He and his assistant quickly stood to attention as the door to the room opened and Alpha Lauzon stepped inside, along with a Werewolf he had never seen before. Judging from his size and demeanor, the new arrival was also an alpha.

"Are you ready to begin?" Alpha Lauzon said.

Nodding affirmation, Hans moved next to the surgical table, eager to commence the testing.

The unknown alpha sniffed the unconscious body on the table. "So how does this all work?"

Han's peered at the man. *American?*

Was this the American Alpha that Alpha Lauzon enlisted to help in their quest? Hans had never been given the name of the allies who invested millions of dollars in helping fund their research.

Not sure how to proceed, Hans looked to Alpha Lauzon to ascertain if he was allowed to speak. When he received a curt nod, he said, "We require two subjects for each test. The control subject and the test subject. The latest variation of Wildfire is introduced directly into the bloodstream of the test subject first. We then monitor the somatic stem cells. This is to determine if there has been a breakdown in the body's ability to maintain and repair the disease. The hope is that it's running rampant and uncontrolled throughout the body."

He nodded at the medical analysis monitors. "Once it's determined that the correct gene has been targeted, the exact same dosage of the variation is introduced into the control subject's bloodstream."

The American Alpha pointed to the unconscious male. "And is this a test subject or control subject?"

Hans patted the patient on the head. "This is Control Subject Thirteen, and we are quietly optimistic at this stage. We introduced the drug one hundred and seventy-two hours ago, and so far, the subject has shown no signs of infection, even though the test subject has."

He cringed when the American Alpha picked up his favorite scalpel from the instruments tray and examined it. Now he would need to start cleaning all over again.

"And if you determine that this is the correct dosage, how are you going to get the right people to take it?" the American Alpha said.

Hans closed his mouth when Alpha Lauzon took over the conversation. "We have procured an organization that supplies artificial sweeteners and caffeine to the food industry. This will be our delivery mechanism to ensure wide-reaching exposure, giving us maximum damage. In fact, we have already distributed the current version of Wildfire in a range of products. Once we finalize the formula, we will already have the mechanism for the quickest distribution."

Alpha Lauzon eyed the instrument table.

A wave of disappointment washed over Hans. Not only had the new arrival disturbed his carefully laid out instruments, now his alpha wanted to perform the procedure.

Alpha Lauzon picked up the oversized bone marrow biopsy needle and smiled. "Wake him." The voice was cold, hard, and free of any emotion. "I want him to be conscious for this."

Hans reached for a small bottle of ammonium carbonate, and waved it under the nose of Control Subject Thirteen. The man strapped to the table inhaled deeply, and the monitors registered a rapid increase in pulse and blood pressure.

It took a full five minutes before the man was fully conscious. When he finally came to, he released an endless bone-chilling scream. The man had been subjected to a number of these procedures, each one more painful than the last. Bone marrow had been removed from so many areas on his pelvic bone, he resembled Swiss cheese.

Hans kept his thoughts to himself, but wished he had never shown his alpha how to perform the procedure. "I think perhaps this time we require two samples, one from the bone as usual, and, it's time for a sample of brain matter."

Alpha Lauzon stood over Control Subject Thirteen and pressed the oversized biopsy needle into the man's body. The needle broke the skin and dug its way through tissue and muscle. Blood oozed and pooled around the dent, trailing onto the table.

The man's face contorted in agony, and he cried out between ragged, painful breaths. Tears streamed down his face. "Stop. Make it stop."

Metal scraped against bone as the needle reached its intended target, and Alpha Lauzon rotated the instrument to get a deeper sample. Subject Thirteen tried to twist away, but the restraints held him down. His uncontrollable scream pierced the silence in the room.

The monitors beeped furiously and red lights flashed.

Merde!

Hans reached for the defibrillator paddles and charged the unit. "He's going into cardiac arrest."

Alpha Lauzon placed the biopsy needle on the table. "Do not let him die. I haven't finished with him yet."

A sense of urgency rushed through Hans, and he glanced at his assistant. He'd just gotten the man trained. The alpha had a tendency to kill his assistants when things did not go right. Everyone stepped back as he moved in and placed the paddles on the man's chest.

"Clear," he said and released the current.

The man's body convulsed. The process was repeated twice before his pulse returned and steadied. The smelling salts were reapplied, and the test subject woke up. Alpha Lauzon stepped back to the table.

Hans let out a relieved breath as he dropped the small glass bottle onto the tray. Their luck had held out. For now. Joining their alpha at the table, Hans nodded to his assistant, and they turned the man's head, holding it in place so Alpha Lauzon could position the needle.

Subject Thirteen, too weak to fight, struggled with the little strength he had left. Before the bliss of unconsciousness took him again, he cried out, agony reflected in his broken voice.

"I hope you rot in hell, bitch!"

Alpha Lauzon smiled coldly, the whites of her teeth a vivid contrast to her perfectly applied dark red lipstick. "You say bitch like it's a bad thing."

THIRTEEN

Breakthrough

Nederland, Colorado

Parker glanced around to make sure they couldn't be overheard. Alice had pulled her and Daniel out of the makeshift hospital to give them an update on her findings. From the dark circles under the doctor's eyes, she could very well believe Alice hadn't slept since the first death under her care.

Alice's mouth set in a grim line as they discussed the impasse in her analysis. She clutched the medical clipboard tightly against her chest. "None of this makes sense. There is a pattern, but I just can't see it." She sighed. "The drug is attacking from a cellular level and directly targeting the Werewolf gene within our DNA."

Parker cringed when Daniel's already staunch stance turned to stone. She felt his rage bubbling just below the surface. While she understood his frustration at their slow progress, anger wasn't going to get them to a solution any faster.

Before Alice retreated from her alpha's current mood, Parker reached out and touched her arm. "What pattern are you seeing, Alice?"

Alice's eyes darted to Daniel and then back to Parker. "It's strange, but some Werewolves have taken the drug with no apparent side effects. Others, like Gail, have symptoms and develop the physical manifestation with the sores, but their body is fighting it, and they are healing, albeit at a slow pace. Then there's the third group where the drug attacks the body to the point it shuts down and nothing seems to help."

Daniel unclenched his fists, but his still rigid shoulders spoke volumes. "Does the time they've been on the drug affect the progress?"

Alice shook her head. "No, it doesn't seem to. We have some that have been on it nearly two months, others only two weeks. Both are getting worse, but it's early days yet. If we can work out why it is affecting the patients differently, we may be able to determine how to fight it."

"What are your current projections?"

Alice pulled the clipboard away from her chest and glanced at her notes. "My guess is that of the twenty-three we have here, we are going to lose half over the next few weeks. There are four like Gail who we need to keep under observation to make sure that their symptoms recede. The remaining we can probably send home after a quarantine period."

"I'll make arrangements for quarantine quarters." Daniel turned to Parker. "I understand that Gail is assisting with identifying the man who introduced her to the drug?"

Parker nodded. "We managed to get hold of the CCTV from the club. She's with Jay and Zeke now. Hopefully, we have some footage of him."

"Keep me informed. Now, if you'll excuse me, the council is waiting for an update."

She and Alice watched as he headed toward the compound.

"There's a rumor Daniel is still on your case about working around the clock," Alice said.

Parker rolled her eyes and snorted. "Christ, isn't anything sacred around here?"

Alice flinched and Parker immediately regretted her outburst. "Sorry. I didn't mean to snap. It just frustrates me that everyone knows everything."

"You have to remember we have no secrets," Alice said. She paused and tilted her head. "Though speaking of secrets... how do you mask your scent?"

Parker froze. In the years since she had discovered the ability, no one had come out and asked her the question. She knew they wondered—it was evident on their faces when they first met her. But no one, not even Morgan or Clara, had ever asked her point blank.

Until now.

She avoided the subject. "I don't know what you're talking about."

Alice waved her off. "Don't get me wrong, I am not condemning you. For a Human, having everyone know what you feel when you feel it is a very unsettling experience." She smiled. "Don't forget, I was Human once. I can remember how frustrating it became when everyone knew if I was happy or sad or angry." She grinned. "Or even horny."

Parker shifted uncomfortably. She could feel her face heat up. "I am not saying I mask my scent, but if I did, that's nobody's business but my own."

Alice took a step back. "I am only asking because I think that's why you and Daniel bicker. He's used to being in command, knowing exactly what people are thinking and feeling. With you, he has no idea what's going on." Alice hesitated and bit her bottom lip before continuing. "You know, Simon is running a pool on who will attack whom first. The question is, what form of attack will it be?"

Parker muttered under her breath as she stalked into Tech House. "That traitor." Simon had the audacity to take bets on whose temper would give way first? "Just wait until I get my hands on him, that flip-flop-wearing hippy."

She stopped in her tracks when she noticed Gail sitting with Jay and Zeke, and pushed down her irritation with Simon. Gail had already gone through enough. She did not need more drama added to her already fragile emotions. When Gail's mouth twitched upwards at something Zeke said, Parker could have hugged the two boys. Gail had been so terrified, it was hard to make any sense of what she was saying. Both her trainees had taken it upon themselves to help Gail relax in their company and not take flight every time someone wanted to speak to her.

Not long after Parker initially questioned her, Gail's condition had worsened. They were convinced that she too would suffer the same fate as the others. When her body fought back, no one was more surprised than Alice. While the teenager was still a little weak, they were convinced she would make a full recovery.

She left Gail with Zeke and Jay to review the footage from the nightclub and resumed her work on tracking the money trail to the culprits. As she checked the progress of her routines, images of the victims who weren't as lucky as Gail flashed in front of her eyes. She picked up a pen and threw it across the room.

The sooner I find the bastards, the sooner the killing stops, and I can go home.

After another failed attempt to break through the firewall Parker pinched the bridge of her nose. *I need to focus.* Much to her disgust, her thoughts kept drifting to Daniel.

She was startled when Zeke jumped out of his chair. "We found him!"

Finally, a break. She reached for her phone. "I'll let Daniel know."

They crowded around the monitor.

"Let me see," Daniel said.

Parker moved to allow him room, and she nodded for Zeke to replay the footage.

Gail, nervous now that Daniel had joined them, pointed to the screen. Zeke zoomed in on the area, and the grainy image sharpened to provide a better picture of the Werewolf.

Daniel stiffened as the image became clearer. His eyes narrowed to slits, and his jaw clenched as he continued to stare at the screen. "Are you sure that's the man who gave you the drug?"

"Yes."

Daniel towered over Gail. "Are you *positive*?"

Gail shrank into herself. "Y...Yes. That's him."

All eyes turned to Daniel. His face was taut, and he clenched his fists. He was barely containing his fury as he slowly and evenly said through his clenched jaw, "I know him."

Parker's brows knitted. She couldn't have heard correctly, could she?

Daniel's lips pursed with suppressed fury, and he continued to glare at the grainy image. Muscles rippled down his face as he resolutely fought to keep tight control of his emotions. She knew him well enough to know his wolf was fighting for dominance, begging to escape and tear the form on the monitor to shreds.

His voice tore from his throat in a deep, menacing snarl. "I know him. Or, at least, I knew him."

Parker glanced around. The omegas and Gail had become frightened by his instant reaction to seeing the image. Each one had adopted a submissive position, in case he lashed out.

She reached for him and placed her hand on his arm, careful to keep her touch light so as not to anger him, or magnify his repressed rage. Daniel's eyes looked to hers and, for a moment, she was unnerved by the storm that was raging within him. Their gaze locked, the battle within him subsided, and she felt his tension ease.

She shook her head at him and nodded toward the intimidated Werewolves. Daniel's eyes followed, but it took him a moment to focus.

Daniel cleared his throat. "I want a copy sent to every Alliance alpha. And get a copy to Alice, too. I want to know how many of her patients recognize him."

She nodded.

Daniel hesitated as if he wanted to say something further. Thinking better of it, he abruptly turned on his heels and stalked out of the building.

FOURTEEN

Family Secrets

Bitter memories and past demons mobbed Daniel's mind, ones he thought long forgotten and buried. But now they boiled to the surface and threatened to overwhelm him. How had he not seen this? The clues were there. How had they all missed it? Morgan and Abraham especially. This would be just as devastating to them and remind them of the past they left behind. A past none of them wished to return to.

He shook himself out of his nightmare. He had work to do. He needed to tighten security around the perimeter to safeguard his pack.

By the time he reached the house, he had already organized additional patrols and security measures with Ray. He was taking no chances. Mentally calculating how many of his pack lived outside the village in the nearby towns and cities, he telepathically linked to Adam and Vic to put the families on high alert. For now, he would need to keep this information limited—he had no doubt that once Werewolves knew who, and what, was actively targeting them, they would stampede back to their packs.

He called out for Simon to follow him as he reached his beta's office, and continued on without waiting for a reply.

Simon stayed silent as they walked into Daniel's office and shut the door.

Daniel took a seat behind his desk and indicated for Simon to do the same, shaking his head at Simon's fidgeting. His beta hated to be kept in the dark.

Daniel put the phone on speaker and dialed. He had to suppress a smile when Simon's thoughts strayed toward him.

Luna, it's to do with Parker. What does he think she's done this time?

He smirked. He was well aware of the betting pool his beta had instigated.

Morgan answered the phone and Simon shifted forward in his chair. His brows furrowed as he glanced at Daniel.

He bypassed any pleasantries. "Morgan, I need you to check your email. Now."

"I'm not at my desk. I'll head over there now and phone you back in five."

Daniel, not a patient man, spent the next four and a half minutes pacing the office, still not explaining anything to Simon. He answered the call before the first ring ended.

"Did you get it?"

Morgan's voice was strained. "Where was this taken?"

"San Diego, about a month ago. He's been identified as one of the pushers."

"Are you sure?"

"One witness so far." Daniel's phone beeped. He glanced at Parker's message and stiffened. "Make that three."

"*Scheiße!*"

Simon's eyes narrowed, and he leaned forward to listen intently. Alpha Morgan only regressed into his native German under extreme stress.

Daniel pinched the bridge of his nose and briefly closed his eyes. "You do know what that means?"

"Of course, I *verdammt* well do," Morgan said. "Have the others been informed?"

"I have only just found out. We need to convene a meeting, the sooner, the better."

"Has Parker gotten any closer yet?"

"She's still working on it. The money has been traced to Europe—it seems to be bouncing around there." Daniel rubbed his jaw and frowned. "That alone should have tipped me off."

Morgan was silent for a few moments. "We can't go jumping to conclusions. It's been a long time. He may have gone rogue."

"I don't think we will be that lucky." Daniel paused. "I want to send Murphy to Europe. We need to know for sure."

A surprised yelp erupted from Simon as he fell off the edge of his chair and landed on the floor. He jumped up and stared at Daniel. *As in O'Neill? Murphy O'Neill?*

Daniel rolled his eyes. Why everyone only talked about Murphy in hushed tones was never clear to him. To be fair, his open defiance of the Alliance was legendary. While he did not like Murphy's blatant disregard for the chain of command, he fully understood where his pain came from. As such, he gave Murphy a lot more leeway than anyone else. The fact that he felt partly to blame for how things turned out twenty years ago may have had something to do with it.

Morgan let out a long exhale. "I agree he's the best candidate, but we both know he won't listen to the council, or do anything to help us."

Simon straightened up his chair. "But that grumpy black-eyed devil will listen to Daniel."

Daniel tapped his fingers on the desk and considered other options. There were none. Murphy had the skills needed and spoke the languages. What's more, he was from an alpha line and could hold his own a lot more than many of the alphas Daniel knew. "I know Murphy. This is bigger than the vendetta he has against the council. He will go. I just have to work out which FBI strings to pull to get him off whatever case he's currently on."

Simon rubbed the back of his neck and frowned. "But why is he going to Europe? Who do you think is behind Wildfire?"

"Daniel," Morgan said, interrupting the question. "Abraham's on the other line. I'll give him a heads up, then phone you back. In light of who's behind this, we need to talk about the danger to Parker. I would feel more comfortable if Clara and I were there to explain it to her."

Morgan hung up, and Daniel looked up to see that Simon's curiosity was on high alert. He felt his friend telepathically reaching out to his fellow betas.

He cleared his throat and waited for Simon to refocus his attention on their current problem.

"Um...sorry," Simon said. "Just making sure that my team is carrying out your last orders."

Daniel raised an eyebrow. "Good try. You wanted to see if they knew any more than you do."

Simon grinned sheepishly. "You can't blame a wolf for trying. So, what's going on? Who do you think is behind this?"

Daniel debated how to tell his friend. The uneasy feeling that had grown unchecked was now at fever pitch. "When are your parents due back?"

"By the end of the month. Why?"

"I want you to get hold of them and tell them to stay put. I'll speak to Alpha Tamas to make sure that if they need to go off pack land, they will be escorted."

Simon's eyes grew wide and he froze. "What are you not telling me?"

He hesitated. "Your Uncle Matheo is on American soil. That means his pack and Alpha Lauzon are as well."

Simon's breath caught, and his eyes flashed with fear that metastasized into the same waves of anger and pain that Daniel experienced. It would be the same for everyone old enough to understand.

Even his mind had initially rejected the thought of who was behind the death of their people. It wasn't possible. But that face could only mean one thing. One name. A name that hadn't been spoken in years.

One name.

One terrifying name.

Unum Sandulf.

One Pure Wolf.

She. Was. Back.

FIFTEEN

Playing with Fire

Midnight was only minutes away. Parker had long since dismissed Jay and Zeke, encouraging them to go for a run. Without the constant interruptions from Daniel, Simon and the others, she was making headway following the money trail, but it was slow going.

Whoever they were, they knew what they were doing. She was like a pinball bouncing from bank to bank, country to country. To solidify her thoughts, she mapped out the trail on the whiteboard, a practice that often helped her think better. She unplugged her laptop and placed it on the high table beside the whiteboard to monitor her attack on the current bank's databases while she mind-mapped.

A throat was cleared behind her, and she jumped. She swung around and discovered Daniel standing in the doorway, holding a tray of food.

"Jessica said you hadn't eaten. I thought I'd bring your dinner down."

Daniel's constant messages were getting on her exceedingly frayed nerves. She turned back to the board. "You need to learn to be patient. As soon as I find out where the money's going, you'll be the first to know."

He laughed, a deep, genuine laugh. "Yeah, well, that's not my strong suit."

She placed an angry cross through one of the names on the board and tossed the marker down. "It's the same as last time—I don't know how many ways I can tell you. You'll be the first person to know once we have traced it, but we're chasing our tails around the European banking system."

Daniel set the tray down. It contained two plates of food. She raised an eyebrow as she glanced at him. One plate was stacked three times higher than the other.

He shrugged nonchalantly. "Thought you might like company." He handed her the smaller plate filled with steak, jacket potatoes, corn, and salad.

The aroma from the food was divine, and her stomach audibly reminded her she hadn't eaten all day. Embarrassed, she changed the subject. "So, how did the Alliance meeting go?"

Daniel eyed her uncertainly. "How did you know about it?"

She waved her fork. "Don't worry, no one here told me. I got a call from Clara this evening letting me know she and Morgan would be arriving tomorrow."

She took a bite of her food, then asked the question that had played on her mind since that morning. "Are you going to tell me who you saw in that picture?"

"No."

Parker's shoulders tensed, and she stabbed at a potato. *When will the secrecy end?* "I thought we had already been through this. I can't do my job unless I am kept in the loop."

Daniel finished chewing before he answered. "Well, believe it or not, I was all for briefing you on it this afternoon. But as Morgan and the others pointed out, this information moves everything to a new level." He paused and looked at her. "Including increasing the risk to you."

Her head snapped up. "Oh?" Now she was more confused than ever.

For once, Daniel's expression was unguarded. He was telling the truth. "Morgan and Clara have insisted on being present when you are briefed." Daniel paused to take another bite of his food. "In the meantime, I know you ignore every command I give you outright, but I'm asking you, for once, to observe my rule about not leaving the pack village."

She gazed at him and tried to ascertain if this was Daniel being controlling, or Daniel being concerned about her safety. She hoped it was the latter. "Okay."

He looked surprised and then burst out laughing. "Well, that must have almost killed you."

She raised an eyebrow. "What?"

Daniel flicked a corn kernel at her. "To actually concede to something I said."

She ignored him and returned to her meal. Just as she had placed her empty plate onto the tray, a beep emitted from her laptop. She went to investigate, and Daniel followed.

"Finally." She let out a deep breath and pointed to the screen. "Looks like it was rerouted through Commerzbank, a German bank."

Daniel frowned. "Do we know if that's where it ended up?"

She shook her head. "We'll only know after we've accessed the Commerzbank account. We'll have to see if it was transferred from there."

"How long will that take?"

"How long's a piece of string? Could be a few minutes or it could be hours."

She moved onto the next leg of the assault on the money trail, but faltered when Daniel stood directly behind her. He watched over her shoulder as she continued typing.

"I'm seeing if there are any ports open," she said.

Daniel moved even closer and continued to watch her work. His arm came around to rest on the countertop beside her, his body almost, but not quite, touching hers.

Good God, man, mind the personal space.

She shifted and tried to alleviate the building tension. "It's kind of like checking to see if any doors have been left unlocked."

Their bodies accidentally came into contact and his touch ignited a low, burning flame. She struggled to concentrate on the task at hand. He was so close, his breath tingled the shell of her ear.

Her heart raced, and she cleared her throat with difficulty. "Once we get a foothold in the network, we need to ascertain where to attack next. Banks have huge networks with multiple databases, so the trick is to work out which database is the one we are after." She paused and ran a nervous tongue over the bottom of her lip.

She felt Daniel tense and turned her head.

He was immobile, staring at her lips with an expression she couldn't read. His eyes slowly moved up to meet hers. She stopped breathing, and her heart faltered, and then hammered in her chest. He was too close—far too close for her liking. She attempted to put space between them by taking a sideways step, but the table prevented any movement.

The heat from his body engulfed her, and she had to fight the urge to lean closer to him. Daniel's hand came up to gently cup her face, and the world moved in slow motion. Her mind failed to register anything beyond his touch. Everything blurred and the only noise was the labored rhythm of her breathing.

He trailed his calloused thumb along her lips, and she involuntarily parted them. His eyes darkened and his pupils dilated, leaving only a slither of green. His thumb continued from her mouth and lightly brushed the side of her neck, pausing to feel her throbbing pulse. An aroused whimper escaped her lips, and his eyes narrowed.

Without warning, Daniel pulled his arm away, and before she blinked, he had disappeared through the door.

Her mind reeled at her body's lingering reaction to him. She held onto the bench with both hands to steady herself, and she struggled to gather her wits.

What the hell just happened?

How could a single touch make her lose her mind?

Thank God, he stopped before anything happened.

She closed her eyes and tried to regulate her erratic pulse.

The door slammed open, and a moment later, she was pulled hard against Daniel's chest.

***

Daniel needed to sate the growing thirst that had only escalated from the moment he met her.

Four steps.

That's all he could get beyond the building before his self-control disintegrated, and he gave in to his hunger and turned back.

Unable to control his need, he pulled Parker flush against his body and relished the feel of her small frame against his. He threaded his hands through her thick hair, tilted her head back, and brought his mouth down. The instant their lips touched, a current jolted through him, and his body hardened.

His mouth began its assault and his tongue pressed for entrance. At first, she moved hesitantly. When his grip on her tightened, she returned the kiss with as much passion and fury as he was inflicting on her. His hands roamed down her back, pulling her tighter against his aching body.

Fire spread through his veins. He snaked an arm around her, then lifted her up, and slammed her against the whiteboard. Without thinking, he hooked one of her legs around his hip so he could press into her more firmly and feel the heat of her body against his. He groaned as she matched his frenzied exploration.

A shrill beep cut through their desire. The urgent, repeated rhythm demanded attention, almost as if the computers were warning him to put an end to this before it was too late.

It took more effort than he thought possible to pull away. He had been standing on the precipice, ready to cross beyond the point of no return. Had the beep come a moment later, it would've taken nothing short of the world being destroyed for him not to finish what they had started.

"I think your computers are calling you," he said, his voice thick with desire.

Parker, unable to meet his gaze, cleared her throat, and backed away from him. "Um…they've probably found an open port." Her face flushed. She turned her back on him and focused on the monitors.

She had been just as affected by their kiss as he was. Or was she? His brows creased. He should be able to scent her desire, and yet he detected nothing.

Daniel let out a low growl and the muscles on his face tightened. He turned on his heels, and headed for the mountains.

He needed space to think.

SIXTEEN

Another Piece of The Puzzle

Parker took uneven breaths when Daniel left, and focused on keeping her pulse in check. It allowed her a reprieve from having to acknowledge what had happened between them. Her stomach twisted. How could her defenses have crumbled so quickly and without reservation? She was mortified—just the memory of how she had reacted to that kiss had her mind reeling.

If you could call it a kiss.

She had been kissed before, and what she had experienced with Daniel was on an entirely different plane. The skills that this one man possessed had made the others seem like mere boys. Goosebumps erupted across her skin. She had lost all self-control, all ability to think beyond that moment. His touch. His mouth. Her desire.

Heat flooded through her as she relived those brief moments. How his body pressed up against hers felt and his powerful arms as they skillfully played with each and every nerve ending along her back.

She closed her eyes and absently touched her lips. The taste of him still lingered on her tongue.

Parker groaned. *Oh God, how can I face him again? We don't even like each other. He is an overbearing, critical tyrant who doesn't trust Humans—especially me.*

She would take the coward's approach and made sure she did not bump into him when she returned to her room. For now, avoidance was the best policy.

In the morning, Parker skulked down to Tech House and breathed a sigh of relief when she made it out the door without running into Daniel. He had either already left, or was not yet up. Either way, she wasn't sticking around to find out.

By the time she arrived at Tech House she had convinced herself to ignore the fact she was acting like a child and only putting off the inevitable.

Zeke and Jay were already at work, talking to Alice and Gail.

She caught the tail end of the conversation. "What's romantic?"

Gail let out a wistful sigh.

Jay threw the teenager a look of despair. "After our run last night, a few of us went into Boulder, and Kyle recognized his mate—a Human. Long story short, we had a bit of a problem keeping him from leaping across the bar to claim her. In the end, it took all of us to get him out of there before they called the police. It fucked up our night."

"Is that normal?" Parker said. "Do Werewolves normally get that aggressive when they find their mate?"

Alice tilted her head, and her lips pursed as she thought about the question. "Depends. Some Werewolves become over-protective, but eventually calm down. Others try and fight the pull, which never turns out well for either of them. And there are the rare occasions when a mate is rejected."

"What's going to happen to Kyle?" Parker said.

Jay shrugged. "Considering she'll probably have him arrested if he steps foot back in her bar, it ought to be interesting." He snorted, then turned back to his monitor. "What a clusterfuck."

"Alpha Locke has commanded him to not say anything to the woman until we can work out what to do. Human mates don't occur very often, but when they do, it's always a bit complicated," Alice said.

Parker was already aware of the panic that set in each time a Human was turned without their permission, or it was discovered they were someone's mate. With each interaction, the Werewolves increased their chances of exposure to the world.

"When did a Werewolf last take a Human mate in this pack?" she said.

Alice bit her lip and stared at a blank space on the nearest wall. "About twenty years ago. Some of the other packs have a higher rate, others less."

Once her acceptance into the Brandenburg Pack was sealed, she had been fortunate that both Morgan and Clara were willing to share information on the history of Werewolves, and their race in general. According to Werewolf lore, Human mates were an extreme rarity. That had all changed after the 1600's with the religious wars that spread across Europe. The Thirty-Years' War in Germany affected many of the Alliance packs.

The Werewolf race, as with the Humans at the time, lost nearly half their population through brutal cavalry attacks from both sides of the religious divide. The packs, while physically stronger, were no match for battalions of well-armed soldiers. If that weren't enough, they lost many more in the witch persecutions that followed. The packs across Europe were devastated. The race itself was looking down the barrel of extinction. Many became insular to protect those who remained, and, of course, nature always finds a way. Over time,

Werewolves found their mates in Humans and were given a reprieve from annihilation.

"We only discovered forty years ago how mating with a Human is possible," Alice said. "The Human mates have the required dormant wolf gene. They are descendants of, or the result of, a Werewolf having a child with a Human."

"That's how Bobby was turned after being bitten. He had a recessive wolf gene within his DNA," Parker said. She reached for her laptop and hooked it up to her monitor. "When Bobby turned, Morgan and Clara wanted to know where the connection was. I think Clara was a bit disappointed when they traced the gene and found it wasn't in me."

"Oh?" Alice said.

She lifted a shoulder in a half shrug. "I think they were hoping that I could someday be turned, or that I would find a mate in one of the packs."

The corners of Alice's mouth tugged upwards. "You need to realize mating is a big thing for Werewolves. They can only recognize their mates once they, and their wolf, reach physical maturity and stop aging in the same manner as Humans. They can spend years searching for their other half."

Parker heard another wistful sigh from Gail as she threw herself down on the Tech House couch. "I still have four more years. I wish I were already there." The teenager pulled a face. "Then I'd be able to find my mate. It sucks big time that my wolf needs to reach full maturity before I can recognize him, or before he can recognize me."

Alice's eyes opened wide, and her jaw dropped open. "Holy frack in a handbasket." She turned and raced out the door. "I need to check on something."

The others, startled at Alice's sudden change, glanced at each other bug-eyed.

Alice would let them know what was going on when she was ready. Parker broke the silence. "Okay guys, that's enough excitement for today. Back to work you two. We need to get into that encrypted database." She turned to Gail. "Weren't you supposed to meet with Simon this morning?"

Gail's eyes flew wide, and she jumped up from her sitting position. All they heard was "Nuts!" as she raced out the door.

Like a well-oiled machine, Zeke, Jay, and Parker resumed their attack on the German bank's databases. At first, it looked as if they were making no headway. The bank's defenses used some of the best security measures they had seen in a while. With each failed attempt, her worry they would lose the trail escalated.

Zeke groaned after another unsuccessful attempt. "Nothing's working. I've tried everything."

Parker threw one of her pens at the wall. "I'm having no luck either."

She got up and studied the whiteboard. Key systems they had discovered within the bank's network were scrawled over the board. Her eyes narrowed as she scanned the board to see if there were any gaps.

"We're missing something."

Zeke let out a frustrated sigh and rubbed his jaw. "No, we have all their major systems mapped out."

A light went on in her brain, and she spun around and smacked her head. "That's it!" She raced back to her computer. "We'll get in through a support system—there's bound to be communication between it and the main network."

After two intense hours mired in frustration, they finally unencrypted and accessed the account transactions.

Zeke and Jay, unable to contain their glee at their accomplishment, broke into their happy dance and chanted, "We are legends."

Her chest ached, and she didn't know whether to laugh or cry. Instead, she sat staring at the screen. Zeke and Jay's voices faded into the background. She dared not move, or even blink in case this was a figment of her imagination.

We're there.

They had reached the end of the money trail. A mixture of emotions overwhelmed her, each fighting for dominance. She was allowed to feel a little elated, wasn't she?

Parker extracted the information that would identify the account holder, and brought up another window to perform a company search. Her shoulders slumped when the results scrolled on the screen.

And there it was, the reason she never allowed herself to get excited.

It was one thing to get to the end of the money trail, but quite another to actually track down the owner of the account. She had seen this more times than she cared to admit—the account holder was a shell corporation. She rested her forehead on the desk and closed her eyes. Her job had only just begun.

Parker cursed. *These bastards aren't making it easy for me.*

With a resigned sigh, she sat up straight and took a deep, calming breath. She placed her fingers on the keyboard. Time to begin the new leg of her search.

She had only just started when Alice burst through the door, brandishing a bunch of papers in her hands and breathing hard. "I've worked out who Wildfire is targeting. Let's go. We need to tell Daniel."

SEVENTEEN

Crumbling Walls

Parker's brows furrowed. She was confused. Daniel did not look surprised at Alice's revelation. Not that she was able to read his face when he put up his stone wall—and the wall was currently defending against any possible breach from external forces.

She was still reeling from Alice's discovery. Rather than make the knowledge public, the two women had thought it best to share the information with Daniel behind closed doors. They had found him in his office.

As soon as they sat down, Alice took a few calming breaths and began. "I know who the drug has been designed to target."

Alice's expression grew pensive, and she wrung her hands together. "I can't believe I didn't see it before."

Daniel raised his hands. "Don't blame yourself." He lowered his hands. "It won't do you any good. Just tell me what you've found."

Alice took a moment to compose herself. "We had three different groups: those who took it and didn't have any symptoms, those who had symptoms and became ill but then recovered, and the last group who became progressively sicker until they were terminal."

"As I am already aware," Daniel said. "What does this have to do with your discovery?"

"The group with no effects were all mature Werewolves whose parents were born Werewolves. The recovery group was the same, with the exception that the infected hadn't yet reached maturity." She paused and nibbled on her thumbnail. "I think the drug is deliberately targeting Werewolves who have been turned or who have a parent that was turned."

Alice shifted forward in her seat and explained in a rush. "Mature, pure Werewolves are immune to Wildfire and pure Werewolves that have yet to reach maturity can fight it. But, once Wildfire is introduced to a Werewolf with mixed genes, the mortality rate is one hundred percent."

Parker cleared her throat. "So, this is a designer drug that is attacking Werewolves based on genetic purity." Her knowledge of biology was rusty, but she was sure that wasn't possible.

Daniel's eyes focused on Parker. "Thank you, Alice. I would appreciate it if you didn't mention this to anyone else just yet."

Alice stood, bowed to her alpha and left, leaving only silence behind.

"You already knew, didn't you?" she said.

Daniel took a deep breath and rubbed his forehead. "I had my suspicions."

She leaned back and crossed her arms over her chest. "And it's related to this thing you can't tell me?" She knew the answer but still needed the actual affirmation.

He nodded.

Her shoulders dropped and she shook her head. She thought they had gotten beyond the cloak and daggers stage. "Don't you think it would've been better to at least point Alice in the right direction?" She recalled the stress Alice had put herself through to find answers, answers that Daniel already had. A wave of anger surged through her body, and she stiffened. "She's been working tirelessly to put the puzzle together, and you had the answer the entire time."

Daniel placed his hands on his desk and leaned forward. "I don't need to explain myself, and I certainly don't answer to you."

She shot out of her seat and placed her hands on her hips. "Don't you think we've already learned the hard way what happens when key people are left in the dark? I would've thought you'd have learned that lesson by now."

Daniel's stonewall expression irritated her even further. She let out a disgusted noise and stormed out of his office slamming his door with as much force as she could. She needed to leave before she said anything she'd regret later.

Parker brooded all afternoon, angry with herself. She had deliberately picked a fight with Daniel and she had no idea why. As usual, her mind had another point of view.

Of course, you do. You were petrified that he would mention last night.

Not able to concentrate, and incapable of pretending to, she decided a walk would clear her mind. She grabbed a bottle of water and headed for the path that would take her into the forest.

She passed the main compound without being seen by the group of children who normally followed her on her daily walks and breathed a sigh of relief. While she enjoyed their company, today she needed the quiet solitude to think. The afternoon sun was warm despite the canopy high above her. She headed farther along the trail than normal and heard the sound of water gushing in the distance.

Parker veered off the path and spotted a small clearing through the trees. When she broke through to the clearing, the beauty of her surroundings took her breath away. Water cascaded down the rocky surface of the mountainside and into a small, but clear blue lake. She spotted a large flat rock on the lake's edge and headed toward it. *I wonder how warm the water is?* She took off her shoes, rolled up her jeans, and dipped her feet in the water. The water was cooler than she expected, but she grew accustomed to it. She leaned back and enjoyed the tranquility and beauty of the lake.

She was so engrossed in her own thoughts that splashing a short way off startled her. A portion of the lake was obscured from view. Whatever the sound was, it was coming from around the corner. Curious, she craned her head and was stunned by the sight of a huge black wolf. The wolf spotted her at the exact same moment.

Frack.

She knew without a doubt that this was Daniel's wolf.

Indecision had her rooted to the spot.

Should I leave before he emerges, or should I stay here and ignore him?

The wolf lazily made his way to the bank and emerged from the water. His fur glistened in the sun. Even wet, the wolf was massive. His muscles were well-defined against the fur plastered to his lean body.

A flurry of nerves shot through her middle as he drew close. Sleek and powerful, he radiated raw, unbridled energy. He halted. Expressionless, his amber eyes stared at her without blinking. It was the same look she had often seen on Daniel's face.

Well, they both have that look down pat.

The wolf took a step closer so they were face-to-face. He leaned in and gently nuzzled the side of her neck, wetting her in the process.

Parker was caught off guard and struggled to push him away. "Get off me, you great oaf. You're soaking, and you smell like a wet blanket."

His eyes alternated between green and amber and she could swear he grinned. The wolf violently shook his body, and water splattered in all directions.

She screamed and attempted to protect herself from the sudden deluge. Eventually, the wolf stopped, and she looked up to find him standing near her, tongue lolling out of his mouth with a definite wolfy grin plastered across his features.

Still cursing, she swatted at the now half-dry wolf and pouted as she attempted to wipe herself down. "Well, that was a shitty thing to do."

The wolf ignored her and nuzzled against her leg.

Still irritated, she swatted at him again. "Go find a stick to play with, you idiot. I need to get dry."

She sat down, dangled her feet in the water, and leaned back on her arms. The wolf, finding a comfortable position, lay down by her side. Parker closed her eyes and lifted her face to the sun.

Once Parker awoke, the wolf got up from his position, sauntered to the water's edge, and dipped his nose to smell it. He looked back at her and leaped into the lake. This time, she anticipated what he was about to do and quickly scrambled backward, avoiding most of the water that splayed back onto the rock.

She called out half-heartedly, "Daniel, I swear to God, I'm going to kill you."

The wolf swam for a while and then sauntered back to shore. This time, he shook himself off from a distance. Then he ambled to a spot just behind where she sat and attempted to retrieve something from between two large boulders.

Curious at the obvious frustration exhibited by the wolf, she rose and went over to investigate. The wolf was unsuccessfully attempting to retrieve a pair of jeans that Daniel must have placed there before transforming.

She pulled the garment out from its hiding spot. "Well, that was a stupid place to put them."

The wolf sat down on his haunches and growled.

Her glance flickered between the wolf and the pair of black jeans in her hands. She was suddenly all too aware that Daniel needed to transform back first before getting dressed. Her face grew hot, and the heat spread throughout her body.

"Oh," was the only word she mustered. She folded his clothing and held it out for the wolf to take.

The wolf took the offering in his mouth and wandered into the nearby line of trees.

Parker returned to her previous position. She was peering into the water when a shadow blocked out the sun. Parker looked up to investigate, and only made out his well-formed shirtless torso as his face was obscured by the light. She gulped and tried not to stare—it was difficult pretending not to notice his perfectly sculptured upper body.

What would it be like to run her fingers across his toned chest and torso, to feel the outline of the scars scattered across his exposed front and back? His uncovered body was as tanned as the rest of him. Water from his still-wet hair dripped and ran down his torso, seeping into the top of the jeans sitting dangerously low on his hips.

Just how low does his tan go?

Without speaking, Daniel sat down beside her, and his legs joined hers in the water. He was close enough that she felt the heat of his skin.

Personal space. The man had no concept of it.

"I'm sorry if you think I am keeping things from you." His voice was low and sincere. "It's not my intention, and I was going to tell Alice, but she worked it out before I could."

Parker sighed. "I know. I overreacted a little bit."

Daniel faced her.

"Okay. A little more than a little."

A bird cried overhead, and they watched as an eagle circled them, and then flew northwards.

Daniel watched the bird disappear into the distance. "I remember the first time my pack saw a golden eagle after arriving in America. We'd been searching for months for somewhere to settle. Somewhere far away from civilization, but close enough that we could still keep an eye on it."

Her feet swished in the water, but she remained silent. He had never spoken about his past and would often leave if a conversation required him to take a trip down memory lane.

"One spring morning, not far from here, my father spotted a pair of golden eagles." Daniel paused to pick up a pebble and tossed it into the water. "As with wolves, they mate for life. He decided that this was an omen, and that this was where we should settle the pack."

She scanned their surroundings and smiled. "Well, he picked a perfect spot. The area is a mini paradise."

He laughed. "You wouldn't have thought so at the time. Remember, this was over one hundred and fifty years ago. There were no roads, no transportation, no under-floor heating, no air-conditioning, and virtually no Humans. It was all untamed wilderness."

She studied the area with new eyes, trying to imagine it when Daniel and his people first arrived. She couldn't fathom what it would be like being a living witness to history. "Do you miss it?"

He thought about the question before he answered. "Sometimes. We could be ourselves without having to constantly look over our shoulders."

Parker's brows edged upward. *He's never spoken so freely about his past before.*

She listened in awe as he described how the valley was developed by the pack, and the hardships they often faced.

Daniel absently reached up and tucked a lock of hair behind her ear. "Life was a lot simpler then. Our wolves roamed as they pleased. We had time to regroup and define who we were as a race, without the constraints of our past."

His touch, whilst innocent, had set fire to her nerve endings. It was an effort to keep her expression neutral and hide the physical effect that lingered even after he severed contact.

"My father taught me to protect the pack above all else. Often that involved holding back information so as not to cause panic." He paused and looked at her. "I suppose that's what I've been doing with you. It's hard to break out of something I've had to do my entire life, but I want you to know I am trying. It's just that I'm not used to trusting others."

Thrown by the revelations, and unsure how to respond, she fingered her necklace and searched for the right words. Without question, this was a conversation he's not had too often. The sincerity in his voice left her in no doubt of that. "Let's face it, you've had the equivalent of a few Human lifetimes to perfect the habit."

Daniel laughed and nudged her with his shoulder. "Well, let's see how *you* fare breaking a habit you've had for over two-hundred years."

Her stomach lurched. Daniel, Morgan, Clara, Bobby, and the rest of the Werewolves would still be around in another two-hundred years. She, however, would be but a memory. Parker took a deep breath and ignored the pain in her chest. "Well, lucky for you I'm Human, so that's not going to happen."

Daniel blinked and fixed his gaze on her. "Morgan mentioned that your cousin's grandfather was a Werewolf."

Parker nodded. She was about to reply, but felt something bite her ankle. "Ow!" She pulled her limb up to investigate. A large mosquito was happily sucking away at her leg.

Daniel flicked the offender off her skin and swung her legs over to rest across his. He reached for the drink bottle behind her, opened it, and poured water over the bite.

She winced "That's hot."

The water within the bottle had heated in the sun.

"I know. The hot water will clean the area and stop the itch."

After he was satisfied the bite was clean, he set the empty bottle down. Her legs still rested across his thighs, and he was gently holding them in place.

"You were about to say?" he said.

"What?" Her entire body was on high alert, her mind a jumbled mess.

His hand absently touched her calf. "Your cousin?"

"O-oh," she said. "Bobby never knew him. His grandmother claimed he died before Bobby's father was born. There was an old photo she carried around with her of the two of them. After she died, he inherited it. The photo came in handy. One of the packs recognized Bobby's grandfather. It turned out he left Chicago around the end of the 1940's and wasn't seen again."

Daniel continued to massage her bitten leg. Electric currents shot up her limb and through every nerve ending in her body.

Jesus, Mary, and Joseph. This man has magic fingers.

She recalled her conversation with Jessica, and curiosity got the better of her. "What was your father like?"

Daniel let out a long breath and shook his head. "My father was driven. He demanded a very high standard from everyone. Apart from when he was with my mother, I don't think I ever saw him smile until the day Jessica was born."

While the words were spoken quietly, his tone spoke volumes. She reached out and placed a comforting hand on his arm. "That must have been hard for you, having to live up to his standard, not able to walk your own path."

Daniel shrugged it off. "It goes with the territory. All alphas are brought up that way. We know nothing else."

"Is that the way you will bring up your children?"

He tensed at her question, a dark scowl flittering across his face for the briefest of moments. She recognized the emptiness and longing reflected in his eyes. Then, as was Daniel's way, his face put up a wall, leaving her doubtful of ever having seen it at all.

He glanced at the late afternoon sun, now hidden behind the trees. "We better head back. Morgan and Clara will be arriving soon."

This was her cue to rise. She attempted to extricate her legs from their position across his thighs. His arm still rested across them, and she tried to nudge it away to allow her some movement.

Daniel tore his gaze away from the sun and looked down at her. She watched as his eyes raked across her hair and face. The intensity of his stare made it hard for her to breathe.

Not even aware she was doing it, she leaned closer to the force of nature beside her. His eyes searched her face intently. He took an eternity to lower his head, only to halt a fraction of an inch from her mouth.

His eyes bored into hers, trying to see into her soul.

The delay, while only a second, was painful, then by mutual agreement, they closed the distance. Unlike their previous kiss, this one was gentle. His tongue was questioning, not demanding entrance. She trembled when she granted him entry and her lips met his. One kiss became two, then three.

Their kiss deepened and white-hot longing flared and burnt bright. Unable to help herself, she reached her arms up and entwined her fingers around his neck. She returned his passion until she had no idea where his lips ended and hers began.

A low moan, deep with desire caught her attention. When he pulled her closer and the sound repeated, she was startled to discover it had come from her.

***

Daniel pulled her closer. All that existed was this moment, and this woman in his arms. She tasted divine. Sweet and hot. He couldn't get enough of her. Hearing her moan only escalated his need. He trailed his lips along her cheekbones and nibbled on her ear. Parker trembled with longing as he nipped at her skin. He dipped his mouth lower and followed her jawline until he was kissing the side of her neck, sucking at her now heavy pulse. The sudden desire to mark her nearly overwhelmed him.

Startled, he froze. His wolf was holding him back. Indecision and doubt washed over him in waves.

She is not our mate, she doesn't even have the gene.

I know

We don't want to hurt her.

I know that, too.

He fought to get himself under control and pulled away. "Parker." He held her at arm's length and searched her face. Her eyes were still dilated, her lips red and swollen from his kisses, and her cheeks flushed with arousal. He wanted to finish what they had started, but his rational mind was taking control. He groaned. They couldn't do this. *He* couldn't do this. He needed to stop whatever this was before it got any more out of control. His chest tightened and a heavy weight pushed down on him. Hurting her wasn't an option, and if he continued down this path, that was the only possible outcome.

"We need to head back. It's getting late, and I have work to do before Morgan gets here." His voice came out gruff and strained as he watched the fire in her eyes flicker and die.

***

Daniel's words hit Parker like a bucket of iced water. She stood up, and they headed back to the village. Neither spoke, though both were deep in thought.

They had almost reached the compound when Daniel paused. "About what just happened—"

She held up her hands to stop him before he could continue. "Let's just forget it happened. We've both been under a lot of strain, and neither of us was thinking straight."

Daniel said nothing. He nodded in agreement, and they continued toward the compound.

She bit the inside of her lip. He was quick to agree with her suggestion. Too quick. Was it because he regretted kissing her? Was it that unpleasant he wanted to purge all memory of it? She blinked rapidly at the sudden sharp pain behind her eyes. While she had to admit it wasn't the smartest thing to do, their desire had been brewing under the surface for a while. Or, at least she thought it had.

When they reached the house, Daniel halted in the doorway, looking decidedly uncomfortable. "Morgan and Clara are almost here. I have arranged for dinner to be served…for the four of us."

His eyes darted to the house and then back at her. He opened his mouth to speak, but snapped it shut and shuffled his feet as he rubbed the back of his neck. She frowned when he glanced back at the house. Perhaps he was rethinking her joining the alphas for dinner?

She sighed. The day couldn't possibly get any worse. "Whatever it is, just come out with it."

"No one will smell your scent on me," he said, "but… you may want to have a shower before Morgan and Clara arrive. They will definitely smell my scent on you, and I am not sure you'll want to have them asking any questions."

Her cheeks flushed, and a lump grew in her throat, making it hard for her to swallow. She was mortified and wished the earth would swallow her whole. Daniel was so embarrassed by her that he did not want anyone to know what had happened. She mustered all the dignity she could gather and made her way to her room before closing the door and fleeing to her bathroom.

What the hell was I thinking? Why did I let him kiss me again? Actually, better question—why did I kiss him back?

Ignoring the obvious answer, she escaped into the shower. There was no way she wanted any of the knowing stares that would come from the Brandenburg alphas. Clara would have a field day.

It took her a full half hour after dinner was put on the table to relax enough to join in the conversation. She chugged down the first glass of wine in record time, and looked up to find both the Brandenburg alphas watching her expectantly.

"Sorry. What did you say?"

Clara eyed her before repeating the question. "*Liebe*, I was just making sure you were eating and sleeping properly. I know what you get like when you're in front of a computer." Clara frowned. "You are looking too skinny. I'm sure you've lost weight."

Morgan placed a hand over his mate's. "Clara, my dear, leave the poor girl alone." He turned to Parker. "I understand you are making progress in tracking down the culprits behind this?"

She smiled weakly and nodded. "We're at the end of the money trail and are now tracking down who ultimately owns the account." She was more relaxed with where the conversation was going. "I think we're close. It's just that there's been some odd information and data we're bumping up against."

She poured herself another glass of wine, sat back, and narrowed her eyes at her companions. "Now, is someone going to tell me about who this Werewolf is that you all obviously know, and why it's such a big secret?"

Daniel, Morgan, and Clara glanced at each other, as if working out where to begin. Clara's concerned expression turned toward her.

That can't be good.

Morgan took the lead. "His name is Matheo Dumas, a beta from one of the packs that was left behind when we came to America."

Alarm bells went off in her ever-vigilant mind. "Dumas? Isn't that Simon's last name?" Her eyes flew to Daniel.

Daniel nodded. "Yes, Matheo is Simon's uncle."

Morgan leaned forward and placed his arms on the table. "A long time ago, the pack was ruled by Alexander Lauzon, an extremely violent and malevolent alpha. He believed in the purity of the wolf, and didn't tolerate what he termed mixed breeding. When the Werewolf race began to find their mates in Humans, he was enraged. He purged countless innocent Werewolves who had been turned or born to mixed-race parents."

Her brows rose. She was finding the information hard to absorb. "But, surely his pack didn't go along with that?"

Clara leaned toward her and gently placed a hand over Parker's. "They were either as mad as he was, or terrified for their own families, and kept quiet."

Daniel took over the conversation. "Two of Alexander's most powerful betas at the time were brothers, Matheo and David Dumas." He glanced down at his hands and took a deep breath.

She sensed this was a memory he would rather not relive.

"Matheo was one of Alexander's acolytes, an absolute believer in the purity of the wolf lineage. David, on the other hand, was the complete opposite."

Morgan nodded. "Alexander was obsessed with the idea that Humans were to always remain in complete ignorance of our existence. If there was even a hint of a Human knowing about us, they were to be eliminated quickly and violently. Alexander would often slaughter the Human's entire family."

Parker, not liking the direction this conversation was leading, had lost her appetite and pushed her half-eaten plate away.

"One day, it came to Alexander's attention that a family passing through the Bordeaux region in France on their way south to Italy may have seen one of the pack members transform. David was sent to investigate and eliminate the entire family."

Daniel poured a much-needed stronger drink than wine for each of them. He handed Parker a glass of single malt. "It didn't take him long to find the family in question, they hadn't traveled too far. You can imagine his surprise when he discovered his mate in the eldest daughter."

He poured another shot and handed it to Morgan. "Knowing he couldn't return to his pack, David fled with his mate, Margaret, and sought refuge with my father and our pack."

Morgan accepted the glass, downed it, and looked across at Parker with a reassuring smile. "Alpha Nicholas granted them asylum, and they were welcomed into the pack. When Alexander heard, he became infuriated. The fact that one of his trusted betas had mated with a Human pushed him over the edge."

"He began attacking other packs indiscriminately until he found out who had taken them in," Daniel said. "Eventually, he made his way to my father, demanding that we release David and Margaret. My father denied his request, and as expected, Alexander challenged him."

"If he had taken more care in training, rather than killing innocents, things might have turned out differently," Clara said.

Morgan shrugged. "Be that as it may, he was no match for Nicolas. During the battle, Nicholas gave Alexander ample opportunities to concede. In the end, his death was merciful and swift—the type of death Alexander had denied so many before him."

Daniel continued. "His daughter, Elise, and his heir apparent, was there at the time of her father's death. She was as brutal and nefarious as he was, and swore she would avenge him. Elise left vowing to remove all impure Werewolves from the face of the earth."

"I heard on their way back to their pack lands, she deliberately revealed herself to Humans just so that she could kill them," Clara said.

She what?

Parker swung her head around to face Clara, her eyes wide with shock. "How could anyone be so cruel and vindictive?"

Clara threw her a weak smile, but her eyes were full of pain. "There are stories about that pack that would stop you from ever sleeping again."

They sat in silence, and Parker stared at her hands. How could she process that level of pure evil?

Clara sighed. "Around the time of Alexander's death, plans were already in place to migrate to the new world. We thought nothing of it, knowing we were leaving them behind." She looked pensive as she glanced at Morgan. "You know, when the packs hear the Sandulf's are in the country, there will be panic."

Her stomach dropped. "I'm sorry. What name did you say?"

Clara's forehead crinkled at her sudden outburst. "Sandulf. Simon's father's old pack is Unum Sandulf. It translates to One Pure Wolf."

She recalled the terabytes of information she had poured through over the past few days. Names and notes she'd scribbled down flashed through her head, and she remembered the odd pieces that had not seemed to fit in with the rest.

"Jesus, Mary, and Joseph!" She jumped up from the table. "Wait here, I'll be right back."

EIGHTEEN

Ever Danced With The Devil by The Pale Moonlight?

Hotel Sofitel, Montreal, Canada

Parked glanced around the hotel bar, readjusted the tablet on the small table, and leaned into the comfortable leather chair. She casually leafed through the thick document she held, and frowned, grabbed a pen off the table, and made a mark on one of the pages.

"Hey, boss, you do know you're only supposed to *pretend* to work?"

She peeked over the rim of her glasses. "Zeke. Did you get this report from a first grader? The spelling is diabolical."

Laughter echoed through her earbuds, then what she could have sworn was Zeke muttering about grammar police.

"The documents and reports are from one of the keynote speakers at an Agricultural and Fisheries Symposium in Florida, boss."

Parker crossed her legs and jiggled her foot as she continued to leaf through the document. "How's the feed? Is it clear?"

To the casual observer, she looked as though she were talking on her phone, or listening to music and working on her tablet. If anyone had walked by, they would have noticed the screen was filled with graphs and charts.

She was actually kitted out with the latest surveillance equipment, and in two-way communication with the rest of the team at their base of operations in a suite at another hotel a short distance away. Both audio and video were transmitted directly to the team monitoring the goings on in the bar.

"We had a bit of interference, but it seems to have cleared up. We've control of both front and rear cameras."

"What about the hotel's video feeds?"

"Not having much luck at the moment."

"And how is the audio?"

"You're coming through loud and clear."

Out of the corner of her eye, Parker spied a waitress heading in her direction.

"*Bonsoir, bienvenue au le Bar. Voudriez-vous commander quelque chose?*"

She looked up at the young woman and smiled apologetically. "*Peut-on parler en anglais, s'il vous plaît, mon français est terrible.*"

The woman smiled and nodded. "Certainly, madam, welcome to Le Bar. Can I get you something to drink?"

She ordered the cocktail of the day, and resumed assessing the other patrons in the room. A few minutes later, she heard a commotion through her earpiece. Daniel had put all his men in place and returned to the hotel suite. His voice, curt and business-like, came through her earbuds. "Any sign of him?"

Parker glanced around the room. "No, but it's early yet."

"I still don't like this," he said. "At the first sign of trouble, I want you out of there. Are we clear?"

Rather than answer him, she rolled her eyes. They were receiving a video feed from both front and rear cameras, so he would have seen her. She held back a smile as she imagined him glowering at the monitor.

It wasn't the first time they'd had this conversation.

When Clara mentioned the name Sandulf, Parker's mind rocketed straight to the account they had tracked the money to. The one that had them chasing ghosts in order to discover who ultimately owned the account, and who was responsible for the carnage.

The shell company that owned the account was Sandulf GmbH. They needed to get back into that account and find anything that could lead them to Elise.

She had grabbed her laptop and quickly returned to the alphas, who were impatient to understand what had gotten her so excited. She explained what she had discovered, and the room went silent. Her evidence confirmed that Elise was behind the manufacturing and distribution of the drug. They just needed to prove the direct link to her and see if the trail would lead them to her.

Now that she had a few more details to go on, she set up her gear at the dining table and began a search of the data they had collected.

Daniel floated close behind her. "You know, hovering behind me won't make it go any faster."

He grunted and muttered something unintelligible as he straightened up and cleared the dishes away to give her more workspace.

Parker caught the look shared between Morgan and Clara. She squirmed in her chair, worried they may have picked up on what had happened at the lake.

Without saying anything, Morgan rose from the table and followed Daniel into the kitchen, leaving the two women alone.

"Bring Parker something to eat," Clara said, "and make sure there are a lot of calories in it."

Parker groaned. She loved the older woman to bits, but her concern for her nutritional intake was exhausting.

Clara got straight to the point once Morgan had left the room. "How are they treating you here? You've been vague over the phone."

She squirmed in her chair and kept her eyes focused on her monitor, sure that Clara would see through her if she looked up. "Everyone has been welcoming, and I've even made new friends."

"And how are you getting on with Daniel?"

Her nerves, already wound tight, were now at fever pitch. Surely Clara couldn't scent Daniel on her. She'd showered. Twice. Did she give something away in her actions? Was it something she'd said? She'd been careful to remain as normal as possible. A bead of sweat broke out just above her eyebrow, but she forced a neutral smile and looked up at Clara. "Fine. Why?"

Clara picked at a nonexistent piece of lint and avoided eye contact. "Nothing dear, no reason."

She let out the breath she'd been holding and refocused on the monitor. *Thank God, she's not going to push the subject.*

Daniel and Morgan returned, but remained quiet as she worked. Morgan settled into an overstuffed armchair and scanned through one of the newspapers that had been left on a side table. Clara, after disappearing for a few minutes, returned and buried her nose in a book, every once in awhile encouraging her to eat something.

As expected, her search revealed no instant results.

"This could take a while," she said. "I suggest you all get some sleep. I'll wake you if I get anywhere."

Daniel dismissed her suggestion. "I'm staying, I've nowhere else to be."

He looked toward Clara and Morgan questioningly.

Morgan looked up from the newspaper he was reading. "I'm good. What about you, my love?"

"Shhh," Clara snapped. "It's getting to the good bit."

Parker, who hadn't paid much attention to what the others were up to, looked over to the book Clara held in her hands and balked. "Jesus Christ, Clara, you aren't reading that, are you?"

Clara glanced up and blinked innocently. "What? I picked it up at the airport. I just wanted to see what the fuss was all about."

"And?"

Clara turned the book to the back cover and scanned the contents. "I don't suppose you have a copy of the sequels, Darker, and Freed, do you?"

She rolled her eyes and returned to her computer.

Parker stumbled onto the final clue a few hours later. "Yes! I knew I had seen the names somewhere."

Three sets of eyes turned to her.

A wide grin spread across her face. "I remembered one of the accounts we traced had credit cards attached."

She peered at the screen as a measure of triumph lifted her spirits. "The name on one of the cards is Matheo Bernard. Different last name, but same first."

Clara and Morgan looked at each other.

"And..." She quickly accessed the transaction details for the account. "Mr. Bernard's card has been used recently." She opened another terminal window and followed the merchant code. "According to this, he is in Montreal... at the Sofitel."

Daniel frowned. "What about Elise? Any information on her?"

She shook her head. "Nothing at this stage, but that doesn't mean it's not there. I just haven't found anything—yet."

Daniel strode over to the large window and stared into the darkness. "Matheo is just a pawn. Taking him down won't get us any closer to where the rest of the pack is. He would die before he gave them up. We need to find Elise."

Morgan let out a deep sigh. "I'm afraid he's right."

From Clara's pensive expression, she echoed Morgan's assessment.

"We'll need to find him and put a surveillance team on him. He'll eventually lead us back to her." Daniel paused and turned to Morgan. "I'll need your best trackers to supplement mine."

Morgan reached for his phone. "They're yours."

Daniel continued with his hastily devised plan. "I have vehicles and weapons stored in Vermont. We can fly there and drive across the border."

Parker frowned and shook her head. How these normally intelligent men had missed a key factor in all this was beyond her. "You know it's not going to work, don't you?"

All three alphas halted their conversation and looked blankly at her.

"Matheo is staying at a five-star hotel in the middle of a large city. Don't you think a bunch of burly men running around is going to be noticed?" She paused and crossed her arms over her chest. "Let's face it, your teams won't blend in with their surroundings. In a building full of Humans, I think he might notice if it's all of a sudden overrun with Werewolves."

Daniel and Morgan glanced at each other.

Morgan sighed. "She's right. He'll detect our scent a mile away."

"I have a better idea," she said. "I can go in. He's not going to take any notice of an additional Human and—"

"No, absolutely not!" Daniel cut in before she could finish. "He is ruthless. I won't run the risk of him learning of your existence."

She flew out of her chair. "You can't dictate what I can and can't do, Daniel Locke. This is the best option for getting in there, confirming it's him, and getting your team to track him once he leaves. And you damn well know it."

Daniel rose to his full height. "I've already said no. He won't hesitate to kill you if he finds out you know about us. It's a risk I am not willing to take."

His eyes locked with hers, his expression icy and determined against her defiance.

The room grew uncomfortably silent.

Morgan broke the standoff with a sigh. "You know she's right, Daniel. None of us will get close, and we don't have anyone else. We need someone on the inside to tell us if he's there." He placed a firm hand on Daniel's shoulder. "We can't lose this opportunity."

From the silent way in which Daniel and Morgan continued to look at each other, they'd continued their conversation telepathically.

"Fine," Daniel said, "but we are taking every security measure." He looked at Parker. "And you are to listen and carry out my every command. Are. We. Clear?" He did not blink once, as his eyes pierced hers.

Daniel broke into her thoughts, bringing Parker back to the present. "I said, are we clear?"

"Don't get your pants in a knot," she said. "Nothing is going to happen to me. This is a busy hotel, and you have a team outside if anything goes wrong."

By the time she was on her second Atomic Champagne cocktail, two hours later, the room was noisy. She, along with Zeke, Jay, Daniel, and Simon—on video, regularly scanned the crowd for any signs of their target.

"Parker, move the camera to the right." Daniel's tone was urgent, and her pulse quickened. Careful not to attract too much attention, she reached down and nudged the tablet to the right. She leaned over and pretended to read something on the screen.

Her brows furrowed. No one stood out as she again scanned the crowd around the bar. "What do you see?"

The bar area was full, all the chairs were occupied, and people were milling around, talking and laughing. Happy hour was almost over, and the patrons vied for the bartender's attention. Servers were busy collecting orders for customers at the small tables scattered around the room. It was chaos.

Parker spotted their target at the same moment she heard Daniel's sharp intake of breath. She froze. "He's here."

She forgot to breathe. It was one thing to watch the vile man through the safety of a computer monitor with miles between them, it was quite another to be in the same room.

Matheo was casually leaning against the bar, openly surveying all the women near him. He reminded her of a predator, his expression turning salacious and lecherous as he raked his gaze up and down their bodies. She felt contaminated just watching him from her safe vantage point across the room.

Gail had been correct. He was an attractive man, used to second looks. There was not an ounce of fat on him, and his body filled out the dark Armani suit in all the right places. His thick, wavy hair was slicked back with copious hair product. When the light caught on a gold chain around his neck she was reminded of her initial impression of his sleazy nature. The top three buttons of his expensive shirt were undone, and an oversized gold necklace was visible, the bottom of the chain resting on a thick mat of dark chest hair.

Jesus, he looks like he stepped out of a Mafia movie.

159

Between his perusals of the women around the bar, he checked his watch and glanced at the door.

"Guys," she said into her earpiece. "I think he's waiting for someone. I'm going to move closer."

"Don't you dare." Daniel's voice was loud and clear through her earpiece. "The plan was for you to confirm he was there and let us know when he leaves. That's it. Change any part of the plan and I'll come in and get you myself."

"No. I need to stay. He might be waiting for Elise."

"Then stay where you are." He was practically shouting at her.

She shrunk lower in her seat. "Keep your voice down. I don't have a goddamn death wish. Humans won't hear you, but he might."

Her earpiece went quiet for a moment. She jumped when the sound of wood splintering erupted through her receiver. She cringed as Daniel's voice boomed into her ear as though he were now in the room, directly beside her. She guessed that he had taken her off loudspeaker, and they were the only ones now privy to the conversation.

"We agreed that you would follow my orders." His voice was icy, low, and with a hint of danger. "All of them."

She tried to reason with him. "I am not a child, and you know we may not get this chance again."

"Parker, I need you to understand the danger you are in. If he figures out you know who, and what, he is—" He paused and drew in a shaky breath. "He won't be merciful."

Parker sneaked another glance at Matheo, who was still leaning against the bar. She scrutinized him and weighed her options. When she made her choice, she let out a breath. "I trust you, and I have faith you've put in place enough measures to get me out of here at a moment's notice if need be."

Daniel swore under his breath and exhaled. "Are you ever going to listen to a word I say?"

She grinned. "Now, where would be the fun in that?"

"This isn't a game." Daniel's voice bellowed. "You are in very real danger with that lunatic."

Parker nearly jumped out of her skin at his angry outburst, and her eyes darted around the bar to make sure no one else heard. "Jesus, are you trying to paint a target on me? I'm here to observe and stay in the background. Nothing more."

A typical male grunt was the only reply she received. She returned to her paperwork but kept an eye on the bar. *This could take a while.*

Her heart leaped when a woman approached Matheo. "Blond, in a body-hugging white dress, with a red Prada Ostrich tote bag," she whispered. "Is that her? Is that Elise?"

There was a pause as she watched Matheo and the woman shake hands, then move to one of the tables located between her and the entrance to the bar. Her shoulders tensed as she watched the interaction. From the way he greeted the woman, she was almost sure this wasn't his alpha. "Is it?"

Her shoulders slumped when Daniel said, "No."

Not wanting to risk looking out of place in a bar without ordering regularly, she emptied her drink into the plant beside her chair, ordered another Atomic Champagne cocktail, and settled back for the duration.

"Do we know who she is?" Parker said. "Is she Human or Were?"

The lack of reply spoke volumes.

After what seemed like an eternity, Matheo and his guest exited the bar and headed toward the main entrance to the hotel. She breathed a sigh of relief and swallowed her anxiety. Something about the man made her skin crawl. "They're leaving through the main door. Be ready."

Daniel barked out orders for his teams to follow both targets from a distance.

Parker tossed her papers and tablet into her briefcase. *Thank God, we're one step closer to tracking down Elise's whereabouts.*

She left money on the table and headed out the entrance. "I'm on my way back."

Distracted, she ran into a large and rigid object and stumbled backward, dropping her bag. She bent down and retrieved the contents strewn across the plush hotel carpet.

"I'm so sorry," she said without looking up, "I wasn't watching where I was going."

It only took a moment for her to throw everything into her bag and rise to her feet, an apologetic smile on her face.

"I hope I didn't hurt—" Her smile froze as she came face-to-face with Matheo Dumas. "—you," she managed to force out. *Shit, shit, shit, shit.*

Matheo smirked as he swept a hungry gaze up and down the length of her body. "Not at all, but you could make up for it by having a drink with me."

His voice was smooth and deliberately honeyed with a distinct European accent.

Her chest tightened, and she found it hard to breathe. *Jesus, Mary, and Joseph. What the hell am I going to do?*

She forced down her escalating panic, composed a neutral face, and hoped her voice wouldn't fail her. "I would love to, but I have a conference call in ten minutes that I can't miss."

Parker made a motion to step around him. Matheo anticipated the move and grabbed her firmly by her elbow. "Why don't you give it a miss, Bella? I'm sure our conversation will be beneficial to both of us."

He did not just call me Bella, did he?

Her pulse raced, and she tightened her grip on her bag to stop shaking. "Unfortunately, it's with my boss, so I don't have a choice." She gave him what she hoped was a smile, though she couldn't be sure. She prayed that Daniel or one of the boys would not start speaking through her earpiece. Matheo would hear it as clear as day. "Next time, maybe?"

Matheo stared at her in a cold, calculating manner. She made the mistake of looking directly at him. She hadn't seen eyes so devoid of compassion, so filled with pure evil, since the night Bobby was attacked. It chilled her to her core and brought up emotions she had long kept suppressed. She needed to tread carefully. Very, very carefully.

He took a step closer and looked down her cleavage. Even with her heels, he was a good foot taller than her. "So, Bella, how long are you in Montreal?"

"Until the end of the week."

"Well, how about you make it up to me tomorrow night?" He pushed for her answer as he ran his hand up and down her arm.

Her stomach churned.

"Sounds like a plan. How about I meet you here at eight?" She tried to appear eager. "And we can grab a bite to eat afterward."

That seemed to appease him. He grabbed her hand and brought the back of it to his lips in an overtly sensual manner.

"Till then." He released her hand, but not before raking his gaze up and down her body.

She shivered with repulsion. Matheo's expression left her in no doubt what was running through his depraved mind. A smile was all she could muster before she fled the room. It took effort not to run, but even if she wanted to, her legs were like jello, and she'd probably trip over her own feet.

She wasn't safe yet. He might be watching her every move, so she went directly to the lift lobby, and pressed the up button. After what seemed an eternity, the doors swished open and she rushed in and pressed the button for the third floor, where, if anyone were to check, she was registered. Unable to stand, she held onto the railing and her shaking body broke out in a sweat.

Her mind had kicked into survival mode. She was afraid Matheo might decide he couldn't wait for the following evening and follow her up to her room. There no protection for her in the building—Daniel and Morgan's trackers were all posted at the exits, far enough away that their scent wouldn't carry to Matheo.

As soon as the lift opened on the third floor, she headed to the stairwell. She looked up and down the corridor to ensure it was deserted and took a deep breath to release the one she had held since bumping into Matheo. Before her legs gave way, she leaned against the door to the stairwell and struggled to get her emotions in check "I'm on the third floor, about to head down to the basement."

She nearly lost her hearing when loud, panicked voices broke loose in her earpiece. She was unable to distinguish one voice from the other.

A moment later, the door behind her was yanked open, and she unceremoniously fell backward into the stairwell. Her body was caught before she hit the concrete floor, and a hand reached around and covered her mouth before she could scream out. She struggled to break free, immobilized against a solid body with inhuman strength.

Oh God, he followed me.

She gagged, then her fight instinct kicked in. She lifted her foot up and brought her stiletto heel down as hard as she could. It made contact with its target, and she grinned.

"Ow, Parks. That was uncalled for."

Relief spread through her, and her body relaxed. It was Bobby.

"I have her. We are heading back now." Bobby ended the call and grunted as he removed his hand from her mouth, straightened her up, and looked down at his sore foot. "These are my best Chuck Taylors, and you put a hole in them."

She took a deep breath to calm her nerves. "I should have put a hole in your foot, too, for scaring me like that."

Bobby opened his mouth to speak, but instead let out a series of coughs.

She looked closer at him. "Are you okay?"

He nodded and waved his hand dismissively. "Just a scratchy throat, that's all." He headed down the stairs toward the parking garage. "I'd better get you back to Alpha Locke, something tells me you're in trouble. Big time."

She pursed her lips and followed him. Her heart was still racing from the scare.

Bobby grinned. "What the hell is that smell?"

When she poked him in the back, Bobby broke out in another fit of coughing, mixed with laughter. "And you need a shower. That perfume is overdone, if you ask me. It's getting right up my nose."

NINETEEN

Oh, What A Tangled Web We Weave

Daniel glared at Parker as she entered the suite with Bobby. He opened his mouth to give her another piece of his mind but then snapped it shut. He wasn't going to have an argument with her in front of everyone.

He grimaced and held his temper in check. Getting through this without completely destroying the hotel room would be a miracle. The moment he realized she was with Matheo, he'd broken out in a cold sweat. Did she have no sense of self-preservation? It had taken Simon, Zeke, and Jay to stop him from storming out to save Parker from that genocidal maniac.

"She's on the move again," Zeke said.

He refocused, and watched the monitor as the blond who had met with Matheo flagged down a taxi. The team pursuing her piled into a dark suburban van and followed from a safe distance.

Daniel leaned forward to get a closer look. "Don't lose her," he said into the open phone line to his team on the ground.

He glanced back at Bobby, who was hovering in the background, a nervous twitch in his eye. From the light sheen of perspiration on Bobby's forehead, Daniel figured he'd better put Parker's cousin out of his misery. "Kyle and the team are waiting for you downstairs. Report back to him now."

Bobby threw Parker an encouraging smile and bolted out the door.

He turned back to the monitors and opened a telepathic connection to Kyle. *He's on his way down. Remember, Vic and her team are on point. You are their back up and are to remain well out of their way. We need Matheo to lead us to Elise, and that won't happen if he knows we're on to him.*

"I should be down there," Simon said. "One Direction doesn't have the experience I do."

Daniel severed the link with Kyle and turned to Simon. "We've been over this." The situation did not sit well with his beta, but they had no choice. Simon was his father's son in not only personality, but looks. Where Matheo was olive skinned with dark hair, David and Simon were blond with fair skin. Matheo would recognize his nephew in an instant.

Daniel, sensing Simon was about to argue, said, "Am I clear?"

Simon remained quiet, but continued to pace the floor.

Feeling the absence of Parker from beside him, he tore his eyes away from the screen and sought her out. Parker had kicked off her shoes and was now sitting on the couch, her laptop open, and a familiar expression on her face. She was on a mission to find information.

He was beyond infuriated that she had put herself at risk, coming face to face with the lowlife. The relief that had washed over him when he heard she was safe had been replaced by white-hot anger. He should never have agreed to putting her in danger. The council had made her his responsibility, and he wasn't about to fail them now.

Satisfied she was safe—for now—his focus returned to the feed coming from Vic's team. He watched Matheo exit a car that had pulled up at the corner of Boulevard Saint-Laurent and Rue Prince Arthur.

"Stay back. Don't get too close," Daniel said.

"Roger that."

Daniel, Simon, and Parker's omegas were glued to the screen when Matheo walked up to one of the well-lit establishments along the road. A long line of people stood on the sidewalk. Much to the crowd's disgust, the over-sized security staff granted Matheo immediate entry. He disappeared into the club.

Daniel was about to bark out a command to Vic when he heard an unladylike snort from the couch.

Parker looked up to four sets of eyes staring at her. She shrugged and pointed at her screen. "According to Trip Advisor this is the bar to pick up women." She then pointed to Matheo's live feed. "It figures that he would know that."

Daniel snorted. Even he found it hard to keep a straight face at her observation.

Now that they knew Matheo's whereabouts for the time being, their attention returned to the mystery woman. The team following the woman in white was discreetly hidden from view, and trailing at least two cars behind her cab, which had now turned into one of the affluent streets in the Westmount district. The cab slowed and pulled into the driveway of a magnificent turn-of-the-century manor.

Large gates prevented the taxi from advancing any farther up the driveway. The woman left the vehicle and proceeded through the gates, which magically opened for her.

"Quick Samuel, what's the address?" Parker said.

Samuel supplied Parker with the information, and she quickly tapped away at her laptop. "Brenda Hollingsworth, twenty-seven. Heir to the Hollingsworth Empire. She works for Daddy, and has had a very active social presence since she was a teen." She looked up at Daniel. "Well, that answers that question. She is most definitely Human."

He frowned. "What do Elise and Matheo want with the Hollingsworths?"

Parker turned back to her laptop. "That's what I am about to find out."

A few hours later, Matheo exited the club. He headed down the street, his watchers staying well back and out of sight.

He sneered when he spotted a lone woman heading in the opposite direction, and Daniel's heart filled with dread. They needed to tread carefully. If they made their presence known, the woman would be safe, but he would be on to them. If they remained quiet, and Matheo took after her, an innocent woman would be scarred for life. Whichever choice he made, he was damned.

"Only show your hand if her life is in danger."

His attention flicked back to the sleeping woman on the couch. Despite her obvious exhaustion, she had insisted on staying up with him, even after he had dismissed Simon, Jay, and Zeke. Fatigue had finally won out, and she fell asleep, though it was a sleep filled with demons and torment. More than once she had cried out, her murmurings too jumbled for even his sensitive ears to pick up.

Daniel sat down on the couch beside her and carefully placed a pillow under her head. He watched his team as they trailed their prey, and absently stroked Parker's hair. She became more restful, and her expression softened with each touch.

Not for the first time, he wished things could be different.

TWENTY

Mother Told Me There Would Be Days Like This

"What do you mean, you've lost him?"

The sound of Daniel's voice shook Parker from her sleep. She raised her head and looked around the room to find him. Sunlight streamed through the window. She checked her watch—it was just after eight a.m.

Daniel was on the phone, deep in conversation, all the while eyeing up a vase on the cabinet.

She pointed at the broken chair and table. "Don't you think you've destroyed enough of the hotel room already?"

"I want you all back here on the double." He pressed the end call button and pocketed his phone. "Sorry, I didn't mean to wake you."

She swung her legs off the couch and stretched. "What did I miss?"

"They lost him on the outskirts of the city."

Parker froze. "What happened?"

"That's what I want to know." He rubbed a hand over his dark stubble. "The teams are heading back here now. Simon's waiting for them downstairs."

She had showered, changed, and was eating her breakfast by the time the team shuffled into the suite.

"Where are the others?" Daniel said.

Simon grabbed two apples from the fruit bowl. "I sent them for a run and told them to get some rest." He threw one of the apples at Kyle. "Here Jonas Brothers, catch."

When Daniel threw an angry glare at his beta, Simon quickly dropped his shoulders and skulked to the other side of the room. The others looked decidedly sheepish and kept their eyes downcast.

Daniel crossed his arms over his chest and glared at his team. "What happened?"

Parker threw them a wan smile in support. Daniel's tone was enough to make anyone flinch.

Vic thrust her hands into her pocket. "We can only track effectively when there is a scent. Without it, we are as blind and useless as Humans." She looked over to Parker. "No disrespect intended."

Parker shrugged. "None taken." Like their wild wolf cousins, Werewolves' sense of smell was far superior to Humans.

Simon reached for one of the maps on the table and pointed to a section of the map. "The team was hidden far enough away and downwind."

Vic pointed to a central area. "Once he left the club, we were expecting him to head back to the hotel." She traced the path. "But halfway back, he went into a parking garage where he got into a vehicle and headed away from the city. He must have suspected that someone was trailing him, because he led us on a merry dance throughout the city before we lost him."

Daniel studied the map. "He's naturally suspicious. If he thought he was being tailed, you would've lost him much earlier."

Parker wandered over to the computers that had recorded the footage of Matheo from the night before. Curious about what happened after she fell asleep, she replayed the videos.

While she scanned through the footage, Daniel strategized over the different routes that were possible, and broke the map locations into zones, allocating them to the teams. He was also placing someone near the hotel in case Matheo returned.

The pack, engrossed in their conversation and planning, did not notice her sudden flurry of activity. She had fast-forwarded through most of the recording, only to pause at the point where Matheo exited the nightclub. A chill washed over her as she watched a malicious smile cross his features.

She shuddered. *What must his alpha be like? How could something be worse than this?*

On the one-hundredth rewinding and scrutinizing of the scene, her eyes were drawn to a small part of the screen. A rush of excitement shot through her body. To make sure she wasn't seeing things, she rewound once again and replayed the section.

How did I miss it?

She felt like doing one of Jay and Zeke's victory dances. Instead, she projected the image onto the sixty-five-inch flat screen.

"The answer is in front of us," Parker said. She moved closer to the screen.

The others stopped speaking, and she pointed at a small device held against Matheo's ear.

"We can track him through his phone." Her mind sifted through what was required. "We need to Bluejack it, and remotely install an app that will provide us with real-time location tracking." She glanced at the paused image of Matheo. "Once I have his data, I'll be able to get into his carrier's database, and find out where he's been, and who he's been talking to."

Although she was jittery with excitement, she hadn't once looked at Daniel. He was already pissed with her. This was about to push him over the edge.

"And just how will you get this onto his phone without him knowing?" Daniel said.

His booming voice made her wince. Daniel's ever-active mind had caught the bit she had avoided telling them. Still not meeting his gaze, she continued addressing the team. "Once I'm within two feet of his phone, Zeke can piggyback off mine to access his Bluetooth. We can get the information we need to download the software and automatically activate it."

The room became quiet. The other members of the team were unsure of how Daniel would react to her plan, considering the events from the previous night.

Daniel crossed his arms over his chest. "And for argument's sake, let's say I allow you to come within one hundred feet of him. Just where will this meeting occur?"

His outwardly calm demeanor unnerved her. "Tonight. Eight p.m. at the hotel bar."

He dropped his arms. His hands clenched in fists, and he stood to his full height. "You must be out of your mind if you think I'd allow you to be in the same room as that killer."

She flinched, and her eyes sought the support of the team, but the cowards were looking everywhere except at her and Daniel.

She resisted the sudden urge to flee, squared her shoulders, and raised her chin. "Daniel, be reasonable. It's the only option. According to the hotel reservations, he's checking out tomorrow. We're running out of time before he goes off our radar again."

"I said no." Daniel crossed his arms over his chest. "And that's my final word on it. I have a responsibility to keep you safe, and you aren't going anywhere near him. Am I clear?"

Her eyes blazed and her lips tightened. "Crystal clear. Tell me, Mr. High-and-Mighty Alpha, do you discriminate against all women, or is it just me?" She slapped Bobby's hand when he tried to pull her away. "Or, do you consider me such a weak Human that I can't possibly do anything to help?"

"P-Parks, I don't think t-that's what he meant." Bobby said.

She cursed at her cousin. "Oh, for God's sake, get a grip. We'll be in a public place with dozens of people in the room. He's not going to try anything."

She turned her attention back to Daniel. "Besides, you can't tell me what I can and can't do. I'm doing this, and that's final."

A deathly silence filled the room.

"Everyone out. Now!"

Simon, Bobby, Zeke, Jay and the rest jumped at the sudden bellow. Not having to be told twice, they bolted for the door and made a quick exit.

Parker narrowed her eyes and pressed her lips together. She was more than irritated at the dismissal. She threw Daniel an angry glare and took a step to follow them.

Daniel growled. "Not you."

She stood her ground. When the door closed, they stood scowling at each other. Her muscles quivered with the strain of being held so tight.

Daniel moved to the window and stared at the street below. "Do you have a death wish?" His voice was exasperated and agitated at the same time. He turned back to face her. "Not only did you not listen to a word I said last night, but you blatantly put yourself in danger. And now you want to do it again? I thought we agreed that it was a one-time deal."

She snapped. "We agreed? You and that damn Alliance seem to think you can dictate my life. Well, let me tell you, buddy, you've got another thing coming if you think I'll stand for it."

Daniel let out a low growl, and his lips parted in a sneer. He paced the room like a caged tiger. "I have a good mind to put you back on a plane to Portland and be done with you."

***

He was torn between two disparate emotions. The tactical commander in him agreed, applauded even, the plan she had outlined. It would allow them unfettered access to Matheo's whereabouts. His team would not be at risk of showing their hand before they were ready.

It would solve all our problems. So, what's the issue?

He closed his eyes and struggled with the battle raging inside him. The Alpha Commander in him had already begun planning the operation, but the man in him wanted to keep as much distance between Matheo and Parker as possible. He had a responsibility to keep her out of harm's way. As much as she frustrated him, she was now firmly entrenched in his life.

His overriding need to protect the packs, and his sense of duty to put an end to Matheo and Elise, finally won over his personal need. He took a deep breath, then let out a long, low sigh. "Okay, we will do it your way. But we are going over every possible detail. I want to make sure we have everything covered, and if you deviate from the plan even once, I'm putting an end to it. You will be on the first plane out of here. Am I—"

"Clear. Yes. Yadda-yadda, I know the drill."

Her face softened. "You may not have faith in me, but I have complete faith in you. I trust you with my life, and I know you will do everything in your power to keep me safe." She added with a grin, "Even if I am only Human."

He rubbed his forehead and sighed. "Okay, what do we need to get him?"

Daniel and Parker compiled a list of items she would need before he called his team in. Once he was comfortable they had covered every aspect of the plan, he dismissed them with a command to rest before the mission.

Simon stayed behind, casually sitting back on one of the couches with his feet up. Daniel noticed that his friend had been particularly quiet throughout the afternoon. He knew something was on Simon's mind, and he did not need to wait long to find out.

"Where's Parker?" Simon said.

Daniel continued to check his lists. "She wanted to get freshened up and find the software she needs for this evening. Bobby and Kyle are with her. Why?"

"Mmmm," Simon said. "You know that Alphas Morgan and Clara consider her part of their pack?"

Daniel ignored the question.

"And you know Bobby's her cousin, right?"

He stilled.

Simon rose from the chair and rubbed the back of his neck. "And you are aware that she has become part of our family, aren't you? The kids adore her, and she's made friends with at least half the pack that live in the valley. Not to mention she's risking her life to help us..."

Daniel's pulse began to race. He did not like the direction of the conversation. It was cutting too close to the truth. "Get to the point."

Simon, not deterred at his mood, shoved his hands into his pockets and glanced down at the carpet. "I see the way you look at her. You will only end up hurting her if you take this any further."

"Don't you think I damn well know that?"

"It wouldn't be so bad if she was any other Human, but she's not. She's Parker." Simon lifted his head and looked straight at Daniel. "While you've ignored her importance to the Alliance, the rest of us haven't. You've been charged with keeping her safe. Nothing more."

His chest tightened, and he broke eye contact, not wishing for Simon to detect his inner turmoil. "If I wanted your opinion, I'd have asked for it." He was finished with this conversation. "I'm pretty sure I gave you a job to do."

Simon left, and Daniel remained deep in thought. Simon was right about one thing—Parker was out of bounds. His feelings were irrelevant. His heart ached as he returned to the matter at hand. To his job. To the protection and safety of those he had dedicated his life to serve.

TWENTY-ONE

Into the Lion's Den

Hotel Sofitel, Montreal, Canada 7:55 P.M.

Parker arrived at the hotel bar just before eight that evening. She ordered a vodka and orange to calm her nerves. Careful to look as though she belonged there, she took a stool at the bar and looked around the room. As per the previous evening, it was full of hotel patrons and local business people congregating after work.

She was mentally exhausted after Daniel's insistence on repeating every aspect of the plan more times than she cared to remember. She had started out confident that her idea would work, but Daniel had bombarded her with every possible scenario to the point where she was filled with self-doubt. Could she pull this off after all?

A young couple was sitting in a secluded part of the bar, locked in a lover's embrace. Her thoughts drifted to Daniel, and their kiss at the lake. She should have been angry at herself—or him. But, no, they were both adults. She knew what he was, who he was. She knew it was impossible for anything to develop between them.

The fact that I've managed to get myself emotionally involved is irrelevant. We are friends and associates. He just happens to be a talented kisser. Very talented.

She was shocked out of her internal debate when an arm snaked around her middle.

Matheo took a seat beside her at the bar, dressed in similar attire as the previous evening. "Bella, I was hoping you would be here."

Despite her churning stomach, she plastered a false smile on her face. "I wasn't sure if you would turn up."

He leaned in, took her hand, and brought it to his lips. "What sort of man would I be if I let down a beautiful woman?"

Her pulse raced, and a wave of claustrophobia washed over her. *God, give me strength.*

"What a gentleman." She extracted her hand from his and resisted the urge to run for the nearest exit. "I don't think we were formally introduced last night."

Matheo raked his eyes up and down her body. "Sadly, Bella, you left before we had a chance to become properly acquainted."

The word properly rolled off his tongue, and his accent enhanced his meaning. She shuddered.

Matheo smirked. "Matheo Bernard, at your service."

She grimaced as he leaned in closer. Heat radiated off his naturally warmer body. The closer he moved, the more her stomach churned, and her inner self rebelled. She concentrated on forcing her erratic pulse and panic under control. The bartender chose that moment to bring her order. Before Matheo could take her hand in his again, she grabbed the drink and put a little distance between them.

"Patricia Smith." She raised her glass to him. "Pleased to meet you." She took a sip before her mouth uttered any of the unflattering words ready to spill out. "So where does your accent come from? It's so sexy."

Even though her gag reflexes were working overtime, a measure of satisfaction rushed through her. She had actually made it sound like she was interested in him.

He reached for his glass, and she was relieved when he tore his gaze away from her and focused on the Southern Comfort. "I was born in Italy, but I have been living in France for quite some time now. And you, Bella?"

She crossed and uncrossed her legs. She was sure she had broken out in a cold sweat. Daniel had her studying a map all afternoon so, if need be, she could answer basic geography questions. "Chicago in the good old U.S. of A. What brings you to Canada?"

Matheo shrugged. "Business." He placed his glass on the bar and leaned closer to her. "But I do not wish to talk business. I wish to get to know you much better, Bella."

Matheo suggestively ran a hand up and down her arm, and she had to fight the urge to lash out at him. Her eyes darted to the large window that overlooked the street. *What the hell is taking them so long?* They couldn't risk her having two-way communication, so the team was relying on the microphone in her cell phone to relay their voices.

As usual, Daniel had teams positioned far enough away to not be detected, but close enough to see inside the building. This time, instead of remaining behind, Daniel had taken up command of his troops, and he was now sitting in a restaurant across the street with a direct line of sight into the Sofitel's brightly lit bar.

Once Zeke and Jay had connected to Matheo's phone, they'd install the app that would run undetected in the background. The prearranged sign they had been successful was a white sticker on one of the glass windows. Daniel would then arrange her extraction.

She turned back to Matheo and continued to make small talk, successfully evading the overtures that seemed to be flying out of his mouth in quick succession. Her skin was crawling. She couldn't wait to get as far away from him as possible. The longer the conversation dragged on, the more her insides writhed.

They ordered another drink, and Parker's heart sank when she noticed a little red sticker on one of the window panes.

Shit, shit, shitty, shit-shit.

She tried not to appear panicked and pretended to listen to Matheo go on about his new Lamborghini. She wiped her clammy hands on her dress and pushed down her instinct to flee.

Bet you the scumbag ordered it in yellow. Shit, what am I going to do? His Bluetooth isn't activated.

Get a grip girl. Memories of Elise and Matheo's innocent victims pushed to the surface. She recalled the feeling of helplessness at witnessing Tony, the first to die in Hell House, and her resolve hardened. This was their best chance to catch the bastards and make them pay. She took a deep breath and focused her attention back on Matheo. She could do this—she *would* do this.

"I always wanted a handsome man to drive me around in a Lamborghini, I think they are so sexy. What color is it?"

Matheo's eyes lit up. "Yellow. I would love to take you out for a spin sometime, Bella."

She leaned toward him and placed a hand high on his thigh, and squeezed it slightly, even as her stomach revolted. "I would love that. Do you have a photo of it?"

Matheo's eyes involuntarily shifted to his phone, which rested on the bar not far from hers. She reached for his phone before he could protest.

"Oh, you do? I just have to see it." She swiped the screen and was presented with a password prompt. She scrunched her nose and looked up at him in what she hoped was a sexy pout. Her hand moved farther up his thigh. "Come on, just a little peek."

Matheo's pupils dilated and he licked his lips. His eyes were practically glittering with desire. He tapped in the four numbers and unlocked the screen. Once open, he accessed the camera roll and located the photos she wanted to see. He turned it around to show her, and she snatched the phone from his hands.

She slipped through the images. "Oh. My. God. That is beautiful. It really suits you. How about I take a photo of us?"

Matheo's eyebrows squished together. Parker got down from her stool and came around to stand beside him. She leaned inward so that their faces were touching. She pointed the phone's camera at them and took a couple of photos.

Sitting back on her stool, she pretended to review the photos and coo over them. "My friends are going to be so jealous when I show them these photos. I'm just going to send them to me. You don't mind, do you?" She disregarded any reply he might have had, and continued her mindless chatter. "And I'm going to put my number in your phone, so you have no excuse not to contact me if you are ever in Chicago."

Matheo was too stunned to notice that she had also activated the Bluetooth on his phone. As she handed him his phone, her own was receiving the message she had sent. Quickly opening the message, she showed him the photos now on her phone, further distracting him from looking at his.

For the next twenty minutes, Parker waited in complete and utter agony while Matheo felt up every part of her body. She could have kissed the hotel's concierge when he walked in looking for her.

"Miss Smith, there you are. Your cab to the airport is here. Can I help you with your luggage?"

"That would be lovely. Thanks."

She turned back to Matheo, whose look of confusion was almost comical. "My flight leaves shortly, and I do need to go. It was lovely catching up. If you are ever in Chicago, you have my number." She reached up and planted a chaste kiss on his cheek.

I wonder if it's possible to use disinfectant on lips?

Matheo quickly recovered from his shock. "But, Bella, I thought we were going to spend the evening together?"

She attempted to make a hasty getaway. "So did I, but my boss called me back, and I need to go." She shrugged. "You know how it is."

Matheo trailed behind her. "Bella, I am sure I can make it worth your while…"

She resisted the urge to roll her eyes at his effort to change her mind. "I have no doubt it would be an evening I would never forget."

Parker exited the main lobby doors to the street beyond, and was relieved to see a taxi driver leaning against his cab.

"You Smith? Going to the airport?"

She handed her bag to the driver and bade farewell to Matheo. They pulled away from the curb and her body finally relaxed. When the cab turned the corner, she let out her breath and leaned forward to address the driver. "There's been a change of plans, can you please take me to the Ritz-Carlton?"

She sank back into her seat and let out a deep sigh. A huge weight had lifted off her shoulders. She felt dirty and violated, but it was worth it. They were well on their way to tracking down the killers behind the drugs and removing all ability to purchase Wildfire online. To top it off, Matheo would now lead them to Elise.

A satisfied smile spread across her lips. *Watch out bitch. We are on our way.*

TWENTY-TWO

There's an App for That

Portland, Oregon

Parker's office phone rang just as she reached the door. Carefully balancing her coffee cup, she made a mad dash across the room for the phone.

"Parker Johnson."

"This is an automated announcement from your local council. We would like you to participate in a very important survey. Please hold the line while we transfer you to one of our live agents."

Seriously?

She slammed the phone down and collapsed in her chair.

It's going to be a long day, I can feel it.

In fact, the three weeks since she had returned to Portland had been the longest in her life. Daniel's team had hoped that once they successfully installed the tracking software on Matheo's phone, they could trail him at a safe distance until he led them to Elise and the source of Wildfire. But that was easier said than done. The team following him was clocking up frequent flyer points at an alarming rate with no indication Matheo was slowing down.

Her part of the job done, Daniel had arranged for her to be escorted to Nederland where the Alliance would be better served if she found out why Matheo had met with Hollingsworth. She was also keeping an eye on the Wildfire online sales.

The mature, rational adult in her had agreed. She had found and led them to Matheo and given them the best chance to follow him to wherever Elise was hiding out. More importantly, she wasn't as trained or as experienced as the other team members, nor did she have the physical strength and endurance. She would only hamper their progress.

The not so mature person in her was slightly miffed at being so easily ousted after they had come so far. In defiance, she had returned to Portland, rather than Nederland, where she now juggled catching up with her normal business affairs and working with Jay to analyze the data coming from Matheo's phone.

Daniel wasn't happy with her decision, but he had relented with caveats. She wasn't surprised when three Werewolves were sent to trail her 24/7.

Parker had been prepared for the uncomfortable phone conversation with Daniel when he discovered she had returned to Portland rather than Nederland. What she hadn't counted on was the distressed call from Alice, immediately followed by Jessica berating her for leaving without saying goodbye. She had spent an uncomfortable two hours trying to convince both of them she did not do it deliberately to upset them. Jessica had been so angry with her, she'd had to look up every second word on Google to work out what Jessica was saying.

She finished off her coffee and proceeded to look over the data from Matheo's movements the previous day.

Beth breezed into her office an hour later. "Girl, you need to get a life. Did you go home last night?"

Parker threw a sullen expression in her PA's direction and returned to what she was doing.

Beth huffed. "Don't look at me in that tone. You have been nothing but secretive and moody since you got back from that assignment. You're in need of a booty call, if I ever did see a need." Beth rested a hand on her hip as she continued. "Perhaps I'll get hold of that fine specimen of a man you are on the phone with every day, and see if he can get you out of your frump."

Parker growled. "Beth!"

"What?"

Parker sighed and rubbed her temples. "Nothing. Why did you come in here?"

Confusion clouded Beth's eyes as she searched for her original purpose. "Oh, yeah, Marc phoned in sick."

She organized another of her employees to cover for Marc, then sat back and considered Beth's comment. She had to admit, her mood wasn't the best lately. *But that's probably due to the excessive hours I've put in juggling my business and the data analysis on Matheo.*

Her phone rang. She looked at the caller display. *At least he's punctual.*

"So, let me guess," she said. "He had a meeting, went to a bar, picked up some unsuspecting woman, had another meeting, and then rinse and repeat?"

A chuckle, deep and warm, washed over her and her knees felt weak.

"If nothing, he is becoming predictable," Daniel said.

After the first week of trailing Matheo across borders and cities, Daniel and the others returned home, leaving only Vic, Adam, and Jeremy behind to continue the shadowing. Much to their disappointment, Matheo hadn't yet led them to Elise. Instead, he seemed to be on some kind of a mission. What, they had yet to work out.

Over the three weeks they had been tracking him, Matheo had visited four more cities in three countries. The pattern was the same with each new city. When he hit the ground, he would meet with a prominent local business person, and then meet with them a second time a few of days later. After the second meeting, he would head to another city.

She and Daniel had set up daily update calls to keep each other informed. He would brief her on the team's findings, and she would supply him with the information she had found on who Matheo was meeting with.

"Any closer to working out what he's up to?" Daniel said.

Her shoulders dropped, and she shook her head. "None, sorry. Zeke sent me the address of Matheo's new friend. It's the same deal as the others. Patterson is the chairman and majority shareholder of a privately-owned company. They have a lot of interests in a variety of industries."

"And there is no way to look for any paper trail?"

"No, unlike public companies, they can pretty much do what they want. They don't have the same reporting restrictions."

Daniel went quiet. "I'm getting an uneasy feeling about this. Elise is up to something. Whatever it is, it's extremely well-planned and executed."

She heard the aggravation in his voice.

"It feels like this is the lull before the storm. We've stopped them from selling Wildfire online. Current reports are showing new cases have diminished almost to nothing. What concerns me is that they know about this. So, the question is, what tactics are they going to use to distribute it now?" Daniel said

She attempted to ease his concern. "Hopefully we work that out before it happens. Do you really think they are so bent on wiping out a complete cross-section of the Werewolf race? I'm struggling to understand how they could do this to their own kind."

Daniel let out a low, disapproving growl. "Elise, like her father before her, is a fanatic. She truly believes that a Werewolf with mixed heritage is an abomination. It was part of the reason the Alliance refused the pack admission to America. They spread discord and prejudice wherever they go."

"No one mentioned that in the stories about the great migration."

"I suppose it's something we aren't proud of. We don't talk about it too often. When we have a few spare hours, I will fill you in on it." Daniel cleared his throat and got back to business. "In the meantime, we need to work out how we are going to deal with current events."

She flicked through the reams of paperwork on her desk. "I finally got into the carrier's database, but that was a dead end. The only record of his calls is the local ones he makes when he is in the city. We know he is talking and texting with Elise, it's just not through the carrier network."

"So how are they communicating? It can't be through telepathic link. There is a limit to the range we can extend it."

"They must be doing it on Viber or some other messaging software." She rubbed her forehead and sighed. "We just need to work out which one, and install something on Matheo's phone that will provide us with the information we need."

"Let me guess," he said. "There is an app for that?"

She grinned and chuckled. Daniel, who she had decided was technophobic, had made an attempt at humor. Something he was doing more frequently. "See, coming out with a modern expression didn't kill you, did it?" With each conversation, his icy exterior had dropped a little more, and she was relishing the daily calls with him. "I'll speak to Zeke to see if we can come up with something and get it installed."

She sighed. "In the meantime, I'll try and access the bank accounts of the companies Elise and Matheo are courting. It's going to take a while—most organizations have multiple bank accounts."

"Make sure you keep me in the loop, and if there's anything you need, just let me know." He rang off.

Despite the dire situation, a feeling of contentment wrapped around her. The warm smile stayed with her as she returned to work.

Less than thirty seconds after she put the phone down, it rang again. Thinking Daniel had forgotten something, she answered without looking at it. "You just can't get enough of me, can you, Alpha Locke?"

"*Liebe*, you need to come home."

Parker's stomach dropped at the sound of Clara's distraught voice. "What's happened?"

Clara hauled in a shaky breath. "It's Bobby. You have to come before it's too late."

TWENTY-THREE

Stan Lee Has Left the Building

Payette, Idaho

A lump was lodged in Parker's throat, making it impossible to swallow. Everything had happened so fast, she couldn't think straight. *How was this possible?* Tears streamed down her face as she shook her head in denial. "No! You can't, I won't stand for it. There must be something we can do."

Bobby winced, and the effort sent his entire body into a fit of spasms. When it subsided, he took a deep breath and let it out slowly. "Parks, you know as much as anyone, there is only one endgame here. Even Stan would be hard pressed to come up with a way through this. I don't have superpowers to make this all go away."

Parker clutched his hand. She would never let it go. Her throat constricted, making it hard for her to breathe. She couldn't accept this. She wouldn't.

Bobby gave her hand a shake. "Look at me, Parks."

She hesitated, then looked up, and her heart ached. Her cousin, who had been more like a brother, lay broken, fighting for his life, on a bed soaked in sweat and blood. Black blotches ravaged the side of his face. The rest of his body was covered in them, too. He was already struggling to remain lucid. At this rate, he would have very little control over what he or his wolf did, within hours.

The Brandenburg pack's doctor had pumped Bobby full of morphine to dull the pain, to allow her the time she needed to get to Idaho.

"But I don't understand how." Her vision blurred, and she wiped away the tears. "You were fine when I saw you last." She hauled in a breath and her eyes opened wide. "Please tell me you didn't try the stuff."

"Give me credit. I didn't take Wildfire."

Her brows pursed together. "Then how did this happen?"

Bobby shook his head. "I don't know. I started feeling ill when we were in Montreal. By the time we had followed Matheo to Mexico City, I knew something was wrong, and I came home."

Unlike the progression of the others she'd seen, Bobby's deterioration was supercharged. Blood had already begun to seep from his ears and nose. His internal organs were shutting down in record time.

"B-but if you would just hold on, maybe we could find something to fight it." She fought to control her emotions, unwilling to think this was the end.

Bobby tightened his grip on her hand. "I want to do this on my terms, before I am too far gone to make the decision."

She let out an involuntary whimper, covered her mouth, and looked at Morgan and Clara, who were standing nearby. Parker wiped her tears. "No. Tell him this isn't the way."

Morgan's lips set into a grim line. "It is his decision. You must respect that. Let him have the dignity to choose the way in which he leaves this world."

Her bottom lip trembled uncontrollably, and she turned back to her cousin. "You can't leave me like this, Bobby."

He let out a cough that wracked his entire body with pain, but he attempted to relax his features and smiled at her. "Be strong. I'll always be with you, Parks, no matter where you are. You may be my little cuz, but you've always looked after me. I never thanked you for that."

She covered her mouth with her hand to stop sobbing. It was bad enough she couldn't control her tears, but to let him see her so distraught was more than she could bear. She choked on her words. "But that's what family is for. You know I love you, Bobby."

A tortured moan erupted from him, and his shoulder popped. His eyes widened and he gasped. "Get her out of here, I don't want her to see this."

The Brandenburg pack's doctor rushed to Bobby's bedside and injected another vial of morphine into her cousin's neck. "He's going to turn, we need to strap him down," he said. "If we are going to do this, we need to do it now."

She fought Clara tooth and nail as she pulled her away from Bobby's bedside. "No, let me go!" She screamed and struggled to return to her cousin. "Let me go!"

As Clara pushed her out the door, Morgan said, "I will let you know when it's done."

Her heart burst, and she let out an ear-piercing wail as her legs gave way. Trevor, her ever constant bodyguard, reached her before her body hit the floor.

Clara's face was stony, though her tears ran freely. "Let's get her up to the house."

Trevor placed her on the couch in the family room. Clara's sudden indrawn breath told her everything she needed to know. Bobby was gone.

"*Liebe*, it is over. He is at peace now." With that, she pulled Parker into her arms. "*Mein hertz*, I am so very sorry."

She buried her head in Clara's shoulder and sobbed uncontrollably for so long she turned numb. This wasn't happening. Bobby wasn't dead. He had just met his idol, Stan Lee, for Christ's sake, he couldn't be dead.

The hollow feeling of loss overwhelmed her, and she lay in a stupor, unable to speak.

A long time later, she stared blankly at the slew of missed calls from Daniel, Jessica, and Alice. Instead of answering, she roamed around the house like a zombie. Bobby had been taken from her too soon. She shouldn't have outlived him. He was a werewolf—he was supposed to live a dozen of her lifetimes. She'd promised his mother that she would look after him, but she had failed.

Memories from their childhood replayed like an old movie. She recalled the summers they spent at the beach before she lost her parents. The time he carried her the entire way home after she'd cut her foot on a broken bottle, and how he'd stayed with her while the doctor stitched the gaping wound, even though he was petrified of needles. How he held her upright at her parent graves as they were lowered into the ground. All her most meaningful memories included him. He had been part of every major event in her life. With Bobby gone, there was no one left who knew where she came from, or who remembered her parents before they were taken from her.

She collapsed to the floor and sat staring into space. She was alone and completely empty.

Morgan and Clara, mindful she needed space, kept vigil with her the entire night. They watched over her as she broke, and held her tightly as she raged against the injustice. They encouraged her to drink when they felt she had become too dehydrated, and they sat with her when she was spent. For once, Clara did not push her to eat.

By morning, she was exhausted. She had run the gambit of every emotion possible in a few short hours. Through it all, she discovered a truth she already knew deep inside. While her biological family was well and truly gone, she still had a family that, while not blood, were there for her, and they would always catch her when she fell.

Bobby's loss hardened her resolve. She wasn't going to lose another loved one to this disease. Someone needed to pay for Bobby's death. The bastards behind Wildfire had picked the wrong person to fuck with.

TWENTY-FOUR

Pandora's Box

Middlemarch Estate

Elijah leaned against the stone wall and watched the American Alpha pacing the length of the patio. He shook his head and rolled his eyes. *It's no use checking your watch. That's not going to make her appear any faster.*

The American Alpha had appeared unannounced and demanded to meet with Elise. They had led him to an outdoor area and posted five armed guards. Now he could wait. Alpha Lauzon would take her time just to show him who had the upper hand.

He returned to playing with his knife, while still keeping vigil over the alpha.

When he detected footsteps approaching, Elijah jumped up and thrust his knife into its scabbard in the back of his waistband.

The American Alpha flinched. He clearly feared Alpha Elise, and rightly so.

Elise's tone was clipped and hard as she strode through the French doors opening to the patio. "Someone better be dying in some new and exquisite way, or every half-breed has suddenly dropped dead, and you just had to rush to tell me about it. Well, which one is it?"

The American Alpha marched over to her. "What are you playing at? Not only have the sales of Wildfire gone down the toilet, but I've been informed that you're no longer manufacturing it in pill format. What the hell does that mean?"

Elijah reached for his knife, and three enforcers stepped between the intruder and their alpha, halting his path and creating a barrier. They were ready to strike if need be.

From her tailored Chanel suit and matching pumps, to the minimalistic jewelry that adorned her neck and the Cartier tank watch on her wrist, Elise could have easily passed as an old money socialite or perhaps even European royalty. The outward appearance she presented to the world belied the true nature of the creature within.

Elise smiled, a smile that did not reach her eyes, and looked down her haughty nose at the American Alpha. "I have no idea what you are referring to."

She took a step closer to the American Alpha and pierced him with an unwavering stare. Her dark brown eyes bore into the other alpha's, and he took a half step back. His gaze darted to the nearest escape route. "You know damn well what I am talking about. I have left you messages for the last four weeks, and you haven't returned one of my calls."

Elijah held back a smirk. Alpha Lauzon matched the American Alpha in height, but had a larger set of balls, he'd wager. Maybe if they were lucky she'd get pissed off enough with the alpha to rip him apart while the rest of them watched.

Elise motioned for Elijah and the enforcers to stand down, moved across the patio, and gracefully sat on the nearest chair. She crossed her ankles, her back straight, and rested her hands on the high armrests. Her dark hair, set in a perfect chignon, was in direct contrast to the white Jacquard fabric of the chair. "Just for argument's sake, let's say I didn't receive them. Why, exactly, have you disturbed my solitude?"

The American Alpha took a step closer to Elise, but before he could complete the move, Elijah let out a menacing growl and stopped him in his tracks. He frowned at Elijah but remained where he was. "You promised me that Wildfire would have taken off by now. The demand has vanished, and my people are telling me that each time they try and re-list it, within moments it has disappeared. And now I hear the supply is no longer available—I want to know what you are going to do about it."

Elise inspected her nails. "You seem to be under the misconception that I answer to you." All pretense of civility was dropped. "I'm sure that this is a momentary lapse in judgment."

The whites of the American Alpha's eyes were like beacons as he realized his error and panic set in. Elijah played with his blade, hoping the American would step out of line so he could have some fun.

He was disappointed when the American Alpha held up the palms of his hands and said, "Please forgive me, I meant no disrespect." He bowed his head, his body contorting into a submissive posture.

Elise uncrossed her legs and tapped her blood red nails on the armrest. "First of all, I promised no such thing. You are here because I allow you to be here. Now, as to your petty matter, that method of distribution was never going to give us the results we required. I only used it to give us a targeted range of test subjects. It was too limiting and restrictive, and it will not solve our real problem."

Confusion clouded the American alpha's face. "What are you talking about? I sunk five million dollars into your project. This was supposed get rid of them."

Elijah zoned out of the American Alpha's rants. He had spent the past twenty years listening to it from Elise and the rest of the pack. They had decided that for too long, they had allowed half-breeds into their community, even letting them hold positions of power. Some packs even extended this impurity up to an alpha. It needed to stop. They needed to bring back order to their race to ensure its survival. Wildfire was supposed to do that for them.

To be honest he did not give a rat's ass. A body was a body. He did not care who he cut or defiled. They all bled red and gave him the same satisfaction, no matter whether they were pure, impure, or even Human. Under Elise's leadership, he had as many playthings as he could ask for, and without having to worry about the stupid alliance or Murphy O'Neill. And for this supply, all he needed to do was whatever she needed.

A cold, short laugh erupted from Elise's lips, dragging him back to the conversation. "You always did think too small."

As Elise outlined her plan for Wildfire, the American Alpha's face grew pale. "This isn't what we agreed on. Even if we win, we won't come out of this unscathed."

Elijah wasn't surprised when the American Alpha made a hasty departure. As he scuttled off, he wondered why Alpha Lauzon had bothered with him in the first place. He was weak and a discredit to their race.

When Elise sighed, he froze. This was never a good sign. She wasn't in a good mood. In fact, if the American Alpha had asked his opinion, he would've advised against speaking to her or approaching her. Keeping as much distance as physically possible, preferably a state or two away, was a good idea right now.

Barely controlling her growing fury, she turned to him. "Contact Matheo. Get him to find out what that imbecile was going on about with the sites coming down—we need to ensure the Alliance is still in the dark. We don't want to show our hand before we're ready."

He nodded and hurried to carry out her orders, but flinched away from a sudden noise. The omega clearing the table was kneeling on the ground, attempting to retrieve scattered pieces of a broken carafe.

"You!" Elise hissed through gritted teeth. "Come here."

The girl looked up and froze. She scrambled to her feet and rushed to stand in front of Elise. She stood still, hands at her side, looking down at the burnt orange tiles at her feet, her face devoid of any color.

The other omegas eyed her with pity, and Elijah's pulse quickened. His body quivered at what was about to happen.

"Look at me when you are addressed," Elise said.

The young girl lifted her head, but was unable to look directly into Elise's eyes. Instead, she focused on the lower half of Elise's face. Her body involuntarily shook from head to foot.

"You do appreciate that was a two-hundred-year-old Waterford crystal carafe you just destroyed?"

"I'm sorry, alpha. It was an accident. I didn't mean to—"

The omega's apology was cut short when Elise reached out with lightning-fast reflexes and dug her talons into the unsuspecting girl's neck, brutally ripping out cartilage and organs, leaving the spine intact.

Elise stared at the part of the woman's body she held in her bloodied hand, and then released her grip. Cartilage, bronchi, esophagus, larynx, and a section of the jugular vein, along with the woman's tongue, now lay in a growing pool of blood as the severed artery on the still standing body spurted in all directions.

Elijah licked his lips and heat flooded through his veins. He looked on with longing while the omega drowned in her blood, and the life evaporated from her as she collapsed on the floor, eyes still open and staring into the abyss. He inhaled the sweet metallic scent that encompassed the immediate area in a spray of red mist, and lovingly fingered his knife, wishing he had been the one to deliver the death blow.

A sense of calm now descended on Elise, and her mood brightened. "Clean up this mess." She flicked her hand in the air dismissively and disappeared into the house. "And replace the carafe. Ridel, this time. I've always disliked Waterford."

M GREENHILL

TWENTY-FIVE

Caffeine by Any Other Name

Portland, Oregon

Parker rubbed the back of her neck as she paced the lounge, phone pressed to her ear. "Answer, goddammit."

She threw the phone onto the couch when it went to voicemail yet again, and continued to pace, her mind in turmoil. *Where the hell is he?* She had repeatedly attempted to contact Daniel, but each time with the same result.

In the two weeks since Bobby's death, she had been on a renewed mission to find Elise's location and learn what she was up to. The pain of losing Bobby was still raw, but she had managed to remain focused with the help of Morgan and Clara. They instinctively knew what she needed, and when she needed it. Her circle of support increased with the arrival of Jessica and Daniel to attend Bobby's funeral. Their presence, while unexpected, was very much appreciated. Since then, she had spent every waking moment racing against the clock to track down Elise and Matheo.

She had begun to prepare dinner when her phone rang. She found it behind the sofa cushions and glanced at the caller display. Relief flooded her. *It's about time.*

"I've been trying to get hold of you all afternoon."

"I know. I've just gotten off the phone with Jessica," Daniel said.

Something in his tone triggered alarm bells. "What's going on? Where are you exactly?" Daniel and Alice had taken off without warning.

"San Diego." He sounded tired and strained.

Parker rubbed her eyes to ward off a headache that had been building throughout the day. "What's happened?"

The line went quiet, and Parker frowned. She was about to check if Daniel was still there when he said, "I was contacted by the local alpha. Five of his pack are sick…" Daniel hesitated. "They're all teenage kids."

She closed her eyes and sunk down on the couch. "How many of them are, um…" Her throat constricted. She could not bring herself to ask the question.

"We're going to lose one of them. Her father was born Human."

Dread spread through her chest and the rest of her body. They had stopped the supply of Wildfire weeks ago, yet the deaths were still mounting and had slowly made their way into the packs. As with Bobby's death, the source of the virus was still unknown.

She closed her eyes and rubbed her forehead. "Any idea how they got infected?"

"That's what Alice is trying to work out. I'm heading back to Nederland in the morning. Alice will stay on for a couple of days to work with the pack's doctor. He needs to know how to deal with what's going to happen. The girl has a hard choice to make and depending which way it goes, Alice will need to show the pack's doctor how to either cope with seeing the disease go through to the end, or how to assist with a merciful death."

"I'm sorry." The words seemed so hollow, even to her ears. Her heart went out to Alice. Her friend had seen too many good people die from this disease. What would they do if Alice broke under the pressure?

Daniel took a deep, ragged breath and exhaled loudly. "Why did you need to speak to me?"

In the shock of hearing about the victims, she had forgotten the reason she had been desperate to contact him. "Oh, yes. We might have a lead on what Matheo is up to. Yesterday, when he landed in Atlanta, he went straight from the airport to meet with Thomas Goodman."

"Isn't he the CEO of the Goodman Group?"

She was not surprised he knew the name. "Yes, but I knew him from something else, and it nagged at me all day. I couldn't put my finger on it until I looked into his personal life, then I discovered why. Thomas has a younger half-brother, Andrew Mallory."

She couldn't believe it when she had made the connection to Thomas Goodman. They had only seen Andrew a few months beforehand at the gala in Portland—Andrew was the same guy Daniel had known.

"And this can help us how?" he said.

"Well, we now have a way of finding out what Matheo was up to." She halted a moment to work through her next steps. "I need to come up with a story to justify why we need the information, and then convince Andrew to get it for us."

"Any ideas so far?"

She considered her options. "I think I've got one that might work."

After a restless night, three coffees, and one of her herbal teas in quick succession, she was more than prepared for her call. "Andrew, this is Parker Johnson."

"I was just looking over the report your team sent over. Excellent work. I'll be taking your suggestions to the next board meeting," Andrew said. "I can't see why we wouldn't go ahead with your proposal."

Parker's foot jiggled nervously under her desk. "Actually, Andrew, that's not why I called."

"It's not?"

"No, this is more of a courtesy call. I can't go into specifics, but I've come across some information I felt you needed to be aware of."

She grimaced, hoping she sounded genuine. Guilt at her deception weighed heavily on her, even if it was for a good cause.

"Oh?"

"I don't want to panic you, but the FBI are investigating a possible terrorist threat. It's come to my attention that your brother, Thomas, met with a French gentleman recently..."

Parker let out the breath she had been holding the entire length of their conversation. Her gamble had paid off, and Andrew was grateful for the heads up. His family was from old money, and they shied away from any possible scandal. He had promised to get back to her as soon as possible.

She did not need to wait long. Within a couple of hours, Andrew phoned her back.

"Thomas confirmed he met with a Frenchman by the name of Matheo Bernard. According to my brother, the supply contract had already been signed with Bernard's boss a while back. He was just there to finalize arrangements and ensure an agreement on the delivery schedule." Andrew hesitated. "Thomas did say that the man made him uneasy, but the deal will save them a considerable amount of money, so he brushed it aside." He paused. "I can't see how any of this could be related to terrorism."

Parker stiffened. This was the moment she was waiting for. If she did not get the answer she needed to her next question, their conversation would've been for nothing. "Did he tell you what the deal was about? Maybe my contact had it all wrong."

She stared at the phone and clenched her hand to her chest. A cold chill ran up and down her spine as the information sunk in.

I have to be wrong.

With her heart in her mouth, she nervously tapped her fingers on the keyboard and hoped the connections she had made during the conversation were incorrect. The data she had obtained regarding the companies Matheo had visited would give her the answers. Or not.

She scanned the files and her pulse quickened. Dread and helplessness overwhelmed her, and yet her mind still alternated between disbelief and abject horror.

No, God, no. Please let me be wrong.

She rechecked the information twice in case her eyes deceived her. A tear fought its way through her resolution and inched its way down her cheek. Bobby and the others never had a chance. Neither would the rest of the victims to come.

Brushing her rising panic aside, she picked up the phone on her desk. "Beth, get me and my shadow on the next plane to Denver."

Parker and her bodyguard, Trevor, arrived at Daniel's village late that afternoon.

Jessica, who had only been alerted to her arrival after her plane touched down, was waiting at the Pack house for them. She rushed over and enveloped Parker in a giant hug. "You got here tickety-boo."

Parker covered her mouth as she yawned. "Once we cleared the city limits, the roads were pretty free."

Jessica's forehead puckered. "How have you been?"

She gave Jessica a half-hearted smile. "As well as can be expected. One day at a time."

Jessica squeezed her arm. "Chickadee, we're here for you. Just let me know when you want to talk." She grabbed one of Parker's bags and headed to Alpha House. "I've set you up in your old room."

Parker halted, not sure whether this was a good idea. "You know, I am okay with bunking at the Den."

Jessica dismissed her protests. "Baloney, you're family." She continued toward the house without skipping a beat. "Daniel only got back a few hours ago. He's gone out with the patrol. We've had a few strange sightings lately, and everyone's nerves are a little frazzled. They left just before you phoned."

She and Jessica chatted as they headed up to the house. When they reached their destination, Jessica handed her the bag she had been carrying. "I'd love to stay and chinwag, but I need to hightail it home. Ray is out with the patrol as well, so Gail is child-minding Mandy. I promised her I wouldn't be late." She engulfed Parker in another hug. "I'm so pleased you're back. Next time, don't you dare skedaddle without giving us a heads up."

Jessica breezed out of the room, and Parker unpacked and settled in. Her stomach growled so she grabbed her laptop and headed to the kitchen. She had an urge for her favorite comfort food—pancakes. And right now, she needed as much comfort as possible if she was to get through the impending disaster.

TWENTY-SIX

Things Just Got Worse

The moon was at its highest point when Daniel and a small team of enforcers returned from patrol. They had gone on an impromptu hunt after finding no sign of intruders along their borders. His wolf had vented its frustration on an unsuspecting deer and was now sated and, for once, quiet.

One foot inside the door and he detected the faint smell of Calendula and honey. His wolf raised its head, but Daniel was quick to dismiss it as wishful thinking. Angry for allowing his thoughts to wander to Parker yet again, he headed to his room for a shower.

His body refreshed, he sniffed the air. The aroma of buttermilk and maple syrup wafted throughout the bottom level of the house. He headed for the kitchen, thinking that Jessica had left him some supper. His heart leaped and he halted mid-stride when he entered the kitchen. *What the...?* Sitting on a barstool at the high breakfast bar, was the last person he had expected to see.

Parker, the reason for his restless nights, pointed to the food across from her. "I made some extras, help yourself."

"What are you doing here?"

Her confused expression mirrored his own. "Didn't Jessica tell you?"

He squared his shoulders and cleared his throat. "No… No, she didn't."

"And you obviously haven't checked your voicemail."

"Battery's dead… When did you say Jessica knew you were coming?"

She tapped a few keys on her computer and glanced up at him. "I phoned her this afternoon as soon as I landed, why?"

Daniel's eyes narrowed. He had spoken to Jessica numerous times since his return; including a half hour ago when he stopped by her house with Ray. "No reason."

He attempted to contact his sister through their telepathic link. She ignored him.

I'll kill her.

Parker slid off her chair. "If it's a problem, I can bunk at Jessica's…"

"No, you damn well won't," he said. His wolf echoed the exact same phrase—at the exact same moment.

Parker sat back down, but looked wary at his bizarre behavior. "Well then, come and have something to eat."

He stalked over to the stack of pancakes, transferred half to his plate, and reached for the syrup.

"Take all of them, I've already eaten. I made the extras for you," she said.

Daniel inhaled the sweet aroma of the still warm food, and his stomach rumbled. He moved the remainder of the pancakes onto his plate, then took a seat beside her at the breakfast bar. "I'm assuming there is a reason for you being here."

Her lips formed a grim line. "Yes, and you're not going to like what I have to say."

The apprehension in her voice had him putting his knife and fork down and raising a questioning brow.

She nodded to his plate. "Eat your food first. Otherwise, you might lose your appetite, and I didn't waste my time for you to throw it away."

Daniel demolished the pancake stack while Parker fidgeted. Whatever she had to tell him, it wasn't going to be pleasant.

Once he finished eating, she grabbed both their plates and skirted around to the sink to rinse them. "I spoke to Andrew, and I know what Elise and Matheo have been doing."

His ears pricked up.

"The Goodman Group is the largest manufacturer of ice cream and yogurt in the South-East," she said. "A fundamental ingredient in their product range is caffeine."

He frowned. "And this means what, exactly?"

Parker closed her eyes briefly, and then opened them again. Her almond eyes were full of fear and concern, which only increased his concern.

"It turns out that Elise has signed a deal to exclusively supply caffeine to the group. They're putting Wildfire into synthetic caffeine and supplying it to food manufacturers. I think that's how Bobby and the others who didn't take the Wildfire pills contracted the disease. It doesn't have the same effect as the pills, but the results are the same."

His heart pounded in his chest. "Are you sure?"

She met his eyes and nodded. "I looked at the business holdings owned by the people we know he's visited. They all manufacture, to some degree, food or beverages that contain caffeine."

His fists tightened and a heavy weight began in the pit of his stomach. He did not want to believe the ramifications. A sudden coldness swept across his body as the full meaning of Elise's plan dawned on him. "And, you are sure about this?"

Her eyes were rimmed with tears as she nodded her head.

He believed her. "We need to warn the packs, they need to be prepared." He rubbed his forehead and worked through a plan to contain the impending disaster. "How much time do we have before we get the next wave of victims?"

Parker bit the inside of her cheek. "Well… based on my calculations, very few of the products we have identified would have already made it onto supermarket shelves. My concern is the companies we don't know about." She frowned, thrummed her fingers on the counter, and stared at her screen. "Those kids from San Diego, is anyone else in the pack sick?"

"No. Alice is still testing the rest of the pack. So far, it's isolated to those five. Alice is sure they all were introduced to the drug at the same time."

"Okay, so it's not something they ate or drank at home. What else is common to the five?"

Daniel's eyes widened. "They all attended the same high-school." He bolted out of his chair. "We need to find out what they all ate or drank at that school."

Parker became quiet, and she rubbed her hands up and down her jeans. "I think it's about time we admitted that we need to bring in help." She looked directly at him, her voice pleading. "This is a game changer. We need something that can fight this disease. We need a cure."

His voice tensed, matching his now aggressive posture "What are you talking about?" No matter how serious this was, he couldn't believe she was suggesting they involve outsiders.

Parker flinched, but recovered, and she squared her shoulders. A determined expression crossed her face. "We need to bring in someone who can analyze Wildfire and come up with a way to fight it. Alice needs help, she can't do this alone. She's already a wreck. You know as well as I do, pumping her patients full of morphine and depriving them of oxygen goes against that God damn oath she took—the woman is coming apart at the seams."

He broke in before she could continue. "We have been over this before. My answer hasn't changed. We can't, and will not, risk exposure."

"So, you would rather wipe out an entire race than take the chance on trusting a few Humans?" Parker slammed the lid of her laptop closed. "Yeah, great plan. I've already lost Bobby. At this rate, I'm going to be outliving you all."

He towered over her, and his eyes flashed before they shrank into angry slits. "Until you have lived through what I have, I suggest that you keep your opinions to yourself."

"You are so narrow-minded and pig-headed." Parker's cheeks flushed and her anger increased. "What if there are drugs out there that can already fight this? Isn't it worth the risk?"

He held his hands up and let out a deep breath. "Will you just stop, I've heard enough. We can't bring in outsiders." His voice was cold and menacing. Anyone else would have understood not to press him.

"Fine," she said. "Let everyone suffer because you are still so entrenched in what happened in the past, but don't expect me to be happy about it."

With that, she picked up her laptop and stormed out of the room.

TWENTY-SEVEN

There Are Three Sides to Every Story

Dawn broke as Daniel placed the phone on its cradle. He had spent most of the night on the phone to each Alliance alpha. The conversations had followed the same pattern of denial and disbelief, and finally a demand for answers.

He did not blame them. That had been his reaction, too. But knowing what the Sandulf Pack was capable of meant that his disbelief quickly metastasized into horror, followed by a deep-seated urgency to protect the pack, the alliance, and their race. He needed to put safeguards in place to identify and warn all those at risk.

Try as he might, he couldn't get his conversation with Parker out of his mind. Her words had haunted him from the moment she stormed out of the room. There was an incessant nagging at the back of his mind, fighting to be heard.

What if she was right? How do we fight something we can't see or touch?

This situation was out of their league. He felt powerless against an enemy that chose to fight with these kind of weapons. Powerlessness did not sit comfortably with him. It was a new and alien emotion, one that he did not like.

Parker being unhappy with him did not sit well with his wolf either. It wasn't that she was angry; it was the look of disappointment etched in her eyes before she walked away that had gotten to him.

He sighed. Guilt. Another new emotion he did not much care for. He headed to the kitchen and discovered a fresh French press coffee had been brewed, and the doors to the outside patio area were already open.

Parker sat at the outside table with her back to him, gazing across the valley. The light of the morning sun reflected on her hair, almost giving the appearance of a halo encircling the crown of her head. It was ironic. The woman really thought she could save everybody.

Her shoulders tensed the moment she became aware of his presence. He took a seat across from her and quietly drank the coffee he had poured for himself, all the while struggling to find the right words to explain his decision.

He cleared his throat. "You know, the early Christians hid their beliefs, knowing that if they were discovered, they would be put to death at the hands of the Roman Empire. We Werewolves watched as the tide was turned years later, when Christians laid havoc against those who didn't believe in their God."

Daniel sat back in his chair, a dull sadness settling in his chest. "Throughout your Human history, you have killed over seventy million people—for the simple reason that they had a different belief system than the dominant religion at the time."

His eyes bored into hers, and he searched for the slightest indication that she understood his point of view. "Since the dawn of time, Humans have ethnically cleansed entire races. Cambodia today is missing an entire generation. The Bosnians, Tibetans, the persecution of Romani, Rwanda, Hitler's slaughter of over eight million people during the Second World War, the genocide of over twelve million American Natives between the 1500s and the 1900s… the list is endless. Humans have systematically eradicated cultures for no other reason than they were different."

He leaned across the table and reached for her hand, his palms clammy. "Humans, by their very nature, can be relied on for one thing—they will destroy anything they don't understand." His touch was light, belying how much he needed the contact.

He recognized Parker's turmoil as she fought against what he had said.

"If they can put to death millions of people because of the color of their skin, their beliefs, or the country they originate from…can you imagine what they would do if they discovered that we have existed alongside them since the dawn of time?"

He hoped that by viewing it from his standpoint, she would be able to understand their reluctance. Humans as a race had a lot to answer for. His chest tightened as he waited for her reaction.

Her expression softened, and her shoulders slumped. She gently squeezed his hand. "I'm sorry," she said softly.

The touch was calming. He sighed, and sat back in his chair. "It's not your fault. If there were more people like you we might have options. But there aren't, and we need to deal with the resources we have at our disposal."

They sat for a minute, each lost in thought.

He winked. "Nice coffee, by the way."

Parker grimaced. "I couldn't quite bring myself to make instant this morning. While neither of us are affected by Wildfire, it just didn't seem right."

The reason for Parker's unexpected visit fell heavy on his shoulders, and he returned to his default no-nonsense tone. "We need to make some changes to keep the packs safe." He stood up. "Which reminds me, we are about to be inundated with Werewolves. The Alliance alphas need answers, and we need to work out what to tell them before they get here."

Parker shot up in her chair. "We?"

He cleared his throat. "You are as much a part of this as anyone else, so yes, we." He snapped the lid closed on Parker's laptop and held out his hand. "We have work to do."

TWENTY-EIGHT

Human Customs

The pack representatives arrived by late afternoon.

Daniel had spent most of the day alternating between containing the escalating panic as word spread within his pack, and working with Parker to prepare for the upcoming meeting.

The moment Parker walked through the large doors of the Pack house, his focus switched to her. He couldn't help it, his unconscious mind gravitated to her. Why, was a subject for another time. He motioned for her to join him. From the thickness of the folders in her arms, she had compiled the required material for each alpha.

The place was in an uproar as she weaved across the room, each alpha vying to be heard over the others. Once she was by his side, he placed a hand on her lower back and dipped his head to her ear. "Ready?"

She clutched the folders closer to her chest and looked up at him. "And if I said I wasn't?"

He flashed a fleeting grin before facing the crowd. His booming voice rose above the deafening noise. "Silence!"

He stood in the middle of the melee. All eyes were now focused on the Alpha Commander, and a nervous hush descended across the room. Alphas and their betas looked at him, expectantly. Those already affected by Wildfire were the ones surviving on little, if any, sleep. Their dark circled eyes and grim expressions only added to the ever-growing fear.

He took a deep breath in and forced himself to appear calm. "Thank you all for coming. I appreciate you getting here so quickly." He paused. It was now or never. "As most of you know, Wildfire has a one hundred percent mortality rate for a turned or mixed Werewolf. Many of you have already been affected by this tragic disease. We have stopped the online distribution of Wildfire tablets, but our people are still dying, even though they haven't knowingly taken the drug."

Never before had he felt so powerless. He squared his shoulders and braced himself for chaos. His duty as Alpha Commander was to protect his people, and yet, here he was, about to tell them he had failed. "We have discovered that Wildfire is being mixed with a caffeine food additive." He looked around at the confused faces, and his stomach dropped. He was about to destroy any hope they might have had. "That means the drug can be introduced into any number of food or drink products that you would buy off the shelf at your local supermarket or corner store."

Confused glances turned to horror, then anger, as pandemonium set in across the room.

One by one the alpha's filed out, a look of barely restrained panic on their faces. They were eager to return to their packs and implement the suggestions and safeguards that he and Parker had outlined.

Morgan approached him. "That went well, considering."

"Hmmm," Daniel said. He wasn't as sure as his friend. "I can understand their panic, but they seem to forget that only a few members of their packs are at risk. Not everyone needs to take the same precautions."

Morgan sighed. "The unknown always tends to make people overreact."

He scanned the room. Parker had been pulled aside by a few of the departing Werewolves. Rather than shrink back from the small, agitated crowd demanding answers, she put their minds at ease, and provided them with reassurance.

Daniel watched the alphas seek advice from a Human. *Perhaps times have changed.*

"Have you heard from O'Neill?" Morgan said.

He nodded. "A few days ago. He wants to check on one more thing before he returns, but he has tracked the pack down. It turns out they also want to know where Elise is."

Daniel changed the subject when Parker made her escape after the final party left the building.

Parker touched Morgan's arm. "Sorry I didn't say hi before."

Morgan pulled her in for a quick embrace. "It's not a problem. There were more important things to do than waste time nattering to an old man." He turned to Daniel. "How is the Matheo trail going?"

"I spoke to Vic this morning. She's been briefed on the current situation. Vic is the only one within the teams following Matheo, that's at risk. I gave her the option of returning, but she has asked to stay on."

Parker looked from Morgan to Daniel. "Well, I know you both have things to discuss, and I have a call with Alice and Alpha Hendriks shortly. Give my love to Clara and the rest. I'll try and make it out for a visit in a couple of weeks."

"You know, you are always welcome." Morgan was silent as he watched Parker's retreating back. "I hear she has been given permission to attend your sister's Eventide ceremony."

Daniel cocked his head. "Where did you hear that? It's not common knowledge."

Morgan shrugged. "You know how it is, Elders talk." Morgan's features became serious. "Your father was a good leader, one of the best." A slow smile emerged as his expression became melancholy. "Not a day goes by when I don't miss him."

He let out a deep sigh. "I know the feeling. I sometimes wonder what he would have made of all this."

Morgan paused, as if searching for the right words. "You were his greatest achievement, the legacy he left behind. But he gave you too high a standard to live up to. It was his one flaw, and I should have intervened in your youth." He sighed and sadness crept into his voice. "I have watched you grow from a child to a man. In all that time, I have never seen you genuinely smile. Happiness seems to have eluded you."

He shot a questioning glance at Morgan. "Are you feeling all right? You're starting to worry me."

Morgan's piercing eyes stared into Daniel's soul. "My boy, it is okay to get some enjoyment out of life. You don't need to walk this path alone all the time."

Daniel crossed his arms. "I don't know what you're talking about."

Morgan nodded at the door Parker had exited. "Don't you?"

"In case it has slipped your mind, the woman is Human, and by your own admission, one without a Werewolf ancestor."

Morgan chortled. "My dear boy. I may be old, but I am certainly not blind. I see the way you look at her. Parker may not be your mate, but you have most definitely developed an attachment to her. And I suspect your wolf has as well."

He narrowed his eyes. "I am not having this conversation."

"You are both too stubborn for your own good. Live a little. Perhaps you can have some joy in your life for once. Perhaps together you can find peace, even if it is only throughout her lifetime."

Morgan's remarks unsettled him, and he was unsure how the conversation had deviated this far. "This isn't the time, nor the place, for a ridiculous discussion such as this. She is an adopted member of your pack, and I have been charged by the council to protect her."

Morgan waved him off. "Nonsense. Now is the best time, as who knows how this whole situation will play out? Besides, have you met the woman?" Morgan chuckled. "Sometimes I wonder who really runs the pack when she's around."

If only he did not know exactly what Morgan meant.

Morgan stroked his chin, deep in thought. "You might want to start with that little Human custom...I think they call it a date."

TWENTY-NINE

Pizza

"Not a problem, just remember to check the labels. If in doubt, don't buy it. Better yet, you could try and avoid processed food altogether." Parker placed the phone in the cradle, inhaled deeply, and let out an ear-piercing scream.

"Feeling better?" Daniel said. His expression was sympathetic with a hint of humor.

She sat back in her chair and rubbed her forehead. "Much."

In the week since the discovery that foods were laced with Wildfire, panic had spread through the packs within and outside of the Alliance. She was inundated with a constant barrage of calls querying whether a particular ingredient, fast food, snack, or drink was safe. Everyone was scared, and justifiably so.

"Let me guess, McDonalds, Pepsi, or Pizza?"

She rolled her eyes. "Pizza. Is that all teenagers eat these days?"

"It appears so."

She had spent the better part of a week sharing an office with Daniel, and had a much better appreciation of the logistical nightmare that came with the responsibilities of leading a pack, running a business, and juggling an impending disaster.

The phone rang again, and she quickly answered. But after the third call in a row about pizza, she was ready to explode. It seemed even those not at risk were reluctant to eat or drink anything that contained caffeine.

Daniel, who had been observing her growing frustration in his usual unreadable manner, raised an eyebrow at her. "When is Gail coming to relieve you?"

The volumes were more than she could handle alone, and she had enlisted both Jessica and Gail's help to take turns staffing the phones.

"Around six."

"I thought that perhaps you might like to have a few hours away from the chaos around here. You look as though you need it."

She sighed and jotted down a few notes. "That's okay, Alice is busy and Jessica is preparing for her Eventide Ceremony, so, there's not much point."

Daniel fidgeted with his pen. "I meant... with me."

Her hand froze on the pad, and she glanced up at Daniel. "Oh."

"If you don't want to, that's okay, I just thought..."

She cleared her dry throat. "No... I would love to. You just caught me by surprise."

He shrugged and nodded toward the window. "I sometimes find that heading out on one of the trails helps me clear my hea—"

He was cut short by the all too familiar sound of the phone ringing.

She reached for the phone. "You know, I now dream of ringing phones. Thousands of them."

Gail was late relieving her, so it was dusk before they left the compound and headed for the tree line. The evening was warm as they walked along a familiar path. When they veered into a dense grouping of trees, she knew they were headed to the small lake. Her breath caught in her throat as they came into the clearing.

Hundreds of tiny glass balls floated on the lake, each with a glowing light in the shape of a small candle. Lanterns hung from trees or rested on the ground, lighting the clearing with a gentle surreal glow. A table for two was set on a grassy patch by the lake, the white linen cloth a stark contrast to the dusk that had fallen across the valley. Her eyes opened wide as she took in the elaborate setting. She didn't know where to look or what to say. Her face grew warm, and she hoped that Daniel didn't notice her embarrassment.

Daniel growled under his breath. "I'm going to kill her."

"P-Pardon?"

He sighed. "I mentioned to Jessica that I thought you needed to get out for some fresh air. She offered to arrange a picnic hamper..." He trailed off and his eyes narrowed. "Thinking about it, she actually was quite insistent."

She surveyed the transformed clearing. "Well, I have to give her credit, she certainly put this together quickly."

Their awkwardness evaporated. They looked at each other and burst into nervous laughter.

"We shouldn't disappoint her, I suppose." He bowed slightly and held his arm out. "After you."

He pulled out her chair and waited for her to sit.

A bottle of Moet rested in an ice bucket beside the table. Daniel poured a glass of champagne in two crystal flutes and lit the tapered candles in the center of the table. "I believe it's customary to make a toast. What shall we drink to?"

She raised her glass. "To putting an end to Matheo and his bitch of an alpha."

They clinked their glasses together and took a sip.

Daniel sniffed at the covered plates. "So, what kind of meal do you think Jessica has planned?"

She frowned as she studied the mystery dish. "I'm not sure, and to be honest, I'm slightly concerned."

Her relief was immediate when the metal covers were removed to reveal nothing more than a Caesar salad. She reached for her knife and fork, and they began the first course.

"Did you sort out Alpha Rossi's problem?" Daniel said.

She nodded. "He has a higher proportion of mixed Werewolves in his pack than most. They were thinking of pulling their kids out of the local schools and homeschooling them until this dies down. I told him to send the kids to school with packed lunches, but with kids being kids, they didn't think that was an option."

Daniel's fork stopped midway between his plate and his mouth. "Why would he want to speak to you about education for his pack? It's got nothing to do with Wildfire."

She raised an eyebrow. "Considering the conversation wouldn't have happened if Wildfire wasn't freaking everyone out, it has everything to do with it. But if you must know, I helped them out a little while ago by updating a teaching state license for a new member of his pack. Her age didn't quite match up with how she looked. So, I made a couple of adjustments."

"How many packs have you helped out, exactly?"

She glanced upwards. "Pretty much all of them."

He continued to eat in silence, but from the way he stabbed his salad with his fork, he was mulling over something. "How did I not know just how far you've become entrenched in our society?"

She met his curious gaze. "It's kept quiet. I'm called in to do a job. I do it, and I get out again." She shrugged. "It's as simple as that."

"I suppose I should have trusted Morgan's judgment when he welcomed you into his pack all those years ago."

She grinned and raised a shoulder. "Mehhh...Where would be the fun in that?"

Daniel relaxed again and changed the topic. Their easy conversation flowed while they finished their first course.

He wandered over to a nearby table and raised the lid on a chafing dish. It contained two heaped plates of Fettuccine Alfredo with sun-dried tomatoes and vegetables.

Daniel snorted. "Well, that's different."

She smiled at his sister's choice. "Actually, that's my favorite pasta dish. I must have mentioned it to Jessica at some point."

He returned to the table, a plate in each hand. The rich aroma of the pasta sauce made her stomach rumble, but she waited for Daniel to take his seat again before she attacked her food.

"Do you think Matheo will ever lead us to Elise?" she said.

He reached for his glass. "The two most powerful warriors are patience and time."

She raised an eyebrow. "Quoting Tolstoy isn't the answer I was looking for."

Daniel shrugged. "That's the only answer I have." He set down his champagne flute. "Time has taught me one thing—they will trip up. We just need to be patient."

"Now you sound like Yoda."

"Who?"

She raised a hand to her chest. "Oh my God, please tell me that Star Wars didn't pass you by."

"So, by the time Simon woke up the next morning, she'd gotten every stick of furniture in his bedroom out to the front yard, and had arranged it exactly as it had been in his room. To this day, he still has no idea how she got him, and his bed, out there."

Her sides hurt. Daniel had kept her laughing by regaling her with some of the many antics that Jessica had gotten into over the years. At some point, they had moved away from the table and sat on the slab of stone by the lake. Their legs dangled in the water, and they watched the small glass globes float by. She was more content than she had been for a long time. Part of her wished for the night to never end.

She smiled at the memory of Daniel's face when he tasted the dessert. The man did not appreciate the tartness of a lemon meringue. However, the fact that he was willing to try it was one of the things she—. Parker's legs stopped swinging in the water, and her body tensed.

No, no, no. I can't be!

She listened to his deep, dulcet tones and groaned inwardly.

Jesus, Mary, and Joseph. Her heart skipped a beat. Somehow, at some point, she had fallen in love with Alpha Daniel Locke.

He turned to her and smiled. "Remind me to show you the cave behind the waterfall one day."

How or when it had happened, she had no idea. All she knew was that this frustrating, demanding, and overbearing Werewolf had become an integral part of her life. And now she couldn't imagine a life in which he did not exist.

The emotion crashed over her like a tidal wave, unexpected and all-consuming.

With this realization came the knowledge that she would never mean anything more to him than she did now. To him, she was a necessary evil helping them through this mess. Sure, they had gotten through their initial animosity. They had even progressed to colleagues, and perhaps even friends. But she knew him well enough to know he wouldn't consider anything more than that with a Human. He was born to lead his pack, and to protect their race. Duty was all he knew.

She glanced sideways at his profile and rested her gaze on his lips. The need to reach up and touch his lips, to place hers against his and taste his essence, to see if the simple act of his touch set her body on fire as quickly and completely as it had during those fleeting moments forever imprinted on her memory, was overwhelming.

Parker shook the thoughts from her mind. She knew she'd be lost forever if she gave in to this weakness. He had gotten under her skin and into her blood so thoroughly that she wondered how she would ever recover.

"Parker, are you okay? You've gone very quiet."

"Um... I'm fine." She searched for an excuse to place some distance between them. "I was just thinking that it's getting late, and we probably should be heading back in."

It did not take them long to clear the table and place everything in the containers and hampers that had been hidden under the small table. Once done, they walked back to the compound side by side, both deep in their own thoughts.

She shivered. A sudden drop in temperature sent a mild chill into the late-night air.

Daniel put an arm around her shoulders to share some of his body heat, and pulled her close. "We can't have you getting sick," he said. "Jessica wouldn't let me hear the end of it, and she mightn't let us sneak out again."

When her heart clenched tight, she knew she was lost.

What have I done?

Parker tossed and turned, unable to fall asleep. Each time she closed her eyes, Daniel's face swam into view. When she did succumb to exhaustion, her dreams were vivid and erotic. She rose before dawn and ventured out to her now favorite spot on the patio that looked across the valley, and tried to catch up on some of her work. Her flight back to Portland was the following day, and she was already behind schedule with some of her projects. Work was going to help her through this.

Images from the previous evening kept pushing to the forefront of her mind, destroying her ability to concentrate. This wasn't how things were supposed to happen. She wasn't supposed to fall in love with a man who would never love her back.

What am I going to do?

She was so distracted, she failed to notice Alice walking purposefully up the path from the compound, until she was barely a few steps away.

"Morning," Parker said. "You're not normally up so early."

Alice's face was drawn, and her eyes were red-rimmed.

She tensed. "What's the matter?"

"I-I need to find the alpha," Alice said.

Parker's stomach dropped and she jumped up from the table and raced after her friend. "Alice, you're scaring me. What's happened?"

"Alpha Hendriks just called me." Her face was haunted and her voice broke. "One of the infected girls just heard her best friend from school is in hospital... She has all the same symptoms."

Parker stopped in her tracks. "But I thought there were only five Werewolves at that high school? And they were already all infected."

Alice let out a small whimper as she turned to face Parker. "That's the problem. Her friend is Human."

THIRTY

Now You Have Him, Now You Don't

Blood surged through Daniel's veins, and his entire body had become a tightly coiled spring ready to break. He fought down his wolf, who threatened to emerge in uncontrolled rage.

The tension in the room was so thick it felt like it had a physical presence. All eyes were glued to him, and he was unsure of how to react, what to say, or even how to feel. Every person in his office was in total denial, not wanting to contemplate the ramifications of what Alice had just told them.

He said nothing, his jaw clenched as his eyes bore into the pack's doctor, as if his mind could eliminate this new problem by mere force of will.

The seconds stretched out and his eyes flickered toward Parker. Even with her Human frailties, she was capable of recognizing the turmoil moving through his mind, his anguish, concern, and anger at those who would viciously and indiscriminately kill in this manner. His gaze locked on Parker. Her emotions mirrored his. Without words, she was projecting the empathy and strength he was coming to rely on.

"Are you sure?"

Alice nodded slowly and gulped. "Alpha Hendricks went to the hospital himself. He couldn't get too close as they had the girl isolated, but the symptoms are the same." She paused before continuing. "All of them."

Simon let loose a feral growl. "I don't understand." He clenched his hands. "It's one thing to target Werewolves, but Humans? They're going to notice the dead bodies piling up. We've contained the Werewolf outbreak from the Humans, but this will become front page news."

This had been one of his first thoughts as well. He paced around the room. "I have no idea what Elise is up to. Even with her addled brain, surely she foresaw this?" He stopped to stare out the window, deep in thought. "Wildfire is very explicit about which Werewolves it affects. I suspect that the same applies to the Humans."

Alice nodded. "I won't be sure until I run a DNA test, but yes, my initial thoughts are that those Humans with a dormant Werewolf gene are at risk."

Silence deafened the room. The ramifications of this new development were far-reaching and more horrifying than their initial assumptions.

Parker stood and made her way to the window. "How many?"

There was a brief pause. "There's no way of knowing. We have no idea how many generations the gene has passed down." Alice's voice rose in pitch as she considered the possible numbers. "If it's like mitochondrial DNA, there's no limit, it could be hundreds of thousands."

He watched as Parker visibly recoiled. While the figure was news to her, it wasn't to him.

Alice shifted in her chair, and her shoulders slumped as she turned back to him. "The San Diego pack is obtaining a blood sample for me. Until then, we're just guessing."

"Once you have the sample, how long?" He needed an answer.

"Provided everything goes well," Alice said, "twenty-four hours before I can confirm if the girl has the gene."

Alice shot Daniel and Parker an apprehensive look before continuing. "Alpha, I've been doing some research into man-made diseases and how they work..."

He narrowed his eyes. Her hesitation put him on high alert.

"If Elise has created the disease, it would be a reasonable assumption that she also has a cure for it."

Cure. The word resonated through his head. "We need to find her. Now."

He turned to Simon. "Where is our pet psychopath today?"

THIRTY-ONE

A Picture Tells a Thousand Words

Erie, Pennsylvania

Matheo pulled his rental car into the main parking area at Millcreek Mall. His temper flared as he struggled to find a space. He hated shopping malls almost as much as he detested the person he was here to see. The American Alpha had insisted on the clandestine meeting rather than discussing his issue over the phone.

Beating an old, decrepit lady for the last handicapped spot, he looked for the Outback Steak House Restaurant on the far side of the complex. He couldn't understand why Elise was adamant they needed this meeting. As far as he was concerned, they no longer had any use for the American Alpha.

He spotted the American Alpha as soon as he entered the dimly lit eating establishment. A waitress approached but he ignored her. He strode over to the secluded booth and took a seat opposite the man.

The American Alpha scowled and glanced around the room. "You're late."

Matheo pierced the other man with an angry glare. "And you are getting on my nerves."

The American Alpha leaned forward and lowered his voice. "Things are getting out of control. You need to tell Elise—"

He let out a low growl. This conversation was a waste of his time. "I have a message for you." He pulled his phone out and slid the device across the table. "This is what will happen to every member of your pack if we hear even the slightest whispers that you have looked in the wrong direction."

The American Alpha picked up the phone and paled. His bloodied and disembodied beta stared back at him. The Alpha glanced around the restaurant, and made sure no one else had seen the image. He swiped the screen to remove the image, and without looking at the screen, dropped the phone on the table.

The American Alpha took a shaky breath. "Tell Elise I have done no such thing. She was the one who kept me in the dark about her real plans for Wildfire. I have sunk millions into its development, and I have as much right as anyone to know what's going on. The Alliance has already stopped the online sales. It's only a matter of time before they trace it back to me." The alpha leaned back, a level of confidence replacing his previous apprehension. "Besides, you should worry more about your own leaks."

He blinked and turned away from the waitress in her shorter than short uniform. "What do you mean?"

"The Alliance is already aware of what you are doing. An alert has gone out to all the packs to take care with the food half-breeds consume."

His jaw clenched. "What did you just say?"

"You heard me." The American Alpha sneered. "They know what you are up to." He pushed the phone across the table. "You have bigger problems than trying to threaten me."

About to let go of the phone, the American Alpha glanced at the image on the screen and froze. He looked up at Matheo, back at the picture on the screen, and laughed. His posture relaxed and he taunted. "Actually, I would be more worried about your own life rather than threatening mine."

His pulse started to race as he brought his fist down on the table. "What the *cazzo* are you talking about, old man?" No one laughed at him and lived to tell the tale.

"Your little girlfriend there." The alpha pointed at the photo. "You have the audacity to accuse me of liaising with the Alliance, and you are in bed with Morgan Bergman's Human pet." His voice sneered in disgust. "That is Parker Johnson. There's not a computer system she hasn't broken into. You, my friend, are... how do the Humans phrase it?" He closed his eyes searching for the words. "Oh yes. That's right. You are right royally fucked."

The alpha stood, a grin on his face. "Oh, Matheo. I'm not sure who I would be more scared of, if I were you. The Alliance's pit-bull of a commander, or your understanding, gentle alpha?" The alpha threw money on the table and strolled out of the restaurant, still snickering.

He sat in the booth staring at the photo of the blue-eyed woman with chestnut brown hair. Matheo looked closer at her ruby lips, curved up in a half smile, and a burning rage bubbled to the surface. He rose and stiffly walked the length of the restaurant, his wolf fighting for dominance.

She. That Human had taken him for a fool.

He dropped his phone into the bin nearest the door. A cold rage flowed through his veins, and the desire to inflict damage was uppermost in his mind. He searched for the nearest area where his wolf could emerge.

I'm going to make that bitch pay.

THIRTY-TWO

Do Unto Others

Portland, Oregon

A scream pierced the otherwise calm office.

Parker raced down the corridor, past employees peering over their dividers. "Beth, are you..." She stopped short and frowned when she turned the corner into the main reception area.

Beth was jumping up and down, hands cupping her cheeks and squealing. A delighted grin stretched from ear-to-ear.

She rolled her eyes and placed her hands on her hips. "Jesus Christ Beth, get a grip. What's going on?"

Beth halted her excited jiggling. "Sorry, Boss. I couldn't help it." She pointed to a giant flower arrangement on the front desk. "Look what just arrived for me."

Beth held up an intricate gold chain that she had been clenching in her hand. "And this came with it." She wiggled both eyebrows. "My new man's gonna get himself somethin', somethin' tonight."

"Beth, you do understand that this is a place of business?"

"Yeah. And?"

Parker groaned. "No reason."

She headed back to her office. *Why in God's name did I hire her? Cause she livens up an otherwise dreary workday. Oh yeah, that's why.*

She shook her head. Beth was such a loving soul, who only saw the best in people, but she had such bad luck with men. This one seemed to make her happy. She hoped he would not crush Beth's heart as callously as the others had.

Since returning to Portland, life had continued its roller-coaster ride. Getting up to speed with her team at the office had occupied her days, and circumnavigating the CDC's firewall and extensive databases had filled her nights. She found that keeping herself busy was the best way to keep Daniel from her mind.

She snorted. Who was she kidding? He was never out of her mind.

She sighed and stared out the window. When Daniel rushed to New York, their daily calls had halted. The number of Werewolves affected by Wildfire had suddenly raged out of control and needed containment before it spilled over into the Human world any more than it already had. While she missed talking to him, she knew it was for the best. It gave her time to place a barrier around her heart.

She forced herself to concentrate on finishing an end-of-project report and became so engrossed in her work, she did not realize when the day moved into night. Except for Trevor, her ever-present bodyguard, everyone had left hours ago. She jumped when her mobile cut through the silence.

She turned the phone over and smiled as she pressed the answer button. "Hey Alice, did you get the files I emailed?"

Once she had broken into the CDC network and found the information related to the Wildfire outbreak, understanding the case notes became difficult. She had forwarded the information to the only other person who might be able to make sense of it.

"I've spent the day pouring through the case reports and lab results," Alice said. "I'm pretty much out of my depth here, but as far as I can tell, it looks like Elise has combined two viruses together—one that's unique to canines, the other a deadly Human virus."

"What does that mean?" Parker said.

"As we suspected, we are dealing with a genetic bomb—it's just that the CDC doesn't know it yet."

She was on high alert and wasn't going to like the answer to her next question. "Dare I ask the name of the virus?"

"Ebola."

Her throat constricted, and it felt like the walls of her office were moving inwards. Blood rushed through her veins, and her pulse raced. She brought a hand up to her forehead. *Oh God!*

"Parker? Parker…are you there?"

Her voice cracked as she spoke. "T-there's no cure for Ebola."

"There's no cure for CDV-1, either. The Europeans have a vaccine, but it's not available in the US."

She was thankful she was sitting. Her legs had begun to shake along with the rest of her body. "So how does this combined virus work?"

"My guess is that the CDV-1 virus searches for the appropriate wolf gene, and if it detects the right set of proteins, it blocks the immune system and releases the Ebola virus."

"What about the CDC's notes? Does it look like they might be able to work it out and find some way of stopping it?"

Alice exhaled slowly. "Because they don't know that it's targeting a specific set of proteins that make up a particular gene, I can't see how."

She rested her head on her free hand and closed her eyes. Her head throbbed. "So, how do we fix this?"

"We can't." Alice's tone was apologetic. "The best we can do is make sure that the Werewolf community keeps away from anything that might contain Wildfire."

She snapped. "And what about Humans? Who's going to warn them?"

"Parker, you know the rules. We can't risk exposure, and I don't have the skills or the experience to solve this crisis."

The line went silent as she considered the options open to her. "Alice, I need you to send me the exact location of the gene and proteins."

Alice hesitated. "Why?"

There was a short delay before she replied. "So I can detect if the CDC stumble onto the gene. I imagine that the Alliance would want a heads up on it."

"Good idea. I didn't think of that," Alice said. "I'll email the details to you in the morning."

She stared at her phone for a long while after the call ended. Could she really sit still and allow this to go unchecked? Images of thousands of bodies lying dead in hospitals, on streets, in homes, and in schools flashed through her mind, and her heart faltered. She let out a small whimper as her mind strayed to Bobby. God, how she missed him. There was a hole in her life that would never be filled.

She reached for her phone and scanned through the images he had sent her from Awesomeness Con in New York. Tears streamed down her face when she stopped at the one of him with Stan Lee. The ear-to-ear smile she missed each and every day ripped open the lid of grief she had held at bay since his death. She wept uncontrollably and grieved not only for Bobby, but for the families of the unsuspecting victims that had no part in the fight Elise was bringing to them. How many dead men, women, and children were walking their last steps? How many Humans were out there, not knowing the grim reaper was about to come calling?

She wiped her eyes with the back of her hand, and drew in a shaky breath. *I can't let this happen.*

Her decision was made. There was only one option open to her, and she needed to take it, or countless lives would be lost.

THIRTY-THREE

A Blast From the Past

Central Park, New York

Daniel had lost count of the number of times he had been to New York over the years. He, and many of the other Werewolves who had witnessed the skyline for the first time from the deck of their ships after the long voyage to America, would always remember the city with fondness.

The city's port was the final destination for the four ships carrying the European Werewolf Packs on the migration from their homeland. The journey had been difficult for all of them, especially their wolves, who were forced to stay hidden from the skeleton crew.

They had paid enough to commandeer the ships for the journey, and not once did the crewmen question why they were carrying so few passengers compared to the capacity of the ships, nor why parts of the boats were off limits to them.

Nor were the packs short on live prey during the voyage. Their vessels were the only ones to dock without a single rat, mouse, cat, or other rodent. He followed the path that led out of the park, and looked up to the skyline. In one hundred and fifty years, buildings had been constructed, demolished, and replaced by bigger and newer buildings. Streets had expanded, and the hills he remembered could no longer be seen. New York had grown from a population of half a million Humans; to eight and a half million Humans and a smattering of Werewolves.

His pocket vibrated, and he reached for his phone. The display identified the caller as Murphy O'Neill. "Please tell me you have answers."

"I don't know where she is, but I can make some educated guesses," Murphy said. "I'm just about to get on a plane. I'll brief you when I land."

Daniel resumed his night patrol of the lower half of Central Park and the busy streets surrounding it. A measure of hope rushed through him. If Murphy wasn't sure he could track Elise down, he would have said so.

At least something was going right, which was more than he could say for this current crisis. The past two days had taken their toll on him. The outbreak in New York was very quickly spreading and escalating out of control.

The team who had been dispatched to monitor new Wildfire cases had sought help. They were unable to keep up with the outbreak and containment without exposing themselves. To make matters worse, the Human authorities had issued a nationwide first-responders alert for an Ebola outbreak. There was no doubt in his mind the disease was the result of Wildfire.

Besides all the Human deaths, local unaligned and rogue Werewolves, who had ignored the warnings, were now infected and terrorizing the streets. The danger increased at night when, in their virus-ridden state, their inner wolves sought comfort from the moon. So far, the progression of the virus, both within the Human and Werewolf races, was isolated to New York, San Diego, and San Francisco, with the majority of the victims in and around New York City.

While they couldn't intervene, or show their hand with the Humans that had succumbed to the deadly drug, they needed to address the outbreak within their own community. He and his team had dealt with the situation the only way they could, quickly, quietly, and efficiently. The infected Werewolves gravitated to either Central Park or to the abandoned warehouses in the Downtown area. He had called in reinforcements from the nearest packs to patrol the areas, locate, and apprehend the victims before they ran the risk of exposure.

Each infected Werewolf was given the same choice: a quick, merciful death; or a painful, prolonged one under guard and lock-up. The ones with a measure of sanity remaining chose the first option.

The destruction of his brother and sister Werewolves was taking its toll, and the weight had become heavy on his conscience. With each death, he found himself picturing a set of expressive blue eyes that helped him focus and deal with the burden that increased with each life he was forced to cut short.

A gust of wind blew around his legs. Daniel stiffened. *Werewolf.* The breeze lifted higher and the scent magnified. *Two Werewolves.*

He followed the scent, confident that his upwind position would keep his presence undetected. He headed toward the south-west of the park and skidded to a halt when he reached a bridge along the tree line near Central Park West. Across the road, leaning against a large boxed planter, were two burly Werewolves. From their stance, they were waiting for someone or something.

Instinct kicked in and Daniel hid among the trees. The wind had again changed direction and died down. While it still wasn't in their favor, he wasn't taking any chances.

Sirens blared over the busy street noise, quickly followed by flashes of red and blue. Daniel watched from his vantage point as police and paramedics swarmed into the building where the Werewolves were stationed. They stood up and stared at the door the police had entered. The door opened and an elderly man in an ill-fitting suit stepped out. From this distance, without the wind in his favor, Daniel couldn't tell if he was Human or Werewolf, but when his eyes rested on the elderly man's companion, every hair on his body stood to attention. A low growl rumbled within his chest when he recognized the vile creature from his past.

"Fuck!"

She hadn't changed in two hundred years. The cold, dead eyes were as evil and as dark as her soul.

An internal battle waged within him. His wolf erupted and fought for dominance. It wanted blood, and it wanted it now.

His first instinct was to charge across the street and separate Elise's head from the rest of her body. Forcing himself back under control, he pulled his phone out and dialed. "I'm at the bottom end of Central Park. Elise and two, possibly three, Werewolves are here. Bring back-up, we need them alive."

Mindful to keep out of sight, he kept to the shadows and trees along the edge of the park, and followed them. Elise and her escorts turned off the main road and headed west. Twenty minutes later they turned down a small one-way street. Daniel peered around the corner. Satisfied there was no immediate danger, and careful to blend in with the shadows, he turned into the darkened street.

Scaffolding hid a building under reconstruction and took up a large section of the street. The darkness from within the tunnel created by the scaffolding, sent a shiver up his spine. The street was empty. No late-night strollers. No residents hurrying home. No vagabonds, no beggars—no Werewolves. Anywhere else, this lack of movement would not be a cause for alarm. However, this was New York.

He stopped short. Elise and her entourage had vanished into thin air. He sent his current position to his team, and continued down the alley. His experience and instinct kicked in as he peered into the dark corners, and his hearing was attuned to every sound in a range of frequencies. His wolf added its skills to the mix, giving them extra range.

Daniel sniffed the air. They had been there a short time ago. The dim light from an open parking garage spilled into the street, but the overpowering scent of gasoline and diesel hid any other odors. Wary that they may have concealed themselves within the opened building, he headed toward the entranceway. A faint rustle from somewhere behind caught his attention. He swung around in time to see his prey emerge from under the covering of the scaffolding.

How did I miss them?

Elise and the older Werewolf stayed back as her two guards stalked him, converging from two directions.

Daniel crouched to gain the extra strength to attack. His eyes narrowed, and he addressed Elise, who had now stepped out of the shadows. "I see you are still letting others do your dirty work."

A cruel smile spread across her flawless face. "Now, now my dear Daniel, there is no need for me to damage my shoes. They are Louboutin after all."

His eyes darted up and down the small street. He needed to string out the time to allow his team to arrive. They needed all four alive. "I am surprised Matheo isn't here defending his genocidal maniac alpha."

Elise dismissed his taunt with an absent wave. "He is off on a little errand to squash another irritant. One, I suspect that you had something to do with."

He was thrown by her odd turn of phrase.

"I told you the last time we spoke, I would have my revenge, and trust me on this… it will be sweet, and a dish definitely well served cold." Elise's accent became thicker the angrier she got.

No longer able to contain his rage, he snapped. "I'm going to rip out your insides and watch as you slowly die, bitch!"

Elise raised her hand dismissively. "Enough of this chit-chat. I'm bored, and that fucking little Human woman in the restaurant pulled a thread on my dress. It's now a complete mess." Her voice became hard as steel. "Finish him."

The guards advanced.

Daniel crouched, ready to pounce. He assessed the Werewolves and picked a target—the one farthest from Elise. He leaped, catapulting his body toward the surprised man. When he slammed into the Werewolf, they flew into a trash can, spilling the contents across the pavement and onto the street. He landed a punch to the man's face, and his head smashed against the pavement with the force of the blow.

A foot came out of nowhere and kicked Daniel in the face. The other guard had closed the distance. He tasted blood and spun to face his second opponent.

They faced off, circling as they each looked for an advantage. Adrenaline pumped through Daniel's veins as he focused on the man's eyes. His patience paid off when Elise's bodyguard roared and lunged at him.

Daniel smiled, sidestepped the hurtling Werewolf, and slammed him head first into the concrete wall.

The Werewolf was temporarily stunned. Daniel turned his focus on the first guard, who had recovered and was snarling, his lips tightened and his teeth exposed.

The glint of something metallic caught Daniel's attention.

Knife.

The Werewolf was brandishing a knife and tossing it from hand to hand. An overconfident expression told Daniel that the Werewolf knew how to use it. A groan from somewhere behind him let Daniel know that the other guard was coming to.

Thinking his opponent distracted, the Werewolf charged Daniel, arm and knife outstretched, ready to plunge. Again, Daniel sidestepped. The blade swiped across Daniel's arm and left a trail of blood seeping through the torn sleeve.

Daniel gritted his teeth and growled. He'd had enough. He could not wait for the others. In one fluid motion, he reached around and grabbed the wrist holding the weapon. A moment later, he was behind his attacker and raised the Werewolf's hand in a diagonal motion across his body. Daniel drew the knife across one side of the man's neck, to the other. The cut was clean and deep. The severed jugular ejected a torrent of blood and painted the road and sidewalk with the sanguine fluid.

The dying guard dropped to his knees and the warm, metallic tang of blood engulfed the alley. He wrapped his hands around his neck to stop the tsunami of blood pouring from his nearly dead body.

Daniel turned to the second guard, who was slowly rising. He took in the sight of his fallen comrade and panic registered on his face. He advanced on Daniel. Not having learned from his dead friend's actions, he leaped and glided feet-first to knock down Daniel. His body hurtled through the air, and Daniel threw his arm out, and the Werewolf stopped in mid-flight, his head locked in Daniel's bleeding arm.

A quick flick, a dull crack, and the Werewolf's spine was separated from his neck. The body became limp and heavy.

Daniel dropped the body to the ground and stood back. The familiar stench of death rose in the darkness. His chest heaved as he brought his breathing under control. He turned to confront Elise, only to discover her missing. His gaze darted up and down the street for any sign of her.

Fuck!

She was gone, leaving behind two dead guards, and an old Werewolf with unruly white hair.

The old Werewolf stood transfixed to the spot as Daniel advanced on him. He visibly gulped and glanced up and down the deserted street.

Before the older man could flee, Daniel brushed the blood from his arm, and said, "I wouldn't if I were you. She has left you to die."

THIRTY-FOUR

The Road to Hell...

Atlanta, Georgia

Parker exited the temperature-controlled airport and stepped into a hot wave of humid Georgia air. Her blouse melded to her skin as she headed to the taxi stand. Her body adjusted to the ninety-degree heat, and a light sheen of perspiration dotted her forehead. She grabbed the nearest cab, climbed in, and gave directions before she changed her mind. The empty feeling in the pit of her stomach grew, adding to her nervousness.

The mid-afternoon traffic was light as the taxi navigated the thirty-minute drive to Druid Hills. The closer they came to her destination; the tighter her chest became, and her breath grew more erratic with each bump, crossroad, and traffic light they passed.

Breathe in. Breathe out. She repeated the chant as she focused on her mission.

She had researched and analyzed every possible outcome of this meeting. Each resulted in the same ultimate conclusion. The only unknown was when.

Today? Tomorrow? Next Week?

She knew from experience that there would be no choice. They would follow procedure, and procedure dictated... Parker shuddered. She did not even want to think that far ahead. If she did, she might have the taxi driver turn around and head back to the airport.

She focused on her breathing again. *I'm doing this to save lives, to protect my friends, and to keep them safe.* The fact that she would probably never see them again pained her beyond belief. Her heart broke a little more each time Daniel's face crept into her thoughts. He would never forgive her for what she was about to do.

Their relationship, strange and tenuous as it was, would be the one thing she clung to in the undoubtedly harrowing days and months to come. The sound of his voice, his fierce pride and sense of responsibility, and the way he set her on fire with a single look. These memories of him would be the one place she would go in her mind to give her the inner strength she would need to get through this.

By the time the taxi approached the sprawling grounds of CDC's Arlen Specter Headquarters, she was focused, determined, and calm.

She strode into the building and approached the nearest security guard at the reception desk in the large lobby. "Good afternoon, my name is Parker Johnson. I have an appointment with Dr. Petra Baghurst."

The guard signed her in and directed her to a waiting area on the far side of the foyer.

She hid a smile as the molecular biologist she was here to see exited the lift a short while later. Petra Baghurst looked a lot younger in real life than she did on the CDC profiles page. People would be hard pressed to believe she was in her mid-forties. From Parker's investigation, the woman was married to her job, was liked by her team, and never seemed to take a holiday.

Dr. Baghurst pushed her hands into the pockets of her white lab coat and frowned. The doctor's eye's darted around the lobby.

She understood exactly why Dr. Baghurst looked confused.

To ensure that she could meet with the doctor in charge of the outbreak, Parker had hacked the team leader's computer, scheduled a meeting in her diary, and placed a couple of fictitious emails in her inbox. The emails implied that they had met before.

The doctor must have been mildly shocked when checking her calendar for that morning to find she had an appointment with a drug representative she couldn't remember scheduling.

She drew in a deep breath and decided to put the doctor out of her misery. "Dr. Baghurst, Parker Johnson. Pleased to meet you."

Dr. Baghurst schooled her confused expression and led Parker to a meeting room. The CDC doctor closed the door and took a seat across the table from Parker. "So, tell me, Ms. Johnson, how may I help you?"

Parker smiled warmly. "Actually, I am here to help you." She passed a sheet of paper across the table, along with her business card.

The doctor hesitated before picking it up and studying the page. "What am I looking at?"

"The one thing that all of the victims of the virus you are investigating have in common."

Dr. Baghurst looked up from the page. "I beg your pardon?"

She leaned forward and placed her arms on the table. "The virus is targeting only those with that protein, in that particular gene."

Dr. Baghurst narrowed her eyes. "Which drug company did you say you worked for?"

"Well, there might have been a little bit of miscommunication." She smiled calmly even though her insides felt like she was sinking into quicksand. "My company consults with a number of organizations on their IT security needs. By chance, I stumbled on some information I thought you should be privy to."

"And where exactly did you find this information?"

"I'm sorry. I can't tell you that."

Dr. Baghurst stood. She was angry. "Look Ms…" She glanced down at the business card. "Johnson, or whatever your name is. I don't have time for conversations like this. They are a waste of my—"

She broke in before the doctor could complete her sentence. "You're currently leading a team investigating an outbreak of a deadly and unknown virus. The results are showing Adenovirus 1, also known as CDV-1, a disease that until recently only affected canines. The infected patients are exhibiting the same symptoms as Ebola, but none of the tests are showing the typical markers. So far, the mortality rate is one hundred percent. You have no clue what's causing it, how it's being spread, or what it is." Parker took a breath. "Oh, and Dr. Kwong is recently engaged, and you took her out to celebrate at the new sushi place down the road."

The doctor gaped at Parker.

"Do you need me to go on?"

Dr. Baghurst sank into the chair.

"As I said before, my company ensures the safety of our client's firewalls and information. We make our clients unhackable. It wasn't too hard for me to get past the CDC firewalls."

Dr Baghurst's eyes shifted back to the slip of paper. She looked up and waved it in the air. "Okay, let's just say I believe you, and that you're not a complete nut case. How did you come by this?"

"As I said before, I can't tell you that."

"Then why are you coming forward with this information?"

It was Parker's turn to consider her next answer. She leaned back in her chair and looked straight at Dr. Baghurst. "Because I can't just stand back and watch countless people die. It's only going to get worse."

Dr. Baghurst crossed her arms over her chest and leaned back in her chair. "And you know this how?"

She reached into her bag and placed two bottles of carbonated colas, a range of chewing gum, and other manufactured food on the table between them. "A virus has been combined with the artificial caffeine in some of these products. That is how the disease is being transmitted."

Dr. Baghurst's brows rose high on her forehead. "Wait...so you're telling me this is a virus that has been deliberately released into an unsuspecting public? And a man-made one at that?"

Disbelief was evident in the older woman's posture as well as tone.

She nodded. "Yes, that is exactly what I am telling you."

The doctor reached for one of the bottles. "You do understand the ramifications of what you are saying if it's true?"

"Dr. Baghurst, I have no intention of hiding. I've worked with the FBI enough over the years to understand what will happen next." Parker counted on her fingers. "One: you'll go back to your lab and discover what I said is true. Two: you'll also discover that the gene and the protein is one you weren't aware of before. It's one that, had you found it, would have been considered junk DNA. You will also find evidence of the virus in some, if not all, of these." She gestured to the items on the table and then looked directly at Dr. Baghurst. "And three: you'll have no choice but to notify Homeland Security, and they will take me into custody."

Parker's heart pounded in her chest as she pulled out a small blue book from her purse and handed it across the table.

This was her last chance to convince the doctor she was sincere. "That's my passport. I have no intention of running, and I have nothing to hide. Despite what you may think, I'm not involved. However, I can't divulge how I came by this information. You have my business card, which you can hand over to the authorities once you have confirmed what I have just told you. But I implore you to get the contaminated food off the shelves as soon as possible."

Dr Baghurst picked up Parker's passport and flicked through it absently. "You do realize this will be considered an act of terrorism? They will press you to find your source...and there is no amendment that can protect you."

Parker contemplated the question. She met the doctor's gaze head on. "What's worse? I don't say anything and countless innocent lives are taken, or I pass on what I know, and suffer the consequences?"

Parker began breathing again the moment the taxi drove away from CDC's headquarters. She rested her head on the seat back and closed her eyes. The meeting had taken a toll on her. She was tired, and her nerves were beyond shattered.

By her calculations, she had twenty-four to forty-eight hours before Homeland Security came knocking. That gave her a limited amount of time to get everything in order. She spent the five-hour flight back to Portland planning the things she would need to do before her arrest. Her personal assets would be seized, but provided she delegated signing authority to her business manager, the company should be safe, and her employee's jobs not at risk.

By the time the plane landed a little after one a.m., she was emotionally and physically exhausted. Rather than going straight home, she headed to the office. The moment she entered the reception area, a wall of heat broke her stride.

Shit. The AC's out again.

The hot air that filled her lungs made it difficult to breathe. Beth's flowers, still sitting behind reception were now dead, wilted from the heat and lack of water.

Beth, why didn't you take them home? You knew they wouldn't last the weekend here.

When she headed toward the back of the floor, an unpleasant odor wafted through the office. She scrunched her nose at the sharpness and her skin became clammy.

Her lips set into a grim line. *Someone's left their damn food out, and the heat's spoiled it.* She sniffed, trying to identify it. *Whatever it is, it's rancid.*

She wandered down the hallway toward the break room. The closer she got to the darkened room, the surer she was of her guess. The stench grew stronger with each step. She swept a hand across her forehead to wipe off the sweat. "How many times do I need to get that damn AC fixed?"

She reached for the light switch in the darkened room. The fluorescent bulbs crackled and flickered into life. She searched the room for the rotting food, and froze. Denial gave way to horror as a bone chilling fear rushed through her body and threatened to overwhelm her.

"No!" ripped from her throat when her muscles relaxed enough to allow movement.

Holding back a scream, she managed a single step forward before she began to shake uncontrollably as her mind registered the gruesome scene. The overpowering stench assailed her nostrils and bile rose in her throat. The hairs on the back of her neck bristled, and she resisted the urge to flee. Pushing the vomit that threatened to erupt from the very depths of her stomach back down, she ran to the middle of the room, dropped to her knees, and reached for the broken and bloodied body.

She pulled the woman into her arms. "Beth, Beth, wake up." Her voice cracked and she realized Beth's body was limp and cold.

Beth's face was unrecognizable, her cheeks purple and swollen. Deep lacerations covered her face and upper body, and blood matted her hair.

She rocked Beth in her arms and sobbed. Her shoulders jolted her body and each cry of despair threatened to crush her heart and lungs.

Her empty gaze took in the rest of the room. Splatters of blood coated the walls. Tables were overturned. Broken glass and crockery was haphazardly strewn across the room. A second body lay in the far corner against a wall like a limp, broken doll. The man's head lay at an odd angle, and his face was hidden from view. His feet wore her bodyguard's trademark sneakers.

"Oh no, Trevor."

She was losing what was left of her tenuous hold on reality, but she summoned all her strength and gently placed Beth on the floor. Tears streamed down her cheeks and dropped onto the face below, muddying the clotting blood. She needed a phone. She needed help. She needed her friend to be alive.

Parker focused on the three-digit number she needed to dial, turned, and stopped short. Her heart lurched in her chest. Fear rooted her to the spot and her legs almost gave way.

Cruel, unbalanced eyes locked with hers. "I've been waiting for you, Bella. Do you like my handiwork?"

THIRTY-FIVE

Prisoner

Middlemarch Estate

Parker's hearing returned before her other senses. From somewhere nearby someone grunted and then shuffled. A moment later a high-pitched scream cut through the silence. While it wasn't anywhere near, it was close enough to hear the terror in the woman's voice, and she became more aware of her surroundings. *Where am I?*

Something was wrong. She couldn't move. She couldn't speak.

Parker attempted to fight through the haze that had settled in her brain like a thick fog on a winter's morning. A dull pain pulsed throughout her body, increasing in intensity until it was a raging torrent threatening to force her back under. She pushed away the acute throbbing pain that threatened to drown her, and focused on her arms. After what seemed an eternity, she felt movement in her fingers, followed by her hand, and eventually down through her limbs and to the remainder of her body.

The stone floor she lay on was cold, damp, and uneven. An agonizing groan boiled up from within her, echoing off the walls and through the chamber, but she forced her body into an upright position and pushed the dizziness aside. With more effort than it would normally take, she forced open her eyes, only to discover that her vision was limited. She touched a hand to her face and was shocked to discover the entire right side swollen, her eye socket tender, and her eyelid almost shut.

Her throat burned when she tried to speak, and she winced with the additional pain. "Jesus Christ, where am I?"

Blood? Why am I tasting blood?

She tentatively touched her lip to discover it, too, was swollen. The last of the mist cleared and her memory returned in full force.

Matheo.

Her struggle to escape.

His cruel and soulless eyes as he beat her unconscious.

She suppressed the panic building within her, before she completely broke down. Her self-preservation kicked in, and she brought her breathing under control.

I need to get out of here.

She looked around. Towering stone walls merged seamlessly with the floor. A small opening high up allowed a fraction of light to enter the room. Shadows danced and settled in areas the sun was unable to breach. She strained her eyes and her pulse raced—shackles hung from metal rings, which were, in turn, bolted to the walls.

"Where the hell am I?

"You got it right the first time. You're in hell."

Parker hauled in a breath and scrambled backward, away from the voice that had sprung from a darkened corner of the chamber.

The faceless voice rushed to placate her. "I am sorry, I did not mean to scare you."

She halted her retreat and considered her next move—this could be a trap. Her labored pants, and the quiet, even breathing of her companion, were the only things breaking the uneasy silence.

The other prisoner broke the impasse. "My name is Joséphine."

The woman's voice was soft, with a melodic quality to it. Her French accent was well defined. "And, may I ask, with whom I am sharing this five-star suite?"

There was something in the tone of her voice that encouraged Parker to relax. "Um, Parker. Parker Johnson." Her voice cracked under the strain.

She crept closer to the shadowed prisoner. The woman, also bruised and battered, was securely chained to the wall. Her hands and arms were outstretched, each arm held in place by a shackle. The woman's long blond hair was matted and dirty. Her blood-soaked clothes were torn, revealing scars in varying degrees of healing.

Parker's concern overrode her sense of danger. "Are you okay?" Anxiety sat heavily on her chest as she pulled at the woman's shackles, attempting to pry them away from the wall.

"Don't worry. It looks worse than it is. I wouldn't bother." Joséphine nodded toward the rusty cuffs "Unless you have the key?"

She sat back, resting on her knees, and contemplated her next step.

"So," Joséphine said. "Who did you get on the wrong side of?"

Parker shuddered—even thinking about him made her skin crawl. "Matheo. You?"

"Elise." She craned her head and sniffed the air. "You are Human."

Parker was still unsure of whether she could trust the chained woman. "And you're…not."

Joséphine's surprise turned to curiosity, and she narrowed her eyes. "They usually put the Humans in the other prison buildings. What makes you so special?"

She gave an uneasy shrug and evaded the question by asking one of her own. "Why are you locked up?"

She saw the conflict warring within the female Werewolf's eyes.

"I know more about your community than you might realize."

Silence hung over the room until Joséphine finally spoke. "Our alpha has been here too long. I came here to bring her back." She hesitated, before continuing. "It turns out that she was up to something quite... uhhh... unexpected. Something I didn't agree with."

"You mean you found out your precious alpha was committing genocide?" Parker's tone was laced with bitterness, the memory of the deaths she had witnessed still fresh in her mind.

Joséphine avoided looking at Parker and focused on the stone floor. "Be that as it may, I was ready to return home to inform the elders of what she had been up to. Not all of us believe in the purity of the We—" She stopped and tilted her head. "Go back to where they left you," she said. "Someone is coming."

She scrambled back to the spot where she had awoken, lay on the ground, feigning sleep, and attempted to control her erratic breathing.

The sound of a key pushing into an iron lock echoed throughout the chamber. Her stomach lurched as the door swung open. Feeling an unknown presence near her, she held her breath, too scared to open her eyes. Someone kicked at her ribs and her breath came out in a whoosh when blinding pain shot through her body.

She cried out as a hand grabbed a fistful of her hair and dragged her up. Bile rose up from the pit of her stomach into her mouth when she came face to face with Matheo. His malicious grin brought her to a new level of terror, and her entire body shook uncontrollably.

"Now, Bella, you weren't pretending, were you?"

She remained silent, the agony so intense it removed her ability to speak.

His warm, musty breath blasted across her swollen face, and his expression turned lecherous. "No matter. Once my alpha has finished with you, that's when my fun will begin."

She attempted to pry his fingers from her hair. "I'd die before I let you near me, you sack of shit."

With a roar, Matheo threw her against the nearest wall.

He snarled, and his body shook with anger. "The only thing keeping you alive is the information Alpha Lauzon wants from you. I will make you pay for making a fool out of me."

"Well, you'd better not kill her, then," Joséphine said. "The alpha would be most displeased—and we all know what happens when she's not happy."

Matheo spat at Joséphine and stormed out the door.

Parker huddled in a ball and rocked back and forth, not wanting to give Matheo the satisfaction of knowing the extent of her pain.

Chains clanked as Joséphine pulled against her restraints. "Are you okay?"

She took a deep breath. "Give me a moment." Her voice shook with the effort to speak.

Joséphine swore under her breath. "I think you had better tell me how you came to be involved in this mess."

THIRTY-SIX

Who's Going To Tell Him?

Payette, Idaho

The fear that settled over Morgan on learning of Parker's disappearance was the feeling of another child taken from him. It ripped into his chest and threatened to stifle the very air he breathed.

He ended the call and stared at a small beetle crawling up a blade of grass at his feet. He was getting too old. For over half a millennia he had led his pack, each member as precious to him as the next. In the absence of his own flesh and blood, they were his children, and he protected them with everything he had.

His long-dead son sprung to the forefront of his mind, and an age-old pain clutched at his chest. He remembered the moment he was told of the death of his only child. Hundreds of years later, the feeling was still as painful, and the memory remained vivid.

He shook himself and headed back into the house. He needed to determine exactly what had happened in Portland.

It did not take long before he obtained all the information the local police had, as well as more pertinent details from Jay and Zeke. He pieced together everything he needed to know and more that he did not.

Exhausted, he left an equally drained Clara to deal with notifying the pack, and returned to his office. An empty feeling settled in the pit of his stomach. Daniel would need to be informed. Picking up the phone, he was almost relieved when the phone went straight to voicemail.

He would talk to the Alpha Commander later.

Morgan flicked through his contact's list to find Jessica's number.

Jessica brought Simon and Alice together, and Morgan broke the news to them. From the silence at the other end of the conference call, they were in as much shock as him.

"Do we know if she is still alive?" Simon said.

"The police found blood not belonging to either of the known victims," he said. "But there wasn't enough to think she was bleeding profusely."

"And they are sure she was there?"

This time Alice asked the question.

His shoulders slumped. "Her mobile, laptop, and handbag were found in the office." They all knew Parker did not go anywhere without her computer.

"Are you sure it was Matheo?" Simon said.

"Yes." He took a deep breath. They wouldn't like what he was about to tell them. "The reception is under video surveillance. Jay got to it before the police did. I will have Zeke send it through to you. It's a little hard to watch."

He heard a sharp intake of breath, followed by an involuntary whimper.

"When are you expecting Daniel to return, Simon?" he said.

"Sometime in the next few hours."

He frowned. "Shouldn't he be back already?"

Simon let out a disagreeable growl. "Fridericks is proving to be more trouble than he's worth, so the trip back by road is taking longer. His phone battery died so we are out of contact." He paused. "Who's going to tell him?"

An uncomfortable silence descended. No one was willing to accept the daunting task.

"You know he needs to be told before it's plastered across all the news channels," he said.

"I'll tell him," Jessica said. She let out a slow breath. "He needs to hear it from me."

Morgan sighed. "I agree. I'd like a word with you. Alone."

A short silence followed as Simon and Alice quietly filed out of the room.

"How do you think he's going to take it?" he said.

"That's the bit I am worried about." Jessica hesitated. "My brother has finally found someone he has a connection to. Parker may not be his mate, but sometimes, when he thinks no one is looking and his guard comes down...The way he looks at her, it takes my breath away. He looks—"

His voice was somber and reflective as he finished Jessica's sentence. "Like he has found something he has been searching for all his life?"

"You've seen it, too?"

"For the briefest of moments, but yes, I have. I do not envy your position."

The seconds ticked by as they contemplated the task ahead. They needed a plan before it was too late.

"If you don't mind my asking, how did Clara take it?"

He glanced over at the photo of Clara on his desk and his heart ached. He hated to see her in pain, and the possible loss of Parker was digging up old wounds. "After she got over the initial shock, anger set in. She's so enraged she wants to take on Elise herself. But that's not the worst of it." He paused. "I have a lynch mob at the Pack House ready to explode. Parker has many friends here, and they all want a piece of Elise and her pack."

He cleared his throat, his voice steely and determined. "If Saldulf wants war, it's on its way."

***

Forty-eight hours on the road with a maniacal Werewolf was taking its toll on Daniel. He was hungry, irritated, and tired.

Ray growled from the back of the SUV. "Shut up, old man, before I shut it for you."

Daniel took a deep, calming breath. The trip hadn't been easy on his chief enforcer, either. They had seen too much death. To be in the same vehicle with the architect of the virus and allow him to live was a strain for both he and Ray. But they needed Elise, and that meant keeping Fridericks alive. For now.

He focused on the road and attempted, yet again, to ignore the incessant ramblings from the back seat. If they did not need the information locked inside the scientist's brain, they would have strangled him, and left him for dead on the side of the road well before they had cleared the New York City limits.

Flying the obnoxious man back to Colorado was out of the question. Their only option was to drive. It had been the longest two days of his very long life—all he wanted right now was a hot shower, a decent meal, some sleep—and Parker beside him. The endless miles of inactivity had given him the time to sift through recent events, and the fact he couldn't get hold of Parker before his phone battery went dead only made it worse.

The truth was, he missed her. He missed the way she would defiantly challenge him when she disagreed with him. He missed the simple act of talking to her, the way she could be serious one moment and teasing the next, or how she made him feel every time she walked into a room. He wasn't sure at what point she had become a necessary part of his life, but no matter how much he resisted, he could no longer deny the emotions that this one little Human elicited.

The question was, what did he mean to her?

There was no denying she was physically attracted to him. Her unbridled passion each time they had touched—each time they had kissed—told him she was as affected by him as he was by her.

While it may be wrong, while there may be no future for them, he no longer had the strength to stay away from her.

Maybe Morgan is right. I'll take a trip to Portland and try this dating thing.

About time, his exasperated wolf broke in.

Shut up.

He focused on the last one-hundred mile stretch to Colorado.

Four hours later, Simon and a few of Ray's enforcers met them as he drove the SUV into the compound.

Before he had a chance to grab the prisoner from the back seat, Simon pulled him aside. "Jessica needs to see you. She's waiting for you in your office."

"I'll head up there once I make sure he's locked up tight."

Simon stood his ground. "I'll do it. She really needs to see you."

Daniel frowned at his beta's odd behavior, but passed the prisoner into Simon's custody and headed to his home. He walked into his office and discovered Jessica pacing up and down the length of the room. Her eyes were red, and her expression was haunted.

His stomach plummeted. "What's going on? Is Mandy alright?"

"She's fine." Jessica's voice cracked.

Her next words crumbled the world around him.

***

"Daniel, did you hear what I just said?" Jessica said.

His reaction wasn't what she had expected, and she was anxious. He hadn't spoken a word throughout her recount of Parker's abduction. In fact, her brother hadn't moved. His eyes were blank, not giving any indication of what was going on in his mind. He looked down at her as if he were a statue. She attempted to reach out to him telepathically, only to come up against a wall. Cold—Thick—Impenetrable.

She tugged on his arm. "Daniel, you're scaring me. Stop being a Bruno, say something."

His face gave an almost undetectable twitch.

"Leave me."

The words were spoken so quietly she almost missed it.

"But Daniel—"

His sudden roar sent chills through her bones. "I said, go!"

She retreated and closed the door behind her. Breaking glass shattered the silence behind the locked door. Dull thuds, then the distinct sound of wood cracking, followed.

Her tears flowed freely, and she skedaddled out of the house in search of her mate. She needed the safety of his arms to shield her from the devastation that threatened to overwhelm the entire pack.

She did not need to go far. Ray was waiting for her outside. By the look of his peepers, someone had already chin wagged. She threw herself into his embrace and allowed her emotions to consume her until she was pooped. When she finally came up for air, other pack members had gathered. All silent, all waiting expectantly for something—anything—to happen.

Her brows furrowed, and Ray pulled her closer. "The pack protects their own. If there is a chance to get her back, even the slightest chance, we'll do it together."

She flinched as a blood thirsty howl resounded from within the house.

THIRTY-SEVEN

Way To Bury The Lead

Middlemarch Estate

The sound of scraping metal woke Parker from a restless sleep. Quickly scurrying into the corner, she brought her knees up to her chest and hugged her legs tight. After four days rotting in this prison, she had memorized the routine.

Each morning three beefy guards entered the cell. A tray of food and a hot drink was placed near Joséphine, but out of arm's length. She often wondered why none of them would get any closer to the chained woman. A bottle of water and a granola bar would then be tossed to her. If she was lucky, they would leave. If she wasn't, one, if not all three, would take turns kicking or hitting her, on Matheo's orders.

Joséphine would scream out for them to stop, cursing them the entire time.

Once satisfied, they would leave. The door would be locked, and the chains keeping Joséphine in place against the wall would be loosened from a distance. Joséphine would be able to stand, walk around, relieve herself, and eat her meal. After a while, they tightened the chains again.

The same process was repeated at the end of the day.

Today was a good day. She was left in peace. Be that as it may, she did not think her body could take much more.

They released Josephine from the chains. "How are your ribs?"

Parker let her legs unfurl from her chest and winced. Her brutalized insides were on fire. She ran the back of her hand across her sweaty brow. "Sore."

"Well," Joséphine said, "if they look anything like the rest of you, they are not in good shape. How's your fever?"

She fought the effort it was taking to stay focused. "Still there, but nothing I can't cope with."

Joséphine inspected the tray of food before she picked it up, sat down near Parker, and placed it between them.

"I hope you like eggs," she said, "because I hate them."

Joséphine had insisted on sharing her meals. She initially resisted, concerned that the woman would be punished. Joséphine laughed the idea off as nonsense and refused to eat unless she did as well.

Hunger had finally won out, and she gave in.

"When do you think Elise will be back?" she said in a cracked and hoarse voice.

Joséphine shrugged. "Today? Tomorrow? The day after? Who knows with the alpha. She is a law unto herself."

Elise had not made an appearance in the five days she's been imprisoned. This fact alone kept her hopes up. The longer the alpha stayed away, the more chance she had of finding a way to escape. While she hoped Daniel, Morgan, and the others were looking for her, she couldn't bank on it. Would Daniel be so angry with her for going to the CDC that he wouldn't bother searching? And even if he did, how would he find her? In all the time they'd been searching for Elise, they hadn't found a single clue to her hideout.

She winced when she moved, and pain shot through her chest. If she did not get out of here soon, she was not getting out at all. The pain throughout her body was getting worse each day, and the little food she was consuming wasn't enough to sustain her body while it struggled to repair itself.

They finished their meal, relieved themselves, and washed up in a tiny basin before the guards returned to secure Joséphine, and remove the tray.

Although the day proceeded as it had every other day, Parker's senses were more on edge than ever. Her skin prickled, and she wasn't surprised when the door swung open mid-afternoon. Armed guards, dressed from head to toe in black, dragged her and Joséphine out of the cell.

The light from the bright afternoon sun blinded her when they stepped out of the building. A sharp pain shot through her body, and the sudden movement made her dizzy. At least two more buildings, similar to the one she had been held in, stood nearby. The barrel of a gun was thrust into her back, sending shooting pains through her chest. When the gun prodded her a second time, she limped in the direction she was pushed.

"You okay?" Joséphine said.

Parker nodded and focused on staying upright.

Joséphine's hands had been restrained behind her back, while shackles and chains held her wrists together. She had five minders herding her toward God knew where.

Why the hell do they have so many guards on her?

They were steered up a set of stone steps and dumped on a large outdoor patio attached to one of the largest manor houses she had ever seen.

She was pushed to her knees. The sudden motion knocked the wind out of her, and she struggled to breathe. She looked up and gasped.

Matheo stood next to an elegantly dressed woman. Everything about the woman screamed power, from the designer clothes and shoes, to the chic but understated jewelry.

The woman stared at her with a face of evil. Never before had Parker experienced such innate fear and terror. She swallowed the bile, but she wasn't strong enough. Her stomach contracted so violently she bent over double. What little food she had consumed that morning flew to the ground in chunks. She sank to her knees and retched until only clear fluid came up. Her throat felt sore from the acid that was layering it, and her mouth tasted of vomit.

Once her body stopped convulsing, she looked up, but immediately regretted it. Cold, soulless eyes glared back at her. Next to Elise, Matheo was nothing.

Elise's gaze moved from her to Joséphine, and Parker let out her breath.

Joséphine guards pushed her forward just as the alpha walked over to her. Something wasn't right. She made a move toward her new friend, but strong hands locked her in place before she managed a step.

Elise stood over the Joséphine, who had been pushed to her knees. Elise's icy smile did not reach her eyes, and a sneer distorted her mouth as she looked down on Joséphine.

Parker watched in awe as Joséphine looked up at Elise, and raised her chin in defiance.

"Hello, mother."

THIRTY-EIGHT

Plans

Portland, Oregon

Simon stormed into Jay and Zeke's office. "That bastard, Matheo, wrecked her house. No room was left untouched."

"We know," Clara said. She nodded toward the two uniformed police officers sitting across from her. "Alan and Mike were just filling us in on what they know."

He nodded to the two Werewolves and scanned the room to see who else had arrived. With little time to set up somewhere for them to meet and plan, they had taken over Zeke and Jay's office, housed in a separate building from Parker's main business. Now it was designated the war room.

Both Jay and Zeke were huddled together, focused on something on a laptop Zeke held. From their haggard expression and red-rimmed eyes, they weren't taking Parker's abduction well. Not that any of them were. But the two computer geeks were like rudderless ships without her.

He let out a long breath and relaxed. At least he wasn't the last to arrive. There were still two, no three missing. Daniel and Morgan hadn't returned from picking up Murphy O'Neill from the airport.

Simon took a seat near Kyle.

"Have you met him?" Kyle said.

He shook his head. "Nope."

Kyle frowned and leaned closer. "Do you know why he's coming here?"

When he declined to comment, Kyle lowered his voice. "You knew? Why didn't you tell me?"

"Need to know West Life, need to—" Simon's ears pricked at a noise outside. The alphas were approaching. Morgan was the first to enter and immediately headed over to Clara.

Simon kept his attention on the door. What did O'Neill look like? All he knew was the Werewolf had freaky eyes. He did not need to wait long. Daniel strode through the entrance, very quickly followed by an imposing man.

Similar in height and build to Daniel, the new arrival could easily have been mistaken for an alpha. From his stance and demeanor, he did not defer to anyone and made no apologies for it.

Murphy O'Neill cased the room with eyes as black as night, and he took up a position away from those gathered.

Daniel cleared his throat and addressed the room. "Most of you won't be aware that I sent Murphy to Europe to track down the Sandulf pack."

As expected, surprise erupted across the room, and questions were fired in quick succession. Simon, already aware of Murphy's assignment, stayed quiet.

Daniel held up his hand for silence. "It was on a need to know basis. I kept his mission quiet to prevent Elise from finding out."

A low murmur spread through the room, and all eyes swung to the imposing man. His expression was guarded and inscrutable. No one spoke as the stone-faced Werewolf came to stand beside Daniel.

"I found them in a small village near Saint Diè," Murphy said. His voice was deep and gruff.

Simon listened intently as O'Neill reported back to the group on his findings.

O'Neill's many years of experience working with the FBI as a consulting profiler was evident in the efficient way he delivered the information.

"Their numbers have dwindled over the years, with many of the younger members choosing to join other packs. Elise and the upper guard first left about twenty years ago."

Simon gulped. So the Sandulf Alpha had been resident in the US for two decades, and the other packs had been oblivious to it.

"They would stay away for months before returning. In the last two years, Elise has only returned for a few days at a time, but she didn't abdicate her position, and the ones who remained were too scared to bring it up."

"Who is running the pack when she's not there?" Simon said.

"In her absence, her daughter, Joséphine."

He hauled in his breath. "Daughter? Who had the misfortune to be mated to that witch?"

Murphy shrugged. "That, no one was willing to discuss with me." He continued to relay his findings. "A few months ago, Joséphine left the pack to get her mother to either return or pass control to someone else. The last they heard, she had tracked Elise down. Everything went quiet after that." His expression, as if chiseled into his striking features, hadn't varied while he spoke.

"Do they know where Joséphine found her or how?" Daniel said.

Murphy shook his head. "No, Joséphine never told anyone her location. I find it interesting that the pack is more concerned with Joséphine's loss than that of their MIA alpha."

Before anyone could voice a question, Daniel addressed the two police officers. "What's the latest development with the police?"

The older of the two spoke up. "Right now, the detectives are going on the assumption that Parker was abducted. They have no idea who the assailant was or why she or the others were targeted. They are looking into her government contracts to see if there is a possibility someone wants access to information she might have. There is no exposure for us at this point."

Daniel's questioning moved to Jay. "What about her other employees?"

"They are pretty shaken up. The two that found the bodies had to be sedated, and the rest are a bit lost. The building is still a crime scene, so no one has been able to get in, and they don't know whether to start looking for other jobs or not."

A muscle twitched in Daniel's jaw. He turned to Simon. "I want a line of credit for her business. Make sure all financial commitments are met and keep the payroll going."

He nodded.

Daniel walked the short distance to the whiteboard. Parker's distinctive writing took up half of the board. He cleared his throat and turned around. His expression was as hard and determined as his voice. "Our primary focus is to get Parker home."

"I am sure all your first responder teams will have told you, there is a nationwide Ebola panic. The authorities are working on the assumption of bioterrorism," Murphy said. He had taken up position at the back of the room.

"Murphy's right," Daniel said. "We need to tread lightly. As far as I am aware, Homeland Security is pointing the finger offshore. But it doesn't help the fact that right now we are fighting this from all angles. Once we get Parker back, we need to work out a plan to contain this. The hospitals are starting to fill up with victims, and that will only result in more public panic."

"How do we begin to work out where he has taken her?" Simon said. He closed his eyes and silently finished with, *before it's too late.*

Zeke, who hadn't wanted to let his mentor down, had worked through the night, despite his wolf's howling. The boy was coming apart at the seams and refused to give control over to his wolf. "We hacked into the traffic cams and tracked Matheo north out of the city. But we lost him as soon as he cleared the city limits."

Daniel rubbed his jaw. "Murphy and I are flying back to Colorado to see what we can get out of Elise's scientist. The rest of you stay here, and see if you can pick up Matheo's trail. Be ready to leave as soon as we have a location."

On his way out, Daniel stopped beside O'Neill. The two men stood eye-to-eye. "Thank you," Daniel said.

Simon rested his elbows on his knees and stared at the floor, and took a deep breath. What if they didn't find her alive? He, like the others, had seen the footage from the night Parker was taken. Matheo showed no mercy to either Trevor or Parker's PA. To be honest, he couldn't be sure that Parker was alive when Matheo carried her out the door like a sack of potatoes. He closed his eyes and his chest tightened. For Daniel's sake, he prayed they found her before it was too late.

Kyle tapped his shoulder. "Dude, you heard him, we have a job to do."

Simon cleared his throat and kept his eyes averted. He didn't need for Kyle to see his current emotional state of mind. "Keep your shirt on One Direction. They can't do anything without me. I have the credit cards."

THIRTY-NINE

The Zealot

Nederland, Colorado

Daniel repressed the urge to reach across the table and rip out the man's tongue. He might be a scientific genius, but that did not mean he was sane.

"The impure will be wiped from this earth." Hans chanted his belief like a mantra, banging a fist on the table. "We will no longer be diluted with their tainted blood."

Daniel leaned across the table, his fists clenched and ready to strike. "I don't care what you think, old man. You will tell me where Matheo took Parker Johnson."

"Alpha Lauzon will lead our race to greatness. She is the future of our salvation."

"Enough." Daniel made his way around the table and towered over the Werewolf he had been interrogating most of the afternoon. "Your precious alpha is only leading you to your death."

Hans Fridericks.

His name was the only information Daniel and Murphy had elicited. The elderly man was a zealot, and he had endlessly ranted about how he and Elise were ridding the world of tainted blood. The Werewolf truly believed he was doing their race a service.

What was even more disturbing was his utter dedication to the cause. The madman had boasted that he had killed his Human mate to ensure that purity be maintained. She was dead the moment he realized she was Human. His only regret was that he did not slaughter her and her family in front of Elise. This would have proven his true dedication, loyalty, and commitment to his alpha.

Daniel had called on all his strength not to slay the butcher there and then. The image of Parker, afraid and in danger was the only reason Hans was alive.

He gritted his teeth. "Where is Matheo Dumas?"

No reply.

"Where is your lab?"

Hans shrugged.

"Is there a cure?"

To that, he yawned.

"How do we stop it?"

With each question, Hans would either recommence his rant or laugh. The sound was grating, maniacal, and set his teeth on edge.

At one point, Hans chanted out formulas. To what was anyone's guess.

He reached his snapping point, leaned over the table, grabbed the scientist by his shoulders, and dragged him across the room. He slammed him against the nearest wall. His wolf rose to the surface, and strained to take control, and he fought to keep his most primal instincts from taking over.

"You will tell me where she is, or I will tear you apart, piece by piece, until you beg for me to kill you."

Murphy telepathically interrupted before he tore the scientist's arm from his shoulder. *You won't get answers if he's dead.*

He slung the killer across the room. *Fine.*

Murphy righted Hans's chair and indicated the downed man should sit. "I am sorry about him," he said. "How about you take a seat?"

Hans hesitated, then pulled himself off the floor and made his way to the offered chair. He flinched when he passed Daniel.

"Now, where are our manners?" Murphy said. "You are a guest, and we have been most impolite. You must be thirsty. Would you like some water?"

Hans glared at them suspiciously before nodding.

This better work, Daniel said.

It will.

He stormed out the door. "I'll get some water."

If they had any chance of getting information, they needed to try everything, even good cop, bad cop. He made his way to the other room where a monitor had been set up to observe the interrogation, and watched as Murphy proceeded with the questioning.

Murphy took a seat across the table. "So, Doctor. It is Doctor, isn't it?"

The prisoner, more relaxed now that Daniel had left, nodded.

"I must say, in one way, I am quite impressed with what you've achieved. I don't condone it, but I can appreciate that developing a disease such as this could only be achieved by a genius," Murphy said.

Hans leaned forward. "But you don't understand, it's not a disease, it's a cure."

His blood boiled. How could that madman condone what he had done to his victims? Pain ripped through his chest at the thought of the lost souls; many of them still children.

Murphy leaned forward and lowered his voice. "It must have been difficult for you, developing something of this magnitude. It can't have been easy, especially with Alpha Lauzon breathing down your neck all the time. She's not known for her patience."

Hans shrugged as if his achievements were predestined. "Not really. My alpha purchased a biotech lab years ago. I was always privy to new medical advancements, and my personal lab is kept up-to-date with the latest equipment." He leaned back in his chair with a smug smile etched across his face.

Murphy mimicked the scientist's posture. "It must have been disappointing to have breakthroughs in your work and not be able to share them with your alpha. I can't imagine that she had time for you over the years."

Hans sat up straighter, a haughty, triumphant look on his face. "You couldn't be more wrong. My alpha shares my vision—she was there at every step." He smiled smugly. "She even assisted on some of the procedures."

Murphy held up his hands. "My apologies. I misjudged the relationship you have with your alpha." He pushed his chair back and stood. "You must be hungry. If you'll excuse me, I'll arrange for something to be sent in."

Daniel's eyes widened. *Food? There is no way he's getting anything to eat.*

A moment later, Murphy joined him in the monitor room. They watched Fridericks chant out formulas.

"During World War Two, Elise, Matheo, and a few of the others were working with the Nazis," Murphy said. "They were assisting with the acquisition of art and gold bullion from institutions around Europe. She took far more for herself than she ever handed over to the Germans."

He raised an eyebrow. "Are you telling me she has unlimited funds?"

"Precisely." Murphy nodded toward the screen. "From the conversation with our friend in there, I would say she has her operations nearby. If she's involved with the experimentation, she's not going to want to be far away. They will need access to something big enough to hide prisoners, as well as buildings that could house a small hospital."

He rubbed his jaw. "She would have bought the place twenty years ago when you said she first left the pack."

"That would be my guess," Murphy said.

"Elise always enjoyed the finer things, so I would imagine it would be secluded and palatial." Daniel paused. "This narrows it down, but where do we start looking?"

"She would need to be in the proximity of a reasonably sized city," Murphy said. "But her Werewolves would need to be near a greenbelt for their wolves to run without attracting attention. She would have placed herself a reasonable distance from any of the packs that know her by sight, but close enough that she could maintain tabs on them." Murphy paused for a moment or two. "I suspect somewhere north of the border, in Canada."

Daniel hesitated. The last thing they needed right now was a wild goose chase. "How sure are you?"

Murphy sighed. "This is what I do. I profile madmen and killers—and a killer is a killer irrespective of whether he is Human or Werewolf. Your madman in there wasn't about to give up his god, but he told us what we needed to know."

He continued to assess Murphy, indecision shadowing him for the briefest of moments. His only concern right now was Parker. "Let's get Parker's omegas onto it. They should be able to narrow it down."

"You make it sound like she's their alpha," Murphy said.

His mouth curved upwards in a half smile. "You've obviously never met the woman."

FORTY

A Rose by Any Other Name

Parker's feverish mind took its time absorbing Joséphine's words. Surely, she had heard wrong.

Every part of her body was throbbing, and she was finding it hard to think straight.

Hello Mother. Her mind was like a broken record skipping back over the same two words.

Hello, Mother. Her breath caught.

How was this possible?

Elise swung her gaze from Joséphine to Parker, her face full of scorn. "I see you didn't tell your little cell mate who you are, my dear."

Elise circled her as if she were prey.

Her pulse quickened. *Do not let her see how scared you are.* She squared her shoulders and straightened her back as much as her broken body would allow.

"So, this is the Alliance's little pet." Elise raked her eyes over Parker, and a sardonic laugh escaped her lips. "Can't say I see what the fuss is about."

In two steps, Elise was in front of Parker, her gaze cutting into her like a surgeon's scalpel. "You, my little Human, have disrupted my plans and upset my beta. Poor Matheo, all he can think about is paying you back for making a fool out of him."

Parker locked eyes with Elise, and a jolt ran through her body. Her conscious mind begged for her to look away before she was unable to escape the pure evil reflected in the depths of the psychotic woman's eyes. She forced herself to stay strong and continued to stare at Elise.

Elise raised a perfectly shaped eyebrow. "Oh look, the little Human thinks she's going to be rescued."

Parker did not move. Instead, she fought to bring her emotions under control. Her current state of mind was giving Elise too much ammunition.

The Sandulf Alpha laughed, a cruel and cutting sound that grated on Parker's nerves. "She actually believes that Morgan and his silly Alliance are coming for her."

Elise's laugh halted. She peered closely at Parker, her eyes moving from surprise to suspicion. "Not Morgan..." Her tone was curious and her eyes narrowed. "The Alpha Commander, perhaps?"

Parker winced and Elise smiled.

"How interesting..." Elise murmured as she stared at Parker. "You and Daniel..."

Elise stepped back and digested the information. From the sly gleam in her eye, she was triumphant in this new knowledge. "The great and almighty Alpha Commander has a Human plaything." She sauntered to a nearby table and poured herself a drink.

Her heart raced. She knew Elise was calculating how she could take advantage of the information.

"It's a pity you aren't his mate. I would have so much more fun destroying him by killing you." Elise shrugged. "No matter, a plaything is the next best catch, I suppose."

Matheo, who had been listening in horror, could no longer hold himself back. "But my alpha, you said I could do with her as I wished once you saw h—"

"Silence!" Elise swung around to her beta. "We may need her as leverage… or bait. I haven't yet decided."

Matheo cast his eyes downward and took a step backward. "Yes, my alpha."

A chill ran up and down Parker's spine as Matheo hurled a look of pure hatred in her direction. She had no doubt he would try to find a way to get around Elise's directive.

Elise's attention returned to Joséphine. "And as for you, my dear, have you come to your senses yet?"

Joséphine looked up at her mother. Her eyes shone pure contempt. "I will never join your cause, Mother. When the Elders hear of what you have been up to, you will be made to pay for your crimes."

Elise stared at the disheveled female Werewolf in silence.

Parker tensed, not sure how the standoff would play out.

Elise dusted a nonexistent speck of dust from her sleeve. "You will join me, my dear. Your choice is a simple one. Rule with me, or die." She spun on her heels and waved a hand at the guards. "Take them from my sight."

Matheo hauled Parker off the ground. She let out a scream at the jolt of pain that ripped through her body. He pushed her toward the prison building and lowered his head to her ear. His raspy breath sent a ripple of fear through her body. "I am coming for you, Bella."

FORTY-ONE

Where is the Cavalry?

Middlemarch Estate

Parker couldn't get Matheo's words out of her head. *"I am coming for you, Bella."* Her doomsday clock had just moved closer to midnight.

The guards hadn't been gone two minutes when Matheo entered their dungeon with a vicious sneer on his face. He ignored Joséphine and stalked over to Parker. She edged backward until her back hit the cold wall.

Hate spewed from his eyes like daggers. "Don't think I have forgotten that you owe me, Bella. I want to see what's so special about you that an alpha would lower himself." His body pressed against hers. His hand dropped from her shoulder, reached into her shirt, and squeezed her tender breast. Matheo's tongue hung over his lower lip. "If I can't kill you, I am going to make sure you wish you were dead."

He was so close, his musty breath fanned her face. She flinched and cried out as his hands roamed over her bruised body. She attempted to push him away, but she did not have the strength in her weakened state. She closed her eyes tight. Her already cracked ribs felt as though they were about to break under the added pressure.

"Get away from her, you bastard," Joséphine said. "Or I will tell Elise you tried to rape me."

Matheo stiffened and halted his advances. He swung around to face Joséphine. "You wouldn't dare, you *chienne*."

Joséphine smiled. "Wouldn't I, now? Let's see how long you last when she thinks you touched her precious daughter."

Matheo let out a stream of curses and turned back to Parker with a calculating look. "I will be back tomorrow, Bella. And next time, that *puta* will not stop me. I have plans for us."

With a savage snarl, Matheo threw a brutal punch into her midriff. She doubled over, her vision white with the pain. Her chest burned from the lack of oxygen as she struggled to breathe. His cruel laugh was the only thing she heard over her gasp for air as the door slammed shut.

"Parker, are you okay?"

She began to cough uncontrollably, and the pain that racked her body made her dizzy and lightheaded. When she calmed down enough to uncurl, her hand, the one she had coughed into, was covered in blood. She met Joséphine's concerned gaze.

Joséphine bent down and helped her up. "You can't carry on like this."

"I know, that's why we need to get out of here." Before it's too late.

The sound of footsteps alerted the prisoners that their evening meal was about to be delivered.

Parker brought a finger to her lips. "When I make a move, keep them distracted."

"What are you going to do?"

"If you want out of here, just follow my lead."

Joséphine nodded.

Like every other meal time, three guards entered. One stayed by the door, and another between the door and Joséphine. The third delivered the tray of food. As he bent down and placed it on the ground, she made her move.

Praying her plan would work, she hurled herself onto the guard's back and screamed as loud as she could. Quickly catching on, Joséphine yelled and hurled abuse at her captors.

The guard she had jumped bellowed. He pulled her off his back and flung her half way across the room. Her body slammed into the hard floor, and the wind was knocked out of her. Curling into a fetal position, she wailed in pain.

The guards released Josephine from her chains and left the cell. She hurried to Parker, all the while mumbling about the stupidity of Humans. "If your plan included a death wish, I think you are one step closer."

Parker rolled over and a low moan escaped her lips, and she hugged her middle. Once the pain had subsided to tolerable levels, she sat up and a triumphant grimace crossed her face.

Joséphine bent down and checked her for broken bones. "I have no idea why you are looking so pleased with yourself." She froze when she saw a cell phone in Parker's hand.

Parker glanced up. "What? Did you seriously think I was trying to kill myself? We need someone to break us out of here. Not to mention the fact Elise is here. They can finally get her."

A wave of nausea hit her, and her vision dimmed. She swayed and nearly dropped the phone. She shook her head to clear the fog that was closing in.

Her breathing became shallow, and Joséphine reached out to steady her. "Parker. Parker, stay with me."

She blinked and looked around. Not sure how long she could hold on, she set her lips into a grim line and focused on the phone. It was a gamble, but she had no other option. Daniel was her last hope. After giving him Elise's location, he would have no choice but to get here in record time, regardless of how angry he was at her. The only question was...could she last that long?

"But you don't know where we are," Joséphine said. "How can you give directions?"

"I don't need to."

Joséphine watched in silence as she worked. When she was finished, she crawled to the door and pushed the phone underneath the opening.

"What are you doing?" Joséphine said.

She edged away from the door. Her world began to swim and her vision doubled. "It's not going to take too long for the guard to work out his phone is missing. He won't think much of it if he finds it on that side of the door."

She swayed, and her vision blurred. Joséphine caught her before she hit the ground.

"Mother's Day must be interesting in your house."

She closed her eyes and gave in to the excruciating physical and emotional pain that had been threatening to overwhelm her since Matheo's assault.

FORTY-TWO

Once More Unto The Breach, Dear Friends, Once More

Oregon Coast Highway

The six Chevrolet Suburban's accelerated up the I-5. Rain pooling on the road flew up from the tire treads as the vehicles passed. The day was as overcast and as dark as the conditions inside the lead vehicle. Daniel hadn't spoken a word since they left Portland. Instead, he had spent the better part of the last few hours, on their way north, stewing on the information he and Murphy had uncovered. It was a gamble, but he trusted Murphy's instinct that Elise would be north of the border near Vancouver, and have Parker close by.

He glanced into the rearview mirror. Alice and John were quietly talking in the back seat, while Murphy, in the front passenger seat, stared out the window at the landscape whizzing by. Both men had spent the better part of the early morning hours confirming details with alternate sources. In the end, the initial report was accurate.

His voice cut through the hum of the engine. "Did you play any part in Parker's visit to the CDC?"

At his sharp tone, Alice leaned closer to her mate. "What visit?"

He grated his teeth together and held back his temper. "So, I suppose you also didn't give her the information on how to locate the Werewolf gene?"

Alice remained quiet.

"The FDA is recalling products that contain Wildfire-laced caffeine," he said.

Alice gulped. "That's a good thing...isn't it?"

His hand's tightened on the steering wheel. "That all depends on your definition of good. The CDC knows which gene the drug was targeting."

Alice hauled in a sharp breath.

He gripped the steering wheel so hard his knuckles turned white. He was livid at Parker for going behind his back and putting them all at risk of exposure. He sighed and released his steering wheel death grip. He also knew she was the type of person who couldn't stand down and not do something about the epidemic.

He rubbed his forehead. Parker certainly hadn't made it easy for him. It took a few phone calls to piece together her movements on the day she disappeared. The Werewolves in the Portland PD had confirmed that a boarding pass was found in her handbag—proof of her whirlwind visit to Atlanta.

His contacts in the government were aware that Parker had met with a Dr. Baghurst, one of the top CDC doctors. The details were incomplete, and Parker hadn't hit the FBI's most wanted list—yet. His only consolation was that the authorities were so focused on preventing the disease from spreading, that they hadn't questioned why the disease was targeting seemingly junk DNA. Yet. That would change.

He closed his eyes briefly. He knew he'd snapped at the team more than he usually did, but he did not care. His only concern was getting Parker back—he would deal with everything else once she was safe. Just the idea of her being at the mercy of Matheo and Elise made his chest tighten.

Murphy cleared his throat and looked at him expectantly.

"What?" Daniel said, a little too loudly.

"Map."

Daniel grunted. "Middle console."

Murphy reached between their seats and opened the lid. He pulled out the folded document, and something dropped to the floor with a dull thud. Murphy reached down to find the fallen object. He passed the retrieved phone across to Daniel. "You have a message."

Daniel grabbed the device and scanned the message. His face turned ashen and he veered the SUV off the road before skidding to an abrupt halt. The trailing vehicles in the convoy pulled over. He exited and raced toward the last SUV as it came to a halt behind the others. He yanked the car door open and pulled Zeke from the back seat. He thrust the phone into the young Werewolf's hand. "I need to know where this came from."

Zeke, wide-eyed, took the phone and glanced at the screen. An instant later he looked back up at Daniel. His expression wavered, and a hint of a smile threatened. He reached into the vehicle, pulled out his laptop, and raced to the front of the SUV. He was a man possessed as he placed it on the hood and fired it up.

"What's going on?" Simon said.

Zeke looked up from his manic typing, his eyes bright and determined. "It's Parker. She's told us where she is."

The initial shocked silence was quickly followed by a jubilant eruption of voices. The somber mood replaced with renewed hope.

Blood circulated through Daniel's veins, air rushed back into his lungs, and he began to breathe again. He frowned and rubbed his jaw as he considered their options. Her message indicated his team would be outnumbered as well as out-gunned.

"What are you not telling us?" Murphy said.

He swung around and met Murphy's dark gaze. "Elise has a small army, and they are well-armed."

Zeke bounced up and let out a yelp. "She's not far, the GPS coordinates are a little to the east of Vancouver."

Daniel darted a glance toward Murphy. He was right. Whatever the FBI was paying O'Neill, wasn't enough.

As if of one mind, they piled into their Suburban's and pulled onto the highway. Just as they pulled out, the heavens opened, and rain pelted down on them. The sky darkened as the miles flew by. Over the next three hours, he reread Parker's message until he had memorized it. Once he had committed it to memory, his mind repeated it, and it became his personal mantra.

>>*D come get me. Be careful. 30+ guards with guns. DO NOT reply. I'm sorry for everything.*

His heart sank. There was a possibility he wouldn't get to her in time. His chest constricted at the thought. He was angry. Angry at her, and angry at himself. Most of all, angry that there was a chance she might never know what she meant to him.

They arrived in Abbotsford just after midday. Not wanting to attract attention, they bypassed the main roads and abandoned the vehicles two miles from the estate. Alice remained behind with the SUV's. She was only there to provide medical aid if they needed it.

The storm was in full force. The sky was an angry ink stain as the rain pelted down on the earth below. Brilliant shocks of white flashed and forked to the ground, in perfect timing with the crash of thunder overhead.

Daniel took a last look at the google earth image of the property on Zeke's laptop and snapped it shut. He handed it back to Zeke and sent out a silent prayer they weren't too late. At least they had a fair idea of what they were headed into. He felt something drip onto his shoulder and realized he was soaked. His fear had so numbed him, he'd not registered just how much rain had fallen. He pursed his lips. He was no good to anyone, let alone Parker, if he couldn't be cognitive enough to realize he was wet.

Growling, Daniel stood to his full height. He had failed to protect her from Matheo. He would not fail her again. He headed for the tree line. "Let's go."

It did not take long for the team to cut through the small forest and locate Elise's estate. They approached in small groups. Each group was assigned an area to scout out and report back. Their only saving grace was the storm would hide their scent.

Morgan and Jeremy returned from their reconnaissance. "There are eight guards outside the main house. Only three are armed."

"What about Elise or Matheo?" Daniel said.

Morgan shook his head. "There was no sign of either of them. The house was too heavily guarded, and we couldn't get close enough to see inside."

The others listened as he gave a rundown of what his team had found. He mapped out the property in the mud, using a small stick. "There are three buildings at the south end of the property, hidden from the main house by a large grove of trees. We counted ten guards—half are armed with Glocks, and the rest have semi-automatics. They all look as though they carry knives."

"That must be where they are keeping her," Morgan said.

Daniel turned to Simon. "What did you find?"

Simon glanced at Kyle. "Backstreet Boys and I counted six patrolling the northern and eastern borders. They don't seem to go farther than the grove."

"We noticed the same thing," Ray said. Jessica's mate nodded in the direction they had been assigned. "There are four guards along the west and south, and they turned back as soon as they hit the tree line."

Daniel glanced at the weapons they had brought with them. He picked one up and balanced it in his hand. The smooth steel was cold to the touch. "If this turns into a gunfight we will lose. They outnumber us, and I would wager they are all perfect shots." He looked up. "Apart from Murphy, how many of you have fired a gun in the last fifty years?"

The team glanced at each other. No one raised their hand. "We need to do this without using those weapons." He nodded at the small pile they had brought with them.

"I don't know about the others," Simon said, "but I'm not liking my odds without them. How difficult can it be? In the movies, all you do is point and shoot."

He picked up one of the Glocks and threw it to Simon. "It's got fifteen rounds. You'll need to unload and reload on the fly, under fire, potentially with chaos everywhere. I want you to unload the magazine and unlock the safety."

Simon inspected the gun. He gave a frustrated growl when he failed to eject the mag from the grip. He put the gun down. "Fine, so guns aren't our thing. But how the hell are we going to get Parker out of there, when we don't even know which building she's in?"

The others nodded. With the exception of Murphy and Morgan, they were all showing signs of doubt.

"We need to work to our strengths—hand to hand combat. If we can get close enough, we have a chance." Daniel glanced upward. "We also have the benefit of the rain. They won't hear or detect our scent until it's too late."

Very quickly, Daniel outlined their plan of attack. "Simon, I want you to take Kyle, Vic, Carlos, and Samuel and stay within visual range of the prison." He turned to the others. "The rest of us will split into two teams and take out the guards along the perimeters and at the main compound. We need to get to them before they can fire and alert the others. Are we clear?"

They nodded.

"If you need to let your wolves out to fight, make sure you can change in time without the enemy getting to you first. But remember, in order to breach those doors, we need to be in Human form." He paused to make sure they understood. "Once the property is secure, we can deal with the armed guards around the outlying buildings."

"But what if they alert Elise to our presence?" Simon said.

"Our telepathic link requires trust—something I don't think Elise has extended beyond those in her inner circle," Daniel said. "Zeke is jamming the nearest cell tower, so they won't have a signal to alert her via phone. Our only risk is if they are using two-way radios."

Kyle peered out of their hiding place and gazed at Elise's compound. "Maybe we should wait and increase our numbers?"

He understood their hesitation. They were outnumbered. Parker's message indicated a greater number than they'd seen so far. If he had to guess, the rest of them were below ground in the bunkers. He checked his watch and shook his head. "I don't think Parker can wait for reinforcements. If we don't go now, we could be too late."

After a drawn-out silence, Simon shuffled forward. "Well, we better get this over with, then." He shrugged. "I give it a 70/30."

"Seventy? You only give us a seventy percent chance?" Kyle said.

Simon pointed at the nearest group of armed guards. "No N'SYNC—they're the seventy."

The unarmed Werewolves, hidden just out of view, looked at each other before dispersing to their targets.

Daniel rubbed the back of his neck. Should he abort the mission? Was it possible that his need to rescue Parker was blinding him, leading him and his men to their death?

Morgan rested a hand on his shoulder. "You know, you couldn't stop them from coming even if you wanted to. They all know Elise is here and she has to be stopped." He drew in a deep breath. "This is more than just a rescue mission. This is what we have been working towards for weeks. It may be our only chance to save our people."

They separated into two teams. Daniel, Morgan, Jeremy, and Murphy headed toward the main house. Jeremy and Murphy broke off to deal with the patrol along the western border, leaving the two alphas to remove all threats from the main residence.

The excess of trees and shrubs gave Daniel and Morgan ample coverage.

With absolute stealth, honed from years of experience, the alphas eliminated the men patrolling the outside of the house one by one. Not a sound was made as each man was pulled into the undergrowth, and their necks snapped.

Their luck did not last long. A guard exiting the building noticed the absence of his comrades and called out a warning.

Daniel, knowing they had lost the element of surprise, jumped onto the patio where four of Elise's men had gathered. Before the large man closest to him could raise his weapon, he breached the distance and, with a targeted kick, dislodged the gun from his hand. He caught the weapon and thrust the butt of the gun straight into the surprised guard's face. Daniel grabbed him, pulled him into a headlock, and snapped his neck before he could cry out a warning.

Distracted, the other three failed to notice silver-haired Morgan jump up from behind and make short order of the Werewolf nearest the edge of the patio.

The remaining two guards, hearing the commotion, headed toward Morgan. With unnatural speed, Daniel pulled a knife from the first guard's scabbard and swiped it across an advancing man's throat, slitting it from ear to ear. He threw the dead man down, and motioned for Morgan, who had dealt with the third guard, to head into the house.

A low growl erupted from within, followed by shattering glass and breaking wood. Daniel looked up in time to see Matheo hurtling through the air toward him—he had launched himself through the closed French doors. Matheo hit him with the force of a freight train, and he was thrown to the ground.

Daniel rolled with the blow and was back on his feet and confronting Elise's sociopathic beta. The two men faced off, each one looking for the advantage.

Pure hate and venom spewed from Matheo's crazed eyes, and he emitted a low, menacing growl from deep within his chest.

Out of the corner of his eye, Daniel noticed Morgan take a step toward their enemy, but he waved his friend off. "He's mine."

Neither he nor Matheo looked away from the other as they circled, waiting for an opportunity to strike. A series of punches and kicks followed, but they both deflected the blows.

Matheo sneered. "You are a weak and pathetic excuse for an alpha, and I am going to enjoy ripping your mutt-loving heart from your body and defiling it, just as those half-breeds defile the purity of our race."

Daniel did not take the bait and continued to bide his time waiting for an opening.

"I suppose you're here for your little Human pet," Matheo said.

His blood rushed through his veins, but he did not show any emotion.

Matheo continued his taunts. "I can't see the appeal personally, but she was begging for more." A sardonic grin wiped across his face. "And who am I to turn down a fuck? Human or not, she was just another piece of meat."

Daniel's fury exploded out of control. He did what he had trained others never to do—in a fit of rage he launched himself at Matheo, and in that moment gave his opponent the upper hand.

Matheo, prepared for the assault, moved at the last moment. As Daniel fell, Matheo brought a large metal object crashing down on his head.

Daniel's vision blurred, and he felt something warm run down the back of his head. He reached behind to discover a gaping wound at the base of his skull. Pain ripped through his body, and he fought to maintain control.

Matheo, still standing, threw down his weapon and grunted. "I knew you were weak and pathetic, but I never realized just how much."

Daniel snarled and propelled himself at Matheo, and they crashed to the ground when he made contact. He grabbed Matheo's head and smashed it onto the tiles, cracking them on impact. He was a man out of control as he targeted a flurry of punches directly into Matheo's face and torso. Blood flowed from Matheo's nose and mouth with each blow.

He pulled Matheo up by the collar and hurled him through the double-glazed windows. The glass shattered, and the shards cut through Matheo's skin and muscle like butter.

Matheo spotted one of the abandoned guns nearby and tried to crawl toward it. Daniel, seeing where he was headed, pushed his opponent down to the ground with one swift kick to his back.

The sound of Matheo's bones cracking was music to his ears. He readied the death blow, but Morgan called out to him.

"She's not here. Elise is gone. We need him alive."

FORTY-THREE

Rescue

Simon breathed heavily and scanned the team to make sure they were all present and accounted for.

Kyle raised an eyebrow. "You puffed already? We've only just started."

"Shut up, New Kids On The Block. I had to save you from that Cyclops. You should be thanking me."

Kyle's grin faded. "What was with that? He should have worn an eye patch at least."

When Daniel moved into place, Simon snapped his mouth shut, and winked at Kyle. He was going to have so much fun reminding his friend of his reaction to the one-eyed Werewolf.

They had assembled in the grove between the main house and the buildings at the back of the property. Their focus now was breaching the three prison buildings. Matheo had been secured to one of the trees—his mouth gagged and arms tied behind his back to prevent him from changing.

Simon ducked down and briefly closed his eyes as his mind wandered to his mate. If he was killed, Lyssa would bring him back to life, just to kill him again for dying on her. *Better not die then.*

When the others moved out, he followed behind. They managed to get across the clearing to the first building before being spotted. One by one, Elise's guards were eliminated, but other guards, sensing something was wrong, poured out of the prison block and searched for their downed comrades.

His blood was pumping when Daniel let out a battle cry. As one, they charged the armed guards.

They had the element of surprise, but the guards fired their weapons before they reached them.

A sharp pain ripped through Simon's leg, and he winced. *That fucker just shot me.*

Another flurry of bullets rang out, and Kyle fell backward, hitting the ground with a resounding thump. Simon threw himself down to check on his friend. "You okay? Where did it get you?"

Kyle grunted and shifted into a crouching position. Blood seeped through his shirt. "Shoulder and leg, nothing that Dr. Alice can't fix."

The door swung open and a small horde of guards poured out. His stomach plummeted as he did a quick headcount. "Fucknuckles!"

Daniel picked up a weapon from a fallen guard and shouted out. "Fall back to the far side of the building." He fired at the guards, who quickly took cover, and returned a volley of their own.

Bullets whizzed through the air, and Simon raced to regroup with the others.

Daniel rounded the corner and threw a semi-automatic rifle at Murphy. Murphy raced to the far side of the building to protect their flank.

Simon did a head count and his stomach dropped. "Where's Grant and Carlos?"

"They went down with the first wave of bullets," Morgan said. "The *verdammt* Were's are perfect shots. Straight through the forehead."

Simon broke out in a cold sweat. They were sitting ducks. "What now?"

He winced as another round flew over their heads. Murphy and Daniel took turns at keeping the small army away from them while they stayed low to the ground.

Morgan crept closer to Daniel and peered around the corner. "At least we know where the rest of the guards are."

Daniel took another shot and swore when his missed. "We need to get those guns off them. We don't have a chance otherwise."

Simon stiffened. For Daniel to admit that, meant they were in trouble. Big trouble. He glanced at the others. From the look on their faces they were equally worried.

"Any suggestions?" Morgan said.

Daniel's eyes darted across the short distance between them and the guards, then back at the building they had taken refuge behind. He took another shot, then ducked back out of sight. Daniel glanced up at the top of the building and opened a telepathic link to Morgan, Simon, and Murphy.

Murphy, do you think you could take that?

Murphy followed Daniel's gaze and nodded.

Daniel handed Simon his weapon. *Take this. If they take a step toward us, fire at them. You don't need to hit anything, just buy us time.*

He nodded and quickly traded places with Daniel.

Morgan, I need you to—

Before Daniel had a chance to finish, Morgan was at the far side of the building and swapping with Murphy.

What are you going to do? Simon said.

We need to even the odds.

He frowned. He was still none the wiser.

Morgan, Daniel said, *if we fail, you need to be ready to fall back.*

Not happening. So, don't fail then.

Daniel let out a grunt then took a deep breath and ran toward the building. In a flash, he was on the roof with Murphy right behind him.

Kyle edged closer to Simon, careful to stay low to the ground. "What are they doing?"

He took another shot at a guard and grimaced. Daniel was right. He couldn't hit the long side of a barn. Hopefully, their opposition wouldn't figure that out too soon. He was about to fire again when two blurs caught the corner of his eye. Daniel and Murphy had reached the side of the building nearest the guards, jumped off the roof, and had landed in the middle of the largest group of guards.

His eyebrows disappeared into his hairline as guns were ripped out of the guard's hands and hurled into the tree line. It had been a long time since he'd seen Daniel in action. The speed at which the weapons were disposed of was astounding.

"*Veni, Vidi*, I kicked some ass."

They had the advantage of surprise. Instead of tackling the guards, they moved on to the next group and relieved them of their weapons.

When Daniel and Murphy had halfway leveled the playing field, Simon bellowed. "Let's go."

They raced toward the throng.

"What do you make of our odds now?" Kyle said.

"Ask me once I find the motherfucker who shot me."

The grounds transformed into a vicious battleground. Bodies fell, dead before they hit the ground. The air, still thick with moisture, turned patches of mud blood red as the fight raged on. Simon overpowered another guard and broke his neck. He turned just in time to see Tony, one of his pack mates, losing ground. He pushed the dead man away and jumped up to help. Before he reached Tony, a second guard entered the fray. A cold chill ran up and down Simon's spine when Tony's throat was cut from ear to ear, and he fell to his knees holding his hand around his neck.

Morgan shouted. "Behind you!"

Simon looked to where the Brandenburg alpha was calling.

Everything happened so quickly it was a blur. Jeremy, one of Morgan's betas, hadn't noticed two guards break away and circle behind him while he fought a third.

One of the guards raised his gun and took aim. The bullet hit the back of Jeremy's head and exploded out the front.

Morgan screamed again and crossed the distance to Jeremy in a heartbeat. He broke both guards' necks in an instant.

The chaotic fighting intensified, but Simon was unable to take his eyes off Jeremy's missing face.

Kyle shouted at him. "Simon! Get your shit together. The entrance is clear."

He shook himself out of his inertia and headed for the prison. He stopped on the way to pull a guard off John. Between the two of them they dispatched another guard with a swift blow to the throat.

Once he was sure the guard wasn't getting up again, he called to John, "Cover me." He headed toward the door and caught Vic's eye. "Vic, we're up. You're with me."

He and Vic moved into position. Daniel and the others, being the better fighters, would deal with the remainder of the guards, giving him and Vic enough time to search the prison complex. If Parker wasn't found in the first building, they would move on to the next.

They rushed through the main entrance and descended the short flight of stairs. The stench from the cells was so overpowering they gasped and fought the urge to throw up before they reached their destination.

Racing through the dungeon, Simon counted fifteen cells. Each one housed one or more prisoners, but not one of them was Parker. His eyes darted back down the dark corridor, toward where they came. They needed to get to the next building.

Simon took a step toward the entrance and stopped. *I can't just leave them here.* He rattled the doors. "Find the keys, Vic."

"I think I saw them at the bottom of the stairs."

Vic raced off and was back in moments.

They made short order of the locks. Each cell was dark with very little light. He stepped in and raced across to the prisoner who was chained to the wall. The man flinched and his eyes went wide in terror. Fear radiated off him in waves.

Simon's brows rose. *Human?* While he was having difficulty smelling anything, he would bet his latest winnings the man was Human.

"I'm not here to hurt you." He looked up at Vic. "See if the keys fit the lock on his chain."

"*Spasiba,*" the man said once he was freed.

"What did he just say?" Vic said.

The man stood and rubbed his wrists. "Thank you. I said thank you."

From the prisoner's heavy accent, Simon guessed he was Russian.

He glanced at the door. They'd already taken more time than they should have. He tossed the key to the Russian. "What's your name?"

The man caught the keys. "Boris."

"Look Boris, we have to go. I need you to free the rest of the prisoners down here. Do you think you can do that?"

Boris nodded and Simon slapped him on the shoulder. "Good luck. When you get above ground, I suggest you head anywhere but here."

They raced up the stairs and headed to the next prison building. Daniel, Murphy, and John were tearing through what was left of the guards. Morgan and the others were at the third building picking off guards as they emerged.

Not seeing Kyle, Simon frowned and scanned the vicinity. When he saw his friend on the ground, leaning against a wall, he grinned and called out, "Who's the puffed one now, Westlife?"

When Kyle did not move, or reply, Simon's heart dropped and he changed course. Blood soaked the wall Kyle leaned against, and the grass was red. Kyle's eyes, still open in death, gazed into nothingness. Simon's vision blurred and everything seemed to move in slow motion as he fought down the panic. How did things get this out of control?

Vic pulled at Simon's arm, and he brushed her off.

She tugged again and screamed at him. "Get a grip. We have to go. Grieve for him later."

He hauled in a breath and fought the heaviness in his chest. He said a silent farewell to his friend and followed Vic. As they went through the door he glanced back at Daniel. *You'd better be alive when I come back up. I don't think I could take another friend dying today.*

The dungeon housed another fifteen cells, but a quick inspection showed only two were occupied.

He frantically called through the first locked metal door they encountered. "Parker? Parker, are you in there?"

There was a movement from behind the closed door, followed by the sound of chains. An unfamiliar voice called out, "Yes, she's in here. Hurry—she's not doing so well."

He said a silent prayer as they scrambled for a set of keys hanging nearby. It took four attempts before the lock clicked, and the door swung open. Simon motioned for Vic to release the prisoner in the next cell. Satisfied they hadn't been discovered, he rushed through the doorway.

The room was dark, and it took a moment for his eyes to adjust. A young woman was chained to the wall. Her outstretched arms allowed no movement in her upper body.

Fresh blood ran from her broken nose, and she looked as though she'd suffered a number of beatings.

The prisoner nodded toward the opposite side of the cell. "She's over there."

His heart broke when he spotted Parker. The woman he had grown to like and respect was huddled against the wall. Her face was bruised and swollen beyond recognition, and clearly showed she had been subjected to horrendous torture. Parker's clothes were torn and bloodied, and cuts and grazes marked every bit of exposed skin.

She lay still, her breathing shallow and labored. She opened her eyes, and managed a weak smile when she saw him.

Falling to his knees, he moaned. She looked too fragile to move. His voice cracked as he struggled to associate the shattered person in front of him with the vibrant woman who had let nothing stop her. "Oh Parker, what did they do to you?"

Vic rushed through the door and seeing Simon with Parker, freed the other prisoner from her chains. The prisoner rushed across the room to inspect Parker's injuries.

Vic crouched beside Parker and swore under her breath.

He headed for the door. "Wait here, I'll check if it's safe to get her out of here."

He raced up the steps and into the open. The rain had stopped. Bodies were strewn across the concrete and grass.

"We found her. She's alive, beaten up, but alive."

All heads snapped in his direction. Without saying a word, Daniel followed him below ground. They had nearly reached the cell when Daniel inhaled sharply and stopped short.

Simon halted halfway through the doorway. He turned to see Daniel's face register a flash of surprise and then astonishment. Indecision flickered as he waged an internal battle.

"Are you okay, Daniel?"

***

The instant Daniel and his wolf realized the scent coming from the prison cell was their mate, they froze. He should be overjoyed. After two and a half centuries, he was less than twenty feet from her. And yet, all he could feel was an overriding need to ensure Parker's safety, and never allow her out of his sight again.

Duty to his people dictated he should claim his mate and allow the others to get Parker to safety. It was what was expected of him. He needed to ensure the continuation of not only his lineage, but his race. His entire life had been in service to his people; he was bred to put their needs ahead of his. But how could he accept her, when his heart belonged to Parker?

For once, he rebelled against his duty. He couldn't and wouldn't live a lie. While he had fought against it, there was no denying the fact that his love for Parker far outweighed anything he could possibly feel for another woman. Mate or not.

The pull of his mate was strong, but it wasn't powerful enough for him to ignore what he felt for Parker. He couldn't imagine a life without her. She was his future, his only future. She was the other part of his soul, the piece that had been missing all these years. No matter how limited their time, he would treasure every moment. Until his last breath, she would be his true north.

He breathed in, closed his eyes, and his mind filled with a sense of calm. His wolf echoed his thoughts, and their decision was unanimous. He took a step away from the door and opened a telepathic link to his beta. *Simon, there's another prisoner in that cell.*

Yes. How did you know? A woman. I have no idea who she is, but she's a Werewolf. Why?

I need you to bring Parker to me.

Simon frowned. *Okay, but why can't you go in and get her? She's asking for you.*

His expression set into a rigid line. *Because...I choose her. I choose Parker.*

You're not making any sense. If you choose her, go and get her.

You don't understand—I am choosing Parker over my mate.

Mate? Simon's gaze snapped around to the cell. *Are you sure? The other prisoner?*

Yes.

Simon turned back to him. *Well, you might have scented her, but from her broken nose, I doubt she's detected anything but her own blood at this point.*

Simon, just bring Parker out here before I skin you alive.

He was taking the coward's way out by not going in himself, but it was better if the other prisoner never knew of his existence—to believe her mate was still out there, than suffer the devastation of rejection.

Simon walked through the opening holding Parker in his arms, and he tensed.

What?

He took a step backward, and his eyes widened.

How? Words escaped him, and he shook his head from side to side.

His heart thumped in his chest as he scanned the damage Elise and Matheo had inflicted on Parker. Her injuries were far worse than he could have imagined.

Simon handed Parker over to him with an apologetic cringe. "Sorry, I should have warned you."

Reverently, he pulled Parker into his arms, and cradled her to him.

Simon stepped back into the dark prison cell. "I'll make sure Vic keeps the other woman down here until you've gone."

He nodded to his beta, then turned and headed up the corridor with Parker in his arms. Safe and where she belonged.

Parker wrapped her arms around his neck. "You're late." Her voice came out in a barely audible croak.

He smiled and gently kissed her forehead as he breathed her in. "Your directions weren't very clear." Even in this state she was feisty.

He carried her up the stairs and into the clearing where the others were gathered. Fury welled up in him—fury beyond anything he had ever felt before. She was more precious to him than his own life. He was supposed to protect her, but here she was, broken and battered beyond recognition.

How could I have failed her?

He paid closer attention to her condition, and his heart sank. From her weak heartbeat, he might still lose her. That scared him like nothing else ever had, and he pulled Parker tighter into his body, as if by sheer force of will, she would survive. He held back his terror-stricken thoughts and refocused his energy on the rage that was overtaking both him and his wolf. That was an emotion he understood. He would make them pay for what they had done.

Morgan rushed over to Parker, concern and then anger washing over his face the moment he saw her injuries. "My dear child, what did they do to you?"

Daniel's head snapped around when John called out, "Wait—where's Matheo?"

His wolf sprung on high alert.

"Over there!"

All eyes turned to where Morgan pointed. Matheo had freed himself and was racing across the clearing while pulling the bindings from his wrists.

A brutal snarl ripped from Daniel and Parker flinched. Everyone took a step backward, and he shook with barely controlled rage. He quickly handed Parker across to Morgan.

His face, stone cold, belied the tension throughout the rest of his body.

He clenched his fists and closed his eyes. In the next instant, he launched himself in the direction Matheo was running. He effortlessly transformed in mid-air. Torn and shredded clothes floated to the ground, well after the massive black wolf landed.

A low growl emanated from his wolf's throat as it stalked Matheo. He and his wolf had one purpose and one purpose only. To make Matheo pay for what he had done to Parker. A snarl was the only warning the wolf gave before it attacked, and carved deep lacerations into Matheo's body. Blow by blow, cut by cut, until no part of him was left untouched. Large chunks of muscle hung from thin threads of skin as Matheo continued to flee.

Matheo's screams were music to his ears. When Matheo clambered back to Morgan and the others, begging for mercy, Daniel's wolf relinquished his control, and he stalked his prey with cold fury.

Matheo swung around to face his executioner. Adrenaline rushed through Daniel as he stopped in front of Matheo, his eyes piercing Elise's beta with pure hatred.

His arm lashed out and bone cracked as his fist punched a hole through Matheo's rib cage. He reached in and clenched Matheo's still beating heart.

Confused, Matheo's gaze lifted. For the briefest of moments, their eyes locked. The corners of Daniel's mouth lifted as he ripped out the beating organ and held it up for Matheo to see. His arm was coated in so much blood, it dripped onto the grass below. When he squeezed his fist tighter, the organ resisted, but unable to withstand the pressure, the heart exploded.

Matheo's body buckled to his knees and he fell, face first, to the ground. Daniel let the pulverized heart fall from his hand to land beside Matheo.

He stared at the ground. His rage had consumed him to the point where instinct had taken over. Both he and his wolf had worked in tandem. While he may have been in Human form, they equally shared in Matheo's demise, something that should not have been possible. He pushed his concerns to one side. All that mattered was that death had finally caught up with a well overdue passenger.

One down. One to go.

No longer consumed with his bloodlust, Daniel turned back to Parker. His mate needed him. He froze at the terror on Morgan's face.

Pain ripped through his heart when Morgan said, "She's not breathing."

FORTY-FOUR

Revelation

Abbotsford Regional Hospital, Abbotsford

He was numb. He'd found her only to possibly lose her again.

The doctors at the ER had taken Parker straight into surgery. Daniel, unsure of what to do in a hospital, followed Alice and John's lead and trailed them to a secluded waiting room. The ticking of the clock on the wall became louder and louder as they waited in silence, each of them fighting with their own demons.

He slumped his shoulders in defeat. *How did I not know?*

Morgan burst into the waiting room a short while later. Worry lines etched his features. He looked from Daniel to Alice. "What's happening, is she okay?"

"She has pneumonia, four broken ribs, and a collapsed lung," Alice said. Her eyes were filled with tears that threatened to spill. "They've taken her into surgery." She placed a hand over her mouth. "What if I made it worse by doing CPR?"

John pulled Alice to him and made a shushing noise. "She wouldn't have made it to the hospital. It's because of you she has a chance."

"Is she going to be all right?" Morgan said.

Alice shook her head. "They couldn't say." Her lower lip quivered, and she broke down in tears.

Pain ripped through Daniel's body. Parker might not pull through. But she had to. He wouldn't allow her to leave him this soon after he'd found her.

Unable to sit still any longer, he rose and paced the room. He reached for his phone. He needed updates from the team trying to keep a lid on the Wildfire outbreak, though the muted TV tuned into a news program only served to reinforce that the epidemic had now truly spilled into the Human world.

He placed half a dozen calls arranging for reinforcements to be sent to the most heavily affected areas, then turned his attention to dealing with a few pressing business matters—anything to keep his mind off what was going on behind those doors.

Time passed with excruciating slowness, and they continued to wait. On more than one occasion, Morgan had to physically restrain him from storming through the hospital and demanding to know what was going on.

After what felt like a lifetime, the door opened, and a doctor in hospital scrubs approached them. The doctor hesitated when the three large men descended on him. He cleared his throat and focused on Alice. "We had a couple of complications, but we've managed to insert a chest tube to reinflate her lung. She is stable, and we are taking her up to ICU shortly. Ms. Johnson should make a full recovery."

Alice breathed a sigh of relief before firing questions at the surgeon.

Daniel heard nothing beyond the words 'full recovery'. A feeling of unadulterated relief swept through his body. His muscles, which had been rigid for hours, let go, and oxygen and blood flowed freely. He took a deep breath. The number of emotions that had coursed through his body in the past few hours were more than he had experienced in his two and a half centuries of living. He was confused and at a loss, with the full ramifications yet to sink in.

Alice was quietly crying against John's chest. The large man, confused as to what his mate was weeping about, kept on repeating, "Didn't you hear him say she was going to be okay?"

Off to one side of the room, Morgan took a moment to collect himself. He then pulled out his phone. Daniel assumed the call was to Clara, who would be beside herself with worry.

Now that he knew Parker would be fine, his state of shock lifted. He wandered over to the window that looked onto the courtyard below and reined in his emotions. His pack expected him to be strong.

I should never have let her near that bastard in the first place.

He jumped when Morgan placed a reassuring hand on his shoulder. "She's going to be okay. Luna wouldn't have given you a mate that wasn't strong."

His head turned to face Morgan. Grey, mirthful eyes met his, a hint of a smile twitching at the sides of his mouth.

There was no point in denying it from his old friend and mentor. "How did you know Parker is my mate?"

Morgan chuckled as he looked out the window. "You just told me."

Both he and Morgan stood side-by-side, gazing on the world below, deep in thought.

Morgan broke the silence. "So, when you rejected that prisoner as your mate and chose Parker, didn't it enter your thoughts that it was Parker all along? Why did you assume it was the other woman? Who, by the way, turns out to be Elise's daughter."

He shook his head and ran his fingers through his hair. "Is nothing sacred?" He was still coming to terms that Parker was his mate—not the unknown prisoner.

"Don't blame Simon," Morgan said. "He's back at Elise's estate making every excuse under the sun to keep her away from you."

"He's what?"

313

"She was insisting on coming with me to the hospital. Simon was acting rather strange, making up ridiculous excuses as to why he needed her there. He could see I was about to take her, so he had no choice but to tell me what happened in the prison cell."

Morgan burst out laughing. "Poor Simon. He must be running out of excuses by now."

Daniel gazed out the window and sifted through the events of the past few weeks. "I keep asking myself how, all this time, I had no idea she was my mate. You cannot imagine the shock when Simon stepped through the doorway with her."

Morgan half turned to face him. "Don't be so hard on yourself. She masked her scent. We all knew it, we just chose never to call her on it." He patted Daniel on the shoulder. "You, my friend, have had a very unique experience. You chose her because your heart and mind told you she was your other half—not because your primal side saw her as your mate."

He frowned, not understanding Morgan's meaning.

Morgan folded his arms and rocked back on the balls of his feet. "When we recognize our mates, our instinct takes over and we accept the bond. Just as we instantly fall in love with our children, and our grandchildren, we automatically fall in love with our mate. The harder task is that we need to learn to like and respect them. That isn't always a foregone conclusion. You have commenced at the opposite end—an enviable and unique position for one of our race."

"How am I going to tell her?" Daniel's heart thudded against his rib cage. "What if she rejects me?"

Morgan smiled. "You are way over-thinking it. Let's worry about getting her out of here first."

Morgan shook his head from side to side and laughed. "Clara is going to be like a woman possessed. Not only does it turn out Parker has the wolf gene, but she also has a mate worthy of her." Morgan clapped him on the back. "Oh, I don't envy you. Clara considers Parker a daughter. Put a step out of place, and you will find she is the mother-in-law from hell."

FORTY-FIVE

A Wolf in Sheep's Clothing

Middlemarch Estate

Simon's head and heart ached. They had placed the bodies of their fallen pack mates in the back of their vehicles for the long drive home. He was finding it hard to believe Kyle was gone. And with no knowledge of how Parker was faring, it put an added strain on them all. What if she didn't make it?

He pushed down his grief and focused on their immediate problem. Time enough later to mourn. Right now, he needed to deal with the clean-up and Daniel's mate, who was pissing him off big time.

Joséphine frowned. "I still don't know why I couldn't go with Alpha Bergman."

"You just can't," he said. "We need to sort this mess out."

He rubbed his neck and surveyed what was left of their strike force. Victory had come at a high price. He sighed and forced himself to focus. They had a lot of work to do within a limited time. So far, everything had gone according to plan, but one wrong move and all that could come crashing down.

Murphy addressed the remaining Werewolves. "We need to clear these bodies—and fast."

"What's the rush?" Vic said.

"Once the FBI discovers Parker is in the hospital, they are going to want to know where she was held. Eventually, they will end up here."

The team stopped and focused on Murphy, puzzled looks on their faces.

"FBI?" Vic said. "Why would they be interested in Parker?"

"The FBI gets involved in all nationwide ransom cases."

Vic's brows rose. "Ransom? Ransom wasn't involved."

Simon rubbed his nose and grimaced. "If everything goes according to plan, the FBI will believe there was a ransom. Zeke is going to use his magic to send a back-dated ransom message and make it look like it came from the other side of Abbotsford. This morning Clara and Jessica withdrew two and a half million dollars in cash. There's no crime in paying a ransom, so they won't think twice about how we got her back, nor the real reason she was taken."

Murphy handed Vic a shovel. "We are going to make sure that there is nothing left here to give them any clues as to what's really going on."

Simon and Murphy broke the Werewolves into groups to begin the clean-up process.

The team worked tirelessly through the night, and it was afternoon before they had removed all the bodies of Elise's guards and buried them a few miles away, deep in the forest.

They ransacked the prisons for anything that might help determine where Elise had gone, and stumbled on a fourth building, hidden well behind the three prison complexes. The interior resembled a miniature hospital and lab. Zeke loaded all the equipment and specimens that might help Alice in the back of one of their vehicles. This included a high spec'd computer Zeke salivated over. They cleared the main house last.

Simon breathed a sigh of relief once Zeke pushed the send button on the ransom email.

Zeke smiled and looked up. "Okay, it will look like the email was sent the day before yesterday."

Simon sent out a silent prayer. The sooner they finished up the better. He was edgy and Joséphine was getting on his nerves. Plus, they still needed to get the bodies of their fallen pack mates across the border and home to Colorado, where they could receive a proper burial. His chest tightened. It wasn't something he was looking forward to.

"If we're done here," Murphy said, "I'm heading to the hospital."

Joséphine made a move to follow. "I'll come with you."

Simon cut her off. "No, you won't."

Joséphine stared at him in a manner that clearly showed she thought there was something wrong with him. For his part, Simon stood his ground. His loyalty to his alpha outweighed anything else.

Before the situation escalated out of control, Vic interrupted. "Hey, where's the other guy?"

"What other guy?" Murphy said.

"You know, the other prisoner we freed."

Simon cocked his head. "You mean the Russians? They're long gone."

Vic threw her arms on her hips. "No, the man in the cell next to Parker."

A mystified expression crossed Joséphine's face, and she shook her head. "There were three of us kept prisoner in that building, all women."

He glared at Vic. "Then who the hell did you let out?"

A loud explosion rang through the air, and they ducked for cover. Three more explosions followed in quick succession.

Simon pulled himself off the floor. "What the hell was that?"

Murphy headed for the door. "Did anyone see anything that might have been an explosive agent when you were clearing out the prison buildings?"

They all shook their heads, and Simon said, "Why?"

"That was a C4 explosion."

They raced out of the house and ran to the buildings that had housed the freed prisoners. Or at least the buildings that used to be there. "Son of a bitch!" Simon cursed and kicked the air. "Who the fucknugget did that?"

A gigantic dust cloud hung heavy in the air. The buildings were now nothing more than broken bits of concrete and metal scattered across the ground. Sunken craters marked the spot where the prisons used to be.

Murphy rounded on Vic. "What did he look like, the man in the cell?"

The sudden urgency in Murphy's tone had the hairs on the back of Simon's neck rising.

"Average height, brown hair, slim more than stocky." Vic paused to recall further information about the man. "Oh yeah, he had different colored eyes, brown and blue, I think."

Joséphine gasped. "What was he doing here?"

Simon frowned. "Who?"

"He is part of my mother's inner circle. Sometimes, I even think that she's scared of him. My guess is that he saw what was going on and pretended to be a prisoner to escape unharmed."

Murphy's voice cut through the air like a razor. His stance was rigid, fury rolling off him in waves. His fists clenched at his side. "Was his name Elijah?"

Simon flinched at the sight of his black eyes turning darker.

"Yes, how did you know?"

A primitive and savage roar ripped from Murphy as he surged away from them and bolted into the forest. The tortured howl of Murphy's wolf reverberated through the air

Simon's brows drew together. *Elijah? Why do I know that name?*

FORTY-SIX

Long Road To Recovery

Abbotsford Regional Hospital, Abbotsford

Turn that stupid alarm off, will you?

Everything was dark. But the high-pitched beeps just wouldn't stop. Beep. Beep. Beep. Parker tried to focus on the rhythm. It sounded familiar. Almost like it was keeping time with her heartbeat.

God, that alarm is irritating. Who turned out the lights?

She stilled when she felt a slight tension on the upper part of her arm, and she became more alert. It wasn't dark. Her eyes were closed, and that god-awful sound was... medical monitors. When the pressure around her arm became uncomfortable, she forced her eyes open to discover a nurse in a blue uniform taking her blood pressure.

The nurse smiled. "You're awake. I'll inform the doctor."

Once he left, Parker willed her body to move, but her arms were as useless as the rest of her body. The fog was clearing and the events of the past few days came crashing over her in broken pieces.

Oh God!

She squeezed her eyes shut in the hopes that would stop her from reliving the nightmare. The beeping monitors picked up speed and kept time with her racing heart.

A much larger hand gently nudged her, and a sense of calm enveloped her. The irritating monitor beeps slowed.

She opened her eyes and looked into familiar piercing green eyes.

Relief flooded Daniel's face, and he gazed down on her with a gentle smile. His voice was deep and comforting as he leaned in and tucked an errant curl behind her ear. "Welcome back to the land of the living."

Before she could reply, the nurse returned with a doctor in tow.

The doctor checked the monitors and her vitals. "I'm Doctor Greyson. Do you know where you are?"

"Hospital?"

"And do you know why you are here?"

She struggled to formulate a response. Even in her addled state, she understood she needed to be careful with her answers. She looked to Daniel, who had stepped to one side, and blurted out the first thing that came to mind. "No, it's all a bit of a haze right now."

Dr. Greyson patted her hand. "That's alright Ms. Johnson, it will come back eventually. The body's ability to protect itself is extremely strong. You should make a full recovery." He made notes on her chart and smiled reassuringly. "You just won't be deep sea diving ever again." He chuckled at his own joke.

Once they were alone Daniel said, "How are you feeling?"

Parker inhaled oxygen through the small prongs resting under her nose. Scattered memories of Daniel's wolf returned. Images of Matheo as he beat her flashed before her eyes. Her body involuntarily shook when she remembered how much pleasure her injuries brought him. "Is he... I mean... is Matheo, you know..." She couldn't find the words.

Daniel reached for her hand and perched his large frame on the side of the hospital bed. "Gone?" His jaw clenched. "Yes, he is."

She swallowed. What was a dream and what was real? She struggled to find the appropriate words. "And, you really... did what you did to him?"

Daniel nodded, his face grim.

She closed her eyes and recalled the moment. While she didn't want to admit it, a part of her had been overjoyed by his brutal death. Matheo had killed her friend, and nothing was going to bring her back. With his death came a small measure of justice for Beth, Trevor, Bobby, and all the others who fell before them.

Another memory rose to the surface. She panicked and set the monitors off again. "Oh my God! Joséphine. Did you get Joséphine out?"

She struggled to sit up, and Daniel gently, but firmly, pushed her back into bed. "Yes, she's fine. Nothing that rest won't heal. In our search for you, we liberated quite a few other prisoners as well."

Parker shivered at the gruesome memory of the bone chilling noises that never seemed to end. "Even from our cell, I heard their screams." She glanced at the door and lowered her voice. "I hope you made Elise's death as painful as Matheo's."

Daniel's shoulders dropped, and he avoided eye contact. "By the time we arrived, she was gone."

A dull ache settled around her heart, and she clutched her free hand to her chest. She'd failed. "I should have gotten the message to you sooner. It's my fault she got away."

Daniel let out a low growl. "Don't you dare take the blame. This is not on you. Elise has been one step ahead at every turn."

She sunk into the pillow, but then tensed. Her mind was still fuzzy and only processing every second thought. "Where are the others? I saw blood everywhere. Who..." She trailed off, unable to put voice to the question.

Sorrow clouded Daniel's face. "We lost Jeremy, Kyle, Tony, Carlos, and Grant."

Tears pricked at the back of her eyes, and she struggled to hold them back. A feeble whimper escaped her lips.

Daniel cleared his throat. "The rest are okay. They are still at the estate. Morgan is at the airport collecting Clara, and Jessica arrives in a couple of hours. You're pretty popular in the Werewolf community."

She cringed, knowing she had put everyone out. "I'm sorry for getting you all into this mess. Elise was there, I swear." Guilt at what happened flared. "There's something else I need to tell you."

Daniel cocked his head and looked directly at her. "You mean your little jaunt to the CDC?"

She braced herself and prepared for his anger. "You know about that?"

"Yes. We will discuss your transgression once you are fully healed. In the meantime, we need to deal with what you will say to the F.B.I.—they will also want to speak to you."

Daniel's easy dismissal of her going against his orders confused her. She attempted to sit up. He may have put off the discussion, but she couldn't. Daniel and the others were in danger if they stayed. "You need to get everyone and get out of here." The pain from her ribs was too much. She gave up and lay back down.

Daniel shook his head. "We aren't leaving and that is final. They think you were the target of a ransom abduction. As far as they are aware, we paid the ransom, and you were released. End of story. There is nothing on the grounds that could prove otherwise, and in the end Elise's men solved a major problem for us."

"How?"

"With the exception of the main house, they destroyed all the buildings on the property. There is no evidence left of what was really going on."

Parker stilled. "They what?"

"When you are better, Simon can give you a rundown on what happened after we left."

She frowned. "But what about the CDC?"

Daniel pushed her back on the pillow and shook his head. "The FBI thinks your visit to Atlanta was related to a client. Our only hope is that the person you visited within the CDC remains quiet on the real reason for your visit."

Daniel leaned closer and outlined the plan they had already put in motion. "It will be another abduction-ransom case, and they'll close the book on it. Murphy knows how the FBI operates and has already told us what to say and how to react. Once they have interviewed you, the doctor has agreed to clear you for travel. You'll be airlifted to Boulder, and an ambulance has been arranged to get you back to Nederland. Alice will take care of you on pack grounds."

An uneasy pressure grew in the pit of her stomach. Why the urgency to get her out of the hospital? "You don't need to go through all that trouble and expense. Besides, I am okay with going home to Portland."

His hard expression told her she wasn't going to win this battle. "It's not going to happen. You are coming home with me, and that's final."

Parker's protest stalled when the nurse came in and fussed over her. Once the nurse left, she began to squirm. Daniel hadn't moved from her side. "You know I can't exactly escape. You should get some rest."

His tone brooked no argument. "I'm not leaving."

He got up and walked over to the chair by the window. He pulled it closer to the bed and reached for her hand. She didn't protest. His touch was comforting, and she was thankful for his presence as she fell asleep.

***

Clara hovered over Parker's bed. "Are you sure she's okay?"

Daniel's gaze wandered over Parker, who was unconscious and unaware of the panic that had set in. "The doctors insist there is nothing to worry about. Alice said the same thing. It's just her body's way of repairing itself."

He had spent most of the past twenty-four hours pacing the small room. While the doctors and nurses assured him she was fine, he wasn't as convinced. Parker's temperature had escalated and she had fallen unconscious not long after coming to the previous day.

His heart broke and it killed him to see her in pain. Her face was swollen beyond all recognition. Her right eye looked like a golf ball, only a narrow slit providing any sight. Her skin resembled every shade of purple, black, and yellow. When the nurses had changed the bandages across the rest of her body, his rage at Matheo and Elise resurfaced. No part of her had escaped damage.

Thanks to Google, he was all too aware of how dangerous hospitals could be. The sooner he got Parker out of here the better. She needed to be back in Nederland where she would not catch any of the diseases that lurked in Human hospitals.

"Willing her to magically recover is not the answer," Morgan said.

Morgan had taken up vigil on the far side of the room and stood with Jessica, who was just as distraught.

Daniel let out a relieved breath when Parker finally awoke. Her eyes opened as much as the swelling allowed, and a tear slid down her cheek as she scanned the room. Her gaze rested on him, but before he could say anything, Clara raced to her bed.

"Oh *Klein*, you're awake. You had us so worried. Never do that to me again, I'm not getting any younger, and you took decades off my life."

He stepped back from the melee and pulled his phone from his pocket, satisfied Parker was okay. Simon and Murphy were well overdue, but before he dialed, Simon tugged at their link.

Where are you? Daniel said.

Downstairs, with Murphy and Joséphine. She's insisting on coming upstairs to see Parker. I don't know how much longer I can keep her away. His tone was desperate.

Daniel remembered the conversation with Morgan and chuckled. In the confusion, he had forgotten to put his friend out of his misery.

Bring her up here.

There was a slight pause. *But you said... Are you sure?*

Simon, just get up here now.

Joséphine rushed through the door a few minutes later. Her obvious irritation evaporated the moment she laid her eyes on Parker. "*Mon Luna.*"

Simon and Murphy eased their way into the room shortly after. Simon, clearly nervous, flitted his gaze from Daniel to Joséphine and back again.

Daniel raised a questioning brow at Murphy.

"We left nothing behind and the bodies are ash," Murphy said.

Daniel breathed a sigh of relief. With the extent of the mop up, it was a miracle they weren't discovered. However, it appeared that Elijah had done them a favor and made some of their job easier. "Are you sure it was him?" He'd already gotten a rundown from Simon, but he wanted to hear the profiler's take.

"Yes."

Daniel studied the other man. There was nothing in his expression that gave away his inner turmoil, but Daniel would lay odds this was tearing Murphy apart. "Any idea where he was headed, or why he wasn't with Elise?"

"None, but with Elise no longer feeding his addiction, he will start killing indiscriminately again."

"What will you do?" Daniel said.

"You know what I have to do, and you know why."

Daniel sighed and turned to face Murphy. "How do you do it?"

"Do what?"

"Survive without her?"

Murphy snorted in disgust. "You call this surviving? I buried my soul when I buried my mate. Elijah took everything from me."

Daniel considered Murphy's words. Even though Parker had been in Elise and Matheo's clutches, he still held out hope that they would rescue her. He couldn't contemplate how he would have survived had they taken her from him. Yet, the man beside him had endured forty years without his mate. Hate was the only thing fueling his existence.

Daniel looked to Murphy. "The one thing I have learned is that sometimes things creep up on you when you aren't looking, and the unexpected can happen." His heart softened for the tortured Werewolf. "A wise man once told me we need to let a little bit of joy into our lives, even if it is for a very short time. Holding on to hate will only get you so far."

"It's all I have. This time, I won't be bringing him in."

"I never expected you to. Just make sure his death is fitting for the pain he has inflicted over time."

He and Murphy stood at the back of the room, each caught up in their own demons. Once Joséphine was reassured her friend was okay, she approached Daniel.

She introduced herself, and Simon tensed, then frowned.

Daniel groaned and made a mental note to inform him that he was in no danger of Joséphine suddenly wanting to claim him as her mate.

Joséphine leaned forward and lowered her voice. "I'm not one to criticize, but you are aware that your beta is not...how do you say...normal?"

Before he could answer, raised voices drifted in from the corridor. He strode out of the room to discover a petite woman demanding entry.

"Can I help you?" he said.

Daniel stiffened when Parker called from her bed, "Dr. Baghurst?"

The small woman pushed past him and strode into the room.

All eyes were focused on the new arrival. Without saying anything, she lifted Parker's chart off the hook and scanned the contents.

What the hell is she doing here?

Daniel nodded towards the door. Simon, Jessica, Murphy, and Joséphine took the hint and made a quick exit.

Simon pushed Joséphine through the door and glanced back at Daniel. *We'll do a sweep to see who is with her.*

Daniel darted a glance to the doctor and frowned. *Anything happens, you get everyone away. Am I clear?*

The woman popped the chart back and slowly scanned Morgan, Clara, and him. He was unnerved at just how intently Dr. Baghurst was regarding them, and an uneasy feeling grew in the pit of his stomach

Dr. Baghurst folded her arms over her chest. "So, if I took a DNA sample from you all, I'm betting I would find this additional gene in each one of you."

Parker stiffened and her gaze flew to his. She cleared her throat, and said, "Dr. Baghurst, I don't know what you are implying, but I believe you need to have a court order to compel us to hand over a swab."

The doctor raised an eyebrow and smiled. "Ah, you would, normally, be correct. But in this case, Homeland Security trumps everything, and the lines are very blurred within their wide range of powers."

That was it. He'd heard enough. "Doctor, why are you here?"

"In my job, I solve puzzles. Based on the results we are getting, I estimate that one-eighth of a percent of the population may have this gene. That's about four hundred thousand people in the US. Now, I keep asking myself—why this gene? It's obviously not *junk*. So, what is it about the people with this gene that makes someone want to go through the effort to kill them?"

Daniel crossed his arms over his chest. He was not happy with where this conversation was leading. "Can I ask you a question, doctor?"

"By all means."

"Why is it so important for you to know? Why do you really need an answer?"

Dr. Baghurst swung around to face him. "Because, as it turns out, I am one of the one-eighth of a percent."

The temperature of the room plummeted. Silence hung heavy in the air. The only noise came from the medical equipment measuring Parker's oxygen levels.

Daniel glanced at Morgan to gauge his reaction, only to discover the other alpha was as stunned as him. Clara clutched Morgan's arm and looked like someone had just walked over her grave. Parker's pulse rose and even under the bruises and swollen face, her color had drained.

Dr. Baghurst arched a brow. "Don't all speak at once."

"What were you expecting us to say?" Daniel said.

"I don't expect you to tell me what's going on right now, but make no mistake, you will be telling me."

Dr. Baghurst studied the monitors hooked up to Parker. She examined her extensive injuries, and her expression softened. "Parker, you came to see me and put your life in danger to save others. While the FBI believes this is a kidnapping, I know better. I would like you to trust me—like I trusted that you had nothing to do with the manufacture of that disease."

The doctor reached into her bag, pulled out a small blue book, and placed Parker's passport on the bedside table. "I'd like to think you can trust me with your secret."

She turned and addressed the room. "Nature dictates that if there's that much hate for someone to go through all that effort, you will continue to be targets in the future, and by definition, so will I."

She was telling the truth. There was nothing in either her demeanor or reactions that said otherwise. Whatever she was up to came from pure intent. He felt a moment of indecision. Had he made the wrong decision not reaching out? Could he have saved lives by listening to Parker and approaching Dr. Baghurst earlier? Not wanting to second guess himself, he moved to Parker's bedside table, reached for a pad, and scribbled something on the paper. He ripped off the page, folded it in half and handed it to Dr. Baghurst. "Be at this address at noon the day after tomorrow. You will be given a copy of a hard drive and journals. I can't guarantee it, but you may find the answers to help you fight this disease."

No one spoke after Dr. Baghurst left.

Parker made herself more comfortable. "Isn't there a risk she might put the pieces together?"

Daniel rubbed his jaw. It was a gamble. One he hoped wouldn't backfire. "If there is something in that computer Zeke found in Fridericks lab that will help Humans, it might help us, too. It's a risk that I am willing to take."

Clara closed the door "How much do you think she knows?"

He sighed. No doubt this would come back to haunt him. "The issue with Dr. Baghurst and whatever suspicions she has, will need to be dealt with another day. We already have enough on our plate keeping our own diseased people away from Humans. Not to mention working out how Elise got away and what she's up to."

FORTY-SEVEN

Unmasked

Nederland, Colorado, 4 Days later

Daniel collapsed in the chair, placed his elbows on his desk, and rested his head in his hands. A combination of relief and trepidation flooded him. He wasn't sure whether to be happy, sad, or worried. He let out a long exhale. They were finally home. Home where he could keep Parker safe and out of Elise's line of sight. Whether he could keep her out of the FBI, Homeland Security, and the CDC's line of sight was another issue entirely.

A warmth spread through his veins, and the corners of his mouth twitched. Even in her weakened state Parker was feisty. She had argued with him right up until they got on the air ambulance, and the doctor had sedated her. He couldn't understand why she thought she was putting him out, and that she should be returning to Portland, not Nederland. She belonged here with him. Where else would she possibly go?

He sat back in his chair and glanced at the door. Perhaps he should check on her?

Growling for not trusting the others, he resisted the urge. She was in good hands. Alice and his sister were tending to her and would stay until he caught up with the pressing issues that had been awaiting his return. Not that Parker would know he wasn't sitting vigil with them. She was still sedated, and it could take hours before she woke up.

He rubbed the back of his neck and refocused. Now that Parker was safe, his mind returned to a more daunting task. He had the unenviable responsibility of planning ceremonies for those who had lost their lives in the battle at Middlemarch. His chest tightened, and he struggled with the grief that was sweeping through his and Morgan's pack. Their fallen had died heroes. While Elise had gotten away, she no longer had an army behind her. Without them she was crippled. Their sacrifice had given his race a reprieve, but it would not be a long one. She was out there waiting to strike again.

Daniel was on the phone when Simon walked into his office later that afternoon. He motioned for him to take a seat. "I'll see what I can do about getting an additional supply of morphine to you." He paused. "I have to warn you, it won't be pretty."

He ended the call and rubbed the back of his neck. "That was the alpha from the Ethiopian pack in Wisconsin. There's a pack member with the disease. They have no doctor, and it's their first case."

Even though they had stopped the online sales, and the food had been removed from the stores, they would still need to contend with those who had already become infected.

"I'll ship out a supply of morphine straight away," Simon said. He surveyed Daniel's office. It still hadn't been repaired from when Daniel was informed of Parker's abduction. Simon tapped the destroyed laser printer with his foot. "You don't do things by half, do you?"

Daniel snorted. "Well, how would you react if your mate was taken from you?"

Simon's smile vanished, and his head snapped up. He cocked his head, and his brows knitted together. "Wait. What?

Mate?" A look of disbelief registered before it turned to confusion. "But you said... I thought that..."

Daniel held up a hand to silence his stuttering friend. "I believe I may owe you an apology."

Simon sank down on the couch and shook his head. "May? Do you have any idea what I had to go through to make sure Elise's daughter stayed away from you? I think she's under the impression I'm completely insane."

"Things were moving a little too quickly, and there wasn't time to let you know the truth."

Simon leaned back on the leather seat and a wide smile spread across his face, something that had been missing since Kyle's death. "The alpha's found his mate. The alpha's found his mate."

"Shut up." Daniel glanced at the door. "No one knows yet—just you and Alpha Bergman."

"Oh." Simon's wicked grin gave Daniel a measure of discomfort. "That means you haven't told Parker?"

"And just when do you think that conversation was possible, considering what she has just been through? Keep it to yourself."

Simon chuckled. "You're worried that she is going to reject you."

His chest tightened.

"You are... Mind you..." Simon winked. "Why she would want an overbearing, bad-tempered Werewolf as a mate is beyond me. You're quite right to be concerned."

A deep growl burst from his chest, and he clenched his fists.

Simon raised his hands in submission, but he was still smiling. "Settle, Cujo." He cocked his head to one side. "In some weird way, I think that we all accepted her as second alpha a long time ago." He commenced chanting again, a grin from ear to ear as he sang. "The alpha's got a mate, the alpha's got a mate."

"What are you—a child?"

He dismissed his beta and went back to work. Simon hummed the chant the entire way down the corridor, his off-key ditty wafting through Daniel's open door.

I think Joséphine might have been correct. There definitely is something not right with that Werewolf.

Simon had only been gone a few moments when Daniel's phone rang.

He raised an eyebrow at the caller display before answering. "She hasn't been here long, and you're already checking up on me."

There was a pause before Morgan spoke. "We have a problem."

The grim way in which Morgan uttered the simple phrase had Daniel's shoulders tensing. "I'm listening."

"Fridericks is gone."

Daniel's brows knitted together. "What do you mean he's gone?" Hans Fridericks had been left in Morgan's custody—pending a decision by the Alliance on what to do with him.

"The house we were keeping him in was attacked early this morning." Morgan's voice turned hard. "I have two dead, and a third severely wounded."

Daniel's hand clenched the phone. "Fuck! How did that bitch find him?"

"That's what we are still trying to unravel. Do you think they're headed to the estate?"

"No." He was confident that the estate was the last place she would return to, especially after blowing it up. "The FBI will have the place overrun by now. She's too smart to risk it. The more important question is, what is she up to now? There's got to be a reason she came back for him."

"It can't be Wildfire. We know about it, and so do the Humans. More importantly, we are all putting measures in place to stop our race from being exposed. What I don't understand is that only the Council and a select few from our packs knew we had him. Even less knew where he was being held."

Morgan's statement hung in the air like heavy rain clouds before a storm. Dark and foreboding.

"We have a traitor."

***

Oh God, my head. A dull pulsating beat thumped against Parker's skull. She opened her eyes, only to shut them again. *Where the hell am I?*

When she pried them open again, she realized she was no longer in the hospital. A moment later the fog cleared. She was in her bedroom in Nederland. She had little time to adjust before Alice and Jessica hovered over her.

Alice smiled. "Hey sleepy head. It's about time you woke up."

Jessica pouted as she squeezed Parker's hand. "You frightened the living daylights out of us. Don't ever do that again."

Alice moved to the medical equipment and picked up the blood pressure cuff. Jessica skirted over to allow her space.

Alice wrapped the cuff around Parker's arm. "You need to keep the oxygen on for a few more days. Your lungs are still not at full capacity, and the trip knocked them around a bit."

Parker's stomach clenched. While a part of her knew Daniel was livid with her for going to the CDC, and most probably wanted nothing to do with her, another small part wished for him to be there.

"BP's good." Alice placed the end of a stethoscope against Parker's back and listened to her lungs. "After breakfast, we'll help you wash, change your bandages, and get you up for a few minutes. We need to build your strength slowly."

"You know you don't need to put yourself out," Parker said.

Alice stared at the end of the stethoscope in her hand, and her shoulders sagged. "I'm not. It's nice to have a patient that isn't going to die on me for a change."

Jessica giggled and clapped her hands. "And we get to have some girl time while you recover, so it's a win-win."

The day flew by. Between her enforced naps, Jessica and Alice insisted on staying with her. She enjoyed the company, but she couldn't help the feeling that Daniel didn't trust her. By the end of the day, she was convinced her two friends had turned into her jailors on Daniel's instructions.

She was relieved when they finally left, and she had some time to herself. So much had happened, it was difficult to separate her emotions from her pain. Her only enjoyment was when Alice and Jessica brought her out to the patio for some afternoon fresh air. She was sick of confined spaces after the prison and then the hospital.

While the evening sun battled to stay above the horizon, Parker relaxed in the recliner and admired the brilliant shades of red and orange emblazoned across the sky. Her solitude was short-lived. Daniel exited the house and headed in her direction.

"I see Mandy and her friends have visited."

Parker's stomach fluttered. Without realizing it, she had been looking forward to seeing him. She glanced at the multitude of get-well pictures and artwork strewn on the table and smiled. "Yes, they were quite sure that bright paintings and drawings would heal me instantly."

Daniel crouched down to eye level and reached for her hand. "Sorry, I've been scarce today. Some pressing matters couldn't wait."

"Don't apologize. You have more important things to worry about than me. Besides, your pit-bulls are quite capable of making sure I don't get into trouble."

He looked around for his sister and Alice.

"I sent them both home. They don't need to wait on me hand and foot. I've had my meds, Alice has confirmed my blood pressure is almost back to normal, and my oxygen levels are improving."

Daniel arched a brow. "So I heard."

His unwavering gaze made her uncomfortable. She couldn't shake the questions that had been plaguing her over-active imagination all day.

Why had he insisted on her returning to his pack grounds?

Why was he adamant that she couldn't return home, or remain in hospital as per the doctor's wishes?

She knew he was angry with her for involving the CDC. Did he trust her so little that he thought she would put his entire race in danger—put her friends at risk? She was crushed to think he had so little faith in her. She would do anything to protect those she loved. They may not be blood, but they were definitely family.

Daniel leaned closer, and he gazed up and down her body. "Are you all right? You look upset."

Parker tensed. Without her special tea, he would be able to pick up on her stray emotions. "I'm fine, just a little tired."

Daniel stood and handed her the small oxygen tank. "Come on, let's get you inside."

He scooped her up, strode through the house, and deposited her in bed. "Have a nap, I'll get something sorted for your dinner."

"What? You cook?" she said. "You can't even make coffee."

Daniel raised a brow. "I'll have you know my outdoor grilling skills are superb."

Worried he might expect her to eat a heavy meal, she said, "I don't think that I could possibly eat anything like that right now."

"I know. That's why Gail is making dinner for you tonight. She's done some Googling, and apparently chicken soup is supposed to make an ill person feel better." Daniel's expression reflected his skepticism on the subject.

She managed a laugh, then grimaced.

Shit, how long are my ribs going to hurt.

Daniel leaned over the bed and placed a gentle kiss on her forehead before leaving the room.

Stunned by his action, she stared at the closed door, the feel of his lips imprinted on her skin.

Control yourself, idiot, he's just making sure I can't do anything to endanger the pack.

Despite her belief to the contrary, she fell asleep soon after he left. When she woke, it was to discover Daniel in the chair nearest the bed.

"How long have you been sitting there?"

He shrugged. "Not long."

Parker frowned. "You know you don't have to keep tabs on me all the time. I'm not going anywhere, and if you are worried about me speaking to anyone, don't. I would never betray any of you."

Daniel's forehead creased. "What are you talking about?"

She sighed. "You know what I am talking about. Don't act like you don't."

Instead of replying, Daniel stood up. "I'm going to get your dinner."

Parker stifled the tears that threatened. *I knew it. He doesn't trust me.* He would not see how crushed she was by his words. This was something she needed to cope with on her own. The sooner she got better, the sooner she could go home and try to get some semblance of her life back.

She wasn't left alone for long. Daniel returned with a tray of food. He helped her up, moved the mobile table across the bed, and placed a bowl on it.

"How is it?"

"Superb, although I think Gail will be disappointed in the morning when I wake up and I'm still looking like this."

Daniel laughed. "Yes, well, we aren't accustomed to the Human condition. The fact that it's going to take you weeks, rather than hours or days to heal, takes a little getting used to."

Parker sighed. "Well, this Human can't wait to get back to normal. The inactivity is already driving me nuts."

"Finish your dinner. Clara tells me you play a mean game of Poker—let's see if we can keep you occupied trying to beat me." Daniel reached into the top drawer and pulled out an unopened pack of playing cards. He smiled. "Oh, and don't think you can cheat. Clara has already filled me in on your tells."

Parker shifted in her bed and struggled to come to terms with his incessant need to ensure she couldn't cause any trouble. "You know, you don't need to babysit me all day and night. I'm sure you have better things to do."

Daniel cocked his head. "Are you scared of losing? Is that the problem?"

"Those are fighting words, mister." Parker scoffed. "Five card draw—Jacks or better to open."

The next few hours passed in a happy blur. She couldn't remember the last time she had enjoyed something as simple as playing a game of cards.

She yawned and Daniel laid down his cards in mid-hand. "I think that's it for me. Besides, Alice has left strict instructions that you need a full night's sleep."

He stood up and cleared away the deck.

She brought the cards close to her face to take a better look and frowned. She was holding a full house and couldn't believe the game was going to end before she won the round. "You just don't want to lose to me anymore."

Daniel crossed his arms over his chest and looked down at her, his mouth a thin line, and his face stern.

She conceded and passed her cards across to him. "Fine then, sleep."

Daniel sat down on the small armchair near the bed and arranged himself the best he could.

"What are you doing?"

"I'm going to sleep."

"On that chair?"

Daniel nodded.

"What's wrong with your room?"

"Nothing, but if you need anything during the night, I'll be right here."

Parker rolled her eyes. "Don't be silly, I'll be okay. You can't sleep in that chair."

"I did last night. It's not as uncomfortable as it looks." Daniel reached over and turned off the lamp. "Now go to sleep. Alice will have my head if you don't get a full eight hours."

She lay in the dark and gazed at the ceiling. When Daniel moved, yet again, to find a comfortable position she let out an irritated tsk. She couldn't listen to the insistent rustle of him moving around in the chair. She reached out with her good arm and turned on the lamp. "Oh, for Christ sakes. If you insist on staying here all night, you may as well sleep in the bed. It's big enough to fit a small army."

"No. I'm fine here."

Parker exhaled. "Daniel, just get in. I need some sleep, and I am not going to get any with you perched on that goddam chair."

They began a staring match, each one waiting for the other to give in.

Parker, who had pushed herself up off the pillow to turn on the lights, was starting to feel the strain on her ribs. A sharp ache radiated down her chest and legs, and she cried out.

Daniel was at her side before her body hit the pillow.

He sank to his knees beside the bed. "Are you okay? What's the matter? Should I get Alice?"

"It's alright," she said through gritted teeth. "I just shouldn't have sat that way."

She took calming breaths and focused on bringing the pain within tolerable levels. Once the agony had subsided, she turned to Daniel. "Now, are you going to get in, or do I have to tell Alice that you argued with an invalid?"

Grunting, Daniel got up and made his way to the other side of the bed. He sat down and bent over to take his shoes off. Then, to Parker's dismay, began to disrobe. He removed both his jeans and shirt, and stood barefoot, dressed only in boxers.

"What are you doing?" Her voice came out in a high-pitched squeak.

Daniel grinned and proceeded to get between the sheets "What? You're lucky I kept these on. I normally sleep without them."

Parker was at a loss for words. Even in her state, she could appreciate the Adonis that had materialized and was now resting in the bed beside her. If her face wasn't already colored with bruises, it would be fifteen shades of beetroot about now.

Daniel turned off the lights and lay in the dark.

He turned on his side and faced her. She was too scared to move, and not sure what to say, or what to feel. How was she going to sleep with him so close?

Daniel broke the silence. "When you were there, did Matheo ever... I mean, did he ever try to..."

"No," she said quietly. "No, he threatened to, but you got there before he had a chance to carry it out."

Daniel exhaled as if he'd been holding his breath.

She turned her head to look at him. He was so close. Even in the dark she made out his strong features. Right now, he was staring directly at her.

"I never thanked you for coming to get me," she said.

From out of the darkness, his hand reached for hers. "I'm only sorry we didn't get there earlier."

They lapsed into silence. Unable to meet his penetrating gaze, Parker looked up at the ceiling.

"You have the gene." His voice was quiet, almost inaudible.

"Pardon?"

"The dormant wolf gene. You have it."

What did that mean, aside from making her susceptible to the Wildfire disease? She chose to make no comment. Her body gave way to the bliss of slumber a short time later, and her mind foggily registered that her hand was still entwined with his.

The following week proceeded in the same manner as the first day. Alice and Jessica took turns at making sure she was taking her medication and adhering to their strict guidelines. During the day, Daniel worked tirelessly and continued to monitor the hospitals as the Wildfire disease spread into the Human world. At the same time, he ensured they kept any further outbreak contained within the Werewolf community. Rather than travel to Denver to handle the pack's construction business, he conducted whatever he could from home. Anything that required him to leave the compound was postponed.

Daniel's late afternoons and evenings were spent with her.

The only exception was the ceremony to honor their dead pack members. She was adamant she had to attend.

The funeral was worse than Parker could have imagined. Not only did it bring back the raw wounds from losing her cousin and Beth, but she was consumed by the fact that Kyle and the others lost their lives while coming to save her. Guilt so overwhelmed her that she struggled to breathe throughout the wake and the ceremony.

She prepared herself for the hostility she would undoubtedly face. After all, she was the reason they were dead. What she wasn't prepared for was all the support. Each time someone approached, it was to thank her for finding Elise's compound and putting a stop to her reign of terror. They were aware that she was behind the CDC's decision to remove the tainted food, but also what she had been prepared to do to safeguard not only their pack, but their entire race.

By mid-week, her lungs were almost back to full capacity, and she was able to get rid of the oxygen bottle. Now she was free to wander and was no longer restricted to bed. Her arm, ribs, and other injuries would take a lot longer to heal.

Most of all she looked forward to her evenings. An unspoken pattern emerged during the week, and solidified a fundamental and unconscious change to their relationship. Once Daniel finished work, he would seek her out, and they would sit and talk until dinner time—often discussing pack matters or the ongoing search for Elise. Sometimes Daniel sought her counsel for the best way to approach pack issues that had arisen during the day.

He continued to sleep in the room with her, and she insisted he sleep on the bed, rather than in the chair.

Soon his being in bed beside her felt natural, and neither put up an argument. Often, she would wake up during the night to discover that his wolf had taken over and sat vigil over her. During these moments, she would reach out, and he would creep closer, edging his way nearer to her until his frame was flush with her body. She would bury her hand in his fur and gently stroke him as he lay beside her. She would fall asleep with the relaxing, steady inhales and exhales from his massive, warm body.

Though she physically healed, her emotional well-being deteriorated. She lived in fear, thinking that the bubble would burst at any moment, and she would have to wake up and begin her life without Daniel. Each time he walked into the room her heart would beat a little bit faster. It was the small things, his attentiveness when asking her opinion, or his anticipation of her needs as she healed.

With the knowledge this would all come to an end, she imprinted these snippets of her days to memory. In her darkest moments, when she needed something to hold on to, she would recall these moments, but she had to stop the fantasy. It had gone on too long. If it were possible, she was falling deeper and deeper in love with a man who felt nothing but guilt for her injuries at the hands of Matheo. A man who no longer trusted her for going behind his back.

The anguish grew each time she saw Jessica and Ray or Alice and John together. The deep bond they experienced was something she was desperate to have with Daniel.

In her manic state, the thought of him with another woman made her physically ill. She was jealous of a woman she hadn't even met, but she couldn't forget that his mate was somewhere out there. He was becoming as essential to her as life itself. In the end, this made her decide to leave before she was no longer able to function.

She spent the entire day psyching herself up for the confrontation that would sever their contact. She needed to convince him that she wouldn't put them at risk.

At dinner, she readied herself.

It's now or never.

"I'm feeling much better. Alice said I could go back to work next week," she said. "Provided I only type with one hand, of course."

Daniel barely acknowledged her.

"In fact, I thought I'd book a flight for this weekend—that way I can settle in before the week starts."

"You aren't well enough to travel."

Irritated that Daniel was again trying to tell her what to do, she said, "I am, and I can't stay here forever. I need to get back to my life and my business. There are people who depend on me."

"They are coping without you."

Her anger simmered just below the surface. He was being dismissive, which only further aggravated her. "Yes, but for how long? Their projects will finish soon, and I need to get more contracts through the door for them."

Daniel frowned. "You could move your business to Boulder or Denver. It doesn't need to be in Portland, and after speaking with a few of them, I think the majority of your team would make the move. I've even scouted a few locations that might suit you."

"You what?" Parker stood. "Why would you go behind my back like that?" She picked up her half-eaten meal, stormed to the kitchen bench, and dumped the dinner plate in the sink. "Besides, I'm not moving anywhere. Morgan and Clara are near me. What the hell would I do in Boulder?"

Daniel jumped up from his chair. "You wouldn't be living in Boulder. You would be here. With me!"

She flinched at the sudden increase in volume.

"Don't be ridiculous." She clenched her fists. "I can't keep taking advantage of your hospitality, and at some point, you are going to have to trust me."

Daniel's nostrils flared. "What the hell are you talking about? I do trust you."

"Then why are you so adamant I stay here?"

She was standing, fists clenched and anger seeping out of every pore. It did not escape her that their stance mimicked each other. Their eyes blazed, and fury exploded in the air.

His face was dark as his voice rose to full volume. "Because my mate is supposed to be by my side, not half a country away!"

She yelled back at him. "You aren't the boss of me. And you certainly have no right to tell me what I can and can't do."

His words finally registered and she stopped dead in her tracks.

Mate? What mate?

She cleared her throat. "I'm sorry, what did you just say?"

"You heard me."

Parker sat down on the nearest chair, but jumped up again. Thinking better of it, she sat back down. She stood up, yet again. Her mouth opened and closed, but no words emerged.

Daniel crossed the short distance between them. His anger abated, he cupped her chin in his hand, and tilted her face up. A hint of a smile touched his lips, though laced with doubt and insecurity. "I never knew how alone I was until you charged into my life and turned it upside down."

His voice, like a smooth wine, spread warmth and hope through her body.

"Make no mistake, you are my mate."

She stood transfixed, and still unable to utter a word. This must be a dream that she was going to wake from, a dream that she would relive for the rest of her life.

His eyes grew fearful. "Say something."

Her voice croaked as she forced herself to speak. "W-when did you know?"

"Know what? That you were my mate, or that I'd found I could no longer live without you?"

Her pulse quickened, and her heart beat faster. "Both, I guess."

"The moment Simon brought you to me at the prison, I knew who you were. Your scent was no longer masked from me." His eyes searched hers as if frantic to read her mind. "And as to the other, it happened so gradually that I don't actually know."

She stood, immobile. Her face was still cupped in his hands. Neither she nor Daniel spoke, the silence drawing out like a taut rubber band, ready to snap.

"I know it's different for Humans, but do you think... do you think you could ever..." Daniel ran a hand through his hair. "What I mean to say is that..."

She cut him off, knowing full well what he wanted to ask.

Her heart was clenched so tightly she could scarcely breathe. She was wrong in thinking he hadn't trusted her. *I misinterpreted all the signs.* She choked back the tears that threatened to fall again. "I needed to go because my heart has been breaking a little more each day, knowing you were never going to feel for me the way my soul, my entire being, feels for you."

She reached up to cup his face with her hand, all the emotions she held for him reflected in her eyes. "You are as necessary to me as the air I breathe. My heart is yours—it will always be yours."

***

Daniel silenced Parker with a smoldering kiss, pulling her closer to him. As he did so, she winced in pain. Feeling her distress, he pulled back, panicked that he had caused her discomfort.

"Are you sure?" he said. "Because I am never going to let you go."

Parker nodded and gave him a broken smile. Through her bruises and swollen features, the truth shone in her eyes. It was as if he had come home from a long, perilous journey. The fears that had built up inside him had evaporated. In their place was the wonderment that this stunning creature before him was his. His to worship. His to love and cherish for a lifetime. His confidant and best friend, who he had no doubt would fight him tooth and nail every step of the way.

His whole body, mind, and soul belonged to her.

Forever.

The End... for now.

Acknowledgements

No book is ever written without support. I would like to express my gratitude to the following:

To my family. My husband and kids, who have been my rock and with me at every step of the way with this story. I love you with everything that I am. You have put up with so much during the journey, it often humbles me how patient you have all been.

Debbie Williams and Angela Zalkalnins, for their unwavering support and cheerleading. I will be forever grateful for you both.

My parents, Olga & Andelko, for their unconditional love. My only regret is dad did not live long enough to see my first published story.

A special thanks to Lina Hanson, Ana Simons, Ann Writes, L. Maree Apps, Vera Loy, Sally Mason, Leigh W. Stuart, Tammy Oja, Kristen Jaques, K Halandras, Erica Laurie, Rosanna Patruno & Cindy Brown. Your wonderful advice and friendship has made me not only a better writer, but a better person for knowing you all.

I would also like to thank Cate, Emma, and Shirley, my editors. Ladies, you taught me so much about the craft, and made the editing process bearable.

Of course, I can't forget my launch team who helped me get Masked into the public arena. I couldn't have done it without you—you have my eternal thanks.

I would be remiss if I didn't acknowledge and thank all my readers on Wattpad for your support.

And for you, the reader who picked up this book and gave a new author a chance to let her voice be heard.

About The Author

After failing miserably at world domination and surviving many years of producing technical documentation, project plans and test plans that no one bothered to open, M (pron. M) Greenhill decided to create something that might actually be read.

She enjoys creating paranormal stories that takes the reader on a journey filled with intrigue, excitement and more twists and turns than are bugs in a Microsoft update.

M lives in New Zealand with her husband and two Overwatch addicted sons. Ever the optimist, she hopes that one day she will own a pair of Louboutin's and that, for once, her husband won't take a short-cut on a DIY project – or even finish one for that matter

Connect with M Greenhill:

Facebook: https://www.facebook.com/MNJGreenhillAuthor

Twitter: https://twitter.com/MNJGreenhill

Web: http://www.mgreenhill.com

Made in the USA
Coppell, TX
28 January 2021